To Terry

I am so happy you enjoy my writing, and I thank you so very much for your support! Terry, next time ms. Lynn will read to you!

    Love you guys,
     Jillian Osborn

HOUSE
~ OF ~
# ILLUSIONS

Jillian Osborn

iUniverse, Inc.
New York Bloomington

House Of Illusions

Copyright © 2009 Jillian Osborn

All rights reserved. No part of this book may be used or reproduced by any means, graphic, electronic, or mechanical, including photocopying, recording, taping or by any information storage retrieval system without the written permission of the publisher except in the case of brief quotations embodied in critical articles and reviews.

This is a work of fiction. All of the characters, names, incidents, organizations, and dialogue in this novel are either the products of the author's imagination or are used fictitiously.

iUniverse books may be ordered through booksellers or by contacting:

iUniverse
1663 Liberty Drive
Bloomington, IN 47403
www.iuniverse.com
1-800-Authors (1-800-288-4677)

Because of the dynamic nature of the Internet, any Web addresses or links contained in this book may have changed since publication and may no longer be valid. The views expressed in this work are solely those of the author and do not necessarily reflect the views of the publisher, and the publisher hereby disclaims any responsibility for them.

ISBN: 978-1-4401-2400-6 (pbk)
ISBN: 978-1-4401-2403-7 (cloth)
ISBN: 978-1-4401-2401-3 (ebk)

Library of Congress Control Number: 2009923833

Printed in the United States of America

iUniverse rev. date: 3/9/2009

PREFACE

The Cornu House, located at seventeen-twenty-three East Waldburg Street in the beautifully historic city of Savannah, Georgia has a rather hellish reputation. Though it may be gorgeous on the outside and ever the more breathtaking within, it's what lurks inside that makes this house an unpleasurable place to live. Just ask those who've stayed there and survived its hellions and never-ending acts of terror.

Many people thought the ravishing house on East Waldburg Street would be a well favored place to live. Unfortunately for their sake, all those hopeful folks were misled by their preconceptions. The same fateful opinion circulated the newest family who'd reside in the house. Given time they, too, would be taken by the madness of illusions and driven straight into the mouth of hell as they were each forced to face their worst nightmare.

Only the strong and willful can survive in this forsaken house. In this twisted legend of ultimate evil you'll come to know that some tragedies tear us apart, while others bring us closer.

CHAPTER ONE

Savannah, Georgia
June 9, 1978

"I can't believe it's really ours!" Andrea beamed as John drove up to the magnificent house.

"This place is really beautiful, isn't it?"

"You know it's always been my dream to live in one of these old Victorian homes. They have so much more character than those boring newer ones."

"Well, if you're happy, I'm happy along with you! I'm glad we were able to find this place. I just hope we have some good neighbors to go along with it."

"We're in Savannah. Everyone's friendly here!" remarked Andrea.

John pulled into the driveway, then turned off the engine. Andrea turned around to the back seat of the van. "Wake up, sleepy head, we're here!" Two bright blue eyes opened and stared back at her. "We're here, Chloe! Why don't you get up and take a look at our new home?"

Chloe rubbed her eyes and slowly pulled herself from the seat. She peered out from behind the window and looked upon the house.

"It's so big, mommy. Won't we get lost?"

"It'll take a little while to get used to. But don't you worry, Chlo, I'll be with you. If we happen to get lost, at least we'll be together, right?"

"What about daddy? What if he gets lost and can't find us?"

John turned to Chloe and said softly, "Daddy won't get lost baby."

"You probably just jinxed yourself, John!"

"What? I always find my way around. I never get lost!"

"And what about that time on vacation, dear? Or was that just a detour?"

"I got us to where we needed to go, didn't I?"

"Yeah, with my help! Go on, admit it, you got us lost!"

"I did not. I knew exactly where I was going."

"You see, Chloe, daddy can't admit he gets lost from time to time. But that's all right, it doesn't mean we love him any less!"

John snuck up behind Andrea and scooped her in his arms. "May I carry you over the threshold, my dear?"

"As long as you don't whack my head into the door!"

"You still won't forgive me for that? We were a little inebriated. You're lucky I didn't drop you as well!"

"That was a funny memory. I think I saw stars for a whole week!"

Chloe stopped and stood before the house while John carried Andrea through the door.

"Look, we made it in and you didn't get hurt!"

"I guess we had some better luck the second time around!" Andrea said while John stood her on her feet.

"Chloe, I'm coming to get you!" John said running out into the yard, "Who're you waving at Babe?"

"The little girl."

"What, little girl, Chlo?"

"The one in the window. She's watching us. I waved at her, but she never waved back."

"Well, that's just her loss now, isn't it? She could have made a good friend today."

"Maybe she's shy, daddy."

"Could be. Maybe you'll see her again later. Which house does she live in?"

"Ours."

"She lives in our house? Are you sure?"

"Uh-huh, she was standing by that window." Chloe pointed.

"Are you sure you weren't seeing things, Chlo? There's a shadow upon that window. It makes it seem like someone might be standing there."

"No, daddy, she was there."

"Well, if you say so. Why don't you go on into the house and pick you out a bedroom!"

"Really? I get to pick out any room I want?"

"Whichever room you'd prefer." John picked Chloe up and took her into the house.

"I thought the two of you had left!"

"We were just outside, mommy. Daddy told me I could pick out my own room!"

"He did? Well, you have a lot to choose from. You better start looking!"

"Will you come with me?"

"Sure, baby, let's go!"

"Andrea, I'll be outside unloading the van."

Chloe pulled her mom up the stairs and ventured into the first room. The walls were coated in a subtle yellow paint with white borders that ran from one corner to the other. The room was filled with dusty sheets and old furniture. An old dresser stood before the wall with the finest carvings that Andrea had ever seen. Behind the dresser was a large matching mirror.

"Aren't antiques beautiful, Chloe? Just think of the time someone put into carving this wood. It truly is exquisite work."

Chloe ran her hand across the dresser and felt the engravings. "It's a little dusty," she said as she looked down at her little gray hands, then showed them to her mom. "See!"

Andrea took a rag and cleaned off chloe's hands. "I think we're going to need a lot of dusting spray, don't you?"

Chloe shook her head. "Can we look at another room now?"

"Take the lead, kiddo, I'll follow."

Chloe ran out the door to the next room while Andrea followed. "I like this one, mommy. It looks like a little girl's room! It even has rosy pink walls!"

"I'm surprised you didn't look on the bed. It appears to me that you have a new friend waiting for you."

Chloe's eyes widened as she looked on top of the pillows. "She's beautiful! Can I hold her?"

3

"She's very old, so be careful, okay?"

"I will, I promise," Chloe exclaimed.

Andrea picked the doll up and handed her to Chloe.

"She looks so real, doesn't she, mommy? What kind of doll is she?"

"This is a porcelain doll, Chloe. You have to be real careful with her. If you dropped her, she could break." Andrea took the doll from Chloe and looked her over. The doll was wearing a velvet green dress with lace around the edges. A small silver pendant hung from her neck and inside was an old picture of a little girl. Tiny black shoes clung to the doll's feet over her little white lacy socks. Her face was ghostly white, and she had unusual topaz-colored eyes. The doll's hair was dark red with thick curls that ran down her shoulders. Her cheeks had a faint pink rouge that brightened her face and her lips were blood red, but not from any paint.

Andrea ran her finger across the doll's mouth. Her lips feel so real, like actual skin, she thought. Suddenly Andrea let out a small cry.

"What is it, mommy? Are you okay?" Andrea looked down at her finger and saw a small bead of blood.

"Don't touch her lips. Something sharp is poking through her mouth."

"I can still hold her, though, can't I, mommy?"

"Just make sure you don't touch her mouth. I don't want you getting hurt, okay? Why don't you go outside and help your daddy unpack the van. You can leave your dolly here for now. When you come back up she'll be waiting for you. Later on you can show your father what we found, how's that?"

"Okay, mommy," Chloe said as she set the doll on her pillows. "I'll be back later."

Andrea made her way into the master bedroom with a large box in her hands. She set the box on top of the dresser, then opened one of the drawers.

The drawer was empty except for a shiny silver locket. She ran her thumb across its surface to brush away the dust. Along the edge she felt for a clasp. Inside the locket Andrea found a frail old picture of a family. The man was well dressed in a distinguished suit. To his left was a beautiful young woman, petite with delicate features. In her arms rested a small child. In front of the man and woman stood two young girls. One was cradling her doll like a sleeping baby.

Andrea studied the doll in the picture and noticed the striking resemblance to the one on Chloe's bed. She closed the locket, then hung it on the mirror. The sun peered into the bedroom and lit upon the locket as it shimmered in the light.

"Mommy! Mommy! The movers are here with the rest of our stuff!"

"Okay, Chloe, I'll be right down."

"Good afternoon, Mrs. Craven."

"Hi, Rich, how are you?"

"I'm fine. Say, where should I set these boxes?"

"Over by the fireplace should be fine. Can I get you something to drink? I know how awful it is out there with that heat."

"If you wouldn't mind, a glass of ice water would be nice."

"Is bottled okay? The water hasn't run through these pipes in so long, it's probably rusty."

"Yes, ma'am, that's nice of you."

"Rich, if you call me ma'am again, I'm going to hit you!"

"Yes, ma'am, um I mean Andrea. Ah, you know me. I have to kid around. Thanks for the water."

"Don't mention it. If you'd like another bottle they're in this ice chest. Just help yourself. You can tell the other guys, too."

Rich noticed Andrea's finger and grew concerned.

"Say, what happened there? It looks pretty bad. You might want to have someone check that out for you."

Andrea looked at her finger and saw what appeared to be a bite mark with red lines running out of the wound. "That's odd. It didn't look that way earlier."

"It looks like you're getting an infection. You need to clean that out right away. Do you have any peroxide?"

"I have a medicine box that should have some. I think it's still in the van, though."

"Why don't you stay here while I go look for it?"

Andrea got a clean rag and waited for Rich to get back with the box.

"Here we go. Why don't we clean that wound first?" Rich walked over to the ice chest and got out a cold bottle of water. "Why don't you hold that rag underneath your hand while I pour the water over your finger. This is a pretty bad bite mark, Andrea. Who bit you?"

"I cut it on a doll that Chloe and I found upstairs. It had something sharp on its face and I nicked myself, that's all."

"This isn't a nick, Andrea. Something bit you. This almost looks like human teeth marks."

"It probably looks that way because of the infection."

"If this gets any worse I think you should see a doctor. This doesn't look right to me."

"There's a little discomfort, but it's not a problem."

"Just keep an eye on it. For now I'll help you clean it out. Okay, this peroxide might sting a little. I'm sorry if it burns."

"It's all right. I've taken to worse wounds than this."

Rich poured the peroxide over Andrea's finger as green pus erupted from the wound. "I'm going to try and get as much of this infection out of your finger as I can. Why don't you see if you have any antibiotic ointment in that box of yours along with some bandages and a Q-tip." Rich finished cleaning the infection, then dried Andrea's finger with the rag. He squeezed the tube of medicine over the Q-tip and applied it to Andrea's wound. "There, we're almost done. I just need a bandage and you're set. Make sure you doctor your finger a few times each day."

"Thanks, Rich."

"No problem. I was happy to help. Well, I best be getting back to work before John thinks I've retired."

"We'll be ordering dinner out later if you care to stay."

"I don't want to impose on either of you. I mean, it's your first day in this house. You're bound to be tired."

"Hey we're all still pretty young here. You know how late John usually stays up. It'd be nice to have you join us for old time's sake."

"Well, all right, I think you've coaxed me into it."

"Since that's settled, shall we finish clearing out the boxes?" Rich followed Andrea out into the yard.

"I hear Chloe already found the perfect room!" John mentioned, as Andrea walked past.

"Oh, she's just delighted! Did she tell you what we found?"

"She mentioned something earlier, but wouldn't say what it was. She told me I had to wait and see."

"You mean your curiosity hasn't taken its toll? Usually you're like a child yourself and can't wait. I'm proud of you!"

"I didn't want to spoil her surprise; she seemed so excited. It's all she's talked about since she left the room."

"I have to say, I'm shocked she didn't tell you what it was. You know how she does; the poor little thing gets so excited she usually blurts out Christmas gifts and other things."

"Well, for once she's keeping a secret, and she's doing a pretty good job of it. Hon, you didn't happen to turn on the water, did you?"

"Not yet, why?"

"I think you should turn on the faucet and let it run for awhile. It'll clean out that rusty brown water that's been sitting in those pipes. Later we'll have clean water for ourselves."

"Just the one in the kitchen?"

"Go ahead and run the one in the bathroom as well."

Andrea looked around the yard for a second and didn't notice Chloe anywhere in sight. "John, where's Chlo?" she asked in a state of panic.

"She's right there by that willow tree." he pointed to an empty site. "She was just there, I swear." He searched over the yard quickly, but found no evidence of his daughter. "Chloe!" he yelled, but received no word of response, "Chloe!" he yelled again. John ran over to his friend. "Hey, Rich! Rich! Have you or Brad seen Chloe?"

"She was by that tree last time I saw her."

By that time Andrea was running toward the house yelling for Chloe. She ran as fast as she could up the porch stairs, then through the door. Andrea bumped into Wade on her way in. "Please tell me Chloe's in here!"

"No, ma'am, Mrs. Craven. I haven't seen her. Have you checked out back?"

Andrea ran out the door to the side of the house yelling Chloe's name when she saw her. "Chloe! Chloe, why didn't you answer us?" Chloe was standing silent and motionless before the house staring into a window. Andrea bent down beside her. "Chloe! Chloe, answer me!" Chloe continued to look upon the window.

"Don't you see her, mommy?"

"See who, Chloe?"

"The little girl in the window. She's waving at me."

"What little girl, Chlo? There's no one up there."
"She is. The little girl's there."
"Chloe, I'm sorry, baby, I don't see anyone."
"It's all right, mommy. She understands."
"Baby, are you feeling all right?"
"I'm fine, mommy."
"Are you sure? You look a bit peaked. Have you been running around?"
"No, mommy, I've been here."
"Why don't you come with me. We'll get you a bottle of water. Maybe you're just a little overheated from the sun." Andrea picked Chloe up in her arms and took her around to the front. "It's all right, John. I found her."
"Where was she?"
"At the side of the house. I think this heat has gotten to her."
"She does look a bit flushed," he told his wife, "Chloe, what were you doing by the side of the house?"
"Looking at the little girl. I saw her again."
"Didn't you hear your mom or me calling for you?"
"No, daddy."
Andrea looked up at John. "I don't know, dear. When I got to her, she wouldn't say a thing. It was like she was frozen there, staring at the window. A minute later she started talking about a little girl."
"Chloe mentioned something about seeing a child in the window earlier today, but I never saw anyone."
"Well, I'm going to take her on in the house and get her some water. Hopefully it'll cool her down some."
"I see you found the little one." stated Rich, "I looked in the house, but couldn't find her. I know you're relieved to have her back. Where was she hiding?"
"I found her at the side of the house. Thanks for your help, Rich. I really appreciate it. You get so worried when you don't know where your child is. I was starting to panic. Thank God she was still here and didn't wander off somewhere."
"I'm glad to hear she's safe. You know, Chloe, you had everyone worried when we couldn't find you. The next time you go off like that, I think it'd be best that you told your mom or dad first, okay kid?"
"I'm sorry, I didn't mean to scare anyone," Chloe spoke bashfully.

"It's all right this first time, Chlo, but please remember to tell me or someone else where you're going next time."

"Okay, mommy, I'll remember." Andrea walked Chloe into the kitchen and got her a bottle of water.

"Here, honey, drink this."

"Do I have to drink it all?"

"Drink what you can."

"Is it okay if I sit on the porch?"

"I guess it won't hurt." Chloe followed Andrea back to the front yard.

"John, Chloe wants to sit on the porch. Will you please keep an eye on her?"

"Sure, no problem."

"Chloe, if you want to get up, please tell your daddy where you're going, okay? Mommy has a few things she needs to tend to in the house, then I'll be with you."

Chloe knotted her head as her mom walked away.

"I'll be back shortly," said Andrea as she went on into the house.

She walked to the kitchen and turned on the faucet. Rusty water burst out like an eruptive volcano, coating the sink with gritty fragments. Andrea left the water running in the kitchen while she ventured into the bathroom.

While she was making her way toward the upstairs lavatory, Andrea heard the sound of small feet running into the rear bedroom. "Chloe, is that you?" Andrea called out. The hall echoed with the laughter of a small child. Andrea stopped in her tracks and called out again. The laughter continued to fill the hall and grew more intense as Andrea made her way toward the back bedroom.

She stood before the door and carefully opened it as the laughter came to a halt. "Chloe, are you in here?" The place was empty except for dusty furniture and papers scattered out along the floor. Andrea shook her head. I know I heard someone, she thought. She shut the door as she left the room and headed to the lavatory. Andrea turned on the faucet and let the water flow until it ran clear.

In the distance Andrea heard the laughter again as she ran into the hall. Confused, she looked around desperately trying to find its source, but came up empty. She ran into one of the bedrooms and lifted the window. Below she could see John outside with the other men. Andrea leaned out the windowsill and yelled down to him, "Is Chloe out there with you?"

John peered up and saw Andrea bent over the window. "Yeah, hon, she's on the porch where you told her to be. Everything's fine."

"Okay, I just wanted to check." Andrea closed the window and walked back into the hallway. She walked past Chloe's room and noticed the door had been opened. "I thought that was closed when I came up here?" She walked on into the room and quickly noticed something out of place.

Chloe's doll was no longer resting among the pillows. Andrea walked over to the bed expecting to see the doll somewhere on the floor where it had fallen, but to her disbelief the floor was empty. "All right, I must really be losing my mind." Andrea bent down on her knees and lifted the sheets, looking beneath the bed. "Okay, that's it. I give up!" She pulled herself up from the floor when something caught her eye.

Andrea gasped when she saw the doll sitting back on the pillows where Chloe had left her. She stared into its eyes baffled with confusion as the doll stared right back. Suddenly to Andrea's surprise the doll quickly blinked its eyes at her. "You're just a doll," said Andrea as she picked it up. "How could you have done that? Your eyes are made of glass."

She set the doll back on the pillows and waited for it to blink again, but it never did. "Okay, maybe this heat is getting to me now and I'm seeing things. That's all it is. Nothing more," she told herself, trying to make sense of what she had just witnessed. She turned around and started away from the bed. As she did, the doll turned its head and formed a hideous grin that bore jagged teeth.

The door shut behind Andrea as she made her way out of the bedroom. Andrea returned to the kitchen and turned off the running water, then walked out to the porch looking for Chloe.

"It's okay, Andrea. John took Chloe to the backyard."

"Thanks, Rich." She walked to the back of the house and found John and Chloe in the gazebo.

"Mommy! Mommy! Can we keep her?" Chloe asked in excitement as she held a fluffy white kitten up to her mom.

"Oh, sweetie, she's beautiful! Where'd you find her?"

"By the pond. She was chasing the dragonflies. Please, mommy, can we keep her?" she begged.

"I don't see why not, as long as your father says it's okay."

"He said it was as long as you thought so, too."

"Well it looks like you have a new pet! You're going to have to take care of her now. You think you can do it?"

"I can take care of her. I'll make sure she has food and water. Can she sleep in my room?"

"Of course she can, dear. So what are you going to call her?"

"Snow!"

"I think that name suits her. What'd you think, John?"

"I think it's perfect," he commented.

"I think we should take her into the house and get her a bowl of milk. She's probably thirsty."

"Can I give her the milk, mommy?"

"I'll have to pour it into the bowl, but you can give it to her."

Chloe held Snow in her arms as the kitten played in her hair. "Look, mommy!" Chloe giggled. "She likes my hair!"

"I see that."

"She tickles!" Chloe continued to laugh.

They walked into the house and went to the kitchen. Andrea heard the sound of running water as they came through the door. "What are you doing back on? I turned you off." She walked over to the faucet and saw steam rising from the sink. Andrea grabbed a towel and turned the knob.

"Why was the water running?" Chloe asked.

"I don't know, baby."

"Maybe someone forgot to turn it off."

"Could be. I guess the last person in here left it running by accident. Well, shall we get Snow some milk?"

"Uh-huh. Don't forget, I'll give it to her." Chloe set Snow on the floor as she ran through the kitchen exploring the place.

"Here you go, Chlo. Try not to spill it, okay?" Andrea said, handing her the bowl.

"I won't!" Chloe set the bowl on the floor, then stretched out beside it and waited for the kitten. Andrea pulled out a chair and sat awhile.

"She's so pretty, isn't she, mommy?"

"She's very pretty, baby. I'm glad you like her as much as you do."

"Excuse me, Andrea, I wanted to know if I should take this box upstairs? It's marked bedroom."

"Yes, Brad, if you wouldn't mind. That would be a big help. You can set it in the first room on the left."
"Is there anything else I could take up for you?"
"Just that box should be fine, thanks."
Brad left and headed upstairs towards the bedroom. He turned the knob to open the door, but something had pressed against it holding it shut. Behind the doorway he heard the faint sound of laughter. Brad listened quietly in the hallway when suddenly three knocks rapped at the door. An uneasiness crept up his spine as a chill set in.

His heart began to race, beating quickly in his chest. He took a deep breath and knocked quietly upon the door when three more knocks beat back. The sound of laughter continued to fill the room, then roamed out into the hall from behind the door. "Is someone in there?" Brad's voice shook as he tried to remain calm.

"Just us," a voice whispered, followed by more laughter.
"Who's there?"
"Why don't you open the door?" the voice spoke again.

Brad grabbed the knob, but it was frozen like ice. He quickly jerked his hand away as the knob turned by itself, then the door creaked open. Brad eased into the room, alert to every corner, but to his astonishment the room was empty. He quickly set the box onto the floor and turned around destined to leave. As he did, the door slammed shut in his face, closing him in.

Behind him Brad felt a pulling sensation tug at his shirt as he rushed to turn around. Standing before him was an alarming image of a ghostly little girl wearing a noose around her neck. An unnerving feeling came across Brad while her eyes locked intently upon him. They were cold and black, sunken deep into her head, and not one ounce of goodness emitted from her body. Her appearance brought evil and unholy thought to mind, and Brad began to shake when he sensed it.

He turned around rapidly and dashed to the door, hoping to promptly get away. He rushed into the hallway when he came upon the doll at the top of the staircase. Brad tripped as it grasped out at his foot, forcing him to fall down the stairs.

Andrea heard the heavy bangs as the noise carried into the kitchen. "What in the world was that?" she wondered aloud.

"I heard it, too, mommy. I think it came from in here." Chloe pointed to the door. Andrea got up and went to the front room, with Chloe not far behind.

"My God, Brad, are you all right?" Andrea asked when she saw him on the floor.

"I'm okay. I just had a little accident," he said as he tried to get up. "I think I did something to my lower back. I might have broken a rib," Brad said in pain as he remained on the floor.

"I'm going to get one of the guys to come help. Don't try to move." Andrea ran to the front door and called out for help. John, Wade and Rich came running in.

"What happened?" John asked in worriment.

"Brad fell. He's hurt."

They rushed over to the stairs where he was lying. "Hey, man, can you move at all?" John asked as he bent down beside him.

"I think I can, but I'm really sore. I had the wind knocked out of me pretty bad. Just give me some time to gather some air."

"What happened? You slip on the stairs?"

"I tripped on the top step and came down the stairs on my back."

"Man, you've lost all your coloring. You're white as a sheet."

"It was pretty scary, I lost my footing so fast; it just happened so quickly, you know?"

"I understand. You felt that scary sensation when you started to fall. You want me to try and help you up?"

"I think I'm all right now. I could probably get myself up." Brad sat up from the floor.

"Why don't you come into the living room and have a seat on the couch?"

"Hey, would you mind taking a look at my back to see what I did? I think I may have broken a rib."

He bent forward and let John examine his back.

"Dude, you really did a number back here. You've scratched yourself up pretty badly," John said as he looked at the skin that had been sanded away. The wounds were moistened with droplets of blood and bruising had appeared through Brad's skin. "You have some noticeable swelling on the lower right side of your back. You might have done something considering how this looks, but I'm not a doctor, so I can't be sure. Andrea, why don't you see if there's something in the medicine box that we can give him to help with his pain."

"I'll be back in a sec."

"Brad, are you going to be okay?" Chloe asked in concern. "I can get you a bandage to put on your boo-boo," she said, willing to help.

"I'll be okay, little one. Thank you, though."

"I fell one time and mommy put a bandage on my boo-boo, then kissed it and told me I'd be okay. But I cried a lot because my owie hurt. Does yours hurt?"

"Chloe, why don't you see if your mom needs any help?"

"Okay, daddy."

"I'm sorry, Brad. You know how kids are."

"Oh, it's all right. She was just trying to help."

"You should stay on the couch. Don't worry about bringing anything else in. The guys and I can do it. Anyway, we're almost done."

Andrea returned to the room and handed Brad a bottle of water. "Take these. They should help relieve some of your discomfort."

"Thanks."

"Would you like a pillow to put behind your back?"

"Oh no, that's all right. I'll be fine," he assured her.

"If there's anything else we could do for you, just let us know. Please feel free to make yourself at home."

Andrea took some boxes upstairs and began unpacking. She cleaned off the dusty furniture in the bedrooms, then began to organize the dresser drawers. Across the hall she heard the faint sound of laughter. Andrea tried to ignore the noise as she continued to clean. In the corner of her eye Andrea noticed someone standing in the doorway. "Do you need something, Chloe?"

"I'm not your daughter," a voice echoed throughout the room.

A chill crept up Andrea's spine as she turned around to confront the intruder, but no one was there. Andrea went back to her work and soon forgot about the strange encounter. She got Chloe's room together, then set out her toys and hung up her posters. As Andrea walked past Chloe's bed an unnerving feeling came over her as though someone were watching her every move. She looked over at the doll sitting properly on the pillows and noticed how its eyes seemed to follow her every move. Unsettled by the feeling, Andrea hurried out of the room and closed the door. She let out a sigh of relief when she made it into the hallway where she finally felt safe. She walked over to the bathroom to set out some towels and soap.

"What did you need help with, hon?" Andrea turned around and greeted John at the door.

"I'm sorry, what?"

"What do you need me to do?"

"I don't need you to do anything, dear."

"You just told me you needed some help in here."

"No, I didn't."

"Yes, you did. You yelled at me through the window."

"John, what are you talking about? I didn't yell out the window," Andrea spoke softly as a sly grin crept across John's face.

"Ah, you just wanted me up here so you could clean my sweaty, handsome face!" He beamed.

Andrea took a bath rag and dabbed his forehead, "Honey, I swear I didn't call you up here."

"But I heard you."

"I never called for you."

"Andrea, is something wrong? You don't seem yourself."

"I don't know. I guess it's this heat. It's making my mind play tricks on me."

"Well, I guess I'm with you on that. My mind's been playing tricks, too. I took some stuff to the basement earlier and I swear I heard two girls talking, but I couldn't understand their conversation."

"Did you see them?"

"I looked around, but never saw anyone in the room with me. To be honest I was sort of spooked. I had an eerie feeling the whole time I was down there, like something wanted me out. I'm telling you now, I don't like that basement. It looks like the one we had in my house when I was growing up. I hated that place. I always thought the basement monster lived there. Out of spite, my older brother would lock me down there until I cried. He knew how scared I was. He did it out of meanness. But that's all right. I got him back! He hates clowns, so you could imagine what I did to him."

"You guys were always playing tricks on each other."

"He always started it, so I had to get him back each time."

"You said you heard two little girls talking downstairs?" Andrea questioned him.

"Yeah, but I was probably just hearing things."

15

"What if I told you I've heard a child up here and it wasn't Chloe."

"You heard them, too?"

"I've only heard one little girl. She won't stop laughing. Every time I hear it, I almost feel afraid. Something about it makes me uncomfortable."

"Do you suppose it's the little girl Chloe keeps seeing?"

"It has to be. I mean, I don't know who else it could be. I'm going crazy with the things I've seen and heard."

"Do you think this place is haunted?"

"I don't know, John, but something's going on here. Wouldn't you have figured the realtor would have told us if this house were haunted?"

"Not unless she didn't know."

"I don't know what to think right now. I'm in a state of confusion."

"If it's upsetting you, we'll talk about it later."

"No, it's not that I'm upset, I'm just questioning my sanity. You know what? Follow me for a second." Andrea led John into Chloe's room. "If Chlo knew I was showing you this without her, she'd be mad at me so don't tell her."

"Show me what?"

"You see that doll?" She pointed toward the bed. "Chloe and I found her earlier today. This is what she wanted to show you later."

"Okay, I see an old doll. What's the problem?"

"That doll's not normal. There's something strange about it. When I walk past it, I can feel its eyes following me."

"Her eyes are made of glass. It just looks like they're following you. It's like an illusion, Andrea. You don't need to be afraid of a doll. I must say, she looks real, though."

"That's not all. There's more."

"What? Are you going to tell me she walks and talks now?"

"When I was in here earlier, the doll wasn't on the pillows, I thought she fell to the floor, so I checked under the bed. When I got back up, she was sitting there like she had never moved. You tell me how a doll can suddenly appear within seconds of being gone."

"Maybe she's a figment of our imagination."

"Then why would we be sharing the same illusion? Not just you and me, but Chloe has seen her, too."

"That is a bit odd. She was actually gone one minute and back the next?"

"She's just a doll, isn't she?" Andrea asked as she took her from John.

"What's up with your finger? It's bleeding."

"Oh, it's nothing, I just got a little cut."

"Why don't we change that bandage and get you a fresh one?"

John walked across the hall to the bathroom while Andrea set the doll back on the pillows.

"Where's the medicine box?"

"It's down in the kitchen."

"Come into the bathroom and get that nasty bandage off. I'll be back in a minute with a new one."

Andrea went to the bathroom, set the lid down on the toilet and took a seat. She pulled the bloody bandage off and exposed the pus-filled wound.

"Oh, Andrea, that finger of yours looks awful. What did you say you did?"

"I cut it."

"On what, a rusty nail?" John bent down and looked at her finger. "Did Chloe bite you? I see teeth marks all along your finger."

"No, Chloe didn't bite me."

"Then do you mind telling me what really happened?"

"It was that doll. At first I thought I just cut myself, but now I think that darn thing bit me."

"Dolls don't bite people, Andrea."

"This one does."

"Your finger is badly infected. Did you put anything on it?"

"Rich helped me clean it and bandage it."

"If this gets any worse, I'm taking you to the doctor."

"It'll be all right."

"Andrea, it's corroded. You know an infection like that could make you sick."

"I know, I know, but what would I tell the doctor? I got bit by my daughter's doll? He'd put me in a looney bin. I'm not crazy, John. You know that, don't you?"

"I understand where you're coming from, but you might have to see a doctor. We'll just say Chloe bit you by accident, that you were feeding her or something, I don't know. Are you sure that doll did this?"

"It wasn't Chloe, John."

"Okay, fine, it wasn't Chloe. Well, are you done up here? I'm going to get back downstairs and check on Brad. You coming?"

"Yeah, I think I'll break up here for a little bit and tackle some of the rooms downstairs."

Andrea followed John down as they walked into the living room.

"Everything's in the house. We put all the boxes that needed to go in the kitchen in there, all the ones for the living room in here and so on."

"Thanks, Rich. You guys are great."

"Ah, we're just helping out."

"Yeah, but you guys have been a big help."

"Hey, we're all friends here. You know we'd do what we could to help," Rich added.

"How's Brad doing?"

"He said he was feeling okay. He wasn't complaining of any pain."

"Andrea and I are going to see how he is. Why don't you come in here and have a seat," John said as he looked around the room. "Say, where's Wade?"

"He was taking a few things to the basement. He should have been up by now. Want me to find him?"

"If you don't mind."

CHAPTER TWO

Rich headed to the kitchen and went over to the basement door. He noticed the light was off going down the stairs. He hit the switch, but the lights didn't come on. "Ah, damn fuse must be blown." Rich peered down into the darkness. "Hey, Wade, you down there?"

Rich listened quietly for a few seconds, but never heard a reply. He looked over to the kitchen counter and noticed a flashlight glowing back at him. "That's weird. I guess you knew I needed to use you." He grabbed the flashlight, then started down the stairs. "Wade, you down here?"

He flashed the light over the room, then noticed something in one of the corners. "Wade?"

Rich slowly walked across the room, shining the light in place. As he came closer, he realized Wade was huddled in the corner with his head buried into the wall, sobbing in the dark.

Beneath his muffled cries, Rich heard Wade repeating something over and over. The closer Rich got, the clearer Wade's words became.

"You're not my mother! I won't do it! I won't do it!"

Rich rushed over to Wade's aid. "Oh, man, what happened to you?" He bent down in front of Wade, then set the flashlight on the floor.

"Rich, is that you?" Wade's voice broke.

"Yeah, man, I'm right here," he said as he put his hand on Wade's shoulder.

"You have to get me out of here."

"No problem. I'll get you out. You got to get up, though." Rich helped lift Wade from the floor. "Are you hurt or something?"

"No, I just have to get out of this basement." Wade's voice continued to break. He turned around into Rich who was standing before him. In the distance Wade saw something in the shadows that caught his attention. "Ah, no, they're still here!" he cried.

Rich turned around. "Who's here?" he asked as he looked over the room.

"Don't you see them? They're hanging in front of us!"

"Man, just calm down. There's no one here."

"They're right there. I see them!"

"Wade, there's no one down here."

"Screw you, man, because I see them. They're here!"

"Let's just get you upstairs."

"They won't let me go! They want me to do it, but I won't!"

"Let's get you out of here. You'll feel better once you're upstairs." Rich hunted on the floor for the flashlight. "Damn it, where'd it go?"

"Forget the damn light, just get me out of here!"

"Okay, we're going."

"Lead me out. I'm closing my eyes." Wade said as he held them shut.

"Man, what's happened to you?" Rich asked while Wade gripped his shirt.

"Are we at the stairs yet?"

"Almost," Rich said as they walked through the darkness. "Okay, we're here."

Wade opened his eyes. "Out of my way, I want up those stairs!" he said bumping into Rich.

Wade waited in the kitchen until Rich came up.

"Man, you look like shit," Rich said as he saw Wade beneath the light.

"You would, too, if you just saw what I did. This house isn't right. There's something really bad here," he spoke as he shook.

"You're having a mental breakdown or something. You need to try and calm down."

"I need to tell John and Andrea. They need to know." Wade walked quickly into the living room. "Andrea, John, you guys need to get out of this house. You shouldn't stay here."

"We need to get out of here?" Andrea asked.

"Is everything all right?" asked John. "Is something wrong?"

"Where's Chloe?"

"She fell asleep on the couch with Snow. Why?"

"Good, I didn't want her to hear this." Wade took a second to gather his words. "You guys really need to leave this place. This house isn't good. This place has evil within it. I've seen it."

"What are you talking about?" John inquired.

"You guys are going to think I'm crazy, but please believe me, what I tell you is the truth. I just saw my mother hang herself in your basement."

"You saw what, Wade?" John asked him.

"When I was five, I witnessed my mother's suicide. She hung herself in our attic. I walked in as she kicked a chair from beneath her feet, then she hung there, twitching before me. I cried out to my dad who was downstairs. He came running up and saw my mom hanging there, still clinging to life. You know that bastard didn't try to help her? He looked at me and said, if your mom wants away from me that bad, I'll let her die. Then that asshole turned around and walked out of the room like nothing happened. I did what I could to get her down, but I was just too small. I didn't have the strength. That asshole abused her so much that she wanted to die. I was left with the old man and his abusive hands. By the time I was nine I couldn't take it anymore. I wanted to be with my mom and far away from him. So I went to the exact spot that she hung herself and tried to do it, too. The old man found me just as I jumped from the chair, ironic because that's when I found my mother. He let my mom die, but for some reason he wouldn't allow me to. My Aunt and Uncle knew what was going on so they fought to get custody of me and became my legal guardians."

"I'm sorry you saw that, Wade, but what does that have to do with our basement?" John wondered.

"I was getting there. I had taken some boxes downstairs. The whole time I was there I heard someone giggling and running across the room. I wasn't scared until I saw her."

"Saw who?"

"This little girl. She looks like pure evil. Her eyes were dark like endless pits, and that look on her face could have made the warmest blood run cold. She slowly crept toward me with her doll at her side, then before my eyes her appearance began to change into that of my mother. It was then she began to talk. Join me! She said eagerly. Wade watch mommy. I'll show you what to do. That's when she hung the rope from the rafter and slipped the noose over her head. Like mother, like son, she said, throwing me some extra rope. She kept telling me that I could do it, and that's all I heard, her voice playing over in my mind like a broken record. I yelled out to her, you aren't my mother! After that the illusion was stripped away, serving only the bare truth, a little girl and her doll both hanging from the rafters. It was the most morbid image I've ever seen." Wade shook his head in disbelief. "I mean, the doll was even hanging by its neck like it committed suicide. This place isn't right. The evil that's here will manipulate your mind and play with your sight."

"Oh, man, I've seen them, too! I was just afraid to say anything. I figured you'd all think I was crazy." Brad told them. "I've seen that little girl and her doll. I swear that damn thing can walk!"

"What doll are you talking about?" Andrea questioned him.

"It's old, real old."

"That's Chloe's doll. We found her in one of the bedrooms," she said mildly.

"Get rid of it! I mean it, Andrea, that thing doesn't need to be in this house. That ghostly girl is attached to the doll. Maybe if you'd get rid of the thing, she'd leave, too. Whatever it is, it's negative. Throw it away!"

"What should I tell Chloe when she asks for it?"

"Just say it got broken and you had to throw it out."

"Isn't this all going a little too far?" John asked. "I mean, a ghostly girl I can understand, but an evil doll that also walks sounds a bit far out."

Andrea turned to John while staring him down. "We talked about this earlier. I told you I thought something was up with that doll. Did you not believe me about it?"

"It's just a doll. There's nothing unusual about it except that it looks astoundingly real. I didn't feel threatened by it, if that's what you wanted to know."

Brad looked toward John. "I didn't have an accident on those stairs.

House Of Illusions

The doll grabbed at me, that's how I tripped. John, I know what I saw, I'm not crazy and neither is Wade. We've both experienced something in this house, and I can tell you right now, Wade's was a lot worse. I mean, what's going to happen to the next person?" Brad took a moment, then looked at Andrea. "Wade's right, you should get rid of the doll."

"That's it, it's going! John, you can go upstairs and get it. After that, you can take it to the trash," Andrea told him.

"Fine. All right, if it makes everyone feel better that it's out of this house, I'll take it," he said, leaving the room.

Andrea turned to her right. "Rich, would you mind going upstairs with John? I'd feel better if someone else were up there with him."

"No problem, I'll go."

"Thanks," Andrea said as Rich was leaving.

He walked up the stairs and found John in Chloe's room. "So did you find the doll?" he asked.

"Yep, got it right here," John said, turning around.

"So this is her?" Rich asked as John handed the doll over to him.

"There is something a bit eerie about her, something strange about her eyes," Rich spoke as he stared at her face.

"That's what Andrea thinks. She said its eyes would follow her. But they're glass. That's what they're supposed to do, give off an illusion."

"There's something that's always crept me out about old dolls like this. I've never liked them too much," Rich said.

The doll looked toward him and stared in his face, remembering Rich's words as they absorbed in her mind.

"Here, you get to take her outside," Rich stated as he handed the doll back to John.

"Yeah, I better get her out of here before Chloe wakes up." John started down the stairs, then out the backdoor and took the doll to the trash. As he was walking back toward the house, John noticed a little girl in the upstairs bedroom looking down. He could feel her distant glare as it blazed upon him. John was overcome by a sudden feeling to quickly look away. He rushed to the back door promptly, locking it shut, then took a few breaths and leaned on the wall until his heart stopped racing. He waited until he was calm enough, then went back to the living room.

"Is it gone?" Andrea asked as she was approaching him.

"It's in the trash."

"Good."
"I think it needed to go," he said softly.
"You do?"
"Yeah, I kind of got this feeling after I took it to the trash."
"Well, you heard Wade and Brad. It needed to go."
"Yeah, I guess so."

"Listen, I'm going to be going. I got to get out of here. It's been a really strange day. I think I'll feel better once I get back home," said Wade. "I'm really sorry; I just can't stay here any longer."

"I think I'm going to go, too. I can't stay here another minute either," Brad told Andrea and John.

They got off the couch and said their goodbyes, then walked quickly to the door.

"We understand why you guys don't want to be here any longer," mentioned Andrea.

"I'm sorry. We don't mean to rush out like this, but I don't think either of us could stay here a second more," said Wade.

"Hopefully everything is resolved now by getting rid of that doll. We'll see you later. You guys take care," Brad told them as he and Wade were leaving.

John closed the door, then he and Andrea returned to the living room.

"I suppose you'll be leaving here soon?" John asked Rich.
"Actually, I was thinking about staying for awhile if that's okay."
"I don't mind you being here. Are you sure you want to stay?"
"Yeah, that doll isn't going to scare me off!"
"Have you seen anything out of the ordinary?" Andrea asked.

"I haven't seen anything yet, and I hope I don't. It was bad enough watching Wade have that breakdown. He seemed sure of what he had seen. If you guys were in the basement with us and saw how he was acting, I think it would have bothered you. Grown men don't normally freak out and cry. The poor guy was huddled in the corner of the basement sobbing uncontrollably. I thought he had lost it at one point. He kept saying they were hanging there the entire time I was with him."

"What do you think about what's happened here?" John asked. "Do you believe it?"

"Like I said, I haven't seen anything, and I hope not to, but that doesn't set aside the fact that I think there's something in this house."

"So you do think there's something here?"

"Yes, it's a possibility. Why don't you guys go to the records department and see if you can find out something about this place? They'll have all the records you'd need. Maybe you'll find something; you never know."

"If things start to happen again or begin to escalate, I think we'll go," added Andrea.

"Have you guys seen anything?" Rich wondered.

"When we first arrived, Chloe kept talking about seeing a little girl in the window. I didn't think anything of it at first until Andrea told me that she kept hearing laughter upstairs. I was in the basement prior to the time you and Wade were there. The place scares me. I got this really uncomfortable feeling that I didn't like."

"Did something happen?"

"I swear I heard two little girls talking down there. Then earlier when I was outside I heard Andrea yelling for me. I came in, went upstairs and found her in the bathroom. She said she never called for me. I thought that was a little strange. It was Andrea's voice; I heard it as clear as day."

"Isn't that when she said she needed some help upstairs?" Rich asked.

"Yeah, it was."

"I heard her, too. I think I even saw a shadow in the window before you went in."

"I knew I wasn't hearing things. See, Andrea? I told you I heard your voice. Rich even heard it, too."

"I don't know what to say, unless whatever's here is strong enough to mimic us."

"But the entity is that of a child," added John.

"I know, but that doesn't mean she can't be strong," Andrea replied.

"What if the spirit is something more sinister and is using the form of a child?" Rich asked.

"I'm not sure. I'm not a professional in this type of thing, but I do know a little."

"What about the doll? She isn't a ghost," John said.

"That's what confuses me so much. If I think about it, I guess there might be a few ways to explain it. But I think the doll's been in this house a long time. Maybe the little girl possesses the doll in some way. I don't know for certain; I'm trying my best to figure it out. There might be some kind of explanation. Honestly, I'm puzzled. Either of you have any input on this?"

"Maybe you're right. The little girl could be attached to the doll, controlling it in some way. But what if the doll had a mind of its own?"

"This is starting to creep me out. The doll's gone; why don't we just drop this? I don't want to think about it anymore."

"Oh, gee, Andrea, I'm real sorry. I didn't mean to scare you. I was just giving you my input."

"I think your thought scared me; you know, the doll having a mind of its own. Anything's possible. It's just scary to think that might be the truth."

"We won't talk about it anymore," Rich added.

"Are you guys getting hungry? I figured we could order a pizza," Andrea told them.

"Sounds great. Just let me know how much it is and I'll help pay on it," Rich said, digging for his wallet.

"Don't worry, Rich. I'll cover it," John told him.

"Too bad. I'll put some money down on it. I don't mind."

"Put your wallet up. I told you, I got it."

"Are you sure?"

"Yeah, I'm sure." John turned to Andrea, "Why don't you call the order in? Is everyone all right with sausage and pepperoni?"

"That's fine with me," said Rich.

"All right, sausage and pepperoni it is. Andrea, why don't you order an extra large and two litters of pop to go with it?"

"Are you picking it up?" she asked.

"Go ahead and get it delivered."

"All right, do you guys want anything else?"

"Yeah. Get some bread sticks, too," said Rich.

"Family size, all right?"

"Perfect!"

"I'll be right back," Andrea said, leaving the room.

"Hey, don't forget to ask for the total." John yelled out to her.

"Since you're nice enough to pick up the bill, why don't you let me pay for the tip?" Rich told him.

"You don't have to do that."

"I want to. It's the least I could do."

"Sure, if you want."

Andrea returned to the room. "Okay, it'll be here within the hour. The total's $23.74. We got the pop free since we ordered an extra large."

"Did you get the bread sticks?" Rich asked.

"Yes, I ordered the bread sticks. They'll be here with the pizza. "

"Good. I was kind of worried there for a minute."

"You thought I'd forget?"

"Yeah, well, you can't blame me. You can't have pizza and not have bread sticks. It's just not right."

"You're a true Italian, Rich!"

"I am?" he thought aloud.

"Just a gesture!" She laughed at his reply.

Rich gazed at Andrea with an expressive look on his face. "We're men. We like to eat a lot."

"Luckily I know that's true."

"You should. You live with me." John said, adding in his reply.

"Man, you always ate more than anyone else." Rich laughed out.

"You should have seen him when I was pregnant with Chloe. John shared in my cravings for food."

Rich turned to John, laughing at Andrea's remark, "Oh, you have to be kidding. You had cravings?"

"Yeah, it was really bad. I wanted the weirdest stuff at the strangest times. I can understand why women get so demanding when they want something to eat at three in the morning. When you, want food, you got to have it!"

"I can't believe it. Not a lot of guys go through that, but you did? That's hilarious!"

"Oh, you think that's funny, huh? I hope you go through it one day, too!"

"No way. It won't happen."

"I'm going to laugh at you when it does, then we'll see how you like it." John said as the doorbell rang. "That must be our pizza."

Rich handed him some money. "Here, this is for the tip."

John opened the door and peered out from behind the screen. The porch was empty, not a single soul in sight. Suddenly, without any warning everyone heard the back door slam shut.

"Andrea, stay here with Chloe. I think someone's in the house." Rich followed John into the kitchen, "I don't see anyone in here."

"Me either," said Rich as he looked around the room.

John walked over to the door. "It's locked."

"It's locked?"

"Yeah, locked. We heard this door shut, though."

"Well, it wasn't the basement door. It's still open from when Wade and I were down there."

"Would you mind shutting it?" John asked.

"Sure."

Right after Rich shut the basement door he and John heard the doorbell ring again.

"Front door," John shouted. He and Rich raced out of the kitchen.

"Hey, how're y'all doin? That'll be $23.74," said the pizza boy, handing over the food.

John handed the pop and bread sticks to Rich. "You weren't at the back door just now, were you?" he asked the kid.

"No, sir. I rang the door just as I got here."

"Oh, okay. Well, here's the money, and your tip's included. Have a good day."

"You, too, sir. Thank you."

John walked behind Rich into the living room.

"Yummy pizza!" exclaimed Chloe.

"And what are you doing up? We were planning on eating all of this food while you were still asleep." John told her.

"No, you weren't." Chloe giggled.

"Yeah, we were. We were going to let you have the leftovers!"

"Daddy, you're silly!"

"I'm just playing, Chlo. You hungry?"

"Yeah, I'm ready to eat. It's been a long day." she said eagerly.

"But you've been sleeping, kiddo."

"I only took a nap."

"Well, it's a good thing you're up. That way you can get some of this pizza."

"Mommy woke me. She said it was time to eat." Chloe looked over to Rich. "Are you staying, too?"

"Sure am. Is that a problem?" Rich asked.

"No, I'm glad you're here. Where's everyone else? Aren't they hungry?"

"They had to get home. They had things to do," Rich told her.

"Oh, okay. At least you're still here. I wanted to show everyone my big surprise."

"You have a surprise to show us?" Rich asked.

"Yeah, but you'll have to wait until we're done eating."

"That must be some surprise then." he added.

Chloe's eyes beamed as she looked at him. "You'll see. I bet you want to know what it is."

"You've got my curiosity piqued, kid, but I can wait."

"All right, everyone to the kitchen!" Andrea yelled. "Take a seat where ever you want." She passed the paper plates and plastic cups around the table. "Okay, you guys, dig in!" She took Chloe's plate and filled it with pizza, then set the plate in front of her. "Here you go, Chlo."

"Can I have another slice of pizza, mommy?"

"Eat this first, then you can have another piece."

Everyone sat around the table and ate, then talked merrily among themselves.

"That was good pizza," John added. "I'm stuffed."

"Yeah, I think we all are except for Chloe. Man, kid, where you putting all that food?" Rich quizzed her.

"In my tummy!" She laughed.

"Are you sure you're not dropping it on the floor?"

"Nope. It's going in my mouth, see?" Chloe exclaimed, showing Rich her chewed up food.

"Chloe, don't do that. It isn't nice," Andrea told her politely.

Chloe threw out her bottom lip to pout. "I'm sorry, mommy."

"It's okay. She's just a kid. They do stuff us adults can't. Man, sometimes I miss being a youngster. I used to hide under my sister's bed and grab her feet as she came in the room. Boy, did that scare her. I bet her screams were heard two blocks away!" Rich said, going back into his thoughts. "Those were the days, having innocent fun and getting

Jillian Osborn

into trouble. Unfortunately those days are now over. It's all in the past, along with many other memories."

Chloe contemplated Rich's word's. "You wish you were still a kid?" she asked.

"Yeah, sometimes."

"Why?"

"Because we're only a kid once. Before we know it, many years have gone by."

"Do you miss hiding under the bed and scaring your sister?" Chloe responded quickly.

Rich began to laugh at her quirky remark. "There are a lot of things I miss. I guess that could be one of them." Rich admitted.

"There are certain things I miss from my childhood, too," Andrea began to say as John interrupted.

"I miss my mom's cooking." he said aloud.

"You sure didn't miss it today!" Andrea added.

"Hey, I was starving."

"Are you saying I don't cook enough?" she asked, playing around.

"You cook enough, but it just don't taste like mom's."

"Why don't you try cooking your own meal for once? Then tell me whose tastes better between the two of us!"

"I know already. You'd win. All I can do is heat up a can of soup. That's what I call cooking." he said modestly.

"And what would you do if I weren't here? Who'd cook for you?"

"Chloe, of course! She cooks on her play stove. She could probably cook some real food, I bet!"

"Do you need me to remind you about a year ago, Chloe playing restaurant and deciding she was going to cook a real meal, so she made us eat her version of potato soup?"

"Oh, yeah. That's when she got in your spice cabinet without you knowing and filled our bowls with all kinds of stuff." John thought aloud.

"Chloe tried to make soup for you guys?" Rich laughed for a second, then turned to Chloe who was sitting at his left side. "I could only imagine how well a six-year-old cooks." Rich looked over to John and Andrea trying not to laugh. "So how was that potato soup? Bet it was the best you ever had!"

"Oh, yeah. She stuck her hand in a tub of butter and put a lump into each bowl, then mashed it into the herbs. The broth was real good. She ran cold water over the ingredients and, you know, that picked up the taste of the butter and herbs nicely. Then she crushed a handful of potato chips and threw that into the bowls, then she finished by adding the salt and pepper."

"Wow! That sure does sound good! Bet y'all enjoyed that a lot." Rich said, trying hard not to laugh.

"Mommy and daddy think I'm a good cook." Chloe beamed as Andrea added to the conversation.

"Oh, it was so good, we had about two bites, then we were full. But let me tell you, this kid can cook!"

"Sure sounds that way."

"I'll be right back," Chloe said as she slid down from her chair.

"Where you going, Chlo?" Andrea asked.

"Just to the other room for a second."

Andrea, Rich and John continued to talk in the kitchen while Chloe was gone.

"I should probably get going soon. It's starting to get late," Rich told them.

"You're more then welcome to stay here," John said back. "You have a long drive ahead of you. Why don't you just stay here for the night? We have an extra bed you can sleep in," John said, offering a room.

"I can't do that. It's your first night in your new home."

The television on the kitchen counter let out the familiar sound of a weather warning. Andrea turned to the TV and listened to the meteorologist's announcement. "There's a storm coming. The station has issued a severe thunderstorm warning in affect until three a.m," Andrea told John and Rich as she walked toward the window.

She peered toward the sky and watched as it was quickly consumed by clouds. "This storm is going to be bad. Rich, I think you should stay here tonight. I don't think you should be getting out in this. It wouldn't be wise."

"I guess I'll..." Rich tried to complete his sentence when Chloe interrupted.

"It's starting to rain!" she exclaimed happily as she came in the room. "Daddy, Rich, I want to show you my surprise!"

They turned around to greet her.

"What're you hiding there, kiddo?" John asked anxiously.

"Isn't she pretty? Mommy and I found her today!" Chloe said, unveiling the doll.

Rich looked toward John, bothered by what was in his sight. Andrea slowly turned away from the window and stared upon the doll in shock.

"Where did you find her?" John asked Chloe, trying hard not to appear afraid.

"Mommy and I found her in my room today."

"Where was she just now when you got her?"

"On my pillows sitting down. You want to hold her, daddy?" Chloe asked, handing the doll over.

"She's real pretty, baby."

"I'm going to play with her all the time. She's my new friend."

"Baby, I don't think this is the type of doll you should be playing with. You see, Chlo, she's very old. If you play with her, she's liable to get broken. I don't think you want that to happen, do you?"

"But she's my friend. I won't hurt her, daddy, honest."

"I know you wouldn't hurt her, sweetie, but sometimes we cause things to happen that we don't mean to. I think it would be best if we put her in the living room in one of the glass breakfronts. That way nothing can happen to her."

"Can she stay in my room? I swear I won't play with her. Please, daddy?" Chloe begged in tears.

"Let me think about it until tomorrow. Maybe she could stay with you, but you have to let me think it over first, okay?"

"Okay, daddy," Chloe said, bowing her head as she sat in her chair.

"I'll be right back. I'm taking this doll to the living room," John told everyone. John knotted his head and motioned for Rich to follow. They walked out of the kitchen and into the living room. "How the hell did this get back in the house?" John demanded.

"I saw you take this thing to the trash. What's it doing back in here? I say we lock it in this case right now," Rich added as John set her on a shelf. "How're we going to get rid of her?" Rich began to panic and tremble.

"I want to wait till Chloe goes to sleep tonight, then get this doll out of here," John whispered lightly.

"What about the storm? You heard Andrea; it's in affect till three a.m."

"If I have to go out in this rain, I will. That doll's not staying in this house," John stated.

"She'll be locked in the breakfront. I don't think she'll get out," Rich replied.

"Oh, man, will you listen to us! We're both about to lose our minds over this damn thing. We're thinking weird thoughts; we're both going crazy. What if the doll decides to break out? Assuming she could. She would venture into any room she pleased. I don't want her in my daughter's room, nor any of the other rooms for that matter. This doll makes me uncomfortable. I want her to go," John said, getting his point across.

"You think it could do that? You know, break out of here?" Rich asked.

"It got back into this house somehow, and I'll tell you what, I wasn't the one who brought it in."

"I'll help you get rid of it."

"We'll have to do it after Chloe goes to sleep. We'll wrap it in a bunch of bags, bind it in rope, then this time bury it in the trash."

"It sounds crazy, but I'll help."

"John, we thought you two disappeared," Andrea said as she walked into the room toward him and Rich. "Chloe wanted to know where you both were."

"Daddy, is my dolly okay?"

"She's fine, baby. We put her in this case where she looks so pretty. See?" he said, picking Chloe up.

"Is she comfortable in there?"

"I would guess so. I set her in there as nicely as I could. What do you think?"

"I guess she looks comfortable."

"It's getting late, Chlo. I'm going to put you in your jammies and get you ready for bed," Andrea said, taking her from John. "You can sleep on the couch until we take you to your room. We'll be back in a minute," Andrea told John and Rich.

"Why don't we take a seat on the couch?" John said to Rich. "We'll wait for them to get back."

"What're we going to tell Chloe tomorrow about the doll? If we've gotten rid of it?"

"I'll tell her that I took the doll out of the case and was looking at it. When I tried to put her back in, I'll tell Chlo, she slipped from my hand and broke. She'll believe it."

"She's a kid. They always do."

"Well, don't you look like a little princess in your purple pajamas!" John said as Chloe and Andrea walked in.

"Look at my house shoes." Chloe said, pointing at her little feet.

"Oh, my goodness, you're covered in purple hair. I better check your legs."

"Daddy!" Chloe giggled. "It's just my house shoes. See?" she said, sliding them off her feet.

"You had me worried there for a minute, kid. I started to think you were growing purple fuzz!"

"I have pink ones, too!"

"Well, good for you. I bet they keep your feet nice and warm."

"Yep, and they're pretty, too!"

"Let's get you on the couch and get you covered up," said Andrea.

"I get to sleep here for awhile." Chloe exclaimed happily. "I'm too scared to sleep in my room. I don't like thunderstorms," she told Rich.

"I don't like them too much either."

"Are you scared to go to sleep?"

"Not anymore, but I used to be."

"Sometimes it helps when you're with your mommy and daddy. Well, good night," Chloe said as she curled in the blanket and rolled on her side.

Andrea, John and Rich talked about the weather until Chloe fell asleep.

"What are we going to do about that doll?" Andrea whispered.

"Rich and I are going to get rid of the thing once Chloe's in a dead sleep."

"You're going to take it out in this weather?" Andrea wondered aloud. "It's pouring down rain. Hail's falling from the sky and the wind is kicking up."

"Maybe it'll die down some later."

"What if it doesn't and gets worse?"

"I hope it doesn't."

"How'd it get back in the house?"

"I guess it walked in, I don't know. I don't have all the answers." John said mildly.

"When could it have gotten in? Wouldn't we have heard something?" she questioned him.

"Andrea, I said I don't know."

"I think I do," said Rich. "Remember earlier when someone was at the front door, then we heard the back door slam shut? I think that's when it came back. We never saw it with our eyes, but that doesn't mean it didn't come in."

"This place is getting even more bizarre. I say we call the realtor in the morning and see if she knows something about this place that we don't."

"What if she doesn't?"

"We'll find whatever records we can about this house." John paused for a brief second. "Andrea, are you feeling okay? You look a bit pale."

"I feel warm."

John quickly got out of his seat and put his hand on Andrea's forehead. "You're burning up!"

"Could you get me some water please? I think I'd feel better if I had something to cool me down," she asked.

"Yeah, I'll be right back." John rushed to the kitchen, went to the sink, then grabbed a glass on the counter and filled it with cold water. He took it back into the living room and handed it to Andrea. "Here you go. Is there anything else I could get you?"

"No, this should be fine."

"What happened to you? One minute you were fine, then the next you're burning all up."

"I don't feel right, John. I'm getting dizzy."

"Why don't you lie down and rest?"

"I think I will. Please, Rich, don't mind me," Andrea told him as she laid on the couch.

"You're no bother. You just get comfortable, okay?"

"I don't mean to be a couch hog."

"Hey, you stretch out as much as you want. I don't mind."

"But I feel like you don't have enough room."

"I have plenty of room. Don't worry about me."

"If you both don't mind, I think I'm going to take a little nap. I feel exhausted from all the work we've done today."

"We'll keep our voices down while you and Chloe sleep. If you need anything later, just let me know all right," John said, covering Andrea with a blanket.

"I'm really hot. I don't need this," she said, trying to hand the blanket back to him.

"It'll help sweat out your fever. That's what you always tell me."

"I don't need it. I'm already sweating enough."

"Too bad. I'm covering you up."

"I'll just kick it off."

"You better not kick it off. You want that fever to go away, don't you?"

"Yes," she uttered lightly.

"Then you're going to keep this blanket on you, all right."

"I'll stay under it," Andrea said softly as she dozed to sleep.

"That didn't take long. She's already out," Rich stated to John.

"Yeah, I see that."

"You want to finish some stuff up around the house while they're both asleep?"

"There's really not that much left to do. We lucked out when we bought the place. Most of the original furniture is still here, along with other things, I guess you could say, belong to the house. It's pretty nice getting a place that's already furnished. It saves us a lot of money. It's not like the stuff in here is junk. There's a lot of antiques in this house. I bet we could get some good money for some of these things if we ever decided to sell. It's all in good condition. An antique dealer would see the value right away."

"Well, I know you got this place at a good deal. I figured this house would have been appraised for a lot more then what you paid for it, though. It's what you notice right away in this house that lets you know you have something of value. Houses aren't made like this anymore. Look how tall these rooms are and how high these ceilings go, and the woodwork in this place is amazing. Rich mahogany doors, brakers and a grand staircase all carved by hand. You just don't see this type of craftsmanship anymore."

"Stuff wasn't mass made the way it is now, Rich. People back then took pride in their work, not to mention the time they spent on just one piece of furniture. Stuff was made better, too. It lasted longer and was more durable then most of the stuff that's built nowadays."

"Yeah. I know what you mean."

"There's an exquisiteness about old furniture and houses that can't be matched to the things that are made now."

"This truly is a beautiful house. I think you, Andrea and Chloe are going to enjoy it here."

"It's always been Andrea's dream to have a home like this. I just thought we'd never be able to afford one this nice," John stood from the couch. "I'm going to get a cold beer. You want one?"

"Yeah, that sounds good right now."

John walked into the kitchen and grabbed two bottles out of the fridge. The rain continued to descend heavily and the wind howled fiercely.

John walked back into the living room and handed Rich his beer. "This storm's pretty bad," he told Rich. "I'm surprised none of these trees have been uprooted."

Rich got off the couch, walked over to the window and peered out. The street lights flickered in the dark like lanterns, then suddenly went out. Rich couldn't see anything beyond that, for the rain was so severe, it had distorted the street and sidewalks.

Hail the size of quarters began to fall, striking the windows as they expired to the ground. A loud crack of thunder carried through the house, shaking the floor beneath Rich and John's feet.

Behind him, John heard a child crying. He turned around and found Chloe awake on the couch clutching her blanket tightly. "What's wrong, baby? Did the thunder scare you?"

"Ah-huh."

"It's all right, Chlo. You want to stay by your mom?"

She shook her head and held her hands up. John scooped her from the couch and placed her on the other side by Andrea.

"Is this better now?" he asked.

"Yes, daddy," Chloe said, wiping tears from her eyes. "Will you put Snow by me? I don't want her to be alone."

"Sure, honey, here she is," John said, laying the kitten beside her. "Try to go back to sleep. When you wake up, the storm will be over."

Another crack of thunder broke through the air as Chloe pulled the blanket over her head.

"What time is it anyway?" Rich asked.

"It's a little past midnight."

"It feels later for some reason."

"Yeah, it does. It's been a long day, that's why," John said, finishing his sentence.

A heavy knock beat at the front door, alarming Rich and John as they stared directly upon each other.

"Who could that be?" Rich wondered.

"Whoever it is, they're crazy to be out in this storm."

Another loud knock struck the door as Rich and John stood in place.

"You gonna answer that?" Rich asked.

John undid the locks and slowly pulled open the door. The porch was empty except for the falling rain hitting the house. John couldn't see beyond the stairs, for the heavy downfall wouldn't permit it, so he quickly shut the door and fastened the locks.

"There's no one out there," he said to Rich. "Maybe it was just hail knocking at the door."

"That wasn't hail. Someone was just here," Rich said.

Two more heavy knocks pounded at the door. Rich brushed John aside and took a look through the peep hole.

"You see anyone?" asked John.

"I don't know. It's hard to tell."

Rich continued to look through the peep hole when John shouted, "What the hell's that?"

"What's what?" Rich asked, wondering what John had referred to.

"Look down!"

Rich dropped his eyes toward the ground and saw the same unbelievable sight as John.

A ghostly white arm had emerged through the door while ice crystals had frosted over the wood, freezing the surface. "What the hell's going on?" Rich yelled.

The hand then opened, dropping a fist full of ice as it formed this message, *It's just starting.*

The ghostly arm faded slowly as it retreated back into the door.

The ice had melted around the surface and trickled steadily toward the ground where it disappeared as it dripped to the floor.

A loud roar of thunder burst in the night while blue-white lightning lit the room, then the power died out. "Oh, this is great! We're now stuck here in complete darkness."

"Relax, Rich. You got a lighter?"

"Yeah."

"Follow me. There's a box with some candles over here." He and Rich lit a few, then set them around the room for light.

"What're we going to do?" Rich asked.

"Stay calm. It's just a little power outage. Everything will be fine."

"I'm not worried about the power, damn it! I'm worried about whatever it is that's in this house. You saw the same thing I did. Something strange is going on here, and to be honest with you, it kind of scares me. I'm pretty uncomfortable with the thought of not having any power. It makes me think something bad might happen."

"Hey, whatever it was startled me, too. I can't explain what we saw. I'm just as afraid of it as you."

"Why don't we forget about sleeping in our own rooms tonight."

"What? You want to stay in here?"

"I'd be fine with that. I don't care if I have to sleep on the floor."

"You don't have to sleep on the floor, Rich. You can have the couch over there."

"Where are you going to sleep?"

"I can sleep in the recliner. Why don't you and I go on and get rid of that doll? That way it'll be out of this house."

"Looks like this storm's finally letting up some. We might as well."

"Why don't you head on into the kitchen and grab a plastic bag along with some masking tape. I'll be there in a moment with our dear little friend." John walked over to the case and unlocked the glass door. A strange coldness emanated off the doll's body as he took her out. He hurried to the kitchen where Rich was waiting with an open bag.

John rolled her in the plastic, then bound her in tape. "That ought to hold her. Let's get her to the trash. We'll bury her in the garbage." John walked over to the back door and undid the lock. "You ready to do this?"

"Yeah, hurry up. Let's get this over with!" Rich followed John out into the rain.

"Pick some of this garbage up so I can put the doll at the bottom of the can." John yelled to Rich.

"Hurry up and toss her in there. I've moved the bags."

John put the doll in the garbage while Rich buried her beneath the other trash bags. They secured the lid, then ran back to the house to escape the rain.

"The damn door won't open." John yelled.

"Push harder!"

"It won't budge."

"What'd you mean, it won't budge?"

"It's stuck!" John yelled back to him.

Rich ran up on the door and tried to push it open. "It's locked. We're locked out!"

John began to beat on the door, hoping it would open. "It's no use. This isn't working!" Just as John was about to give up, the door swung open, welcoming them back into the kitchen.

"What happened to the candles that were burning?" Rich asked.

"The draft must have blown them out. It's all right, I still have my lighter. We can see with that."

The two men walked carefully through the kitchen, making their way into the living room.

"God, I'm glad that's over!" Rich said in relief.

"That makes two of us." John looked over to the couch and saw an empty seat. "Where's Andrea?" His heart began to race and a sense of dread crept over him. "She's not on the couch!"

"Maybe she went upstairs."

"Andrea wouldn't have left Chloe in here alone."

"Let's just check upstairs in case. Maybe she's in the bedroom."

"I'll check, but I want you to stay here with Chloe. Hand me that candle over there." He pointed to the table.

John quickly walked up the stairs and noticed a dim light coming from the bathroom. "Andrea?" he asked softly as he opened the door. He saw her sitting on the floor next to the toilet. "Are you all right?" John walked into the bathroom and stood by his wife.

"I'm sick. I don't feel too well."

John kneeled by Andrea and felt her head. "God, honey, you're burning up. We need to get you something for this fever."

"No, I don't want anything. I'll just get sick."

"But you need to take something."

"Just get me a cold rag."

"Andrea, you're burning up with fever. Let me get you some medicine."

"No, all I want is a cold rag," she spoke weakly.

John placed the cool rag on Andrea's neck.

"Just help me get back downstairs to the couch. I want to lie down."

John walked her down the stairs, then helped her get on the couch.

"Is everything okay?" Rich wondered.

"She's sick."

"Is there anything I could do?"

"She just wants to lie down. She needs something to lower her fever, but she refuses to take anything."

"I think I have the flu. I break out in chills, then I'll get all hot again. If you don't mind, I'm just going to go back to sleep. I feel weak," she told them.

"That's the best thing for you right now," John replied.

"Why don't we all just call it a night? I'm pretty tired myself," Rich added.

"Yeah, it's already late. We have a long day ahead of us tomorrow. We better get some rest."

CHAPTER THREE

It was 7:00 a.m. when Andrea felt a light tug on her right shoulder. She opened her eyes to greet Chloe who was standing before her. "What is it, baby?"

"I'm hungry, mommy."

"Give me a moment, then I'll be up." She noticed the rest of the living room was empty. "Where's your daddy and Rich?"

"Upstairs. They didn't want to wake you."

John came down the stairs with a box of trash in his hands. "I'm sorry, Andrea. I told her not to wake you."

"She just wants some breakfast."

"I told her I'd get it when I came back down."

"It's okay, I'll make her something to eat."

"You still don't look well, Andrea. Why don't you sleep in? I'll tend to Chloe," he assured her.

"No, it's okay. I'll tend to Chloe myself."

"Do you feel well enough? Because if you don't, don't worry about it."

"I'm up. I'll tend to her. You just finish up whatever it is you're doing."

"If you start feeling sick, I want you to lie back down. I have some trash to take out. I'll be back in a minute." John went out the back door.

As he started down the walkway he noticed a middle-aged, regal man standing in the alley with a Malamute at his side.

The man was nicely dressed and the smell of expensive cologne carried in the breeze.

"You must be my new neighbor for the month. I'm Tucker Blackwell. I live to the right of you."

"Nice to meet you. I'm John Craven," he said, extending his hand. "I'm sorry, I don't believe I heard you correctly. Did you say I was your new neighbor for the month?"

"You heard right, son."

"Well, I was thinking the family and I would stay a bit longer."

"No one ever stays in that house for too long. I'd be surprised if you made it past a week."

"I'm sorry, sir. I don't think I follow."

"Rumor says that place is haunted. I've seen families come and go from that house just as quickly as the seasons change. That house isn't fit to live in. It should have been burned. Never the less it's a beautiful home; unfortunately, it's just not the best place to be."

"What happened to the other families?"

"Most of them ran off scared in the night. Folks who've lived there and came out of that place alive will tell you they've seen things in that house that just weren't possible, as though dark illusions had been conjured up from within its walls."

"Ghosts?" John wondered aloud.

"Ghosts, goblins. Something's there and it won't ever leave."

"Do you know what it is, Mr. Blackwell?"

"All I know about are the stories that people have told. Whatever's there is beyond my comprehension. By the way, you can call me Tookie. That's what I'm known as around here."

"Is it just you and the wife who live here?"

"I lost Evelyn three years back to cancer, God rest her soul. She fought for six years before it claimed her life," Tucker managed to say.

"I'm sorry to hear that, sir."

"Unfortunately, it was her time, and in the end I think she was ready to go. We can't live forever, son. That's life for you, though. We must all come and go at some point in time. So it's just been Sam and me in the house," Tookie said, petting his dog on the head.

"I bet he makes a good companion," John added.

"Sam's a good old dog. He's been a loyal friend from the first day I got him."

"Say, that was some storm we had here last night. Are they always that bad?"

"Last night?" Tookie pondered. "I never heard any storm."

"It was pouring here till about three in the morning."

"I was wondering why your lawn and sidewalk were so wet. I didn't get any rain by my house, and I live next door. That house of yours must have already started playing tricks on you. My warning to you, son, is that whatever you see in that house, don't believe it. That place will feed you nothing but lies."

"Thanks for the info. I'll remember your advice."

"Do you have any children?"

"Yes, one. Chloe. She's six."

"Keep an eye on her. Whatever's in that house is drawn to children. It'll try to use her and turn her against you and your wife by feeding her one lie after another."

"You don't say? Well, Mr. Blackwell, I hate to cut this short, but I must be getting back. My wife's been ill since yesterday. I better be going. It was nice meeting you."

"It was my pleasure. You and the family are welcome over anytime you'd like. If you ever need to talk, I'm just next door."

"Thank you for your kindness. You're welcome here, too." John shook Tookie's hand and petted Sam on the head, then headed back to the house.

He walked through the back door and found Andrea resting her head on the kitchen table. "If you feel that bad, why don't you go back to bed?"

"I had to get Chloe something to eat. My job of being a mother comes first."

"She's eating. Go on and lie back down. I'll watch Chloe until you're better. Now go!"

"Thanks, John," Andrea said, pulling herself up from the chair.

"I'll bring you some medicine in a few minutes." John looked over to Chloe, who was eating a bowl of cereal. "Try to leave your mom alone so she can get some rest. She's not feeling good. You can help Rich and me around the house while your mommy's sleeping."

"What should I do?" she asked.

"You can start off by helping Rich and me uncover some of the furniture upstairs, then you can help me figure out where to put it. We'll rearrange the rooms and sweep the floors."

"That sounds like a lot of work."

"We can do it. It's always faster when you have help!"

"Can I play with Snow for a little while? She's upstairs on my bed."

"You can play with Snow, but you have to finish your breakfast first. Maybe later I'll take you to the pet store and we'll get her a toy mouse to play with."

"Ok, daddy. Can I go upstairs now? I'm done with my cereal."

"Sure, go on."

Chloe went up to her room when she heard Rich in the bathroom. "What are you doing?" she asked him.

"Just trying to clean the lime and rust out of the tub. I already did the sink. It's all clean. That's how the tub will look once I'm finished."

"I'm going to my room to play with Snow. Daddy said he'd take me to the pet store later. Do you want to come?"

"Yeah, I'll try to go."

"Well, I'll see you later. I'll be in my room."

Chloe walked toward the bed as the door closed shut behind her, locking her in the room.

John was downstairs washing Chloe's dishes from breakfast. He poured up a cold glass of orange juice, then took it to the living room and handed it to Andrea. "Here, honey, take these. They'll help reduce your fever."

Andrea took the glass from John, then swallowed the medicine.

"Are you hungry at all? I'll make you some breakfast."

"I hardly have an appetite now."

"Let me know when you get hungry, and I'll make you something."

"I think I'll take a bath after while. Maybe I'd feel better."

"Rich is working in there now. He'll have the bathroom ready for you soon. I'll be upstairs so you rest for now. Yell if you need anything."

John went to help Rich. As he walked past Chloe's room, he heard her voice clearly from behind the door.

"I think we'll be best friends, too!" he heard her say, then John heard a raspy voice unknown to him.

"Illusion and I have waited a long time for someone like you."

The voice sent shivers down John's spine as it spoke. He took a deep breath, then put his hand on the doorknob and tried to turn it. "Chloe, you open this door right now!" he demanded.

The door unlocked, then opened freely as it invited him in. Chloe was sitting on her bed as John rushed over to her. "What's going on in here? Who're you talking to?"

"It's okay, daddy. I was talking to Savannah."

"Savannah? Who's Savannah?"

"Savannah's the little girl who lives in my room."

"Is she the little girl you were seeing in the windows?"

"Yes, daddy. She told me she lives here with Illusion."

"Who's Illusion, honey? Can you tell daddy who that is?"

"Illusion's her best friend, daddy! They're like sisters."

"What does Illusion look like, Chloe?"

"She looks like a little girl, daddy!" Chloe giggled. "She's a lot shorter than Savannah, but she's older."

"Where did they go?"

"Savannah left when she opened the door, but Illusion's still here."

"Where is she, Chloe?"

"She's right here with me."

"I don't see her."

"That's because she's hiding, daddy. She's sitting behind my pillows." Chloe reached out, then pulled back a familiar object, stunning John's sight.

The color in his face faded, and he was struck with a sense of dread, which he felt in his gut. "Illusion's the doll?" he asked while chills crept up his back.

"Yes, daddy."

"Why do you call her by that name, Chloe?"

"Because that's the name she goes by."

"Where did you find that doll, Chlo?"

"She was waiting for me along with Savannah. Daddy, I swear I didn't take her out of the case. She was already in here."

"I know you didn't, baby. You're not in any trouble. Why don't you hand her to me and I'll put her up."

"Please don't take her from me, daddy!" Chloe begged. "She wants to stay with me."

"Chloe, I don't think I should leave her with you. I don't think that's a good idea right now, all right, honey?"

"But I've taken good care of her. I won't break her, I promise!"

I don't know what to do, John thought. If I take her away, she'll just end up coming back. "What do you and Illusion talk about, Chloe?"

"Everything. Her and Savannah are my best friends. I don't have anyone else, daddy. Please don't take Illusion from me." She squalled.

John looked into Chloe's tearful eyes and felt saddened by her cries. "I bet you'll meet some little friends your age, Chlo. It'll just take some time to find them."

"But I have friends now, daddy, and I like them."

"I tell you what. I'll let you keep Illusion up here under one condition. You're only allowed to play with her for fifteen minutes, then you're to put her up."

"Okay, daddy."

"I'll let you know when your fifteen minutes have passed," John said as he was leaving the room, "I want this door left open, too, Chloe. I don't want you going off and closing it, okay baby?" John walked across the hall to check on Rich. "How's it coming in here?"

"I'm just finishing up."

"It's looking good. You know Andrea and I really appreciate your help."

"Don't mention it." Rich said washing off his hands. "Well, you got a clean bathroom."

"That's good. We could all use a bath right now."

"You ain't kidding!"

"Listen, Rich, I need to talk to you for a quick second."

"Yeah, what's up?"

"Let me shut this door. I don't want Chloe hearing."

"Hear what?"

"I'm just going to have to be blunt on this," John said, shaking his head.

"Is something wrong?"

"That damn doll made her way back into my house," he whispered to Rich, whose eyes were widened by disbelief.

"No way, man! We got rid of that thing last night! She's in the trash."

"It's with Chloe in her room. I don't know how it got back in. It's been to the trash twice. What do I have to do to get rid of it?"

"Why don't we bury it?"

"Either that or burn the damn thing. I don't want it in my house. There's also something really strange about this place, Rich. You know that storm we had here last night?"

"Yeah? What about it?"

"I talked to a neighbor earlier. He said there was no storm here last night, but there's evidence outside my house. It rained here and only here, nowhere else."

"What the hell's going on?"

"I think whatever's in this house didn't want you leaving last night."

"You think it manipulated the television and caused it to rain?"

"Well, yeah, isn't that what you'd think? I believe whatever's here made it happen. We just didn't know it at the time."

"We have a real problem, don't we?"

"I say we stay alert to everything that happens here. It's hard to know what's real and what's not. Mr. Blackwell said this house plays tricks and not to believe everything you see."

"Where's that doll right now?"

"I had to leave her with Chloe. I know it wasn't a good idea, but I didn't know what to do. Chloe told me that its name was Illusion. The doll talks to her, Rich. It's not supposed to do that."

"You have to get that thing away from her now."

"I know," John whispered lightly. "That's my daughter in there with that thing." The door slightly opened behind John's back. Standing in the doorway was Chloe clutching Illusion tightly in her arms.

"Daddy," she said softly.

"What is it, Chlo?" he asked, trying to stay as calm as possible.

"Daddy, Illusion said you're talking about her, and she doesn't like it. She says you should stop."

"Why does Illusion think we're talking about her, Chlo?"

"She told me that you and Rich were saying bad things about her.

She doesn't like it and neither does Savannah. They said you better stop it right now." Chloe turned around and walked back to her room, then shut the door.

John ran down the hall after her while Rich followed. John grabbed the doorknob quickly. "Ah, the damn things hot!" he said, releasing his grip.

Rich ran to the bathroom to fetch a hand rag. John wrapped the towel around the doorknob and twisted it open. "I told you to keep this door open, Chloe." he yelled.

"I'm sorry, daddy. Illusion wanted it shut."

"Your fifteen minutes is up, Chlo. You better hand me the doll."

"We haven't finished playing." She cried.

"I told you fifteen minutes. You'll see her again tomorrow."

"But daddy!"

"Sorry, baby."

"Where are you taking her?"

"Your doll just needs some rest. Why don't you play with Snow?"

"She's sleeping."

"Well, wake her up and get her to play. I'm just going to put Illusion back in the case. You can have her again tomorrow, but she needs to rest for now, okay Sweet Pea?"

"Okay, daddy. Savannah and I will play with Snow."

John felt dread creep up his spine when he heard Chloe say the name. "Savannah?" he asked, choking up.

Chloe began to giggle. "Yes, daddy. She's standing behind you and Rich!"

They turned around to a large mirror hanging behind them. Before their reflections stood a young girl. She stared back with a cold, hard gaze stuck to her face. Her eyes were pitch black, and her skin colorless.

Her blood red lips were set in a rigid grin as though it had been molded on her face.

"I need no introduction," she said wickedly.

John and Rich looked on appalled by her sight. They felt each goosebump rise from their skin as they covered their arms and legs. They could feel the hair stand up on their necks while cold chills swept across their backs. As quickly as it was there, the girl's image vanished.

"That was my new friend, daddy!"

"I'm sorry, Chloe. I don't like your new friend."

"Savannah told me you'd say that. She said you wouldn't understand, that you'd judge her because she looks different. She told me you'd be afraid of her and that you wouldn't like her."

"She doesn't look like a nice little girl, Chlo. I want you to have nice friends your age, and real for that matter."

"But she's nice, and she likes me because I'm not scared of her."

"Chloe, Savannah's not real. She was just an image that appeared in your mirror."

"But she's real, daddy!"

"She's just an illusion, baby. She's make believe."

"No, she's not!"

"Chloe, I think your dad's right. Savannah isn't a real person," Rich added in.

"But she's here! I can see her! I always see her, even when you can't!" Chloe said, looking deep into Rich's eyes. "Savannah says you both know she's real, yet you both deny her before me. She tells me you're no different than the others. You're all the same, scared chicken shit!" Chloe shouted out.

"Chloe, you have no business talking to Rich or me that way! And where'd you learn that language? Because of your foul mouth you won't get to play with Illusion tomorrow."

"That's okay, daddy. Illusion will come to me."

"I'll see that she doesn't. You stay in here and play with Snow. I'll be back to check on you in a little bit." John and Rich walked out of the room. "You leave this door open, you hear?"

"What's going on up here?" asked Andrea.

John turned around as Andrea saw the doll in his hand.

"Where did that come from?" she asked with her eyes fixed on Illusion. "I thought you got rid of it."

"She came back. I have to put her some place where Chloe can't find her," he whispered. "Chloe's being brainwashed by this thing. It's going too far. Whatever's in this doll has taken hold of her."

"What do you mean?" she asked, following John to their bedroom with Rich not far behind. "The little girl and this doll are trying to make her believe they're her friends. I've seen Savannah..."

Andrea interrupted, "You've seen who?"

"Chloe said the little girl's name is Savannah, and the doll goes by Illusion. Savannah looks like the abomination of pure evil, Andrea. That's the best I could explain her to you. She's a vile and wicked child. I don't know about Rich, but she frightened the hell out of me."

Andrea looked over to Rich, who was standing across the room. He took a deep breath. "There's something disturbing about her. She embraces you in a sensation that makes your skin creep and then your blood runs cold."

Andrea looked back to John, then asked, "You think we should leave?"

"No, we're going to fight this, and we're going to get rid of it. This is your dream home, Andrea. I won't let it fall through our fingers because something here frightened us away. We can beat it," John assured her.

"But how can we fight something when we don't know what we're dealing with?" she questioned him.

"We're going to find out what it is and hopefully put an end to it. There has to be some type of information out there that could tell us who Savannah was."

"While you start to do that, I'm going to take a bath. I think I'd feel better. Do both of you still feel okay?"

"I feel fine. I haven't been sick," John told her.

"Me either. I feel okay."

"You're both lucky you don't have this. I hope you don't take it."

"I'm sorry you're sick. Go on and take a nice hot bath to relax. Don't worry about anything here," John said.

"All right. I'll see you both when I get out."

CHAPTER FOUR

ANDREA WENT ON INTO THE BATHROOM and started her water. The tub filled with bubbles that rose through the air while the room occupied the scent of peony bath gel. Andrea bent over and turned the faucet off, then slipped into the tub.

She rested her head on its porcelain surface, then sponged some water around her neck, moistening her skin. She unwound more as she sank into the water as its warmth was drawing her in. She closed her eyes and dampened her face. The room was tranquil and warm, soon Andrea had relaxed away to her own personal retreat.

Fifteen minutes passed. Andrea sank deeper into the tub when she felt the water rush up to her lips. It was strange, however. Her tastebuds detected a coppery taste with salty undertones. Andrea opened her eyes, then realized she was submerged in a bath filled with blood. Andrea began to panic, thinking she was seeing things. The bloodied water began to splash from one end of the tub to the other. Andrea was frightened at that point and rushed to get out of the tub.

She felt something take hold of her leg, then slowly crawling from within the bloodied water was a young boy. He cried out to Andrea. His sight had terrorized her more, forcing her to shake uncontrollably. She looked on at the young child, seeing only his gaping wound.

The boy's head was split open and his brain matter seeped through. The child continued to squall, but Andrea disregarded his outcries as she fell from the tub. Andrea watched on from the floor as the boy rose from the bath. He outstretched his arms toward her, beckoning her to come near. She let out a bloodcurdling scream as she slid away. The boy continued to stand there as he cried out for her. Andrea heard feet running down the hall.

"Andrea, it's John. Are you all right? I'm coming in." He quickly opened the door to find his wife shaking unruly in the corner. "Oh, God, Andrea, what happened to you?"

"It was awful! I don't want to ever see that again. I was so scared." She cried.

"What did you see?"

"The tub filled with blood and a young child came out of it!" Andrea continued to cry, "Please, John, we must leave from here tonight!"

"It's okay, honey, you were just seeing things. It's an illusion. Don't believe it. It wants you to think it's real, but it's not," he said, trying to calm her.

"That was no illusion, John. What I saw was real. When he touched me, I felt his grasp."

"He?"

"Yes, the little boy."

"You're not talking about Savannah?"

"No, John, a young boy came out of the tub crying."

"There's a little boy here, too?"

"Yes, I just saw him."

"I'm so used to it always being Savannah or Illusion; now we have another one to worry about. Who do you think he is?"

"I don't know. He's still just a baby, no older than three. I don't think I was scared of him; it was more how he looked that frightened me. He seemed like a child crying for his mother. His head looks like it was smashed open. It was horrible, John. He was in so much pain, but I was too afraid to do anything. He was just a baby." She continued to cry.

"Shh, it's all right," he said, trying to console her. "Is this where he grabbed you? You have bruises on your leg in the form of small hands."

Andrea looked down at the marks. "He held onto me so tight, then I fell out of the tub."

"Let's get you out of here. I'll take you back downstairs." John walked Andrea out of the room as they headed for the stairs. "Let's get you on the couch where you'll be more relaxed. I'm going to the kitchen to make you a sandwich. Rich will stay with you until I get back," he told her.

Andrea nodded, motioning to John an okay.

"Is there anything I could get you?" Rich asked in concern.

"A normal house." She laughed. "I don't know how long we can stay here. This place scares me. I don't feel comfortable."

"It'll be all right, Andrea. Things will get better," Rich told her. "Hey, maybe it's here because I'm here!" he said, trying to make her laugh.

"Well, if it is, you better leave now!" Andrea laughed back. "No, I don't really think that at all. Whatever's in this house has been here, probably for a long time, I'd presume." Andrea shook her head, then continued, "I never thought my dream house would turn into a nightmare."

"Why don't you fight it, like John said? Don't let it run you off. You've waited a long time to live in a place like this. Don't shatter your dreams of living here just yet."

"I love this house. I loved it the first instant I laid eyes on it. I still love it, but I've grown afraid of being here."

"Don't think that way. Try to stay positive about it. This is your house now. Take charge and don't undermine yourself."

"Thanks, Rich. Maybe you're right. I need to learn to stand my ground and be in control. You have to beat it someway, right?" she told him as John returned to the room.

"Here you go. Made you a ham sandwich. Has everything on it you like."

"Thanks," she said, taking the plate from John.

"I got you a bottle of water to drink along with some chips. Eat what you can. What you don't finish, I'll wrap up. You can have it later. I'll be back in a moment. I'm going to check on Chloe."

John went up to her room. Chloe's door was wide open, and she was there on her bed fast asleep. John walked over to her quietly, trying not to wake her. He put his hand on her forehead to see if she was running a fever. After seeing she was all right, he left and returned to the living room.

"How is she?" Andrea asked.

"She's out like a light," John assured her. "I felt her forehead to see if she had fever, thinking maybe she was coming down with what you've got, but she's fine. I just left her sleeping. I didn't want to bother her."

"As long as she's all right."

"Yeah, she's in lala land, so she won't be up for awhile. How was your sandwich? I see you ate it all."

"It was really good. I think I needed some food in my stomach."

"Do you want me to make you another?"

"No, this was fine. I don't want to over eat."

"Here, let me take your plate then." John went to the kitchen and washed the dishes in the sink. He returned to the living room when the doorbell rang. He looked over to Rich, who was staring back.

"You don't suppose it'll happen again?" Rich asked. "You know, the door and all?"

"I see someone outside the screen. They're fairly tall."

Behind the door was a familiar face.

"Hello again, John!"

"Oh, Mr. Blackwell. How are you, sir?"

"I'm fine, just fine, thanks. Listen, I recall you telling me earlier that your wife had been sick. I wanted to bring her some flowers as a get well gift. I also brought a little something for you as a house warming present. It's not much, just some peaches off my tree. They're real good. Better than what you'd find in any market. These are prize-winning peaches here, the best of the best. Anyway I just thought I'd drop this by. Will you see that your wife gets these flowers for me?"

"She's just here in the living room if you care to come meet her."

"Well, all right then, if you insist. I'll just be a minute."

John welcomed Tookie into his house. "Right this way. Andrea, I have someone I'd like you and Rich to meet. This is our neighbor, Mr. Tucker Blackwell. This is my wife, Andrea, and my best friend Rich."

"How do you do?" he asked. "John and I met earlier today. He told me you've been ill. I just wanted to bring you some flowers and give you my regards. I also brought some peaches off my tree. I thought y'all might enjoy them."

"Well, thank you very much, Mr. Blackwell. That's so kind of you," Andrea replied. "The flowers are absolutely beautiful."

"I'm glad you like them, dear. I thought they'd brighten your day. Please call me Tookie. I live next door, so if y'all ever need anything, please let me know. Well, I should be going now. I just wanted to bring this by."

"No, please sit down, I'd like you to stay," Andrea told him.

"Are you sure? Because if you're not feeling up to it, I could always come by and visit y'all another day."

"No, I insist that you stay. I feel better now, I had something to eat."

"Only if you're sure you feel up to it, miss, I don't want to intrude."

"No, please go on and have a seat anywhere you'd like. Make yourself comfortable. Would you like something to drink?"

"Coffee would be nice, if I'm not a bother," Tookie asked politely.

Andrea looked toward John. "Would you mind getting his coffee?"

"Sure. How do you take your coffee, sir?"

"Ah, cream and sugar if you have any."

"Coming right up. Can I get anyone else a cup?"

"I'll take another bottle of water," Andrea told him.

"Rich, can I get you something?"

"Coffee would be fine. Cream, no sugar. Do you need any help bringing it in?"

"I think I can manage," John told him before leaving the room.

"So, Mr. Blackwell, how long have you lived in Savannah?" Andrea wondered.

"About eleven years now. After I retired, Evelyn and I moved here from Atlanta."

"Your wife is welcome to come by if she'd like," Andrea told him. "You could use our phone if you wish, and John could go get her for you," she offered.

"I'm afraid I couldn't reach her that way. I lost Evelyn three years ago. She'd been ill for six years."

"Oh, I'm terribly sorry. I had no idea," Andrea said, sympathizing to him.

"That's quite all right, miss. My dog Sam stays with me at the house. If it weren't for him, I don't know what I'd do. He gives me reason to go on."

"That's good you have a pet there with you. There's nothing sadder then an empty barren house. My mother was severely injured in a car accident four years ago. She had succumb to her injuries after being in the hospital for two days."

"Oh, my dear, I am so sorry to hear that." Tookie frowned.

"My dad was a torn up mess after losing her. A year had passed when I decided to get him a dog. I thought it was the best thing I could do for him since he didn't want to leave the house. That dog has filled him with the life that he lost. He loves that old mut so much."

"Animals have a way of healing people," he told Andrea and Rich. "They have a way of perking us up when they sense that we're down."

"How long has Sam been with you?"

"I've had him for about eight years. He was a birthday present from Evelyn. I carry a picture of him in my wallet along with hers." He handed Andrea the pictures for her to see.

"She looks like a heart-warming lady."

"That was my Evie. She was sweeter than sugar," he said with a smile. "Sam's on the other photo beneath hers."

"He's beautiful. Is he a Malamute or Husky?" she asked, handing the pictures to Rich.

"He's an Alaskan Malamute. He's truly a magnificent dog and a great friend," Tookie told them.

Rich handed the pictures back to Mr. Blackwell. "How old was he when you got him?" Rich wondered.

"He was about four and a half when Evie brought him to the house."

"Here you go, Mr. Blackwell," John said as he handed him his coffee.

"Thank you."

"Here's some cream and sugar if you need more. I'll be back in a minute."

"So, Mr. Blackwell, what line of work were you in?" Rich asked.

"I was a lawyer for thirty-three years when I finally decided I needed a break."

"Do you ever miss work at all?"

"Evelyn made me forget about it. We spent a lot of time together. That's what we wanted. A peaceful, non- hectic life, and that's what we found when we moved here."

"I wish our lives were more peaceful here," Andrea told him.

"So it has begun?" he asked her mildly.

Andrea shook her head. "I'm sorry, what?"

"I don't know why this house still stands. Nobody ever stays here long. Some kind of powerful force has its grip on this place. Something bad, real bad," Tookie warned her.

"I know what you speak of. What is it?" Andrea questioned him.

"All I know is that it's not good. This street would be better if this house weren't standing. Something powerful already owns this place. It likes children for some reason. I heard a couple moved here in 1905. They had an adopted daughter about ten years of age and two younger sons. The girl remained in this house pretty much all her life, her marriage had failed and she had no children. Her parents were sick, so she came back home to take care of them. She lived here until her death, which was a little over three years ago. She made it to the ripe old age of eighty."

"What happened with the house after her passing?"

"After that the house went from one family to another. I never knew the woman to speak oddly of the house, but everyone else who lived here did. Most of those folks didn't stay for too long. There was one couple, however, who lived here two years. Brunswick was their last name. Nice young couple like you and John. Sometimes they talked about things that went on in this house, but nothing like some of the bizarre occurrences that would happen to the other owners. Maybe they weren't plagued by it as badly because they had no children. Mrs. Brunswick was sterile and unable to conceive. That was the only difference between the Brunswicks and the other folks. Everyone else had a family. Whatever's here lays dormant until a child is presented. The nicest girl or boy can turn violent in this place. I don't know much more. I hope what I told y'all will help."

"Why didn't the city demolish this place?"

"They don't see anything wrong with this house. It's all about money to them. A family will stay here for a little bit, then a new one comes along and the cycle starts over again. Most of the time they run off scared in the night. About a month after the original owner had died, a family moved in. Unfortunately, a suicide took place within these walls."

"A suicide?"

"A woman went mad and killed herself. Before she died, her family said she kept talking about seeing images of her dead father. She went on about how her father was ashamed of her and that in his eyes she was a disgrace. She thought she was useless, then she finally went over the edge and took her life. Her husband took the kids and moved out not long after. Then the house went back on the market drawing a new family in, allowing the real estate agency to bank on more money and letting the city keep theirs."

"That's terrible," Andrea thought aloud.

"I think it's time this place goes down. I've seen what this house has done to people. I can't bear to watch as another family's life gets torn apart. Please take heed to my warning. Leave this place while you're still sane. I'll help you burn it, whatever. You and your family can live with me in my house until we get you settled somewhere else."

"Mr. Blackwell, sir, my wife and I appreciate your offer, but we're going to fight this thing. I won't let it run us off," John added.

"Then for your daughter's sake, leave. It'll beat you if you decide to stay here and fight. It's far too strong."

"Has this house ever been blessed?" John asked curiously.

"The men who came here all dropped dead on the porch. On three different occasions a holy man was here. They each fell into death the same way, heart attacks at the front door. None ever made it into the house."

"Has an exorcist ever come here?" John wondered aloud.

"An exorcism must be approved by the church, but no blessing was ever granted for one. Are you looking to obtain an exorcism?"

"If that would help drive out the things in this house, but that doesn't mean I wouldn't fight it myself."

"Don't think I didn't warn you about this place then, son. I just want to make sure you and your family stay safe."

"Thank you for your concern. If we can't make it living here, I promise I'll help you bring this place down."

"Then I'll hope for the best for you and your family. You're all welcome at my house anytime of the day." Tookie looked at Andrea, who was sinking into the couch. "Are you all right there, miss?" he asked in a concerned voice. "You don't look real well."

"I'm feeling sick again. It's all hit me so fast."

John felt Andrea's forehead. "Your fever's back. I'll get you something to take."

"No, no, don't worry about it. I'm too dizzy to drink anything. I just want to lie down and not move."

"I'm sorry you're feeling ill again. I do hope you're feeling better soon. I'm going to leave you now so you may get some rest. It's about time for Sam's walk through the park," Tookie said, glancing at his watch.

"I'm happy I got to meet you. When I'm better and on my feet, we'll get together again. I'll make dinner one night."

"That sounds nice. Then I shall bring by a bottle of wine from my personal collection. I have a great selection. Just let me know what you like. You go on and get some sleep."

"Thank you again for the gifts. I wish I could visit longer," Andrea told him.

"Next time, dear, I hope you feel better." Tookie patted Andrea on the shoulder, then shook Rich's hand. He followed John to the front door with a piece of paper in his hand. "This is my phone number if you should ever have to call me. I'm usually home unless I take Sam for his walk."

"Thank you, sir."

"Hey, I told you before, call me Tookie."

"Thanks, Tookie. I mean, you brought flowers to my sick wife. That was considerate of you. I'm about to get one of your prized peaches. They all smell so good. Thanks for sending some over to us."

"When those are gone, y'all come over. There's plenty more where those came from. You can pick what you want; I have a couple of trees in my backyard."

"I might have to take you up on that if they're as good as you say."

"I don't think you'll be disappointed. Let me know what you think after you've eaten one. I'll see you later; have a good day."

"Be careful there, Tookie. We'll see you next time." John watched him walk off, then closed the door.

"Mr. Blackwell seems like a nice man," Andrea told him as he entered the room. "He dresses well, too, and wears nice smelling cologne. He's a nice looking gentleman. I'm surprised he never met someone else."

"Maybe he didn't want to be with anyone else. Evelyn was his life. I bet he's waiting on the day that they could be together again."

"Oh, John, it's so sweet you think that way. Would you do the same for me if I were gone?"

"You know I couldn't make it a day without you. My heart would shatter into a million pieces the instant you left."

"Oh, no. Here we go with that mushy talk." Rich laughed.

"I think all this deep talk is making someone sick!" John said, eyeing Rich.

"If two people could ever really love each other, it'd have to be the both of you. Cupid's arrows knew exactly where they were going when they hit you two. You guys are love-struck on each other. I don't think I'll ever feel that."

"You just turned thirty, what two months ago? It'll come along at the right time," John told him.

"It's just that I wanted a family by now. I don't want to be forty years old when my first child is born. I'd be fifty and have a ten-year-old kid. I still want to be young when I teach my son how to ride a bike or swing a bat."

"And what if your wife bore you a daughter?" John wondered.

"Hell, I'd teach her how to ride a bike and swing a bat, too!"

John's face began to blush. "What if she preferred to play with her toy stove instead?"

"A toy stove, huh?"

"Yep! And she wants you to play."

"I guess I'd train her to be a chef."

"When she makes you a bowl of potato soup, will you be prepared to eat it?" John asked Rich, trying to keep a straight face.

"Oh, not Chloe's potato soup story! You guys really ate that?"

"The few bites that we could."

"So I guess if I had a son, he'd break things rather then fix them, huh? Yeah, I think I'll hold off on wanting to have a kid for awhile longer." Rich decided.

"Andrea and I thought we'd let you borrow Chloe for a few days. And what'd you know, here she comes. How was your nap, baby?"

"Fine. Will you take me to the pet store now?"

"We'll go in a little bit."

"What's wrong with mommy?"

"She's still sick, honey."

"Who's going to cook dinner if mommy's sick?"

"I guess I'll put some hotdogs and hamburgers on the grill. Is everyone fine with that?"

"You'll have to go to the store, John. I don't have anything here," Andrea told him.

"I can go to the store after I take Chloe to get a couple things for Snow."

"I'm going to take a nap for awhile."

"If you aren't better by tomorrow, I'm taking you to the doctor. I'm taking Chloe to the store now. We'll be back shortly. Rich, you coming?"

"I think it'd be better if I stayed here with Andrea, don't you?"

"Yeah, you're probably right. I'll try not to be too long," John told them as he was leaving the house.

"All right, I'll see you and Chloe when you get back," Rich said before he closed the door. "Are you okay, Andrea? Is there anything I could get you?" he asked as he sat down.

"No. If you don't mind, I think I'm going to go up to my room. I'm getting tired of this couch. I'd rather be in bed."

"Do you need help getting upstairs?"

"I think I can manage, but thanks." Andrea wrapped up in her blanket, then left.

She walked down the hall toward her bedroom when she noticed the attic door had swung open. A faint light peered out from behind the door, lighting the hallway. Andrea moved closer toward the entrance when she heard a woman's voice faintly call out to her.

"Andrea," the voice whispered softly.

A mild breeze intertwined with the essence of rose water passed down the attic stairs, brushing against Andrea.

"Who's there?" she asked.

"Come to the attic," the woman's voice mildly commanded.

"Who are you?" Andrea wondered as she stood in the doorway waiting to hear a response. She started up the stairs as the boards creaked beneath her feet. Finally she made it into the attic and took a look around. "Is someone here?" Andrea asked aloud. The room was piled with boxes and old dusty furniture. In the corner of the room was a large claw foot mirror with a body of armor standing by it. Andrea was pulled toward the objects as though an invisible force had drawn her near.

She looked on at her reflection, not fazed by anything else that surrounded her. The appearance of a dress had come into sight as it floated steadily beside her. Andrea turned her head to her side, but nothing was there, just an empty space. She set her eyes upon the mirror once more and to her astonishment saw the dress still hovered there. She watched as a woman's neck appeared out from within the dress, then the image of a head and face began to take form.

Floating beside Andrea was the bodiless ghost of a young woman. Andrea looked upon the mirror at the woman's face when she realized she had seen her before. The young woman continued to float there without speaking a word.

"Who are you?" Andrea choked up, but asked.

Slowly the young woman's hands then grew out away from her sleeves with her right hand fisted tightly. She continued to float there quietly in the reflection of the mirror when she drew her eyes toward the floor, alerting Andrea to follow. She twisted her wrist, then opened her hand releasing the object she had in her grasp.

Andrea heard it fall to the floor as she looked down to see it. Beside her foot rested a rather small and rusty old key. As soon as it hit the ground, the woman's image had vanished.

Andrea bent over to pick up the key, then examined it. It was no more than two inches long with rust wearing away at its surface. Andrea held the key tightly, then started across the room. As she did, Andrea came upon a rotting board that gave away beneath her foot. She felt a searing pain in her ankle as her foot went through the board. Andrea lost her balance as she fell backwards into a box.

She fought for awhile trying to free her foot from the rotting hole, then finally pulled it loose. She rubbed at her ankle trying to ease the pain when she noticed a small trunk hidden beneath the floor boards. Andrea slid her hands down into the dirt-infested hole and pulled the object out as she set the trunk into the open space beside her.

The trunk had turned grey from attracting decades of grunge and dirt. Andrea blew upon the surface stirring up the dust particles she'd sent into the air. Inhaling the dust into her lungs, Andrea had gone into a coughing attack. When she finally caught her breath, Andrea rubbed her hand along the box to clear away the rest of the dirt. Beneath all the build up were beautiful carvings that had been etched into the wood.

Andrea looked over the details closely before she attempted to open the trunk, but unfortunately to her surprise it was unwilling to open.

Andrea brushed her fingertips along the front of the box when she came across a brass keyhole. Andrea remembered the old key the woman had left behind. She picked the key up off the floor and placed it in the hole. Andrea slowly gave it a little turn, then heard when it had unlocked. A cloud of dust floated into the air, releasing with it a moldy odor that had been set loose from within the trunk.

Inside Andrea found a handmade journal that had been tied off with lace and ribbon. Andrea undid the knot, then proceeded to open the diary carefully, trying not to harm the binding. The pages were old and worn at the edges with crinkles running down the parchment. Andrea felt the paper with her fingertips and found that it was rough to the touch.

The scent of ink still dampened the pages as Andrea detected its fragrance. She turned to the first entry, then started to read.

─── **CHAPTER FIVE** ───

The first of April, nineteen hundred

WE'VE LIVED HERE FOR NEARLY THREE weeks and I can say it's been great. I've finally found the home of my dreams. I still can't believe I live in it. This place is dear to me, and it's a beautiful home for my family.

I was out in the gazebo earlier today while taking a little break. The weather was beautiful with the sun shining golden rays upon the earth. My surroundings were peaceful as I sat in the company of the birds. I desperately needed that time to myself.

Griffin's been sick since early this morning with a fever and chills. He was terribly cranky, crying throughout the day. His screams rang on in my ears as I started to take an awful headache. After Wallace arrived home from work, he took over the father position, granting me some much needed time to rest. I felt as though the fresh air had cleared my mind, forcing my headache to lessen. Thankfully it worked, and I soon felt better.

Savannah came out into the yard to show me her new possession. I thought it was a new doll that Wallace had bought for her. Instead Savannah claimed they found it somewhere in the house. When I asked her where they got it, Savannah told me the doll was in a cabinet in the attic.

Wallace was putting up a few things to store away when he and Savannah came across it. It's a beautiful doll, but there's something about her eyes that send me the chills. I know how ridiculous that must sound. I could understand it more if it were a clown and I were scared. But she's a beautiful doll, not some unsightly jester in a suit. Really, what is there to be afraid of? She's only a doll.

I guess I'm just over-reacting. How silly of me. Maybe tomorrow will be a better day and Griffin won't be sick.

Until then, keep a page open for me...

Signed Always,
Scarlette

Andrea went deeper into the journal as she dug for more information and continued to read on.

The eighteenth of April, nineteen hundred

That doll continues to take my little girl away from me as we grow farther apart each day. Savannah is not the child Wallace and I have been raising for eight years. She's changed; she's different.

There's a coldness that circulates within her spirit now accompanied by a distant gaze that's set deep in her eyes. I could almost swear her vision was clouded, she's become so detached. Another change I've seen in my daughter is the attitude she carries about. Savannah has never behaved the way she does now. It's like she's suddenly turned into this rebellious child, always talking back, not minding her manners, making rude comments or gestures, and even getting into trouble at school. I don't like what I see in Savannah nor what she has become. She's even started hurting her baby brother. It frightens me.

She'll get mad at Griffin for no reason than slap him in the face. I don't know what's caused this behavior in her. Is it possible for a doll to influence a child in this way?

There's so much I just don't understand. I pray that one day I'll have that happy little girl whom I once knew back, but I fear that won't be for awhile. What must I do? I need a miracle. Thank God I still have one daughter who acts the way she should.

As Always,
Scarlette

Andrea was alarmed by the words of the journal. She decided to take it to her room, and there she continued to read on as she got comfortable in her bed. Andrea soon forgot about the pain in her ankle as she quickly became engrossed in Scarlette's journal.

The twenty-sixth of April, nineteen hundred

My fears continue to plague me as I worry so about Savannah. There has been no change for the good. Things just seem to keep getting worse.
Savannah has become even more harmful and disobedient than before. I thought about taking the doll away from her today, but when I tried, Savannah bit me and drew my blood.
My wrist is bruised from the attack and a broken blood vessel rests under my skin that aches and burns. Savannah fought me to keep the doll, and in the end she eventually won.
I'll have to take the doll away while Savannah sleeps. It's my only hope if I have a chance. Wallace believes Savannah's going through a phaze and that it has nothing to do with the doll, but I know it does. Wallace thinks I'm going crazy and that I'm the one who has the problem.
I am saddened by him because he does not see the truth. That doll of Savannah's, which she calls Illusion, has a wicked evil in its eyes. If I could sense it, why hasn't Wallace?

Always,
Scarlette

Andrea got off the bed and walked to the dresser. There, hanging on the mirror, was the locket she had hung the day before. She opened it to the picture inside and saw the image of the woman from the attic along with her family.

"So you're Scarlette?" Andrea said softly as she looked at her photo. "Why have you chosen me to read your diary? Of all the other families who have lived here, why was I the one you led to it?"

Andrea walked back to the bed with the locket in her hand, then picked the journal up. As she came upon the next page, she heard a light knock at the door. Andrea looked up and saw John entering the room.

"Rich said you wanted to come up here to get some rest."

"I was getting tired of the couch. I thought it would be better if I came in here."

"Are you feeling any better?"

"I guess so. My mind's been occupied since I've been up here."

"I wanted to let you know that Chloe and I were home. She spent nearly all my money on things for Snow. Food, toys, a red collar with white stones, and even a fluffy bed. You name it, Chloe had me buy it. I told her to leave me enough money to get some things at the grocery store, otherwise we wouldn't have any food for tonight."

"So did she leave you enough?"

"Just barely. She's like you, spend, spend, spend." he laughed. "Don't worry, I was able to get everything we needed, though. I picked up a bag of chips, some condiments to go on the dogs and burgers, pop and a few other things I thought we could use." John paused as he saw the journal. "So ah, what're you reading there?" he asked, pointing at the diary.

"I found it in the attic. It once belonged to a woman who lived here long ago."

"Where at in the attic?" John wondered.

Andrea raised her eyebrows while she looked upon him. "It was in a trunk in the floor."

"You mean on the floor?"

"No, I mean in it. The trunk was beneath the floor boards when I found it."

"How did you know it was there?"

"I didn't. My foot went through a rotting board as the floor gave away. I believe it was supposed to happen. I saw the woman who wrote this journal before the floor caved away." Andrea opened the locket and handed it to John. "You see that woman there in the picture?" she asked, followed by John nodding. "Her name is Scarlette, and Savannah was her daughter. The little boy I saw earlier in the tub was her son Griffin. Something bad happened to all of them in this house. I saw Scarlette in the attic. She gave me a key to open the trunk in the floor. She wanted me to find it. I've been reading it ever since."

"So what's it say?"

"The first entry was on April 1, 1900. Scarlette wrote that she and her family had recently moved into the house. She talked highly of the place, stating it had been her dream home. That day, April 1st, announced the arrival of Illusion. Scarlette has that name written in her journal, the same name you've heard Chloe mention. Scarlette had also written that her husband, Wallace, along with Savannah, had found the doll in the attic. Right away she sensed something wasn't right with it. There was something about the doll's eyes that had frightened her. After finding Illusion, Scarlette stated how quickly her daughter began to change."

"Did she get rid of the doll?"

"Savannah attacked her when she tried, biting Scarlette on the wrist. The little girl even battered her younger brother for no reason, I guess to just strike out. According to Scarlette it seems as though the doll is what made Savannah change. The more time she spent with Illusion, the more apart she and her mother became."

"Is there anything in the journal that claims to get rid of that doll for good?"

"I don't think so. If there was, do you actually think that doll would still be here? This journal was written in 1900. Illusion has been here ever since, maybe even longer. Who knows?"

"There's no history of that doll or its maker in that journal?"

"Nothing. Just that it was already in the house."

"Where do you suppose it came from?"

"It must have always been here. Maybe we could find out who owned this place before Scarlette and Wallace. There has to be some sort of information that could give us insight on that doll."

"We can try to find out what we can. Let's hope there's some kind of information out there that we can read."

"We'll have to get Rich to watch Chloe. I don't want her coming with us when we go."

"I agree. Why don't you come on downstairs? I'll get the food going on the grill."

"I'll be down in a moment. I want to put this journal in a safe place."

"I'll see you downstairs then. If I'm not in the kitchen, I'll be in the backyard," John said before leaving the room.

As he was passing by Chloe's bedroom, the door immediately slammed shut by unseen hands. John walked over toward the door and opened it. Inside he found an empty room. The only thing that struck him was the difference in the temperature. Chloe's room was filled with an uncomfortable coldness that chilled the bone. John felt unwelcome, so he quickly shut the door and started down the hall. As he approached the staircase, John heard Savannah's wicked laughter seep out from beneath Chloe's bedroom door.

John stopped and looked back down the hallway as the smell of death took to the air. Before his eyes the lights dimmed, then slowly died out. Within the darkness John saw a figure form before his sight. A strange gurgle-like noise came from Savannah as she stood beside the door clutching Illusion in her arm. John looked down upon her as he was overcome with fright.

Slowly she descended the glooming hall, floating steadily through the air. "Your wife still hates you!" Savannah spoke eerily. "She would rather seen you die that dreadful night on April fifth."

"Shut up!" John yelled. "You speak of nothing but lies!"

"I only speak the truth. You're the one who speaks of lies."

"I don't believe a word you say."

"Face it, you're the one who killed the twins."

"No, I didn't!" he cried. "Andrea started bleeding before I got her to a hospital. There was nothing they could do. The twins had no heartbeat."

"If you had arrived sooner, they'd still be alive. It's your fault because you didn't hurry to the hospital in time. Your wife blames you for the twins' demise."

The lights began to buzz, then came back on, and in the poof of a second, Savannah and Illusion were gone. John took a deep breath and milled over his thoughts. He started down the staircase when he heard one of the bedroom doors shut. John rushed back up to the top of the stairs when he saw Andrea was coming down.

"Are you okay, John?"

"I'm fine."

"You sure?"

"Yeah, I'm sure. I'm fine; come on. Let's go grill some dogs and burgers. Rich, you got that grill started?"

John and Andrea walked into the living room to find a space of empty seats.

"Maybe he and Chloe are already out back," Andrea implied.

"Let's take a look."

Andrea followed John to the backyard where they found Rich slipping wood chips into the grill.

"How's it smelling?"

"Smells great! What're you using there? Hickory chips?"

"That's right. Mr. Blackwell gave us a bag from a tree he had cut. He said he owns some timber. This here's from one of his trees. Them burgers and dogs are going to pick up the flavors well."

"Where's Tookie now?"

"He went back to his house. He was putting some seed out for the birds when he saw me starting the grill."

"That was nice of him. Well, let's get this food on the grate and get it cooking."

"Rich, did Chloe come out here with you?" Andrea asked.

"She's over in the gazebo."

Andrea walked over to Chloe who was sitting in the grass. "What're you doing, Chlo?" she asked when she noticed something in her hands.

"It had a broken wing, mommy."

"Chloe, I know you want to help the little birdie, but please put it down."

"But Savannah said when a bird has a broken wing and can no longer fly that it's better off dead. She told me she learned that from Illusion."

"Chloe, how dare you say such things."

"But it's true. Why should it live when it can't fly anymore? I'm just trying to help it, mommy, that's all. Honest."

"What did you do to that bird, Chloe?"

"Savannah told me to squeeze its neck," she said while brushing her fingers upon its feathers.

"Oh no, Chloe, I can't believe what you've done!"

"Are you mad at me?"

"Of course I'm mad, Chlo. You took that bird's life. It'll never see its mommy or daddy ever again."

"It won't?" She pouted.

"Chloe, what you did wasn't right. I want you to stop listening to Savannah this instant, understand?"

"But Savannah's my friend."

"No, honey, she's not. A real friend wouldn't have told you to hurt an animal, or even a bird for that matter."

"But I thought what I was doing was right. Am I going to be punished now, mommy?"

"Let's talk to your father about that. I want you to tell him what you've done."

"He'll get mad at me, too." She began to cry.

"What's with the tears, long face?" John asked her as she stood before him sobbing.

"I didn't know, daddy! I thought I was helping it!" she cried out.

"Helping what, baby?"

"The little birdie," she said, bowing her head in shame.

John looked up to Andrea. "What about a bird?"

Chloe fought back her tears, then slowly said, "I killed it because it couldn't fly."

"You did what?"

"I'm sorry, daddy, I really am. Savannah said for me to do it."

"That's it! I don't want you talking to her. She's a bad influence, Chlo. You aren't to have anything to do with her anymore. One way or another, she's leaving this house. I'm going to see to it."

"She won't ever leave, daddy. This is her house. She told me."

"What do you know about Savannah and Illusion?"

"Just that they live here. Savannah told me she moved here with her family, but Illusion was given life in this house. She's been here the longest."

"Did Savannah tell you what happened to her family?"

"They're all dead," Chloe said, twirling her hair around her finger. "Am I going to be punished for killing the bird?"

"I think you should bury it, then tell the bird how sorry you are for killing it. I'm going in the house to get some gloves." John looked back at Rich as he walked toward the house. "Can you keep an eye on the food?"

"Yeah, sure."

"Why don't you and I find a place to bury the bird?" Andrea told Chloe.

"Why can't we put it in the garbage?"

"We're not putting it in the garbage. You heard your father. You're going to dispose of it properly."

"So I have to bury it?"

"That's right. Where'd you want to dig the hole? How about over here beneath the azalea bush?" Andrea said, clearing a space.

"I still think we should throw it in the trash."

"Chloe, are you not listening to me?"

"I heard you."

"You're going to bury it and that's the last you're going to talk about putting it in the trash."

"Whatever."

"What's gotten into you?" she asked, thinking back on Scarlette's words of Savannah's ungodly change.

"Nothing, mommy. What's gotten into you?"

"Are you getting smart with me?"

"Why don't you ask me another question, then we'll see if I am."

"That's the last straw, young lady. You don't get to play with Snow for the rest of the day."

"What's going on over here?" inquired John.

"I told Chloe she couldn't play with Snow anymore today. She was getting smart with me."

"No, I didn't, daddy! All I said was that this is a good place to bury the bird. I never got smart."

"Chloe, that is *not* what you said, and you know it."

"Daddy, mommy should go lie down. I think her fever's coming back." she told her father sweetly before turning to her mom. "She doesn't even remember what I said."

Andrea's mouth dropped to the words Chloe had just spoken. "Chloe!" Andrea shouted.

"You should go lie down, mommy. You don't look well."

Andrea looked up and saw John shaking his head in agreement with Chloe. "You believe her?" she questioned him. "John!"

"I'll tend to this. You go help Rich with the food."

"Fine then, you deal with Chloe," Andrea said as she walked off. "Have fun."

"Daddy, is mommy mad at me?"

"I think she's a little upset with what you've done."

"I know better now. I know what I did was wrong and that I shouldn't have done it."

"I'm glad you learned your lesson. Now take this little shovel and dig a hole for the bird."

"Is this deep enough, daddy?"

"You better dig some more of that dirt out so the hole will be big enough." John helped Chloe dig deeper into the soil, then he set the carcass into the hole where he laid it to rest. "Go on and cover the hole with the dirt you just dug up."

"Like this?"

"Yes, that's good. Now, pat it down."

"Am I doing it right?"

"Here, watch out. I'll do the rest." John finished packing the dirt into the ground, then looked up to Chloe. "Do you want to put a flower on the grave now and say a few words?" He cut a few tea roses off a nearby bush, then handed them to Chloe, who then laid them nicely upon the grave.

"I'm sorry, little birdie, for breaking your neck. I hope you can forgive me. May you now rest in peace," she spoke kindly.

"That was nice, Chlo. Let's try to put this behind us now. I hope nothing like this ever happens again."

"It won't, daddy, I promise," she said, coaxing him into her lie.

"Good. Now wash your hands and get ready for dinner." John walked behind Chloe as they made their way toward the house.

"The food's already in the kitchen. I'm just turning off the grill."

"All right, Rich, I'll see you inside." John walked into the kitchen, then waited for Chloe to finish washing her hands. Andrea set the table and filled the glasses. Rich came in through the back door, then took a seat by the table.

"Need any help?" he asked aloud.

"That's okay. I just about got it all," Andrea spoke back. "I figured we could do something like a buffet. I'll set everything on the counter."

"Good thinking. The table will be less crowded."

"You guys come up here and help yourselves now. There's ketchup, mustard and relish up here. The onions and tomatoes are in these containers. We have pickles and lettuce, too. Whatever you need. Oh yeah, here's some cheese singles just in case anybody wants a cheeseburger. So come on and get it while it's hot!" Andrea looked over to Chloe. "What can I get for you? Do you want a hot dog or a hamburger?"

"A hot dog and..."

"I know, a zig-zag of mustard coming up." Andrea prepared Chloe's hot dog. "Where are you sitting?"

"By daddy!"

"You hear that, John? Chloe wants you to sit by her."

"Okay, Sweet Pea, just let me get my food and I'll sit by you."

Everyone got their plates filled, then took a seat at the table.

"Can someone pass me the potato chips?" Rich asked.

"Here you go," John said as he handed him the bag. Rich piled his plate with chips, then passed the bag around the table. Everyone was enjoying their meal and talking among each other when Chloe got up from her chair. She walked over to the counter, then put a hot dog in a bun.

"I would have fixed you another one, Chlo," Andrea said as she watched her from across the room.

"It isn't mine."

"Who'd you make it for?"

"Nobody you could see," Chloe said sarcastically as she held the hotdog in her hand. A second later it floated into the air. Andrea's mouth dropped when she realized the food was being eaten by an unseen guest. John and Rich looked on in disbelief as the hot dog vanished before their eyes. Chloe began to giggle. "It's only Savannah."

"Chlo, I want to know more about her. Why is she here?" John asked his daughter calmly.

"I've told you before. It's not my fault you weren't listening."

"Don't you get smart with me, Chlo," he said to his daughter sternly. John stared into Chloe's eyes as he watched her pupils distend, then she slowly blinked them twice.

"I'm sorry, daddy. I don't mean to get smart with you," she spoke kindly. "Can I have a hug so I know you're not mad?" Chloe leaned into her father as she wrapped her arms around his back. Then slowly she proceeded to rest her head upon his shoulder while she squeezed him tightly.

Chloe drew up her eyes until they were level with her mother's. A coiled grin crept upon Chloe's lips as she glared directly into Andrea's face. An eerie sensation crept up Andrea's spine that made the hairs on her neck stand up.

"Chloe, you're about to squeeze all the air out of my lungs. Can you loosen up a little?" John asked before breaking her concentration.

"I'm sorry, daddy!" Chloe giggled aloud.

"Have you been working out there, kid? I swear you're getting some muscles!"

"No!" Chloe giggled again.

"Then it must be all those vegetables you've been eating."

"You really think so?"

"I don't know what else it could be."

"I'm going upstairs to play with Snow now, daddy. I bet she misses me."

Andrea waited until Chloe was out of the room before she broke down to John. "That's not our daughter anymore," Andrea said, shaking her head. "The evil that's here has changed her. We've only been here one day, John, and this thing already has Chloe in its grip. Doesn't that scare you?"

"She's fine, Andrea. I don't see any negative changes in her except for the fact that she was getting smart, but then she apologized."

"What about the bird she killed? Rich has known Chloe since she was a baby. He knows she wouldn't even harm a fly."

"Andrea's right, John," Rich added, "It's not in Chloe's nature to hurt or even kill an animal. I've seen the changes in her myself, and honestly man, it's a little scary. What normal little girl would kill a bird?"

"I understand what you're saying, and you're right. It's not like Chloe to hurt an animal. It worried me, too, that she killed that bird today. I wish I could forget that she even did it, but the thought of knowing is always going to be in the back of my mind," added John.

Chloe had been listening in on the entire conversation while sitting on the staircase. Standing up to her right was Savannah clutching Illusion in her arms. Both were wearing looks of disgust on their face.

"I've told you before, they didn't trust you. Now you've heard it for yourself," Illusion whispered in an unpleasant tone.

"Illusion's right, Chloe. And when they don't trust you, they won't love you either."

Chloe narrowed her eyes with hate while she sat there with a distant look on her face.

"They've all turned their backs on you, even Rich," Illusion spoke wickedly. "Beware of your foes." she spoke again, convincing Chloe of her lie.

"I'm gonna use your bathroom. I'll be right back," Rich told John and Andrea before he got up from his chair.

Chloe heard the shuffle of his shoes as he came down the hall, so she tiptoed into her room, then stood by the door. Rich saw her peeking from behind the doorway as he slowly passed by.

"Are you playing peek-a-boo with me?" Rich asked while looking down at Chloe. She looked out into the hallway with a cold expression upon her face, then purposely slammed the door without saying a word.

"Well, I see you're in no mood to talk," Rich mumbled as he walked into the bathroom. He finished his business, then proceeded to wash his hands at the sink. In the mirror Rich noticed the door creeping open.

"I'm in the bathroom. I'll be out in a minute." He dried his hands off, then walked over toward the door as he heard a man's voice call his name. Rich peered into the hall, but found no one in sight as the voice continued calling for him. Rich stood in the hall and looked around. "Who's calling me?"

He listened to the man's voice as he followed it to the back bedroom. Rich stood before the door unsure if he should go in. The man's voice had grown louder while Rich thought what to do. He brought his hand up, then knocked at the door. "Is someone in here?" Rich asked as he began to knock again, then the door had swung open allowing Rich to peer into the darkness. "Hello? Somebody here?" He walked into the room and felt along the wall for a light switch. The voice continued to call his name, then the door slammed shut, locking him in. "Oh, God, I can't see! Where's the damn switch?" Rich's heart pounded in his chest as fear set in.

"It's over here," the voice whispered.

"Who the hell are you?"

"Oh, Richy, I'm terribly ashamed of you. You don't even recognize your Uncle Fred's voice."

"My uncle is dead!"

"I'm right here, Richy. Say, why don't you find that light switch? It's pretty dark in here. You know I'd like to see your face when I talk to you."

"There's nobody here. There's nobody here. It's just my imagination. It's just my imagination." Rich panicked over and over.

"Of course I'm here. Why would you say that? I guess I'm just gonna have to give you some physical proof."

Rich tried to open the door, but it didn't budge. Suddenly he cried out in shock as an icy hand patted his shoulder, chilling his bones.

"See? I told you I was here. Do you believe me now?"

Rich turned to the door and beat at the walls, screaming for help. "Get me out of here!"

"You can't leave. We haven't even talked. Stay for awhile. We need to catch up on the past."

"John! Help!" Rich yelled as he beat harder at the walls. "Somebody get me out of here!" Rich listened to John's feet as he ran down the hall.

"I'm coming!"

"Open this damn door now! Break it down if you have to!"

"I'm real hurt, Richy. You just had to call John and break up our family reunion," Uncle Fred said calmly.

"I can't get the door to open, Rich!" John shouted.

"Well, try harder!" Rich screamed back in terror.

"Watch out! I'm going to try to kick in this door!" John leaned back, then started to kick when the door opened abruptly. He lost his balance suddenly, then fell backwards to the floor.

Rich emerged from the dark room and rushed to help John up, then they rushed downstairs.

"This place has some serious problems," Rich said, shaking in fear.

"What's wrong?"

"Freaky shit happens here, man. I don't know any better way to say it."

"What happened to you up there?" John asked as he looked toward Rich who was sitting silently.

He took a moment and several breaths before he opened up to John. "Do you remember me ever talking about my Uncle Fred?"

"Yeah, but why are you asking about it? I know how you hate talking about him or even hearing his name."

"This house is really messed up. This place isn't right. It plays with your mind and eyes."

"Is everything okay, John? You never returned to the kitchen to tell me if things were fine," Andrea said, peering into the room.

"I'm sorry, hon. Everything's okay."

"Is something wrong with Rich?"

"He got crept out by something. He'll be okay. Everything's all right."

"But it's not all right. I told you this house has some serious problems."

"What happened, Rich? What's wrong?" Andrea questioned him.

"When I was twelve, my Uncle Fred took my three cousins and me on a camping trip. That night he killed my eleven-year-old cousin Rob, my nine-year-old cousin Lily and my seven-year-old cousin Cooper. I was the only surviving victim. Fred was arrested, and then questioned for what he did. He said he lost it because my aunt was divorcing him, and he didn't want her to get custody of the kids. He decided to kill them, then went through with his plan. I was shot because he was afraid I would tell. He ran off thinking I was dead like my cousins. But I lived and he didn't. His fate was sealed by the hands of the court. My Uncle Fred has been dead for eighteen years, but I just talked to him in one of your bedrooms. That's one problem I can say is wrong with this house. Need I say more?"

"Oh God, Rich, I had no idea. I'm so sorry to hear that."

"I forgot how it felt to truly be afraid of someone. You have no idea how badly I wanted out of that room. At times I felt as though I were having a heart attack. I couldn't even see the bastard; it was dark! But I heard his voice clearly, and I felt his icy, dead touch. I haven't felt that afraid in a long time. I don't know how much longer I can stay in this house."

"You don't have to stay here, Rich. If you want to leave, you can."

Everyone looked toward the stairs and found Chloe standing there.

"Why haven't you left if you don't think you could stay? I could show you the front door, or if you'd prefer, I can show you the way out the back."

"Chloe, how dare you speak so rudely," Andrea yelled.

"Mama, you shouldn't yell. Your shouting scares me," Chloe said sarcastically.

"I think you need to apologize to Rich, Chloe," John told her with a serious tone, "And you're not leaving this room till you do, so speak up."

"I'm sorry I made you mad, daddy."

"Chloe, you don't need to apologize to me. You should apologize to Rich."

"Oh!" Chloe exclaimed before turning to Rich. "I'm sorry." she said kindly. "I'm going back to my room now to get ready for bed. May you all have a good night."

"That's another problem right there. Chloe isn't right. You need to get her out of this house right away. She's turning into someone else," Rich spoke calmly to John. "Savannah and Illusion have taken control of Chloe, and I'm afraid they'll destroy her. They'll leave you with a daughter you don't even know at all. Don't wait until it's too late."

"I'm going up to make sure she's in bed," Andrea said as she rose from the couch. "If I'm not down soon, will one of you come check on me?" she asked before leaving the room. The guys shook their heads back and forth, then Andrea went on her way.

She crept quietly up the stairs then walked down the hallway toward Chloe's bedroom. As Andrea reached out to the brass doorknob, she felt the grasp of a man's hand upon her shoulder.

"Scarlette?" he asked as his voice floated on air.

Andrea turned around slowly, never once blinking. She then felt her heart beating heavily within her throat as she came upon the man's face. It was bleached with discolor and his eyes were pale grey as though he were looking through haze. Andrea quickly leaned her back into Chloe's door when suddenly the man's face vanished. Andrea took a breath, then calmly opened the bedroom door and peered in.

Chloe was lying still in her bed as Andrea watched the covers rise from her chest as she slept. Once Andrea realized Chloe was asleep, she gently shut the door quietly behind her. Chloe opened her eyes, knowing her mother had left.

"Let's play!" Savannah said as she emerged from the corner of the room with Illusion in her arms.

"What do you want to do?" Chloe asked.

"We want to play with Andrea," Illusion told her in a wicked tone. "It's time to create her fear!"

Andrea was just starting down the stairs when she heard a child's voice calling out to her.

"Mommy!" the voice carried down the hall.

Andrea stopped and turned around expecting to see Chloe standing by her door, but the hallway was empty.

"Mommy!" the voice spoke again as Andrea saw the child's shadow run through the hall from one doorway to another. "Are you coming?"

"Chloe, what are you doing? I thought you were in bed asleep." Andrea started down the hall to the room the child had entered. "What's this about, Chlo? It's too late to play games."

Standing by a window was a little girl Andrea had never seen. She was around five years of age with dark shoulder-length hair. Her big blue eyes were filled with wonderment as she stared across the room.

"Hi, mommy!" the little girl spoke merrily.

"How did you get in here?" Andrea asked.

"I always follow you and daddy where ever you go."

"Who are you?"

"You don't know your own child?" the little girl asked in confusion, then began to pout.

"I'm sorry, hon. I'm not your mommy. But I can help you find her. Do you know where you live?"

The little girl looked at Andrea with tear-filled eyes. "This is my house, here with you and daddy."

"Sweetie, I'm sorry, I don't know you. Will you tell me your name?"

"I'm Ivy and that's Adrienne," she said, pointing out toward the door.

"What?" Andrea turned around slowly.

Standing behind her was another little girl who was an exact replica of Ivy.

"I'm Adrienne." She giggled.

Ivy walked over to her sister where they stood before Andrea.

"This can't be," she said in disbelief. "It's not possible."

"Actually it is," Ivy assured her.

"We were still growing in your stomach when we died. Of course, we were babies..." said Adrienne.

"Or something of that form," added Ivy.

"We had to choose an appropriate age for ourselves. That way we could talk to you."

"We didn't want to be real old."

"And we didn't want to be too young."

"So this is the shape and form that we took."

"As far as appearance goes, this is how we would have looked if we were five and a half." Adrienne state truthfully.

"You don't know how lonely we are."

"We want you to be with us."

"We're alone, Adrienne and I," cried Ivy.

"There's no one here to take care of us."

"We've walked along your side for all these years when you couldn't even see us."

"We need our mommy."

"Come home to us," Ivy begged Andrea as she revealed an axe she'd been hiding behind her back. Andrea's eyes widened in terror while she looked upon the sharpened blade.

"It'll only take a minute, then it'll all be over."

"Then you could start a new life here with both of us."

"Daddy and Chloe don't need you anymore. We do," Adrienne said with a stern tone in her voice.

"But first you must allow us to cut off your head," Ivy said as she crept slowly toward Andrea, holding the blade in sight.

Andrea made a move toward the doorway, then made it into the hall where she ran into John.

"Whoa, Andrea, slow down there. You've just about run me over!"

"Get me away from that room!" she cried. "They're going to kill me!"

"Who's going to kill you?" John asked in concern.

"Ivy and Adrienne!" she yelled. "They have an axe."

"Who's Ivy and Adrienne?"

"The twins, John. Remember?"

"Our twins?"

"Yes, our twins that we lost!" Andrea cried hysterically.

"Shh... try to calm down. Let's not wake Chloe up. Come on, I'll take you downstairs."

Rich watched as John walked with Andrea into the room.

"Oh, God, I knew it! Something bad has happened. Are you all right?" Rich asked when he noticed her tears. "It's that doll again, isn't it? She and Savannah are messing with you."

"It wasn't them," she cried. "I can't take this house any longer. I know those weren't the twins, but it seemed so real. We're either leaving this place, or we're going to find someone who can help us."

While she continued to talk, Rich heard the sound of a small child running down the stairs, followed by a recurring cry. Andrea and John picked up on the sound soon after, when the footsteps were heard in the room. Slowly Griffin materialized before their eyes as his translucent body passed by them.

"Mommy! Mommy!" he cried for attention. "Vannah hurt me!" he cried even harder.

Everyone watched as he exited the room, vanishing before them.

"That was Griffin, the little boy from the bathroom." Andrea sobbed. "He's just a little boy," she said between tears. "I wanted to help him, but I was too afraid. What if he's trapped here along with the rest of the family?"

"But what about the other people we've seen? Are they trapped here, too? Or do Savannah and Illusion have enough strength to conjure up their image? I saw my dead uncle in this house. In life he wouldn't have known this place even existed. Wade saw his dead mother hanging in your basement. I don't know who's come by to see John, or maybe they haven't dropped in yet. Savannah and Illusion have total control on this place. It's your house by their game. They'll make you see and hear things as they pick at your mind." Rich paused briefly, then blinked his eyes, "They're not ghosts or even spooks. Savannah and Illusion are by far different."

"What would you call them then?" John asked while Rich raised his brow and took a deep breath.

"I'd say they're demons."

"But demons are monsters, Rich. They don't resemble little girls and their dolls."

"Demons can take on any form they wish. If it was their will, they'd take on the form of a child or a doll, for that matter."

"That all sounds a little far-fetched."

"Really, John? Then what is believable in this house?" Andrea added. "There's something strange going on in here. And let me assure you, it's not about floating objects or doors closing by themselves. It's about even weirder shit than that. Wake up, John, and take a look around! This house has something horribly wrong with it!"

"I know there's something wrong here. But I don't believe they're demons," John said, shaking his head.

"What about Illusion then?" Rich asked. "What is she?" he questioned him. "She's not just a doll, John. Even I know that much."

"But that's the thing, she *is* a doll!" he argued back. "Oh, who am I fooling? I don't know. Maybe Tookie was right. This house isn't fit to be lived in," John said, looking down at the floor. "Andrea, what are those droplets by your feet? Did you spill something?"

Andrea looked down and saw drops of blood on the floor tainted with spots of green pus.

"Where did that come from?" she wondered. Andrea thought for a second, then looked at her hand. Seeping through her bandage, blood was dripping away from her finger. "What's going on? Why am I bleeding?"

"When did you change that bandage last?" John inquired.

"Sometime yesterday," she said while removing the gauze. "This is bad, John," she said as she showed him her finger.

It was swollen and red with bursting bubbles oozing out pus and blood.

"I think it's time we washed it out again. We should have done this earlier. Your infection has gotten worse, I'm afraid."

"What if we can't get it out?"

"I'll have to take you to the doctor then. He could give you some antibiotics or a shot. That should clear it up if we can't." John looked to Rich. "I'm going to take Andrea up to the bathroom and get her some fresh bandages. We'll be back in a few minutes."

CHAPTER SIX

Rich decided to turn the television on while he waited for Andrea and John to return. He flipped desperately through the channels, but was unable to find any programs worth watching. "This is crap. I don't believe there's nothing on." Right after Rich said that the channels began to flip by themselves until it stopped on a certain program.

"Fred Sullivan was executed today for the murders of his three children and for the attempted murder of his nephew, Rich Sullivan."

"Oh what the hell?" Rich wondered aloud. "He was executed eighteen years ago. This program shouldn't be running."

"When asked what his motives were for the murders, Sullivan's words were precise. I did it to save my family."

"This can't be!" Rich yelled. He picked up the remote and started pressing the power button. "Turn off! Turn off! Damn it, why won't you go off?" Rich shouted to the television.

"Rich Sullivan, the surviving victim, gave his testimony in court on September 2, 1960. The evidence was thoroughly reviewed in detail for the summer slayings of eleven-year-old Rob, nine-year-old Lily and seven-year-old Cooper Sullivan. The decision of Fred Sullivan's fate was determined by the hands of the court. On September 19, 1960 the assembly found Sullivan guilty of a triple homicide and for the attempted murder of Rich Sullivan. It was announced by Judge Pryce, Fred Sullivan was to be sentenced to death by electrocution."

"I don't want to hear anymore." Rich demanded. "Why won't you go off?" he cried to the remote.

"When asked today, moments before his execution, for any last words, Fred Sullivan said, one day he'd find a way to return. Reporting for channel eight news, this is Taylor Keaton."

The television then turned itself off when the room became silent. Rich stood near the television, frustrated and afraid. His heart beat heavily in his chest while he trembled with fear.

Rich walked into the kitchen, then stood before the sink. He reached for a clean cup and filled it with cold water. The eighteen-year-old newscast played over in Rich's thoughts, interfering with his mind. What the hell's controlling this house? he thought a few seconds upon.

Rich peered innocently through the window when he noticed a person standing beneath the moonlight. Rich stayed in place and watched while the man's face became visible through the glass.

"Hey there, boy! Did you miss me?"

Tears began to form in Rich's eyes while he stared into Uncle Fred's face. "You're not here!" he cried. "You're not even real!"

"I thought we had a good long talk about this earlier, Richy."

"Go away! You're not welcome here!"

"I just came by to finish the job, boy!" Fred said with an unnerving glare.

The air around Rich stood silent before he heard the distinctive announcement of a shotgun being loaded. Fred pointed the barrel toward the window, intending to shoot his nephew in the head.

Rich dropped to the floor in a state of panic while the gun went off, blazing pellets through the glass. Rich slid across the floor on his stomach, hoping to escape the terror.

"I'm going to get you, Richy!" Fred yelled as he leaned into the window. "I see you there, boy!"

Rich heard the shotgun being loaded again and knew it was time to get away. He crawled as fast as he could across the floor, barely making his escape into the dining room. Rich made his way beneath a large mahogany table where he concealed himself and hid. He fought there to catch a breath as he attempted to calm down. Rich looked around the dimly lighted room for any sign of Uncle Fred. He sighed in relief when realizing he was alone. Rich waited a moment before he started to move, then felt the icy hand upon his back.

"We haven't played hide and seek since you were a kid. But I like the way we play this version even better."

Rich realized Fred was kneeled down right beside him when he started to slide from beneath the table. As he did, Rich tried to kick Uncle Fred in the face, but his foot passed right through him.

Fred started laughing at Rich's attempt to hurt him. "Don't you know you can't harm me, boy?"

Rich scurried into the living room and ran straight for the stairs. In the distance he heard Savannah and Illusion's laughter. Rich hurried up the stairs for the bathroom. He found the door open with Andrea and John standing inside.

"We were about to come down," John said. "I just needed to get this bandage on her finger."

"You're never to leave me alone in this house again. Do you hear me?" Rich stated. "My Uncle just about killed me down there!"

"Oh, God, Rich, I didn't know. I figured you'd be all right. I didn't think we'd be up here long. Are you okay?"

"No, I'm not okay! I just had a shotgun pointed at my head!" he responded quickly.

Andrea cried out to Rich's spoken words, "Why won't it stop?"

"Listen, I can't stay here another night. I have to leave. I think it'd be best if y'all came, too." Rich stated. "I'll help you clean up the mess in the kitchen, but after that I'm gone."

"What mess in the kitchen?" John asked Rich.

"The one Fred made with his gun."

"He was actually shooting it?" Andrea questioned him.

"I don't know how you didn't hear it. He was firing a freaking shotgun!"

"We never heard anything up here, Rich," John told him truthfully. "You know I would have come to help you, but I didn't know you were in trouble."

"I know you would have. I'm not blaming you of anything. This house is just tricky, that's all. I'm lucky to be alive right now. Fred was set on killing me."

"If you're that uncomfortable, Rich, you can go. You don't have to help clean up any mess."

"I told you I'd help, and that's what I'm going to do. But like I said earlier, I'm gone after that."

"Why don't we go downstairs then? I know you don't want to be here another minute," John told Rich.

"I'm sorry, man. I just can't stay here." They all went down to the kitchen.

John's mouth fell in shock as he gazed upon every shard of glass visible in the room. Empty shotgun shells were seen scattered along the floor, but no holes were ever found.

"My God, John," Andrea said while viewing the room. "Look at all this glass."

They all stood there for a minute and looked upon the mess before they got to work.

"I think that's all of it. Unless there's a few small fragments that we don't see, but I think we got most of the glass cleaned up." Rich stated as he disposed of the shards. "I guess this is it for me. I wish you'd consider coming, too."

"This is our house now, Rich. We don't have anywhere else to go. We have to stay here and fight this. I wish you could understand that," John said mildly.

"I understand. I'm just afraid for you all. This house can kill people, or at least whatever's in it could. Just promise me that if things get worse, you'll all get out. Mr. Blackwell said you could stay with him until you found another place."

"I know he did, Rich, but all our money went into buying this house. We couldn't afford to move again, not right now anyhow."

"Keep in touch then, so I know you and the family are all right. I'm not going to drive home tonight; it's too long a ride. I'll probably just stay in a motel. I'll give you guys a call in the morning. I want to make sure you made it through the night."

"Thanks for staying with us. We enjoyed your company," said Andrea. "I'm just sorry you have to leave so soon."

"I enjoyed seeing y'all."

"I apologize," Andrea added.

"For what?" Rich questioned her.

"For your unpleasant stay in this house."

"I have some good memories, though. Believe me, my entire stay here wasn't unpleasant."

"Are you sure?"

"I'm positive."

"You're not just saying that, are you?"

"Of course I'm not. I got to spend time with my friends," Rich told Andrea while giving her a hug. "You take care of that finger, all right?" Rich then made his way to John. "You guys come and see me next time."

"We will, Rich. Thanks for helping us move in."

"I guess this is it then. I'll see you guys in a few months, huh?"

"We'll be there. You have a safe trip. We'll talk to you tomorrow."

"See you guys later," Rich stated before he left.

"Looks like it's just us here now," John told Andrea as he closed the door.

"You think we'll be all right?"

"I sure hope so."

"I hope you're right."

"Well, what's it going to be tonight? The couch again or our bed?"

"Our bed, don't you think?"

"Sounds better than the recliner."

CHAPTER SEVEN

"Wake up!" Chloe said, shaking Andrea. "You need to make my breakfast." she rudely demanded.

Andrea squinted as she looked at the clock. "Chloe, it's not even 6:00 a.m."

"I don't care," she said hastily. "I want French toast now. And you better not forget to fry some bacon."

"What's with the yelling?" John asked after he was awakened by Chloe's remarks.

"I'm sorry, daddy. I didn't realize I was yelling."

"Well, you were. Now what's this about?"

"I'm just hungry, that's all. I asked mommy to make me something to eat. Then she yelled at me because it's not even 6:00." Chloe pouted to her dad.

"I never yelled at you, Chloe. Why would you say such a thing?"

"She did yell, daddy, honest. Don't believe what she says."

"Well, I'm sure she didn't mean to, baby."

"John?" Andrea said. "Did you hear me shouting?"

"Mommy will be down in a few minutes, Chlo. Then she'll make you some breakfast. Why don't you go see if any cartoons are on while you wait for her?"

"Okay, daddy." Chloe said merrily. "I'll be on the couch."

"You don't really believe her? Do you, John? I never raised my voice," Andrea whispered to him.

"I never heard you raise your voice once. I was just trying to stop the yelling."

"Have you noticed that when she gets an attitude with me, she never gets one with you? Don't you find that a bit odd, John?"

"Yeah, I've noticed it. It's like yesterday when she killed that bird. It's like you're the bad parent, and I'm the good one. I think she's playing with us, Andrea."

"I don't think she's playing with us, John. Chloe acts rudely around me now and she'll lie to you in front of my face."

"All I can say is that we keep an eye on her."

"I better get downstairs before she comes up yelling again."

"I'll be down in a few minutes," John told Andrea as she got up from the bed.

"Make it quick, will ya? You know where I'll be." Andrea slipped her house shoes on her feet and walked down to the kitchen.

She gathered the ingredients to make the French toast just as Chloe came into the room.

"Took you long enough. I told you earlier that I wanted my French toast now. It should have been made already. You're too damn slow!" Chloe said to Andrea hatefully.

"Chloe!" Andrea yelled back. "How dare you talk to me that way. You owe me an apology right now."

"I don't have to apologize for anything, you bitch!"

"That's it! I've had it with you, and I've had it with that mouth. Go to the living room!" Andrea demanded.

"But what about my breakfast?"

"You won't have it till later. Unless you can apologize to me now; then I'll make it."

"Forget it! You're not worth my breath! I'll just tell daddy how cruel you're being to me. He'll make my French toast!" Chloe walked prissily out of the room, then began to conjure up tears.

She met John on the staircase as he was coming down. "Oh, daddy, mommy's being so awful. She won't make my breakfast. I'm so hungry, daddy, but mommy would rather have me starve to death than feed me."

"I truly doubt your mommy would let you starve, Chlo."

"But she won't fix my breakfast."

"There has to be a reason why she won't make it, hon."

"She's acting like a you-know-what."

"And what's that, Chlo?"

"I can't say it, daddy. It's a bad word. I'm a good girl and I don't say those things."

"That's funny, I thought I heard you yelling at your mom just a short while ago."

"It wasn't me, daddy. I don't yell at people. I'm a little princess," she said, batting her eyes. "Illusion and I were watching cartoons. Want to watch one with us?"

"Not right now, Chlo. Maybe in a little bit."

"Fine, then. I'll be on the couch while you and mommy eat breakfast."

"Aren't you going to eat, too?"

"She won't make my French toast. I told you that already! Don't you listen?"

"Chloe, it's too early for you to have an attitude. I told you, your mommy won't let you starve. I'll let you know when the food's ready."

"Maybe I don't want anything now."

"That's fine. I'm not going to force you to eat. You'll eat when you're ready," John told her before he walked into the kitchen. "What's Chloe's problem now?" he asked, walking up to Andrea.

"She was mad because I wasn't down here right away," Andrea whispered. "John, she called me a bitch."

"She called you a *bitch*?" John asked in shock.

"Yes, because I told her she should apologize to me."

"Do you want me to have a talk with her?"

"It wouldn't do any good. She doesn't listen to anything I say. It goes in one ear and out the other. She'll do the same with you if you'd try telling her something."

"If she continues to act this way, I'm going to sit her down and we're going to have a little talk."

"You can try, but nothing you'd say will faze her."

"We don't know that for sure until the time comes."

"I really doubt you'll get anywhere, John."

"She told me you were going to let her starve."

"I told her she wasn't going to have any breakfast until she apologized to me. She acts like it's beyond her to say I'm sorry. Even though she didn't, I still made her breakfast. I wouldn't let her go hungry."

"I know you wouldn't, dear," stated John as he looked upon Andrea's hand. "Do you want me to change your bandages after we eat?"

"I almost forgot about that. I guess so," Andrea said, looking down at her finger.

"I'm going up to get the bandages then."

John passed by the living room and over-heard Chloe talking.

"I just don't know what to do yet, but we'll figure something out."

Chloe listened while John passed by, then turned around. "Where are you going?" She asked politely.

"Upstairs to get your mom some more bandages," he responded as he stopped to stand there. "What were you talking about?"

"Nothing, daddy."

"You must have been talking about something."

"No, not really." She paused briefly. "Why don't you go on and get mommy her bandages?" Chloe told her father nicely. As he walked up the stairs Chloe mumbled, "I hope her finger rots off!" She giggled to Illusion. "Isn't Savannah going to watch cartoons with us?" she asked fluffing up Illusion's dress.

"She has something to tend to," Illusion whispered back with an eerie voice as she gazed upon Chloe's face.

"Then she'll be down, right?"

"Soon, real soon."

"Good, because I don't want her to miss *The Mouse That Lived In My Shoe.*"

Meanwhile, John was gathering the bandages and peroxide to take down to Andrea, then he proceeded to go back to the kitchen.

"John, would you mind taking out this garbage for me?"

"Nope," he said, grasping the bag. John unlocked the back door and walked out into the yard carrying the bag in hand, then took it to the trash. As he walked back toward the house, he heard an unusual noise coming from behind the cellar. As John got closer, he noticed the old wooden doors desperately trying to be opened.

Heavy knocks beat upon the cellar and muffled cries were heard from within. Thick smoke seeped out through the cracks and encircled the air around John's head.

"Please help!" a man's voice cried out. "I can't breathe down here!" He panicked after he said that. The man began to cough as he choked on the smoke.

"I'll get you out of there!" John shouted through the door. He tugged at the cellar with all his might, but couldn't get it open.

"Please hurry! The flames are getting closer!" the man cried in agony.

John could smell the man's burning flesh as he continued to pull at the doors. Agonizing cries filled the air as the man wept behind the cellar. The screams John heard were so horrible that they plagued his mind with sadness. "I promise, I'll get you out!" he hollered to the man. John gave the doors one final tug as they swung open without any problem.

Huddled on the stairs in a fetal position laid a burnt man. The fire continued to burn rapidly near his body while John felt the tremendous heat from their flames.

"We have to get you out of here!" John yelled. "Give me your hand!"

The man continued to lie on the stairs with his chin tucked into his chest. His breathing was raspy, and strange noises gurgled in his throat. John scrolled his eyes quickly over the man's body and saw how badly seared his skin was from the fire.

In some places, parts of him peeled off, while bubbles boiled over the rest of his body, causing severe pain.

The man reached out to John, begging for help as he opened his hand. He took hold of John's forearm, squeezing him weakly. A second later that squeeze turned tight. "Have you decided to come with me, Jonny boy?" the man inquired while slowly drawing up his head. He locked his eyes upon John as he stared deeply into him.

A trail of tears streamed down John's face and fell onto his shirt. The man slowly pulled himself up from the stairs and stood before John. The sight was utterly disturbing, even though John continued to look on.

The man hardly had a face, nor any features for that matter. Skin clung to him where it peeled away. Deep burn marks sank into his face, blistering his withered skin.

"Why didn't you help me the first time this happened?" his father scorned him. "Then I wouldn't be in this agonizing mess."

John continued to gaze into his father's eyes, never once looking away. "I couldn't save you!" He cried. "I tried to help, but the doors were jammed!"

"That's crap, Jonny," he said, baring his set of sooted teeth. "You left me alone to die!"

"I did my best to break the doors with the axe, but I was unable to get to you in time."

"Those are lies, son, all lies!" He blew up in anger. "That mouth of yours still fibs even as an adult. I can't believe my wife gave birth to someone so shameful."

"Dad, you were already gone when I got to you. The fire was out of control. I did everything I could have done." He sobbed with intense emotion. "I didn't want you to die! I walked into those flames and I now live with the scars, because I attempted to save you. A part of me died when you did. My life was never the same after that day, and neither was mom's!"

"Nuff said. I didn't come here to talk." His voice gurgled while he spoke. "I'm here to condemn you to the flames that once consumed me." He laughed sinisterly. "It's time to come home to daddy, kid!" He threw his arm up with lightning speed, applying intense pressure to John's neck and throat.

John fought back as his father tried to drag him into the endless inferno.

"Don't struggle with me, Jonny."

"I'm not ready to go!" he yelled before stumbling to the ground. John had a chance to get away, so he made his escape. He started to the house as fast as his feet could take him. As he got to the door, he turned around before entering.

John saw no sight of his father anywhere in the yard. The cellar doors were closed and the flames had gone away. All was once again normal, the way it had been when he had first come out.

John took a deep breath and shook his head in disbelief.

"How's Mr. Blackwell?" Andrea wondered as John walked into the room.

"What?" he questioned her.

"I saw you talking to him. I just wanted to know how he was doing."

"I didn't talk to him," he said quickly. "I haven't even seen him today."

"I saw you both talking by the fence. Well, I guess it was him. I couldn't really see through the trees."

"Whoever you saw, it wasn't me."

"I'm pretty sure you don't have a twin brother lurking around here, dear."

John dropped his eyes toward the table and saw Chloe sitting in one of the chairs. A strange smile had formed on her lips while an uneasy gaze had set in her eyes. An eerie feeling came over John while Chloe took a bite of her French toast. "See, kiddo, I told you mommy would feed you."

"Daddy, why are you sweating?"

"I got really hot when I was outside."

"Oh, because it looks like you were standing near a fire," she said getting smart.

Andrea walked over to John and set his plate on the table. Along the back of his neck Andrea noticed the sooty black outline of a person's hand.

"There were no fires in the yard or in the cellar either," John hinted to Andrea, hoping she would understand.

Chloe pulled Illusion out from a chair and set her on the table, then turned the doll around to face John. His heart beat wildly as he stared upon her porcelain face.

Illusion looked back with a stone cold expression as she gazed in his eyes, looking deep into his soul.

"Mommy, can I have some more juice?" Chloe asked.

Andrea got up and walked to the refrigerator. She grabbed at the juice when it disappeared from the shelf. Andrea looked into the fridge with shock. "Where'd it go?" she asked softly. While Andrea dug through the shelves, Chloe exposed a lit match, holding it out for only John to see.

An evil grin crossed Illusion's lips while the flame burned not more then five inches from her delicate face. She slowly moved her eyes to the direction of the match, locking in on the orangish-blue flame. John was taken with fear, afraid to say anything, so he continued to sit there.

Chloe leaned forward to blow out the match while the look on Illusion's face wore off.

"I finally found the juice," Andrea announced as she walked back to the table. "Did somebody blow out a candle?" she asked when she detected the smoke. She noticed the look on John's face right away and quickly became worried.

"I don't want the juice anymore. Take it back to the fridge," Chloe demanded. "I'm going upstairs now. I don't want either of you bothering me."

Andrea waited until Chloe was away from the room when she asked John what happened. "You have soot on your neck," she stated as she wiped it away. "John, was there really a fire outside?"

He sat there unable to talk as he stared at his food.

"Aren't you going to eat?" she asked as he continued to stare at his plate. "Will you at least talk to me?"

"I'm sorry, Andrea. I'm just a little shook up right now."

"You're okay now. Whatever you saw is gone," she said, rubbing his shoulder lightly.

"Illusion's really alive, Andrea. I don't know how that could be," he spoke in confusion. "I saw her eyes move, and this hideous smile crept upon her lips. She may look like an innocent doll, but I can swear now that she's not!" he said, trembling. "Illusion has a set of jagged teeth hidden behind her delicate smile. I believe you now. I know that thing can bite." John shook his head as a single tear ran from his eye. "Andrea, what the hell have we gotten ourselves into by moving here?"

"Something else has upset you, John. I can see it in your eyes."

John took a moment before he finally opened up. "I had a rather unpleasant visit from my father. The entire time he was blaming me for his death. It was horrible. I took a step back into memory lane to a frightening incident that had once taken place. He tried to pull me into the fiery cellar so that I, too, would burn in the flames as he did. I fought to get away before I slipped and fell. I'm afraid he would have pulled me into the fire if I didn't get away from him. This evil that's here is set on killing us, Andrea. What if it does?"

"What do you want to do? You heard Mr. Blackwell tell us about the men who had heart attacks on the front porch and died."

"Maybe we should go ahead and check into newspaper clippings and old records of this place. We'll see if we could get someone to watch Chloe for a few hours so we could go. Do you feel up to it?"

"When do you want to leave?" Andrea asked while John glanced at the clock on the wall.

"It's barely 7:00 now, I'd say in a couple hours or so."

"We don't really know anyone around here, John. You think Mr. Blackwell might watch Chloe for us?"

"I hope so. It would help us out if he could."

"Do you know where the number is to call him?"

"I posted it by the phone. I'll give him a call around 8:30. He should be in from taking Sam on his walk."

"What are you going to tell him?"

"The truth, of course. We need to know what happened in this house. Pray we find what we're looking for," John spoke in a serious tone. "As for now, we'll try to have a normal morning if possible. I want to get some work done in the front yard. You going to be okay in here?"

"I haven't read Scarlette's journal for awhile. I have some free time to do that now."

"I thought you were done with that."

"I still have more entries to read. Maybe I could finish it today."

"Where's the journal?"

"In our room. It's in the cabinet next to the bed."

"I have to go up and change. I'll bring it down to you." John passed by Chloe's bedroom, then suddenly stopped. In the hall John could hear Chloe yelling from behind the door.

"That's what you get!"

John rushed over and grabbed the doorknob, then went into the room. "What's going on in here?" he quizzed Chloe briefly. "Why were you yelling?"

Chloe got up from her bed and walked over to her father. "What is it, daddy? Does my shouting scare you?" she quizzed him back. "I think I recall telling you and mommy earlier not to bother me," she said rather rudely. "Now that you're here, why do you bug me?"

The room had grown quiet except for the unusual sound of a kitten crying. John heard the muffled cries, but couldn't detect from where they were coming. "Chloe, where's Snow?"

"She's in here, daddy."

"I know she is, but where did you put her?"

"She hides while you seek!"

John started tearing Chloe's room apart, digging though clothes, drawers and cabinets. "Where is she?" he yelled.

"You're so cold, daddy!" Chloe giggled. "But you're getting a little warmer."

"Chloe, shut up and tell me where she is!"

"Warmer! Warmer! Okay, daddy, you're burning up!"

John stopped by Chloe's window anxiously looking over her room. He finally realized that Snow's cries were coming from inside the wall. He stared at an antique picture facing Chloe's bed, then quickly jerked it down. Behind the picture John found a small hole in the wall containing a wooden box. John pulled the box out and quickly opened the top. He found Snow wrapped in a bunch of rags and small towels. "What were you going to do, suffocate her?"

"Well, since you said it!"

"Why would you do that?"

"All that kitty snot she left on my arm made me mad. I wasn't going to really kill her, daddy, if that's what you thought."

"Snow is not to stay with you anymore. I don't want to even see you playing with her, do I make myself clear?"

"You better watch yourself, daddy. Grandpa Ray knows how to get into the house." Chloe snickered briefly in his face.

"You're to stay in your room alone. Do you understand? Snow's coming with me."

Chloe yawned to John's remark. "Then you better be going now, shouldn't you?"

John glared at Chloe before leaving the room. He carried Snow to his bed and laid her down. "You poor little kitty," he said, rubbing her head. "You'll stay with Andrea and me."

Snow flipped around to her back, begging for a tummy rub and began to purr. "You're a cute little thing, aren't you?" He walked over to the closet and dug through the hangers for some work clothes, then changed. He remembered Scarlette's journal as he scavaged through the cabinet next to the bed. John finally found it in a drawer buried beneath a few of Andrea's night gowns.

He scooped Snow up into his hand and carried her down to Andrea. "Look who comes to see you!"

"Hey, little fuzz ball!" she said, taking her from John.

"Keep her away from Chloe."

"Why? What's wrong?"

"She was going to suffocate Snow. I told Chloe she's not to play with her or keep Snow in her room anymore. She's to stay with us at all times."

"Oh, my God, John, I can't believe she was going to kill her. Why?"

"She said Snow made her mad. That doesn't mean she should try to kill her, though. Chloe's mind is demented. First the bird, now this. What's next?"

"I'll make sure Snow stays with me," Andrea assured him. "Before you go out, could you watch her for me? I want to change clothes."

John waited with Snow on the couch as Andrea went up to change. He tossed a small fuzzy ball around and played with the kitten. Snow chased the ball all over the sofa until she took it away from John. He pulled the ball back and continued to play.

Andrea walked into the room giggling at John. "I think she likes you!"

"She likes this ball. Snow could play with this thing till she grows tired." John said getting up from the sofa, "I guess I'll be going out then. You planning on staying in here?"

"This seems like the best place right now."

"Here's the journal then," he said, handing it over to Andrea. "I'll be in to check on you later."

CHAPTER EIGHT

ANDREA GOT COMFORTABLE ON THE COUCH as Snow walked over and laid on her lap. Andrea undid the ribbon and cracked open the journal. She opened the diary to the next entry.

The twenty-eighth of April, nineteen hundred

As hard as I may try, nothing I have done will get rid of that doll. She simply keeps coming back. For what reason, I do not know.

Wallace is finally starting to see things in a true light, I've prayed that he would. Savannah said a few things that haven't set well with him. Just yesterday she kicked him in the shin and stepped on his foot for getting the wrong type of ice cream on her cone. Savannah wanted vanilla; instead he brought chocolate.

Collette and Griffin are frightened by her. I know they sense her evil. Today Savannah got mad at her sister and pulled out a thick mass of hair, Collette cried for twenty minutes. That was only the beginning. Later she took a boiling kettle from the stove top and set it upon Griffin's skin, burning his arm.

Jillian Osborn

Why won't this madness end? What has my family done to deserve this? Please, I must know. How can I make it stop?

Waiting for an answer...
Scarlette

Andrea flipped a little deeper into the journal.

The fourth of May, nineteen hundred

My dear God, my worst thoughts have come true. Never would I have completely believed it, but I've witnessed the truth. This morning around two o'clock I thought I was awakened by Savannah. My inquisitive mind got the best of me so I walked into the hall. As I came upon the staircase, I could see into the parlor. As I peered into the moonlit room, to my fear and horror I witnessed Illusion walking across the ground below. Every inch of my being was frightened beyond control as I stood there to panic.

In her hand I noticed the shiny silver object she carried by her side. Under the moon the sight was most clear as the scissors reflected beneath the light. I hurried to Griffin's room, taking my son from his crib. Collette heard me as she stood between the frame of her door. I told her she must hurry and get to my room. I rushed behind her with Griffin in arm. Wallace awoke as we came through the door. I told him to gather Savannah from her bed, then we fastened the lock and held onto the kids.

Illusion paced through the hall all night trying desperately to get into our room. At one point she thrashed the shears beneath the opening of the door, stabbing at the floor.

We waited in the room for the first light of day. We felt the comfort of the sun, but then dread fell upon us; a new day had begun. New terrors lurk around. With each day it gets worse.

As we came into the hall we found where the scissors had been driven deep into our door with tremendous force. The walls were slashed and torn away from Illusion's aroused fit of rage. I pray each day that this were over. I merely wish to bring an end to this curse. If there is a way, I need to soon find it, for I fear the time is running out. A wasted minute can turn into hours, and wasted hours can lead into days.

I fear I don't have the time. My family needs a miracle to intervene in our lives.

Wishing for that miracle to come along...
Scarlette

The sixth of May, nineteen hundred

I was in the attic today when I came across the secret door that led into the most ungodly, irreligious room. What I saw has deeply disturbed my sight and corrupted my mind.

In the center of the room stood a large butcher's block stained in massive amounts of dark red blood. Spread along the countertop were melted black candles that had been securely held into place. Chalked onto the wooden floor boards were some of the most unusual symbols.

Strange charts clung to the walls, along with parchment scrolls and other odd writings. In the back of the room was a massive case that harbored several doll-making supplies, along with a few alfits. Hung from the rafters in neatly placed rows were different types of herbs, roots and flowers.

I walked over to an armoire that stood before the butcher's block where I hesitated a moment before opening it. If I could go back and not be tempted to reveal what it was hiding behind those doors, I wouldn't. Inside on the shelves were apothecary jars that contained human body parts carefully perseverved in formaldehyde. Each jar was labeled with their alarming contents. Here are the names of several jars that I recall from reading, brains of a madman, tongue of a liar, heart of a killer, eyes of a deceiver and the lips of a dishonorable mouth. What kind of horrible events took place in this house? I fear to even ask that question, and I dread even more to know the answer.

Resting next to the jar labeled heart of a killer was a leather bound journal. I opened it to read the contents, but was unable to do so for the journal was written completely in Latin. I put the journal back, then sealed off the room, vowing never to enter that God forsaken place again.

Whatever happened here was beyond gracious and cheery. It was truly unrighteous and diabolical. I hope nobody ever stumbles upon that room again. That place is a secret I'll take to my grave, but I shall keep the information safely in the contents of this journal with strict confidentiality.

Always,
Scarlette

Does this room really exist? I believe what I've read. I know it's all in truth. Why would Scarlette lie? Andrea thought. I wonder if I could find it? If I could, maybe I'd be able to understand this mystery. Looks like I'm on a mission to find that room. Andrea got up and hid the journal beneath the cushion of the couch.

She started up the stairs, then headed to her bedroom where she sat Snow down to sleep.

CHAPTER NINE

Now Andrea stood before the attic as she stared upon the distending staircase. Andrea felt a flutter of butterflies in the pit of her stomach as a nervous sensation stirred within her. Andrea took a deep breath and fought back her fears. "I can do this," she assured herself, "I'm not afraid." Andrea slowly walked up the stairs. With each step she took, Andrea came closer to the attic door until it was right in her face. She entered, then stood in the center of the room to have a look around.

Andrea searched the walls, but found nothing unusual. She then decided to move some boxes and furniture away, hoping to reveal the door, but again nothing. Andrea was getting exhausted from all the heavy lifting, so she proceeded to take a seat in an old rocking chair. It was then Andrea noticed a brass dove hanging from a nearby wall. Shocked to see it hanging there, Andrea walked over to it. She looked the area over in much attention, hoping to find the door.

Andrea began to knock upon the walls, searching for a hallowed sound. "Where is it?" she yelled as she began to beat even harder. The brass dove on the wall got jarred by Andrea's heavy knocks and fell to the floor. She bent down to pick it up when she noticed something unusual on the floor beneath a large trunk. Andrea tugged the trunk aside, exposing a large trap door in the floor. "What do we have here?" she asked herself, "This must be it," Andrea said while taking hold of the old iron door pull. "Well, here goes nothing," she said as she lifted the wooden frame. A sinister cold escaped the room as Andrea raised the door.

She peered into darkness, afraid and unnerved by the unsettling feelings that came over her. Andrea took a few moments before she started down the staircase into the endless hole filled with clingy spider webs and particles of debris and dust. As she walked into the dark, Andrea felt along the wall for a light switch when she finally found it at the end of the staircase. Andrea closed her eyes and choked up for a second. "May God be with me now in this time of need for I know what horrors will be viewed before me," Andrea spoke softly as she proceeded to flip the switch. She kept her eyes shut tightly for a second more before deciding to get a clear perspective of the dwellings before her.

Andrea opened her eyes slowly to take in the view of the room, and in that instant she was presented with a vision of overwhelming horror. "What is this terrible place?" she uttered to herself while staring upon the stained butcher's block. "This is truly a room where sinister activities and events took place. Such vile occurrences have happened here in my home. How do I rid this evil that has since grown into something so powerful and out of control?"

Andrea looked over the disgraceful room, horrified by the sinful images so clearly in her sight. She passed by the butcher's block trying desperately not to peer upon the blood stains soaked into the wooden surface. As Andrea walked by she could smell the coppery scent of blood as though it had been freshly dispersed upon the table. The smell was sickening as she inhaled the putrid odor that raised away from the countertop. Andrea made her way toward the case containing the doll supplies and carefully looked them over. She noticed the similarities between the unfinished dolls and Illusion. "What the hell was going on in here?" Andrea looked over each of the charts and parchment scrolls presented on the walls of the room. Most contained images and odd diagrams that Andrea couldn't comprehend. Weird symbols and strange writings were also seen on many of the charts and scrolls that perplexed Andrea.

She stood before the armoire where she readied herself before viewing its appalling contents. A cold chill ran across her back while shivers took control of her body, forcing Andrea to shake.

Slowly she began to count, hoping that would cause her to forget her fears. "One," she said and took a deep breath followed by a brief pause, then, "Two." Pausing again Andrea takes another breath, then puts her hands on the doorknobs. "Three!" she said and the doors swung open. Reflected in Andrea's eyes were the apothecary jars that contained body parts from the dead. Andrea gasped when revealing the disturbing subjects she knew were there. She was by far more appalled from seeing the specimens themselves than when reading about them in Scarlette's journal. Andrea choked with disgust for she couldn't believe the names written upon each shameful jar. "Why would someone keep these types of things?" she said, cringing. "This is some really sick stuff."

Upon the jar that contained two human hearts, Andrea saw the leather-bound journal that Scarlette once touched. She snatched the journal, then quickly closed the armoire, shutting away its awful contents. Andrea turned around into the butcher's block when she saw Ivy and Adrienne sitting on it. Her mouth dropped in fear as they returned an unnerving glare.

"Good morning, mommy," Ivy said softly.

"How have things been?" Adrienne added in.

"Today would be a marvelous day to come home to us." Ivy giggled.

Andrea was too deeply afraid to make any movement so she stood before them frozen with fear. She gazed toward the stairs for a quick second before looking back at the twins.

"It's no use, mommy."

"We've closed the trap door."

"So you can't get out," Adrienne said sternly.

"We won't leave you alone."

"It's our law."

"You'll come with us."

"We won't take no for an answer."

"That's certainly unacceptable."

"Therefore you cannot try to escape at this time." Adrienne looked at Ivy who had a smile on her face, then they both turned to Andrea.

"We even thought of you, mommy."

"We painted the axe handle blue."

"We know it's your favorite color."

"Come closer to see."

"It'll only take a minute." Ivy said while displaying the axe.

"Then it shall all be over."
"The procedure's quick!"
"We swear."
"We wouldn't lie."
"So come with us, mommy."
"Are you ready to die?"

The twins slid off the butcher's block, then made their way toward their mother.

"You aren't my twins!" Andrea shouted.

"I assure you, we are." Adrienne spoke in a wicked tone.

"No, you're not!" Andrea yelled back, then the disguises were ripped away. Standing before her was Savannah, clutching Illusion.

"Oh, Andrea, it's such a pity to see you run away from us. We just want to play. No harm intended."

"Unless it goes that way," Illusion said with a hostile voice.

Andrea hurried up the stairs, leaving Savannah and Illusion behind her as they laughed at her fear.

"No matter where you are in this house, we'll always find you," mentioned Savannah.

Andrea pushed on the trap door as hard as she could until it finally gave way, then she was able to escape Savannah and Illusion's wrath of terror.

Andrea drug the old trunk back over to the floor and sealed away the door. Andrea ran into Chloe, who was standing in the hallway purposely waiting for her.

"Oh, mommy, you look frightened. Did something scare you?"

Andrea looked at Chloe, upset by her sarcastic tongue.

"Go back to your room."

"What's that in your hand?"

"It's nothing, Chloe. Now go."

"It must be something. I want to see it."

"It's just a journal."

"I want it. Give it to me."

"I told you to go to your room."

"That's not yours. You have no right to take it. Give it to me now!" Chloe demanded.

"I'm your mother, and I said go to your room."

"Fine then, you stupid bitch! You can't read that journal anyway. It's no use to you."

"I'm tired of your crude mouth. Get out of my sight," Andrea said as she passed by Chloe.

"Oh, mommy, you're so mean. You've crushed my feelings."

"I'm going to hurt that butt of yours if you don't shut that mouth."

"You hurt me, Savannah and Illusion will get you for sure."

"Aren't you supposed to be in your room?" Andrea said as she walked down the stairs, dismissing her daughter.

Andrea walked to the front door and saw John in the yard. He waved at her through the glass as Andrea was coming out. "I think you need to wash Chloe's mouth out with soap."

"Is she being disrespectful again?" John inquired.

Andrea knotted her head to his question. "I hate to see what our daughter's become, John. I don't like to yell at her, but I had to. I can't take another day of this."

"Try not to think about it, dear."

"How can I not? Ever since we came here, our lives have been ruined. It won't stop, John. It'll never stop. What should we do?"

"Try to keep our family safe. That's what's important. We'll beat this; we can do it."

"I'm not so sure that's possible, John. Not after what I've just found. We're dealing with something old and powerful. We don't have the strength to put up a fight."

"Don't look so blue, honey. Where there's a will, there's a way. Besides, we have God on our side. We can get through anything as long as he's with us."

"What if we grow apart, John? What if this thing turns us all against each other? You've seen how it's changed Chloe. What's it going to do to us?"

"Have a little faith. Don't break down on me now," he said as he held Andrea's hand.

"I'm just afraid, John. I grow more worrisome each day."

"It's all right to be scared, Andrea. Just don't allow it to take you over," he told her softly as he noticed the journal on the stairs. "What's this?"

"It's some kind of journal."

"Where did you find it?"

"One of the entries in Scarlette's journal talked about a secret room in the attic. I found it. I saw the same disturbing images Scarlette described in the pages of her diary."

"What did you find?"

"There's a room hidden beneath the floor of the attic. There's a trap door underneath a large trunk. That's where I found the entrance. It's the most unpleasant place. Bad things happened in there."

"What do you mean?"

"It's a shrine dedicated to black magic or something. There's a table in the room that's stained with blood. I think it was used to sacrifice the living. Across from it is a cabinet that contains jars with human body parts."

"Body parts?"

"Everything's still there. People's eyes, brains, hearts and more. It's creepy, John."

"Maybe it was a laboratory for a scientist or doctor."

"Doctors and scientists don't keep doll-making supplies in their labs."

"What?" John asked in confusion.

"There are shelves that hold doll making supplies. It's bizarre. There were strange charts on the walls and odd symbols covering the floor boards."

"How long did you stay in there?"

"My reason for going was to find this journal. Scarlette talked about it in her diary. The entire book is written in Latin."

John opened the diary to the first page. It read, *Mei Liber Libri Consisto Niger Deliciae, Per Cyrus Cornu*

"Do you know what is says?" John asked curiously.

"I haven't got a clue."

"So what are we supposed to do with a book that we can't read?"

"I thought there might be some useful information in it. I figured maybe we could find someone who knows how to read Latin and translate it for us."

"Andrea, how do you expect to find someone who knows Latin around here?"

"I don't know. I thought maybe you might have an idea."

"You know how rare that possibility is?"

"Then where would you start?"

"I'd look for someone who studies it or has a degree."

"Like a professor?"

"Yeah, someone who knows their stuff."

"Why don't we see if a professor at one of the universities could help?"

"That's not a bad idea, but I don't know if someone would be willing to help us."

"Still, it's worth a try. What do we have to lose?"

"I see your point. I guess we'll try to find someone later. I hear the phone ringing."

"You want me to get that?" Andrea asked John.

"Don't get up. I'll answer it," he replied as he started into the house. "Hello?"

"Hey, John, I wanted to make sure everyone was all right. I wanted to call you before I left the motel."

"Hi, Rich. It's good to hear from you. We're all right even though things continue to get worse."

"I was afraid of that. How's Andrea?"

"She can't take it here much longer. She's ready to break. I'm afraid I'll be like her in another day. I try to keep it together, but things grow even weirder with each passing hour. I don't want to question my sanity, you know? But if things continue going the way they are, I just might have to. I mean you see shit you think is real because it's right there before you, then you try to doubt it because you know it's not possible, but then the realism kicks in again and takes over."

"Someone came to visit you?"

"Yeah, my dad."

"Oh, gee, man, you see? It's playing with you now. You have to get out of there. It'll try its best to destroy you all if you don't."

"I know," John said. "What happened with my dad nearly destroyed me. Seeing him and listening to what he was saying was tearing me apart."

"Don't listen to the lies. You have to keep yourself together."

"I'm trying, Rich, I really am."

"How's Chloe? Any changes?"

"Not any for the better, I hate to say. Andrea doesn't know Chloe anymore. Either do I. She lies to me so much and says bad things to her mom, and Chloe expects me to believe that she doesn't. It's like she's become a rebellious teenager, yet she's only a child."

"I'm worried about you guys, man. Please tell me you'll all be careful while you're there."

"As much as we can."

"I still wish you'd change your mind about leaving that place."

"There's always time to."

"Just don't wait until it's too late. You catch my drift?"

"I got you."

"Well, I'm leaving here now and heading on home. I'll talk to you when I can."

"All right, Rich. You have a safe trip."

"I'll try to do that."

"Thanks for calling."

"No prob. Later."

"Bye, Rich," John said as he hung up the phone.

He glanced over to the clock so he could check on the time, then picked the phone up again and waited for a dial tone. He pressed in a few numbers and it began to ring as he waited for an answer.

"Good morning, Mr. Blackwell."

"Hello there, John. Now you know I'm going to have to hang up this phone if you don't stop calling me that."

"I'm sorry, sir. I guess I always try to remember my manners."

"You're a respectful man. I won't hassle you for that." He laughed. "Let's try this again."

"Okay, Tookie!"

"That's more like it, son. So what can I help you with this morning?"

"Andrea and I were wondering if you could do us a favor."

"What'd you have in mind, son?"

"We wanted to see if you might be willing to watch Chloe for a couple of hours, if that isn't a problem."

"Not at all. I'd enjoy some youthful company."

"You're sure you don't mind? You're the only person we've met since we moved in. We really don't have that many choices."

"I'd be happy to help you. Son, if you don't mind me asking, is everything all right? You sound a bit stressed."

"It's just this house, Tookie. It's starting to drive my family apart.

Andrea and I wanted to do some research on this place and hopefully find some answers."

"I'll watch Chloe for y'all. I hope you find what you're looking for." Tookie paused for a second, then continued, "Sometimes the truth can be a scary thing for the person who's seeking answers to such questions. Are you and Andrea prepared for what you might find?"

"As prepared as we can be, I guess. We need to find out the secrets to this house before it kills us. One day may be too late. We might as well do something about this while we're still breathing."

"If you need any other assistance, I'd be more than happy to help you and your family out. Just say the words and I'll be there to aid you when y'all need it."

"I appreciate your services with this matter. Would it be all right if we brought Chloe by in an hour?"

"Whenever you're ready. Sam and I will be here waiting."

"Thank you so much, Tookie. You have no idea how much help you are to Andrea and me right now."

"I'm glad I'm here to help you. It's like I said the first day we met, I can't watch as another family has their lives destroyed by that house. I want to help before it's too late."

"We'll be by in an hour. Thanks again, Tookie."

"Okay, son. Sam and I will see y'all then."

Andrea was walking into the house just as John hung up the phone. "Who called?" she asked.

"Rich. He wanted to see if we were all right."

"Did he get home safely?"

"He called from the motel. Said he wanted to call us before he left. I called Tookie after I got off the phone with Rich. He said he wouldn't mind watching Chloe for us."

"I don't need no damn babysitter!" Chloe yelled from the staircase.

John turned around to face her. "It'll only be for a little while, Chlo."

"I'm old enough to watch myself. I'm not going!" she demanded. "I'd rather stay here with Savannah and Illusion than to go off to some old man's house. You never know what an old man might do to a child. I know you're more sensible than that, daddy, or at least that's what I thought."

"Mr. Blackwell is a nice man. How dare you for saying that, Chloe!"

"Well, it's the truth. There are dirty old men in this world who like to mess with little girls. I won't be one of those victims," she said as she ran off to her room.

"Chloe, get back here!" John said, running off after her.

"Forget it, John. Just let her go."

"I can't believe her, Andrea. Did you hear what she said?"

"I heard her. She's just trying to get away so she doesn't have to go over there. Don't worry, we'll get her out of her room after while."

"Are you so sure of that?"

"We'll break down her door. One way or another, we're going to get her out of there."

"You think we'll have to go through some drastic lengths to get her out?"

"I hate to say it, but yes. It's not like she'll come willingly."

"Yeah, you're right."

"I know."

"If I have to climb a ladder and go through her window, I will."

"Let's not think that far yet, John. Maybe we could talk her out of her room without any problem."

"Are you contradicting yourself?"

"Why do you ask that?"

"You're the one who said she won't come willingly."

"I did say that, didn't I?"

"Yes, dear, you did."

"I guess we'll find out what happens when the time comes."

"Where's Snow?" John asked as he looked around the room.

"Oh, I took her up to our bedroom earlier."

"Should you check on her?"

"Yeah, I probably should."

"If she's not in there, you know Chloe has her."

"She better not. Not after what you've told me."

"You better go," John told her.

Andrea went upstairs. As she passed through the hallway she heard the distinct sound of water running in the bathroom. She opened the door and peered into the room when she noticed Wallace's ghostly image standing near the sink.

"Scarlette, is that you?" he cried out.

Andrea continued to look at him as he turned around to her with bloody eyes. She was frightened and upset by the distressful sight.

"Savannah tried to claw my eyes out. I can't see!" he continued to cry on in pain. "Please help me!"

Deep claw marks covered his face and eyes as blood dripped out of the freshly scratched wounds. Andrea looked in the sink and saw the bloodied rag he'd been using to wipe his face.

"It stings and burns!"

"Wallace, I'm coming!" Scarlette yelled as she raced down the hall.

Andrea backed up as Scarlette made her way into the room to help him.

"Oh, my God, what has she done?" she cried back.

"I can't see. I think she's blinded me!"

"What can I do to help?"

"Call the doctor," he begged. "Please hurry."

Scarlette rushed out of the room as she and Wallace vanished before Andrea's eyes. Andrea stood there for a moment in shock at the event she had just witnessed. She started back down the hall and went to her room. She opened the door and right away noticed that Snow wasn't on the bed where she left her. Andrea began to panic as she looked around the room desperately trying to find the kitten. Finally she heard a faint meow come from the window as she made her way toward it.

"Snow!" Andrea said. She was greeted with another faint meow as she saw her hiding behind the curtains. "Oh, Snow, I was so afraid something bad happened to you."

Andrea picked the kitten up and held her tightly in her hands. She looked out the window and saw birds hopping around in a nearby tree. "Were you watching those silly birds?" Andrea asked her. "Here, I'll set you back in the window so you can continue to watch them. I'm happy you're all right," she said as she scratched the kitten's head. Andrea left the room and closed the door behind her.

"Is Snow okay?" John asked.

"Yeah, she's watching the birds in the window. Everything's fine," Andrea assured him.

"I wish everything would be fine when we have to get Chloe out of her room."

"No matter how much she might fight us, we cannot let her take Illusion over to Mr. Blackwell's house."

"I agree." John glanced down at his watch. "Do you have anything you need to get done?"

"I just have to get my shoes on, that's all."

"Go ahead and get them on. I'll see if I can get Chloe out of her room."

Andrea headed toward her bedroom while John stood before Chloe's door.

"Chloe, will you open this door please?" John asked nicely as he waited for a reply. "Chloe, did you hear me?"

"I told you I wasn't going anywhere. Leave me alone!"

"Chloe, please open your door."

"No!"

"Chloe, unlock this door right now!"

"It's jammed, daddy. It won't open. Looks like I'm stuck in here. Ain't that a shame?"

"You're testing my patience, Chlo. I asked you nicely to open this door."

"And I told you it was jammed!"

"Fine then, we're going to do this my way."

"Having problems, John?" Andrea asked as she walked down the hallway.

"She won't come out."

"So what do you have in mind?"

"I'm going to have to go through her window."

"Oh, John. I wish you wouldn't do that."

"You have any better ideas?"

"I guess not. Just be careful, okay? It's a long way down if you should fall."

"I won't fall, Andrea."

"I hope not, but be careful anyway."

"I will, honey. I've been on ladders plenty of other times and I've never fallen off. You better stay here, I'll open her door once I get inside."

"I'll see you on the other side then. Be careful, please. I don't want to have to take you to the emergency room today."

"You won't have to. I'll see you shortly." John walked down to the kitchen, then went out through the back door. He made his way over to the old shed and hunted for a ladder. This should work. John thought.

He carried it over to Chloe's window and laid it against the house. John started up the ladder when he came across one of the windows of the lower section of the house. Through the glass John saw the badly burnt image of his father peering back at him. Ray Craven opened the window and started up the ladder after his son. John hurried as fast as he could, hoping to escape.

"Aren't you happy to see your father again, son?" Ray yelled to him. "You don't have to climb away from me. I just want to talk to you," he spoke sternly, followed by a wicked tone of laughter. "You can't escape me, John. I'm right behind you!" he said while reaching out for John's ankle. "I told you, boy, you can't get away." The ladder began to shake violently as John fought to keep his balance.

"Chloe!" he yelled. "You better open this window now. Daddy needs your help!"

Chloe walked over to the window and peered out at her father. "What's wrong, daddy? Can't you stay still?"

"Open the window!"

"I'm afraid I can't do that. Illusion won't permit it." She then turned her back and walked away from the window.

"Damn it, Chloe!" John yelled while he fought to shake his dad away. He knew the only way he could escape was to break the window.

Andrea heard the sound of shattering glass as she stood before Chloe's door. "John, are you all right?" she yelled to him. "Please say something!"

Andrea felt her heart beating heavily in her chest as she waited to hear his voice. She hurried down the hallway just as the door creaked open behind her. Andrea stopped, then turned around to find John standing in the doorway.

"I'm okay." he told her.

"Oh, John, when I didn't hear your voice I got worried."

"Everything's fine. I just had to break the window."

"Are you sure you're all right? I heard you yelling, then I heard glass shattering."

"I saw my father again, but I'm safe. I got in the house."

"John, your hand is bleeding!"

"It's nothing. It's just a few scratches." John looked in on Chloe as she sat on her bed. "Why didn't you open the window for me?"

"Because I couldn't, that's why!"

"You know, maybe your mother and I shouldn't take you to the park."

"The park!" Chloe exclaimed as her expression changed.

"We were going to take you there, but now I don't think we should."

"But I want to go to the park."

"If you acted like a nice little girl, we'd take you."

"I'm sorry, daddy. I didn't mean to make you mad. Can we go to the park now?"

"I don't know, Chlo. Maybe you should stay in your room for today."

"No, daddy! I want to go to the park! I'll be a good girl, I promise."

"Let's see what your mommy thinks," John said as he turned to his wife. He raised his eyebrows as he looked into her eyes. "Well, Andrea, what'd you say?"

"I guess we could for a little while."

"I promise I'll be good." Chloe picked Illusion up from her pillows. "We're ready to go now."

"Oh, no, baby Illusion can't come to the park. She's liable to get dirty. It's best she stays here," Andrea told her.

"She can't come with us?" Chloe pouted.

"She'll be here when you get back, then you can play together."

"I'm sorry, Illusion, but mommy's right. You would get dirty." She set the doll on the pillows, then kissed the top of her head. "I'll see you when I get back."

John took hold of Chloe's hand as he led her into the hall. "Don't forget to close the door," he told Andrea.

She followed him as they came into the living room.

"Why don't you go ahead and take Chloe outside. I'll be there in a minute."

"Good idea," Andrea said as she and Chloe walked to the front porch.

John picked up the phone and called Tookie. "Is it all right if we drop Chloe off now?"

"Sure, come on by. I'll have the door open."

"Thank you. We'll see you shortly." John locked the door as Andrea and Chloe walked down the stairs.

CHAPTER TEN

"Where are we going?" Chloe asked.

"To the park, of course."

"Aren't we going to drive there?"

"It's a nice day. I thought we'd take a walk," John told her, coaxing Chloe into his lie.

"Oh," she said mildly as they came upon the next house.

"We need to stop here really quick," John told everyone as they followed him.

"You know, mommy, it's really weird."

"What's weird, Chloe?"

"I don't feel the coldness anymore."

"What coldness, Chlo?"

"The coldness I feel when I'm in the house. I feel so warm now."

"Is it the sun?"

"No, mommy, I don't think so. I started to feel it as soon as we left our house."

Andrea looked up to John. "They can't control her out here. As long as she's away from the house, she's fine."

"Chloe, what does the coldness do to you? How does it make you feel?" John wondered.

"It's like when you're sick and you have the chills, I guess, but you feel the coldness deeper inside."

"You don't feel that way now, do you?"

"No, I'm warm."

"Chloe, your mommy and I have someone we want you to meet."

"A new friend?"

"He's a little older then those you're used to, but yes." John knocked on the door.

"Y'all come on in!" Tookie exclaimed as he walked to the door. "Well, you must be Chloe."

"Yes, sir, that's me. What's your name?"

"I'm Tookie, and that over there's my dog Sam. Do you have a doggy?"

"No, sir, I have a kitty named Snow. We found her in our backyard."

"Well, isn't that swell. I guess she knew you were moving in, huh?"

"You think so?"

"I sure do. Y'all come on in here and have a seat on the couch," he said politely, then turned to Chloe. "Say, I bet you like orange juice. Am I right?"

"Yes, sir, right next to apple."

"I have some fresh squeezed orange juice in my kitchen. Would you like a glass?"

"I've never had fresh squeezed orange juice before."

"I think you'd like it. I'm going to get you some."

"Thank you."

"Aren't you just the most well mannered little girl!"

"My mommy and daddy taught me to be."

"Well, they've done a good job because you're an angel."

"My Aunt Debbie calls me that!" Chloe giggled.

"I'm sure she does. Could I get anyone else some orange juice or perhaps a cup of coffee?"

"I'll take some coffee please," Andrea told Tookie.

"How would you like that, dear?"

"Sugar, and lots of cream."

"Coming right up. Is there something I could get for you, John?"

"That orange juice is sounding pretty good."

"Okay, two glasses of orange juice and one cup of coffee, sugar and lots of cream coming up."

Tookie returned a bit later with a tray in his hands, carrying the coffee and juices.

"Mr. Blackwell, I've been admiring your house. This place is stunning!" Andrea said, commenting on the dwellings around her.

"Why, thank you, my dear."

"So who was the decorator?" Andrea pondered aloud.

"Evelyn did most of it herself," he explained. "We both shared a passion for refurbishing antiques. There's a significant place for each of them in every room of this house. Evie loved anything that was old and had character."

"She definitely had taste. You both did a gorgeous job." Andrea's words were interrupted by the doorbell as the chimes echoed throughout the house.

"Will y'all excuse me while I answer that?"

"Oh, sure," Andrea said in response.

Tookie walked over to the large door ready to greet whoever was there. He looked out to find an empty porch as he peered from behind the doorway. "Hello, is somebody there?" Tookie asked while he walked outside. He noticed a small note left beneath the doormat and picked it up. He undid the letter, then proceeded to read the note, in large red ink it said simply, *We're here.*

Tookie disregarded the note and walked back into the house.

"Is everything all right?" Andrea asked.

"Just the neighborhood kids leaving me silly notes, that's all. I'm going to catch them one of these days."

"They've been causing you some trouble?"

"They've been sneaking into my backyard and stealing my peaches. I wouldn't mind it so much if they just came and asked for some. You know how kids are these days. Most of them have no respect anymore. But your Chloe here is another story. You both keep a good eye on her. I told you before that house will try to manipulate her anyway it can."

"It already has," John commented on Tookie's statement.

"Mommy, what are daddy and Mr. Tookie talking about?" Chloe questioned her.

"Nothing, dear."

"Didn't they say something about me?"

"They were talking about how much of a good little girl you are,"

Andrea added as she stared at John and Tookie. "Mr. Blackwell, is it all right if Chloe plays with Sam for a few minutes?"

"Sure, she can play with Sam."

"Thank you, Mr. Tookie," Chloe spoke in return.

"I have a jar of treats if you care to feed him some."

"He won't bite me, will he?"

"Oh no, Sam's never bitten a soul. He's a good old dog."

"I like him. He's so pretty and fluffy."

"Well, if Sam could say thank you he would. Right Sam?"

"He doesn't talk?"

"Oh, no, my dear, I'm afraid not. But if you ever meet a talking dog, you let me know about it, okay?"

"I will, Mr. Tookie."

"Good answer. You and Sam sit here and play while I talk to your parents."

"Okay." Chloe answered softly.

Mr. Blackwell walked back over to the couch and took a seat near Andrea. "Now, where were we?"

"When Chloe heard you were going to watch her, she ran straight to her room. She said she wanted to stay home with Savannah and Illusion rather than coming here. I know how awful that must sound. I'm sorry. I thought you should know that Chloe is a totally different person when she's in that house," Andrea told him.

"Who did she want to stay with?"

"Savannah and Illusion."

"Who might they be?" he pondered aloud.

"Savannah is the name of the little girl who used to live in our house back in 1900. Illusion is the name of her doll. They're both bad, but I believe Illusion is the true source of the evil. That doll has a mind of its own, she's alive somehow. I know that sounds outrageous, but it's the truth. I found Scarlette's diary. That was Savannah's mother," Andrea explained. "I've been reading her journal."

"Scarlette kept a journal?"

"Yes. Scarlette described the changes in her daughter's personality not long after Illusion's arrival. There's some sort of secret room in that house. It's the worst place I've ever been. Evil doings went on in there that are beyond my thoughts. I found a leather journal written in Latin by whomever lived there first. Unfortunately John, nor I could read it. We thought we might look for a translator who could understand it."

"You said Latin, right?"

"Yes, sir, I did."

"I have a brother who's a retired Latin professor. He could probably help you. I just need to talk to him."

"Are you serious?" Andrea asked with widened eyes. "John and I were thinking about sending it out to a university, hopefully to see if we could find somebody to help us. Instead, you brought the invitation to us."

"I'll call him a bit later to see if he'd be interested in helping you. Knowing my brother, he should jump at the opportunity right away."

"Where does he live?" John asked curiously.

"Victor resides in Charlton with his wife Clara. They used to live in Princeton, New Jersey until they decided to retire and move to Charlton in 1969."

"What did his wife do?" Andrea wondered aloud.

"Clara was a neurologist, and a good one at that. She always treated her patients like family. She was well respected in the medical field and by those around her."

"She sounds like a wonderful person. Do she and Victor visit often?"

"Occasionally. We usually get together for dinner and pass the time away. Victor and I have always been close. We share a good connection with one another. I couldn't have asked for a better brother."

"Who's the oldest?"

"Victor's the baby. He's three years younger than I. Our birthdays are close so we share them together."

"How close?"

"My birthday is on December 10th and Victor's is the 15th. We always have a big feast with the family. It's like having Christmas ten days early."

"Do y'all get together for Christmas, too?"

"Always. If the birthday parties are celebrated here, Sam and I go to Victor and Clara's house for Christmas, and vice versa."

"When you talk to him, please let him know that John and I would be more than happy to pay him for his services."

"Victor doesn't work that way. He wouldn't want to make a profit off y'all. He loves to help people. What he does, he does out of the goodness of his heart. He loved teaching at the university because he was able to share his knowledge with those who were willing to learn. He was passionate about his work. It was dear to him."

"Well, we hate to keep taking up your time. We better go so we can get back. John and I thank you again for watching Chloe for us."

"It's not a problem. You go and find out what you can about that house. We'll be here when you get back. It's no rush, so y'all take your time."

"Thank you," John and Andrea both answered at once.

They got off the couch and walked over to Chloe, who was still sitting on the floor with Sam.

"Now you be a good girl for Mr. Blackwell while we're gone. We'll be back as soon as we can."

"I'll be good, mommy."

"That's my girl." Andrea said before kissing Chloe on top of her head.

"We'll see you shortly, kiddo."

"Okay, daddy!"

"We shouldn't be too long," Andrea told Tookie.

"Take your time, dear. You don't want to miss something because you didn't dig deep enough." Tookie walked John and Andrea to the door. "See y'all later."

The Cravens walked down the sidewalk and made their way toward their van.

CHAPTER ELEVEN

"John, do you know where the library is located?"

"It should be somewhere in town, but if we can't find it, we can always ask someone for directions."

John and Andrea drove around until they came across a large building.

"I think we found it." John said happily. "And look, I didn't get us lost."

"I'm proud of you."

They walked in through the doors, then made their way toward the front desk.

"Good morning. Is there something I could help y'all with today?" the lady behind the counter asked.

"Yes, could you please direct us to the archival collections?" asked John.

"Yes, sir, I can help y'all with that. The archival collections, research, and reference department is located in the basement of the library. Just take those stairs over there until you see a sign that says basement. Mrs. Silverton will be down there. She can help you."

"Thank you very much. You've been a big help."

"You're very welcome. Y'all have a nice day now."

John and Andrea headed for the staircase and made their way

down to the basement. Working alone behind a desk was a tiny, frail, older woman.

"Excuse me, are you Mrs. Silverton?"

"That would be me," she spoke softly. "Can I help y'all with something?"

"Yes, ma'am, we need to do some research on our house. Can you show us what to do?"

"I sure can. Follow me." she led the Cravens back into the room. "Are you looking for newspaper articles?"

"We're looking for anything pretty much," John told her.

"We just moved here from Tennessee. We wanted to know some history on our new home," Andrea replied.

"I'll show y'all how to use this machine here. Maybe y'all could find some articles that might be useful to you." Mrs. Silverton showed John and Andrea how to scroll through the newspaper clippings. "How far back do you want to go?"

"We're looking for anything around 1900. Maybe even earlier than that."

Mrs. Silverton scrolled through the articles until she came across some from the time that Andrea mentioned. "Here you go, kids. Just use this knob to scroll up and down. If you need anything else, please let me know."

"Thank you. We appreciate your help."

"I'll be at my desk if y'all should need me."

John flipped through the articles one by one as they appeared on the screen. "Andrea, I don't think we're going to find what we're looking for."

"Don't give up. We'll keep looking."

"But I don't see anything that jumps out at me."

"We must be patient. Keep searching."

"Maybe we're looking in the wrong area," John said as he scrolled to the next article.

"Don't speak so soon. I think we found something." Andrea looked at the article before her and John.

The date was July thirteen, 1900. The headline read, *Bizarre Murder-Suicide On East Waldburg Street.*

"That's it, John. We have something!" Andrea said as they began to read the article.

"The bodies of Wallace, Scarlette and Savannah O'Connor were found yesterday evening. Apparently a murder-suicide took place in the family's home on East Waldburg Street. There are no known motives to why this tragedy happened. From what evidence we have, the murderer was eight-year-old Savannah O'Connor. The scene described by the Savannah Police Department was extremely horrific and beyond anything that they had ever seen. The bodies of Mr. and Mrs. O'Connor were found in separate rooms as well as the body of young Savannah O'Connor. Wallace O'Connor's body was found in the kitchen where he had been mutilated beyond recognition. Scarlette O'Connor's body was resting at the bottom of the attic stairs where she had apparently been pushed to her death. The fatal injury Scarlette had suffered was a broken neck that had completely rearranged her head. It was the most appalling sight beheld by those who witnessed the aftermath. The most bizarre of the deaths was that of little Savannah O'Connor. Her lifeless body was found hanging from the rafters in the darkened basement along with her favorite doll at her side. It seems as though Savannah did not want to enter death without taking her favorite dolly with her. This unfortunate tragedy happened not more than a month after the tragic death of three-year-old Griffin O'Connor. The only remaining family member still alive is five-year-old Collette O'Connor who was staying with a close family friend at the time of the murders. Authorities say that young Collette will have to be placed in an orphanage until a family is willing to adopt her . It is not yet known what orphanage she will be placed in, but when the information becomes available, we'll be sure to let the people of Savannah and neighboring cities know. Our condolences go out to young Collette in this time of sorrow."

"She killed them, John. Her own family. I wonder what happened to little Griffin? What did she do to her baby brother?"

"There's probably an article in here about his death. We just need to find it."

"Can you imagine the horror that family felt knowing that their child was going to kill them?"

"What if we end up like them? I mean, the cycle has started again, but this time it's with our family. Why?"

"You think history might repeat itself?"

"No doubt about it. The signs are already there for us to see. We need to do something about this before it's too late."

"Stop!"

"What is it?"

"Look, it's the article about Griffin."

Andrea and John read the article over silently in their minds.

Misfortune Hits Close To Home.

"I'm afraid to read any further, John. I've seen what he looked like in the tub. It was horrible; that poor child."

"Honey, you don't have to read it if you don't want to."

"I probably shouldn't because I know it'll bring me to tears, but I feel like I need to know what happened."

"I take it you're going to read it then?"

"Yes."

Andrea and John started to read the article before them.

"The body of three-year-old Griffin O'Connor was found in his home in the early hours of June tenth by his parents, Wallace and Scarlette O'Connor. The cause of death will be announced by the coroner sometime tomorrow afternoon. As of now the word on his death appears to be accidental. Young Griffin was found floating face-down in a pool of bloodied water in the family's bathroom. A gaping wound was found on the child's head, possibly due from falling into the porcelain tub. Mrs. O'Connor claims that her child's death was no accident.

"The tub was much taller than him. There is no way he could have reached the faucets to even start the water. Griffin was a heavy sleeper. He never woke up during the night unless he was sick. I don't believe my child hit his head on the bathtub either, not with the amount of damage done to my poor baby's skull. Someone crushed his head with a heavy object, I'm sure of it."

Authorities did a complete search of the O'Connors home, but found no signs of forced entry. Despite the facts, Mrs. O'Connor still insists that Griffin's death was by far no accident. She firmly believes that the cause of her son's death was a senseless act of murder."

"Andrea, are you all right?" John asked while he noticed the stream of tears running down her face.

"Griffin was all alone when Savannah killed him. She truly was an evil child in life as she is in death. How can an eight-year-old even think about killing their three-year-old brother? She was ruthless and savage. A bad seed had taken its form in her."

"She wasn't always like that, though. You got to think, Illusion's the one who turned her into what she is. Maybe there wasn't any hope for the O'Connors. There was no way to escape the outcome of their lives, but maybe we have hope. We might be the ones who can put an end to this nightmare. Where they failed, we can succeed."

"They're too strong, John. We'll end up losing the battle."

"As long as we don't give up, we can't lose," John explained.

"There's another article about Griffin on the screen."

John scrolled down a little farther and pulled up its entire contents.

"Autopsy Reveals That O'Connor's Death Was In fact An Act Of Murder. Dr. Patterson revealed the autopsy report not long after viewing the body of three-year-old Griffin O'Connor.

"During the examination I came across noticeable ligature strangulation marks around the child's neck. He suffered a massive abrasion to his cranium caused by blunt force. The object used was more than likely a brick or heavy stone similar to those found in yards or allies. Griffin sustained the tremendous head injury first, followed by manual strangulation as he was held under water. The cause of death was asphyxiation."

At this time Mr. and Mrs. O'Connor are the prime suspects in the murder of their son Griffin. A further investigation of this case is being examined by the proper authorities. Mr. O'Connor commented on the accusations being placed upon he and his wife.

"These accusations are ludicrous. There is absolutely no way my wife or I would have harmed our son. The contemplation would have never crossed our minds. We loved Griffin dearly; he was our son. We are not killers. Scarlette and I are good parents, we love our children. They are our life."

Wallace's tearful comment was ended by his uncontrollable cries of heartache. Mrs. O'Connor spoke up after her husband's demise.

"The town's people know how much we love our children. They, too, can tell you that Wallace nor I are capable of taking the life of one of our own."

With that said, the O'Connors have spoken with their tearful statements. The outcome to this case lies in the hands of the authorities. We will release more news when the proper information is presented to us."

"Scroll down to the next clipping, please," Andrea asked politely.

"This one's about the death of a general store owner on June twelfth,

1900. I don't think we have to read it. The article has no concern to what we're looking for."

"Wait a second before you go to the next clipping. I swear, I saw Savannah's name mentioned in that article." Andrea looked over the paper, then suddenly stopped. "There!" She pointed out. "Right there, see? Savannah's name is mentioned."

Andrea and John read the paragraph.

"Savannah O'Connor was the last person seen coming out of Mason's General Store. Witnesses say they saw her alone, but with the company of her doll. When interviewed, young Savannah stated that she had gone to Mason's to buy some candy.

"I had fifteen cents to buy some penny candy." Savannah explained, *"I walked to Mr. Mason's store. When I got there, I found the place empty. I rang the service bell a few times, but he never came out. I think he went to Henry's Barber shop. That's why he wasn't there when I came in."*

There is no word yet on who would want to brutally murder such a dear old man. All the people who knew Donald were fond of him for his tender heart and helpful soul. Authorities say that Mason's son, Ronny, found his father's body in the stock room of the store.

"It was the most horrible sight having to find my father in the shape that he was. I'll never get those images out of my mind. Whoever did this to him is sick. I don't know how a human being could do such things to another person. My dad always wanted to leave this world peacefully. Instead he had to suffer. The person didn't have to kill him," explains Ronny. *"If they wanted the money so badly, he would have given it over without a fight. My dad was a peaceful man. He was very simple and loving. Now I'll never be able to see him again and neither will his grandchildren. Whoever did this has taken away someone who meant so much to me. Please, I beg whoever you may be, turn yourself in."*

Authorities stated that Mr. Mason's wedding band had been removed from his finger and is now missing. An autopsy is underway to find out the cause of Donald Mason's death. Further information will be presented when it comes along."

"I bet she killed him, John."

"Why would she kill an old man?"

"I don't know, but don't you find it a bit odd that she was the last person seen coming out of his store?"

"Maybe he did or said something that set her off."

"I know she did it, her and Illusion. I just wonder why?"

"To me it sounds like Illusion turned Savannah into a killing machine."

"Do you think she killed other people?"

"I hate to say, I wouldn't doubt it."

"Excuse me, I thought y'all might also be interested in these," said Mrs. Silverton as she handed John and Andrea a few books. "These are record books that date back from the eighteen eighties. I thought y'all might be interested in taking a look at them."

"Thank you for digging these up for us," Andrea told the old lady.

"If you need any earlier ones, let me know and I'll find those for you."

"This should be good for now."

"Have you found what you were looking for?"

"A few things. We just need to keep searching."

"Take your time," Mrs. Silverton said before she walked away.

"Andrea, here's another story about the general store owner."

Coroner States That Mason's General Store Owner Was Beaten To Death, read the headline.

"Oh, how awful. That poor man."

"Donald Mason was brutally murdered in the stock room of his general store on June twelfth. Ronny Mason, Donald's son, found his father's body not more than forty-five minutes after his father's fatal slaying. Unfortunately there was no success to be made as Ronny desperately tried resuscitating his father who, sadly at that time was already gone. The murder weapon, which appears to be a wooden baseball bat, has been missing from the crime scene. If anyone has knowledge of the baseball bat used in the slaying of Donald Mason, please contact the Savannah Police Department at once. Dr. Patterson revealed the autopsy report taken yesterday afternoon after the complete examination of Manson's body.

"Over seventy percent of Donald Manson's body was dominated with severe trauma. He had suffered a compound fracture to his right forearm, two fractured wrists, four broken ribs, two shattered kneecaps and several lacerations to his face. Among the facial lacerations, I came across an orbital rim fracture that caused a significant amount of damage to the brain. The magnitude of external force directed to Mr. Mason's face damaged his brain tissue and caused substantial bleeding. The cause of death was a

subarachnoid hemorrhage comprised from the bleeding between the layers of tissue protecting the brain."

No suspects have been apprehended at this time for the murder of sixty-eight-year old Donald Mason. It's in the best interest for our community that the person responsible for this crime turns himself in. Funeral arrangements for Donald Mason are being made by his family in this time."

"Did we pass up the obituaries for the O'Connors?" wondered Andrea. "I thought we would have seen them by now."

"I probably passed them up earlier by accident. Do you want me to look for them?"

"If you can."

John scrolled through the articles until he came across the obituaries. "Here we go. They were here all this time. We just didn't see them."

John and Andrea looked at the pictures next to the O'Connors obituaries.

"They looked like the perfect family, even Savannah. She looks so innocent and sweet. Who'd have thought she'd turn out to be the most evil child on earth?"

"Looks are deceiving, especially in her case," John commented.

"I still can't get over the fact an eight-year-old girl could be tempted by murder, then actually go through with it."

"She was literally brainwashed, that's what happened, and that's what drove her to kill."

"I just don't understand how a normal little girl could kill four people, though. Consider the strength she'd need to kill her father, for instance. The article stated that Wallace had been severely mutilated."

"Think about the power Illusion had over her, Andrea. She was able to dominate, as well as influence Savannah to the extent that she wanted. Maybe she gave her some sort of evil power that made her stronger. Illusion took Savannah to the edge, and it was there where Savannah was seduced into darkness. For what reason, I don't know, but hopefully we'll be able to find out. What other articles do we need to find?"

"Is there anything on Collette? What happened to her? Was she ever adopted?"

"If they have another article on her, I bet it's going to be a tough one to find. What year should we look in?" John inquired.

"Oh, I don't really know. Let's see, Collette was five when the murders took place." Andrea thought about with much intention. "Why don't we see if there are any articles from 1902? That'd put her at being seven years of age. Maybe someone adopted her by then."

"It's worth a try. Let me see what I can pull up." John scrolled through the articles one by one, but found nothing of value, "There's nothing mentioned in 1902. Bad call. You have another year you want to try?"

"Um, try, I don't know, 1904 I guess."

"Your call, 1904. I'm pulling up some articles now." John passed through them, keeping a close eye on each headline that he read. "Nothing," he said as he passed to the next. "Still nothing," he said. "I'm not finding anything on Collette. Oh, wait a second. This might be something here." John scrolled up a little more.

O'Connor Girl Finally Has A Place To Call Home.

"That's it, John! Good work," Andrea expressed happily.

"Collette O'Connor returns to her former house where her family was killed just five years earlier. Bizarre? That's what we say, but those are the facts. The bodies of Wallace, Scarlette and Savannah O'Connor were found on July twelfth, 1900 in their home on East Waldburg Street. The crime was rumored to have been a murder-suicide. Just a month before the deaths of the O'Connor's three-year-old Griffin O'Connor's body was found floating in the family's bathtub. The story took the residence of Savannah and the neighboring cities for a shock. Nothing like this had ever been committed in Savannah until that dreadful day. There were about three other killings that took place in Savannah in which no suspects were ever apprehended. The first was a general store owner by the name of Donald Mason. Mason's body was found on June eleventh, 1900 by his son Ronny in the store's stock room. The second was Adelle Collingswood, the town's dearly beloved piano teacher. Adelle's body was found by Myrtle Bristow, who at that time was dropping her daughter, Abby, off for her midday lesson. Myrtle Bristow found Adelle's body draped over her piano with iron rods driven into both of her eyes and her hands were completely severed by piano strings. She was found on June twenty-third, 1900. The last person was the milk man, Cole Jameson. Mr. Jameson's body was found riddled with scissor holes by Kipp Radcliff on July six, 1900. A roll of tape was found wrapped around Jameson's mouth to prevent him from screaming. Radcliff found Cole

Jameson sprawled on the stairs to his porch that fearsome morning. The one thing that ties these cases together is the name Savannah O'Connor. Apparently O'Connor was the last person seen coming out of Mason's General Store. When viewing Adelle Collingswood's appointment book, authorities found that Savannah O'Connor had a piano lesson just a half hour before Abby Bristow. Around the time of Cole Jameson's death, a neighbor of Radcliff's reported hearing a man from outside his window say clearly, *"Mornin, Miss Savannah, you're up pretty early."* Is it a coincidence that Savannah's name was mentioned in all three of these murders? After all she did kill her family. Authorities came to the conclusion that Savannah O'Connor took her baby brother's life in the morning hours of June tenth, 1900. Collette O'Connor, who was staying with family friends at the time, became the only family member able to escape an untimely demise. Collette was placed in St. Agatha's Orphanage at the tender age of five. On March ninth, 1905 adoption papers were finalized by the Court under the Honorable Judge Ennis Allaway. Mr. and Mrs. McGowan are now the proud parents of ten-year-old Collette O'Connor. The McGowans recently moved here from Fernwood, along with their two young sons, Layne and Garret. Without any knowledge, the McGowans took up residency in the O'Connor's former home. The house on East Waldburg Street stood vacant for more than two years. The McGowans saw the potential in the place and decided to call it home. Today Collette O'Connor rendered back to her first known residence, the house on East Waldburg Street, but hopefully she won't descend to the pain of her tragic past as she moves forward with her life."

"What are the odds of that?" Andrea mumbled to John.

"I would have never imagined she'd return to that place, not after what happened there with her family. Maybe it was her destiny to move back."

"Oh, my God, John, do you remember what Tookie told us?"

"About the house?"

"He told us about a couple who moved into the house back in 1905. Do you recall him saying that the family had an adopted daughter and two young sons?"

John grew quiet and retreated back into his thoughts. "You're absolutely right. A ten-year-old girl moved into our home with her new family in 1905. Tookie said she lived there mostly all of her life until her death a few years ago." John's realization swept him away. "Collette O'Connor was the eighty-year-old woman who lived in our house."

"And nobody has been able to live there since her death." A cold chill swept across Andrea's back, "Collette found a way to keep the evil at bay. It's like she had power over her sister, and an even greater power over Illusion."

John thought quietly for a second. "What'd she figure out? How'd she do it?"

"She became the sentinel of the house, a guardian against evil. It was her fate to keep Savannah and Illusion away. Collette delivered her duties to the end of her days. The evil that once lay inactive, has been unleashed upon us now that Collette's gone. It's invited itself in with a much hostile force, and it's set upon tearing our souls apart any way it can."

"Do you think we're dealing with the devil?" Andrea pondered. "What would you call Illusion?"

"Devil sounds tangible. Maybe the man or woman who made her found a way to set Lucifer's soul free in the form of something innocent."

"Why don't we check out the record books? Maybe we can find out who built our house and go from there."

"Mrs. Silverton brought us a few books. Why don't I look through one while you look through another?"

"Good idea. Why don't we move over there to that table where we'll have more room?"

"Here's your load. Start searching." Andrea cracked open the first record book on the top of her stack while John did the same. They did their research throughout each book for nearly two hours until John came across something that caught his eye.

"I wasn't sure we'd ever find anything, but finally I did. Take a look at this, will you?"

"What'd you find?"

"Read here," John told her as he pointed to the section in the book.

CHAPTER TWELVE

"The Cornu House, located at seventeen-twenty-three East Waldburg Street, was built on August third, 1886 for Cyrus Cornu. Cornu, originally from Spain, had a Ph.D. in Theology and was one of the world's leading professors in the field of Metaphysical Philosophy. Professor Cornu moved to Savannah on May twenty-ninth, 1886 from Barcelona, Spain. Cornu came here not long after the tragic loss of his wife, Catalina, and the couple's ten- year-old son, Estavan. Catalina and Estavan Cornu were on their way to the market to buy some produce when they were tragically crushed to death by falling material off a partially dilapidated building. Cyrus Cornu was saddened by the event and eventually came to Savannah to start a new life. On November first, 1899 the body of Professor Cornu was found in his home on East Waldburg Street. The apparent cause of death was SCD, layman's terms, sudden cardiac death. Professor Cornu went into cardiac arrest sometime during the evening hours of October thirty-first, 1899. It was evident that he had been taken by fright which ultimately led to his death. There were no clues to what might have frightened Professor Cornu on that Halloween night. No indications were ever found for what really happened in those last hours. The life and death of Cyrus Cornu made the house on East Waldburg Street a legend."

"I bet he gave Illusion life on that Halloween night. What do you think?" John asked Andrea.

"I think we're insane, but I agree with you. I bet his journal could tell us more about what Illusion is and why he made her."

"Let's hope Tookie's brother is willing to help us."

CHAPTER THIRTEEN

Meanwhile, at Mr. Blackwell's house:
"I know they'll be more than thankful for your help, Victor. I'll talk to John and Andrea when they get in and see if they'd be willing to meet with you tonight."

"Call me as soon as you have an answer. I'll be waiting by the phone."

"All right, you be expecting that call. I'll talk to you then," Tookie said before he hung up.

"Mr. Tookie, I'm all done with my lunch. Can I look around your house now?" Chloe questioned him.

"Oh, sure, feel free to browse around."

"Is it okay if I go upstairs?"

"How about I give you the grand tour? Would you like that?"

"Oh, very much," she expressed happily.

"Well then, dear, follow me."

Chloe followed Tookie up the staircase as she rubbed upon the railing.

"This banister was hand-carved by a gifted craftsmen," he explained.

"Ours is pretty, but not nearly as nice as yours."

"Looks like you have an eye for elegance, my dear one."

"I like pretty stuff. Everything you have is pretty."

"Well, thank you. I'm glad you like it here."

"Our old house in Tennessee was boring, but mommy says our new one has character."

"Older houses usually tend to. That's what sets them apart from the newer ones."

"Do you have any dollies, Mr. Tookie?"

"Actually, I have several that Evelyn collected over the years. Would you like to see them?"

"I'd love to!"

"Right this way, deary!" he said as he led Chloe down the hallway. "This was Evelyn's doll room."

Chloe's eyes grew big with surprise as she gazed upon each doll with admiration. "They're all so pretty, Mr. Tookie. Which is your favorite?"

"This one here has always been my favorite." he exclaimed.

"Why's that?"

"Well, you see, when Evie and I found her we both decided that this doll resembled her almost perfectly. Evelyn and I ended up naming the doll after her."

"So the doll was named after your wife?"

"That's right."

"I wish I had a doll that looked like me."

"Maybe one day you'll find one."

Chloe walked along the room looking at each doll as she quickly became mesmerized by their haunting beauty. Chloe noticed a familiar face staring back at her from one of the shelves. "Hey, that one looks like my dolly I have at home."

"Which one would that be, dear?"

"The one up there in the green dress." She pointed.

Tookie walked over to the shelf and picked up the doll. "Mmm, that's unusual. I don't recall this one."

"She looks like my dolly. The next time I come by I'll bring her with me. Maybe they're sisters."

"Could be. That may explain why they look alike."

"Do you have any other rooms with dollies?"

"I'm afraid this is the only one," he told her.

Chloe threw out her bottom lip. "I wanted to see more," she said sadly.

"Do you like teddy bears?"

"Yes." She smiled as her sadness began to fade.

"I have a collection of vintage teddy bears in another room if you care to see them."

"You do?"

"They're in my study."

"Will you take me there?"

"I most certainly shall. Come along."

"Mr. Tookie, your house is full of wonderful things. I enjoyed the room filled with dolls."

"I hope you take a liking to the next."

"Where do we have to go?"

"Down the hall to my study."

"What's a study, Mr. Tookie?"

"It's my personal library, where I read, do my research, take notes or write papers. It's also the place where I go to just simply think."

"That sounds neat. I don't think we have a library in our house. I haven't been in all of the rooms yet."

"I bet y'all have one."

"You really think so?"

"I wouldn't doubt it. Now, come along and tell me what you think."

Tookie opened the door into his library. Staring back at Chloe were massive shelves filled with books and other writings. Sitting along the shelves were vintage teddy bears as they sat and guarded the books behind them.

"Wow, Mr. Tookie, I've never seen teddy bears like these before."

"It's because they're old. Some even older than me!"

"Where's the oldest one you have?"

"That would be my teddy bear named Bailey who's over here."

"Can I see Bailey? I promise I won't drop him."

"Sure you can, but remember you must be gentle. He's very old."

"I will." Chloe beamed as she held him in her tiny arms. "Mr. Tookie, I think Bailey smells a little funny," she stated, honestly.

"I'm sorry about that. I'm afraid Bailey has picked up the scent of his age. He's no longer a young cub of a stuffed animal. Bailey was made seventy-six-years ago. Unfortunately that attunes to his smell,"

Tookie explained to her. "But marvelously he's still here and doing fine under my watch."

Just then Tookie's words were interrupted by a quiet knock on the door. Tookie turned around puzzled at the fact that someone was standing in his hallway. Then it sprung to his mind. "That must be your parents," he said as he walked across the room. He took the knob in his hand and gave it a turn. The door opened only to reveal an empty hallway. "We're in here." he said loudly. "John! Andrea!" Tookie turned to Chloe. "They must have gone downstairs. I'll see if I can catch them."

Tookie left the room as Chloe stayed behind in the library. Chloe took her time looking at the rest of the bears. A few minutes had passed when Chloe wandered out into the hall. As she made her way passed Evelyn's doll room, she heard someone softly call out to her from behind the door. Chloe continued to listen to the voice as it drew her in.

"Who's there?" She looked around, but found no one in sight. As she was about to leave, Chloe heard something fall from one of the shelves. Chloe stopped and turned around. Walking across the floor toward her was Illusion. "I thought that was you! It is you, right, Illusion?"

"Of course it's me," Illusion said gratingly.

"When did you get in?"

"Your mommy and daddy were still here at that time," she spoke with an unsettling tone.

"Why didn't you tell me earlier?"

"I needed time to study Mr. Blackwell's fears." Illusion's eyes grew dark and menacing. "Now I know them."

"Don't hurt Mr. Tookie, please, Illusion, he's my friend," Chloe begged the sinister doll nicely.

"I've told you before, the only friends you have are Savannah and me. You've been away from our house far too long."

"Where's Savannah?" Chloe demanded.

"Downstairs."

"Call her up here."

"Must you insist?"

"I want to talk to you both."

"I'll call her up here, but then we're going to play."

Within moments Savannah appeared before Illusion and Chloe.

"Shall we begin the game?" Savannah asked in a wicked tone equal to Illusion's.

"No! Wait," Illusion spoke.

"Wait?" Savannah roared.

"Yes, wait."

"But for what reason must we wait?"

"It appears that we have a reluctant among us," Illusion said, turning to Chloe. "She doesn't want Mr. Blackwell harmed."

"Why can't we harm him?"

"She claims he's her friend."

Savannah laughed at the remark from Illusion's mouth. "He's not your friend. That man doesn't even like you. He's pretending to get along because your parents brought you here. Illusion and I are your friends. All the others are deceivers!" Savannah spoke wickedly. "But still she doesn't want him harmed."

"So what must we do?" Illusion asked.

"We must give her the changeling." Savannah walked up to Chloe with Illusion in her arm while cold air emanated around them. Savannah then crept into Chloe's face where she calmly seduced Chloe into her kettle of boiling lies.

"We're the ones who are there when the deceivers are unwilling to spend time with you," Savannah said while she hypnotized Chloe with the black of her eyes.

"We're the ones who care when the deceivers won't make an attempt to." Illusion's eyes darkened with each passing second, and soon Chloe fell under their spell. In the distance Chloe heard the sound of footsteps coming down the hall.

Tookie noticed the door into the doll room was open and went in. Inside he found Chloe playing with Evelyn's doll.

"I'm sorry, Miss Chloe, but I don't like anyone to play with this doll. I hope you understand," he said as he took the doll from her hands.

"She's just an ordinary doll. She can't feel any pain."

"That's absolutely right, dear, but I would if something were to happen to it."

"Mr. Blackwell, do you have any peaches?"

Tookie quickly caught onto the name that Chloe called him and found that fairly odd.

"I do. They're growing out back in my yard."

"I'm going downstairs to watch cartoons. I want you to go out a pick me one now."

"Chloe, are you all right? You look a bit pale."

Chloe looked up to Tookie as she gazed upon him for a second with dark-cold eyes, then quickly dismissed him as she passed on by. "What are you waiting for? Go get me a peach!"

Tookie waited as Chloe vanished down the stairs before he glanced into the room. He found nothing to be out of place, not even the doll which had apparently gone missing.

Tookie started down the stairs where he found Sam and Chloe. "Oh no, dear, you mustn't be so rough. Sam likes to be pet upon softly."

"Are you finally going to get me that peach?"

"That's why I was coming down here."

"You better rush on before this mut here gets it!"

"I beg your pardon?" Tookie asked before completely dropping his jaw.

"I meant his treat, that's all. Why? What did you think I meant?"

"It's about time for Sam to go outside. We'll be back in a minute." Tookie whistled for Sam to get up. "Come on, boy. Time to go out!"

Sam followed Tookie into the backyard. Beneath one of his many trees, Tookie saw a woman sitting alone.

"Excuse me, Miss," he said as he approached the lady from afar. When Mr. Blackwell got close enough to the woman, she stood and greeted him beneath the golden tree. "This can't be," he spoke aloud. "Please excuse my stare, but you look exactly like her."

"My Tucker Blackwell, I've come back to you," the lady said sweetly as the words floated off her lips like a soft tune.

"Evelyn, is that really you?"

"In the flesh. I've been waiting a long time for this chance to see you again."

"But how can this be?"

"Your love for me has brought me back."

"I still don't understand."

Sam dashed over to Evelyn and Tookie, and within those seconds he sensed something morbidly wrong. Sam stood beside Tookie as a loyal dog should to his master. That's when he began to bare his canine teeth and growl fiercely at Evelyn.

"Sam, what's wrong with you? It's me," Evelyn said as she tried to bargain with the dog.

As much as Sam tried to send across his warning, it went unheard by Tookie who was blind to the facts.

"It's all right, Sam. Calm down, boy."

"Why don't you send him off, Tucker? There's no use trying to talk when we have a jealous dog between us."

"Go along now, boy. It's okay. I'll get you when I return to the house."

"Now then, my dear Tucker Blackwell, where were we?"

"Evie, I've missed you so much. But as hard as this is for me to say, I must say it."

"What is it, Tucker?"

"This period in our lives is over, but it shall renew once I come home to you."

"Don't you miss me, Tookie?"

"Every day, Evie, but you're gone now. Our lives can't exist together on this plane any longer. It doesn't work that way."

"That's why I've come for you."

"What do you mean, you've come for me?"

"I need you with me, Tookie. My Heaven isn't the same without you."

"Evie, I can't go with you, not yet anyhow."

"Tookie, my bones ache. The cancer still keeps me locked in its tormenting clutches. Do you remember when you'd rub my aching body?"

"I couldn't bear to see you in pain, Evie. It killed me over and over again to see you suffer."

"I need your warm hands to ease my aches and pains, Tucker. Without you, I continue to suffer with the cancerous anguish that eats at my body. Comfort my burden pain. Say you'll come home to me."

"You know I'd come to you in an instant, but right now I can't," he said with tears.

"Don't say you can't!" Evelyn snarled as she suddenly turned vicious. "I will fix the problem that stands in your way."

"What are you talking about?"

"Life, Tucker Blackwell! That thing that holds you here! It separates you from me and I from you! There's only one way to end it." She spoke with an unnerving glare, "Take your own life and be free from your cares."

Tookie gazed into the soul of death as Evelyn's eyes became vessels of darkness. "What are you?" Tookie asked, unafraid to look away.

"We are the conveyers of strife, the couriers of persistent lies and the advocators of illusions."

"What business do you have with me?" Tookie questioned the demon that took the form of his wife. "And I tell you now, don't feed me your lies. I won't allow you to trick me."

"Tucker, it's me, Evelyn, your beloved wife."

"Then recite the prayer we'd perform together."

"You make me sick, you despicable old man!" Evelyn yelled in anger. "You'd better run. That dog of yours is in Chloe's hands! It's better to watch! Trust me, you can."

Tookie started off running as fast as an old man could. "Sam, I'm coming boy!" he yelled. "If you forced Chloe to hurt my Sam, so help me God, I will find a way to send you to hell myself!"

"Hell is far too full of dishonorable souls. It doesn't need us; that's why we're here. We're at the top of the list in dishonor. We attained a pass to stay here for however long we please."

Tookie thought about the images that might be of Sam as the reproduction of them carried on in his mind like a played out movie stuck on rewind. He became frightened while he thought more and more clearly with what might come to be of his loyal companion.

As Tookie made his way to the back door, he collapsed to the ground, repeatedly grabbing at his heart as he fought for a breath of air. "I can't give up. I won't," he said, crawling into the house. "Sam! Where are you, boy?" he asked while he lay there close to death, but continuing his fight.

CHAPTER FOURTEEN

"Do you think Chloe had a nice time with Mr. Blackwell today?" Andrea asked John while they drove down the block.

"She took to him quite well, don't you think?"

"I'm so happy for that. I was afraid we'd never get her over there."

"Just a little persuasion got the job done," John said as he parked the van.

"I don't want to take her back into that house, John. Not after finding out what we did. We finally got our little girl back. I don't want to lose her again."

"We can't just dump her off on Tookie."

"I didn't say that," Andrea commented.

"I didn't say you did. Chloe's our daughter, and we're her parents. We have to tend to her ourselves."

"I know that, John. I just meant that we need someone to watch her until we can end this nightmare, if we can."

"We'll put an end to it. I just don't know how long it'll take to do so," John told her as they got out of the van.

"Don't forget Chloe's package," Andrea told John as she ventured over to the sidewalk.

"I'm getting it out now." John caught up to his wife as they walked to Mr. Blackwell's house.

"I wonder why he won't answer?" Andrea thought aloud. "He should have been to the door by now. You don't suppose something happened?"

John handed Andrea the package and got in front of her. "We're going in. Stay behind me."

They walked into the living room first and found Chloe sitting alone on the couch watching cartoons.

"Chlo, where's Tookie?" John asked curiously.

"I should have known. You've both returned."

"Chloe, honey, that doesn't answer daddy's question."

"I didn't say it was going to," she said with a little sarcasm.

John glanced at Andrea quickly, while he turned away from his daughter. Andrea shook her head, unknowing of what to say as she looked back at him. John turned his head back toward the couch to look upon Chloe once more.

"Chloe, where's Mr. Blackwell?"

"He's in the kitchen," she stated to her father openly. "The forecast for today said things weren't looking so good."

As soon as John and Andrea understood her reply, they both made a quick beeline to the kitchen.

"Tookie!" John called out. "Tookie, we're coming." John stopped between the corridors when he saw Mr. Blackwell across the room sprawled out on the floor. "Oh, my God!" he yelled as he raced to Tookie's side.

"My heart, son. It's my heart. I need my medication," Tookie said with exhaustion.

"Where is it?" John panicked.

"Counter by the toaster."

Andrea ran to the countertop and searched through the bottles of medicine.

"I wrote heart pill, in black letters."

"It says heart pill, Andrea! You're going to be fine, Tookie. Andrea's getting your medicine now," John told him as he tried to keep Mr. Blackwell calm.

Andrea carried over the antiangina medication. John helped Mr. Blackwell get the medicine under his tongue to dissolve. Then he and Andrea tried to wait as patiently as they could for the nitroglycerine to break down into Mr. Blackwell's bloodstream.

"If y'all didn't come sooner, I'd be a dead man right now."

"It's okay, Tookie. We're here now, and you're doing fine," John told him kindly.

"Why don't you save your breath so you can get strong again? We'll stay here," Andrea said. "When you're ready to get up, we'll help you."

"Will someone find Sam for me? I'm worried about him," Tookie pleaded with the Craven's.

"I'll go while John stays here with you."

"Oh, thank you, Andrea."

"It's all right. I'll find him for you." Andrea got up and wandered through the house calling out to Sam. "Chloe, have you seen Sam anywhere?"

"Can't you see I'm watching cartoons?"

"Chloe, I asked you a question. Now answer me," Andrea told her as she walked closer to the couch. As she crept closer to Chloe, Andrea noticed something horribly familiar sitting at her side. "How the hell did that get here?"

"Savannah brought her over."

"You left Illusion at the house, Chloe."

"And now she's here. So what?"

"Did you do something to Sam, Chlo? Speak up!"

"If I did, do you actually think I'd tell you?"

"Your father's going to have your hyde if you hurt Mr. Blackwell's dog."

"Don't you think you better run along now, mommy? You know, time is running out, because you choose to stand here and waste it."

Andrea left the room and went upstairs continuing to hunt for Sam. She opened all the doors and called out Sam's name, but unfortunately found nothing. Andrea made it to the last door which happened to be Mr. Blackwell's bedroom.

"Sam, are you in here?" Andrea walked into the room checking behind the closet doors, then directed her attention to beneath Tookie's bed. As she was pulling the covers away from the floor, Andrea glanced through the window at a fire which had seized her eyes and complete attention.

Around the ground near one of the trees, Andrea saw a mound of grass that had been set ablaze. Andrea moved her eyes toward the trunk of the peach tree and saw poor Sam tied above the searing flames. "Oh, my God!" Andrea raced down the stairs. "John, I need you now!" she yelled. Andrea rushed off into the yard as John followed.

"Andrea, what's going on?"

"Sam's been tied to a burning tree! Hurry, John!" Andrea found the tree that looked upon Tookie's window. "How're we going to get him down?" she cried.

"I have a pocket knife. That should do us some good, I hope."

"John, hurry!" Andrea cried out again.

John leaned into the tree, hoping to stay clear of the fire. He then took his pocket knife and sawed along the rope that binded Sam to the tree.

"Is he coming loose?"

"I need your help!"

"What can I do?"

"Hold onto Sam and start pulling at the rope!"

"John, the flames!"

"I know, honey, but I just about got him!"

The rope around Sam loosened more, and Andrea was able to free him. "Is he all right?"

"I think so, but his fur has been scorched a little." John walked over to Andrea and took a seat on the ground. "Go inside and get me some cold wet towels."

"For what?"

"I need to put them on his fur," he told her.

Andrea followed John's directions and went back to the house to fetch a few towels. John patted Sam on top of his head to assure him he was there. "You're going to be fine, boy," he told the whimpering dog softly. "I'm not going to let anything happen to you."

"Here're the towels, John," Andrea said as she returned to his side.

John laid the towels across Sam's body to cool him down.

"I brought out a bowl of water, too."

"Put it by his face. We'll see if he'll drink some."

Sam raised his head to the bowl and started to lick the water in giant gulps.

"Sam's a little warm from the heat, but I think he's okay."

"That was a real close one, John. What if we weren't able to get him down?"

"Then Mr. Blackwell would have been terribly hurt."

"What about the fire?"

"Stay with Sam. I'll see if I can find a hose." John noticed Tookie coming from the house. "Sam's all right. He's by Andrea."

"Oh, good. I was so worried." Tookie walked until he saw Andrea.

"I'm so sorry about this, Mr. Blackwell."

"Sorry for what?"

"I didn't think they'd show up here."

"Who, Andrea?"

"Savannah and Illusion. They're the ones who did this."

"Please, dear, don't worry. Sam is fine."

"I feel so bad, though. We brought this evil into your house."

"But you didn't know it was strong enough to come here. It's not your fault. Please understand."

"They've taken Chloe again. They've possessed her or whatever it is that they do."

"Fire's out!" John yelled from nearby. "I just hope your tree is okay, Tookie."

"The tree isn't what's important. It's knowing that we're all right. I have plenty of other peach trees in my yard to bear fruit."

"I'm glad you're all right," Andrea said while giving Tookie a hug.

"Hey, at my age you must learn to be tough."

"I must say, you certainly are. I think some of that toughness has rubbed off on Sam, too," John joked around.

"Sam's a fighter like me. I think some dogs take on the personality traits of their masters."

"Well, Sam definitely has your endurance."

"Let's get back in the house."

"I agree. There are some things we must talk about," John told him brazenly.

"I take it y'all found out what you needed to know?"

"We came across an awful lot," Andrea said back. "Things that disturb me."

"The articles were that bad?"

"We came across so much stuff that I was afraid to know."

"Come on in. We'll see if we can find a place to talk."

"What about Chloe?" John wondered to Andrea.

"I think she'll stay glued to her cartoons. I'm going to sneak into the living room and make sure that's what she's doing."

Tookie looked over to John. "Why don't you and I have a seat in the kitchen. We'll talk in here. I think it's about time for some coffee, too. What do y'all think?"

"Coffee sounds really good right now."

"I'll get that pot brewing. I candied some peaches yesterday. Would you care for a bowl?"

"Sure, why not."

Andrea returned to the kitchen.

"Well, what's Chloe doing?"

"She's fast asleep on the couch with that damn doll in her arms."

"Illusion's here?"

"Apparently so."

"We're damned."

"Look on the bright side; at least Chloe's asleep. That'll give us some much needed time to talk."

"Do you care for some coffee, Andrea?"

"Yes, please," she told Mr. Blackwell quickly.

"Here's yours, John," Tookie stated as he set the mug on the table. "I was going to get John a bowl of my famous candied peaches. Would you care to try some, too, dear?"

"That sounds marvelous."

"I hoped you'd say that. I'm going to heat them in the stove so they'll get nice and warm." Mr. Blackwell walked over to the table and handed Andrea her coffee. "Those peaches will be warm in a minute," he stated while he waited before the warming stove.

Sam walked up to Tookie and nudged him on the hand.

"Hey there, boy!" he said while giving him a pat. "Here you go, Sam. Your favorite treat!" Tookie washed his hands at the sink, then checked on the peaches which appeared warm enough to eat. "Here y'all go! Take a bite of these and tell me what y'all think."

John and Andrea savored the scent that rose to their nose through the rising steam.

"Wow, these smell like heaven!" Andrea admitted.

"It's my own recipe. I must say, they're tasty!"

"So you're a lawyer and a chef?" John spoke outwardly.

"I was once a lawyer, then one day I became Chef Tookie!"

"Nicely spoken."

"Wow, the flavor's incredible!" Andrea said, praising with compliment.

"I can make those a little better if you want."

"I don't think it could get any better then this."

"Let me see if I could change your mind." Tookie walked over to the ice box and took out a pint of ice cream.

Andrea's mouth began to water. "You know, Mr. Blackwell that just might do the trick."

"Homemade vanilla ice cream always does. And it has real vanilla bean. That should please your taste buds."

John stared at Andrea's bowl with delight. "Tookie, do you mind if I get a scoop of that after you've finished with Andrea?"

"Why, sure you can, son!"

"Oh, John, wait until you taste this!"

"It's that good?"

"The perfect pleasure!"

"Here you go, John. What'll it be? One scoop or two?"

"I think two would be sufficient."

"Well, son, what do you think?"

"I got to give it to you, Tookie, this is better than what you'd find in any restaurant."

"Well, thank you. That means a lot."

"How did you make these?" Andrea wondered.

"I started off with my prize-winning peaches, covered them in sugar, along with a little peach brandy, then added some vanilla bean. I set the bowl on the countertop where the peaches made a flavorful syrup, I then added a little lemon juice and a few dashes of cinnamon, allspice, nutmeg and clove. I stirred the mixture, placed it in a baking dish, then cooked it until it was good and ready!"

"Your recipe's incredible. This is truly a delight!"

"It must have been. I see John there's already done with his bowl."

"Hey, if it's something good, I'm gonna eat it."

"Do y'all feel like telling me what you found out today in the records department? I truly am anxious to know of your findings, if you don't mind me saying so."

"Oh, God, where would we even start?" Andrea thought aloud.

"It might help if you talk about the first thing that comes to mind."

Andrea took a moment to gather her thoughts.

CHAPTER FIFTEEN

"There was a family by the name of O'Connor who moved to our house in 1900. The husband's name was Wallace and he had a wife by the name of Scarlette. They had three children, Savannah, Collette and Griffin. One day Savannah was in the attic with her father when they came across an unusual doll in a cabinet. Mentioned in the preserved pages of Scarlette's diary, she wrote about the doll which Savannah called Illusion. As Savannah started spending time with Illusion, her demure had suddenly altered abruptly. Scarlette was the first to witness the wicked changes in her daughter. Savannah became disobedient, willful and unruly. Scarlette started to feel the coldness that began to circulate within Savannah's spirit. Savannah started to lash out at her younger siblings, Collette and Griffin. She would physically attack them just to hurt them for no reason. Scarlette tried desperately to get rid of Illusion, but nothing she'd do would get rid of the doll. As time went by, things grew worse in the O'Connor home. One night Scarlette had seen her biggest fear."

"Don't tell me that Savannah accidently killed one of her siblings," Tookie stated.

"That part will come later. Right now let me tell you this. Scarlette woke up one night to find Illusion walking alone in the parlor below."

"Illusion's the doll, right?" Tookie questioned her.

"Right."

"But dolls back then couldn't walk."

"Exactly."

"I don't understand."

"Illusion is alive, Mr. Blackwell."

"Go on with your story."

"Under the moonlight Scarlette noticed a pair of scissors in Illusion's hand. Scarlette rushed to gather the kids, then took them to her room. They stayed together until the first light of morning. When they opened the door to the hallway, they found where Illusion had slashed away at the walls and floor with the scissors."

"The doll's apparently possessed."

"Yeah, but by what?" John asked Tookie.

"Something that's not very pleasant."

"In the early hours of June tenth, 1900 the body of Griffin O'Connor was recovered by his mother. Scarlette's three-year-old son was found floating in the bathtub, surrounded in a watery pool of his own blood. He had been hit in the head, then held under the water by his throat."

"Oh my goodness!" Tookie stated as he grew saddened by the story. "Those were the types of things I hated to hear about in court. It sickened me."

"There's more, but I won't go on if you don't want me to."

"No, no. I want to hear it all."

"Are you sure?"

"By all means, please continue."

"On July eleventh, 1900 Savannah went completely insane and took the life of her parents. Wallace O'Connor's body was found in the kitchen where he had been severely mutilated. Scarlette was found at the bottom of the attic stairs where she had been pushed to her death. Her neck was severely broken due to the fall and her head had been turned to her back. In the basement officers found where Savannah had hung herself. Hanging next to her limp body, Illusion hung from a noose."

"Where'd they find Collette's body?"

"That's the twist. Collette was staying with family friends the night of her family's death. But I'll get to that in a moment. I have several other things I'd like to talk to you about. John and I came across some other articles pertaining to murders in this town. Savannah O'Connor's name was linked to each one."

"Are you saying she killed those people?"

"The first was a man named Donald Mason, who owned Mason's General Store. Savannah was the last person seen leaving his store by several witnesses. She was alone, they said, but in the company of her doll. Mason's son, Ronny, found his father's body in the stock room of the store. He had been severely beaten with a bat. More than seventy percent of his body had bruising on it. He was found on June twelfth, 1900. The second person was a piano teacher named Adelle Collingswood. Her body was found by the mother of one of her students, Abby Bristow. Adelle's body had been draped across her piano, she had iron rods driven through both of her eyes and her hands had been completely severed off by piano strings. Authorities found Savannah's name listed in Adelle's appointment book. Savannah's name was recorded above Abby's, just a half hour before her lessons. Adelle's body was found on June twenty-third, 1900. The last person we know of was a milk man by the name of Cole Jameson. He made a delivery to Kipp Radcliff's house when he was attacked with a pair of scissors and punctured full of holes. A neighbor of Radcliff's reported hearing Jameson's voice through his window telling Savannah good morning."

"You mean to tell me this young girl and her doll killed six people?" Tookie wondered.

"The sad thing is, there may have been more, but we don't know that for certain," John told him.

"Can this story get any worse?" Tookie asked them both.

"Unfortunately, yes," John said.

"How old was this Savannah you're talking about?"

"She was eight, so young at the time but never the less, she was a seed of true evil," Andrea told him.

"Well, I'd say so if she did those things you spoke of."

"Now this is where Collette comes back into the picture. She was only five when her family was killed. Collette was placed in an orphanage known as St. Agatha's until a family came along to adopt her. In 1905 at the tender age of ten, Collette was adopted by the McGowans, a family who had recently moved here from Fernwood. Unknowingly the McGowans bought the O'Connor's former home, then ultimately Collette was subjected to return to the place that destroyed her family. You know this story well, you're the one that told it to us. I've just filled in the missing pieces."

"Collette McGowan was really Collette O'Connor?" Tookie stated with shock.

"That's right, and Collette found a way to prevent her sister and Illusion from doing any harm while she was there. Now that she's gone, other families are having trouble staying in that house. Make sense?"

"Who'd have thought Collette would return to that house and become a sentinel?"

"John and I were as shocked as you. We figured it was her destiny. That's why she was led back to that house."

"That makes sense. I can't believe it. No wonder she never talked about odd things happening there. She wouldn't allow it to have any control under her watch. How did she beat it for so long?"

"That's what we don't know," John told Mr. Blackwell sadly.

"If she found a way, so can y'all."

"I'm afraid time is running out, though," Andrea told Tookie. "John and I feel that the tragedies that fell upon the O'Connors will happen to us."

"Oh no, no, kids. You mustn't think that way."

"Savannah and Illusion are stronger than they were before. They can conjure darkened images of your deepest fears. That's how they prey upon us. They know our nightmares," Andrea explained while John interrupted.

"Tookie, do you remember meeting my friend Rich the day you were by?" John asked him directly.

"Yes, I remember him."

"When Rich was a kid, his uncle took him and his three cousins camping. That night Rich's Uncle Fred went mad and took the lives of his three kids, Rob, Lily and Cooper. Fred tried to take the life of his nephew as well when he shot straight into Rich's body. Fred Sullivan was caught for his crimes and sentenced to death. He was executed eighteen years ago, so apparently he's been gone a long time," John explained to Tookie.

"That's terrible, but I'm proud to hear that justice was served on the behalf of Fred's kids and nephew. "

"While Rich was staying with us he saw his dead uncle in our house."

Tookie's mouth dropped to the floor in shock.

"Fred tried to kill Rich with each chance that he got. Savannah and Illusion have a way of taking on the image of anyone from our past. They use those familiar forms to their advantage as they force us to confront our torment, suffering and pain. Another friend of ours has seen his dead mother, I've seen my deceased father and Andrea has seen our twins."

"You had twins?"

"Ivy and Adrienne. Those were the names that John and I had chosen," Andrea said in sadness. "I was six months into my pregnancy when I had the miscarriage."

"Oh, my goodness, Miss Andrea, I'm deeply sorry to hear that."

"We've continued to stick together as a family even though Ivy and Adrienne are gone."

"That you must, my dear. They're the ones who give you the strength to carry on."

"The few times that I've seen Ivy and Adrienne they've frightened me."

"But they're babies. What causes you fright?"

"To see my twin girls coming after me with an axe in hand is unnerving, Mr. Blackwell."

"Were they still babies when you saw them?"

"No, they're now five," Andrea told him.

"Tookie, what happened here today?" John questioned him. "Chloe was fine when we left her here."

"I took her into Evelyn's doll room, and it was there she talked about a doll that looked exactly like the one in your home. We left the doll on the shelf and ventured into my library. Someone had knocked on the door while we were in there. I thought maybe y'all had come back. I went looking, but neither of you I could find in my house. When I returned upstairs, I noticed the door to Evelyn's doll room was open. Ultimately I knew Chloe had gone back in. When I found her, I quickly detected a change. She had become quite rude and demanding. I left her on the couch so I could pick her a peach. When I got outside, I came across a woman resting beneath one of my trees. As I came closer to her, I realized it was Evelyn. She looked like her in every way and even had her voice to go with it. At first I wanted to believe that the form in front of me was my wife, but down inside I knew it wasn't possible. She came across as a lovely lady, then suddenly her personality shifted and her eyes blackened before me. I wasn't afraid to stare upon the beastly entity. In fact, I confronted it. Whatever this thing is, it's definitely strong. It told me that Chloe had Sam, so naturally I panicked. As I went running to the house, my heart was overwhelmed with anxiety and fear, and I collapsed at the back door gasping for air. Y'all made it back here just in time. If you didn't, well, I think you know what would have happened."

"I apologize again for bringing this wickedness into your home," Andrea said softly.

"You didn't bring it here, my dear, and neither did John nor Chloe. It came here on its own."

"I just don't understand how it got in. Were there any signs?"

"I think I might know when they came here," John told Tookie and Andrea as he thought for a minute. "Do either of you remember the phantom visitor who came by before we left?"

"I thought it was one of the neighborhood kids stirring up trouble," Tookie admitted.

"I don't think so. They tricked you and made you believe it was one of those silly kids when in fact it wasn't. The same thing happened at our home as well."

"Then the only reason they're here is because of Chloe?"

"I think so. Savannah and Illusion will return to their house when we leave," Andrea commented.

"What do you suppose they want with your daughter?"

"They want to make her just like them, I'd guess."

"I wonder how Collette fought this madness?" Tookie wondered, "Is there anything else to this story?"

"Actually, there is. After John and I researched the articles about the O'Connors and the other murders, we read through several record books. John came across the name of the original owner of the house, Cyrus Cornu. The leather journal that I found has his name on it."

"I went ahead and talked to my brother about that diary, he wants to meet with y'all later tonight, if possible."

"That would be great," Andrea answered.

"I knew that would make your day. I'll call him a little later and let him know what time to come by. He's extremely interested in seeing this book that you speak of."

"He'll have to pray before he starts to read it. Something tells me that this diary is far from being holy."

"Did y'all find any information on this Mr. Cornu fellow?"

"He was originally from Spain; Barcelona, to be exact. He moved here in May of 1886 following the tragic deaths of his wife and son. Apparently Cyrus had a Ph.D. in Theology and was one of the world's leading professors in the field of Metaphysical Philosophy. On October thirty-first, 1899 Professor Cornu went into cardiac arrest and died in his home. His body was found the following day," explained Andrea.

"This man was a professor?"

"That's what the records indicated."

"What was he dabbling with and why? There had to be some form of rational explanation for his motive."

"Maybe he just went insane, made a bargain, then in return leveraged his life to a demon," John added.

"But what was the bargain for?"

"I honestly don't know, but I think his journal will tell us the truth."

"Wasn't there another journal that you found in the house, Andrea?"

"Scarlette's. It'd been hidden in the attic floor for all this time."

"Mr. Blackwell." John paused for a second. "Out of all the other families who have lived there, why were we the ones chosen to fight this?"

"It's like a puzzle. You have to put together the pieces for it to make sense."

"You told us before that it preys upon children. There has to be some reason behind that."

"It seems as though this maleficent force is set upon corrupting and ultimately destroying the innocence and purity that children exude. Its goal is to bring about chaos and confusion to the pure and harmless, and ultimately bend that child's will."

"Right now it seems like there's no hope on stopping this. You said before that there were three holy men who stepped foot on the stairs of our home, and each had dropped dead of a heart attack. I don't think John nor I could fight something that has more power then us."

"But you're missing the point, my girl. It's all about faith and hope. Yes all three of those men suffered heart attacks upon coming to the house. They weren't capable to do battle with what waited for them. Each man was up there in age. They weren't strapping young lads in the prime of their lives. You and John are still young. Your energy force is vibrant and your will to fight is as strong as you want it to be."

"Do you really think we can beat this? Honestly?"

"If it's your will, then yes." Tookie thought for a moment. "Is there any way I could see these journals that you speak of?"

"Of course. I'll run home now and get them. I should probably check on Snow as well, just to make sure the little thing's all right."

"Andrea, why don't you wait here and I'll go," John told his wife. "I don't want you going over there."

"It's okay, John. Savannah and Illusion are here, remember? Besides, I hid the journals. I don't know if you'd be able to find them."

"What if they follow you back to the house?"

"Chloe's here. They'll only go where she goes. I should be safe."

"I hope you're right," John said as he gave consideration to his thought. "Go ahead, but try to make it quick. If you're not back soon, I'm coming to get you."

"I shouldn't be long. Just give me enough time to find them and check on Snow."

"Try to hurry then. For an odd reason something doesn't feel quite right."

"Mr. Blackwell, is it okay if I leave through your back door?" Andrea wondered.

"Why, certainly, dear. The door will be open. Just come back in."

Andrea walked into Tookie's yard and made her way toward the alley.

"I'm going to check in on Chloe," John said as he got up from his chair.

"Would you like me to get you another cup of coffee, son?"

"Yeah, sure, Tookie, if you don't mind. I'll be back in a minute or two." John walked quietly into the living room and found Chloe still asleep on the couch. In her arms John saw Illusion. He crept toward the doll, then carefully pulled her loose from Chloe's grasp.

John crept backwards for a moment, then snuck away to the kitchen where he greeted Tookie at the table.

"Is this the doll?"

"This would be her," John said as he set Illusion on the table.

"I knew Evelyn didn't have a doll like that. I understand now why she looked out of place."

"That damn thing isn't just a doll. It's an abomination of something wicked."

"Tell me, John, why'd you bring it to the kitchen?"

"I want to see if I can break her. I don't know why I haven't tried before. She's made of porcelain, after all. She'll crack into pieces when she hits the ground."

"John, I think you'll end up angering her if you try. What if she doesn't break? Consider that, son."

"This thing has ruined our lives enough. There's a likely chance she's going to break."

"John, I advise against this. You don't know what you're dealing with."

"What are the odds of a doll like this being unbreakable? You know that fact as well as I. I'm getting rid of this thing once and for all." John took Illusion and held her above his head. "Here now this nightmare ends!" he shouted as he threw the doll to the floor. "Why didn't she break?"

"I told you, son, you don't know what you're dealing with."

"She should have broken, Tookie."

"Not that one."

"But she's still a doll!" John went mad for a moment and stomped upon Illusion's face in a fit of rage. "Break damn you!"

"John, calm down."

"I said break!" he yelled at the top of his lungs while Tookie stood from his seat.

"John, you must stop this at once!"

Echos of wicked laughter filled the room as they drove John deeper into madness.

"What's going on?" Tookie wondered.

"The other half has come."

Suddenly the room grew dim with light and a shadowy figure was seen moving along the wall.

"You can't destroy what cannot be broken," Savannah said harshly as she peeled herself out from the paint. "Illusion and I are forever."

Her voice rang throughout the room as her appearance frightened the onlookers. "You've made a fatal mistake, John Craven. Loosen your foot from Illusion's face or she will gladly disunite it."

John backed away in fear as his heart beat heavily. Illusion's eyes darkened as she stood from the floor and walked over to her dear Savannah.

"You cannot conquer the invincible, you stupid fool. Chloe is ours for the taking. We've made her one of us," the doll said in a raspy voice as Savannah held her close. "Nothing you can do will save her, and I do mean nothing," Illusion spoke again, sending her point across to those who were there to hear it. "We'll meet again."

"Not too soon," Savannah said with an unnerving glare.

"But never too late," Illusion said as she spoke those final words before they vanished.

"Oh God, Tookie, what are we going to do?"

"Let me call Victor to see when he'll be available. Your only hope might be in that diary."

"I have to admit, Tookie, I'm scared as hell."

"They are frightening, I must say, but you mustn't be afraid. Your fears will only allow them to grow. It'll give them full manipulation over you and anyone else they might come into contact with. You can't endanger yourself that way. If you fail, the battle is over due to your lack of belief in these words of faith, hope and will."

"Tookie, I truly used to consider the thought that I was strong, but since all of this has happened I think of myself as a speck of dust in the face of fear. I'm afraid nothing's going to be left in me when an unfortunate time comes calling. I'll continue to diminish into traces of scrap and fall into a hole of self-pity because I couldn't be strong."

"Son, you have to tell yourself that you're strong. You must believe that. You can't give up; I won't let you. I've told you since day one, I'll help you any way that I can. John, you can trust me. I'm your friend. You and Andrea have my word on it. Please let me help you and your family."

"Tookie, I understand that you'd like to see the house burn to the ground. But I put all of our money into that place. The rest was going to be used on renovations. I don't have the money to invest in another home at this time. I just can't do it."

"Son, I told you, you have my word. I'll help you in any way that

I can. I'm well off. Money has never been an issue. Both Evelyn and I came from prominent families. We were taught that when someone is in need, we're to help them. I don't care if you can't pay me back, your family's safety is important to me. That's all that really matters."

Just then the back door swung open. "It's just me," Andrea said as she walked in, "I was gone twenty minutes and not once did you come to check on me. After ten I was pretty sure you'd be there."

"We had some trouble here," John said modestly.

"Trouble? What kind of trouble? What has Chloe done now?"

"It wasn't Chloe."

"Damn it, John, just talk to me!"

"Savannah and Illusion paid us a visit. It was my fault. I shouldn't have done it. I should have listened to Tookie."

"Mr. Blackwell, will you please explain what's going on?"

"John thought he could break Illusion on the floor. Instead it made her and Savannah upset."

"So what happened?"

"They said they were invincible," John told his wife. "They're unstoppable, Andrea. The damn thing wouldn't even break! I tried, I really did! There's no way we can beat them. They're here to stay."

"Andrea, dear, why don't you come here and help me for a second," Tookie said while he brewed a fresh pot of coffee. "I'm afraid John is suffering from a mental breakdown," he said softly. "He's on the verge of losing his determination to fight this. Please don't let him give up, I beg you. You must give him the reassurance that he needs; otherwise, I'm afraid he'll shut down."

"I understand."

"Well, then, here's your fresh cup of coffee. Shall we have a seat?"

"After you."

"My dear, a true gentleman always lets the lady go first, so please, after you." Tookie followed Andrea to the table. "Now if you don't mind, I'd like to see Cyrus's journal."

"This is it," she said as she handed over the diary.

"Tookie, do you have a newspaper or something I could read to take my mind off this?" wondered John.

"I have a newspaper on the counter. I'll get it for you."

John cracked the paper open and started to read. "What the hell's going on?" he shouted.

"What's wrong, John?"

"This isn't even today's paper! How'd you get this?"

"It was thrown on my doorstep this morning."

Andrea got up from her seat, then stood behind her husband. "This newspaper's from February 14, 1974." Then Andrea saw the familiar picture. "That's my parent's car," she said with disbelief. "That's the car my mom was driving when she had the accident. Give me that paper!" she demanded.

"Are you sure, Andrea?" Tookie asked politely.

"This is the article about her car wreck. I don't believe this." Andrea started to read aloud, "Marien Harris of Fayetteville, TN was involved in a car accident around 1:00 p.m. yesterday afternoon. Apparently Harris was on her way to Sophie's Candy Kitchen to obtain Valentine's Day gifts for her family. On her way, Harris ran into sixty-four-year old Melvin Gray. Now wait a minute, this isn't right. My mom didn't hit him. Mr. Gray suffered a heart attack and ran through a stop sign. He crashed into the driver's side, then rammed my mother's car into a light pole. What else does this article have to say?" she wondered as she began to read the paper aloud. "Harris failed to stop and ran into Gray's car, sending them both into a ditch. Marien Harris died on her way to the hospital. Upon viewing Harris's car, authorities found a half empty bottle of Brandy on the floorboard. As for Melvin Gray, he was rushed to St. Anne's where he is now in critical condition. I don't believe this! This entire article is wrong! Mr. Gray suffered a heart attack and died at the scene. My mother was rushed to St. Anne's where she died a few days later."

"They're responsible for this, Andrea, Illusion and Savannah. They're messing with you by putting this here. They're going to drive us insane with this shit!"

"John, watch your mouth. You're in Mr. Blackwell's house."

"But it's true, Andrea. We're just another pair of victims to them."

"John, are you allergic to any anti-anxiety medications?" Tookie wondered.

"No, not that I'm aware of. Why?"

"Take this. It'll help calm you down."

"Do you take this for your anxiety?"

"Don't get me wrong, son. I love Sam a lot, but it hasn't been the same since Evelyn's passing. I suffer with anxiety and depression, not always, but things could get bad for me from time to time. Trust me, if you take this, you'll feel better."

"Since you say so, I might as well."

"Here, this might help also," Tookie stated as he handed John a booklet.

"What's this?"

"Go on, here's a pencil to help you."

"A word search booklet?"

"Ah, I'm an old man. I have to do something around here to pass the time. I always enjoyed word searches. They keep you busy. Maybe you'll start to like them, too."

"Thanks, Tookie."

"Do as many as you want." Tookie took his seat at the table and joined Andrea. "Now, dear, why don't we forget about this misconceived newspaper and do a little reading. You can catch up on Scarlette's diary while I take a look at Cyrus's journal. Sound all right to you?"

"Actually it does. Who knows when I'll get another chance to read it."

"I'll also be calling Victor shortly. I just want to take a look at this so I can explain it a little better over the phone."

"That's all right with me, Mr. Blackwell. Take your time. I see John's engrossed in his word search. Thank you for helping him."

"That's why I'm here."

"Well, I guess I'll be reading now." Andrea picked up the diary and opened it to the next entry.

CHAPTER SIXTEEN

The seventh of May, nineteen hundred

I FEAR TO EVER STEP FOOT *in that attic again. That room has given me nothing but nightmares. I wish we could move, but I know that we can't.*

Since yesterday I've had the worst feeling that something terrible is about to happen. I can't seem to shake this unsettling dread. As always, Savannah continues to grow further and further away as she slips deeper into darkness. None of the little school children want to be around her. They dislike her and stay away. She picks fights not only with the little girls, but the little boys as well.

Her teacher, Mrs. Wells, speaks often of Savannah's disorderly behavior. She's placed in the corner each day for punishment. She continues to swear and beat upon her younger siblings. I don't believe there's anything I could do to change her back into my sweet little girl.

Worried to death,
Scarlette

The eleventh of May, nineteen hundred

I know that Savannah is responsible for my findings today. I had been out in the backyard weeding and planting flowers for a garden. I walked over to the shed to get a few things when I detected the foulest odor. I followed the putrid scent behind the wooden shed where I found a pile of firewood. There was something strange about the way it had been laid out. It appeared to have been moved around as though it had been hiding something. My curiosity got the best of me and I started to remove the logs. Beneath the massive pile I found the mutilated carcases of different animals. There were birds, snakes, mice and rats, and even my neighbor's two cats, Milo and Buttercup.

Mrs. Norwich has been worried to death ever since her two cats went missing sometime last week. I couldn't bear to tell her the truth that I found them. Their poor little bodies were tortured to death. Does Savannah actually have the brutality in her to do something like this? A long time ago I would have said no, but things have taken a drastic change.

Taken with fear,
Scarlette

The sixteenth of May, nineteen hundred

A notice went out today from Constable McPherson about a missing child. Mrs. Wells had also sent notices out to all the families regarding the disappearance of eight-year-old Kelsey Cowan. Mrs. Wells noticed that the Cowan girl never returned from recess. A search party was sent out in hope of finding the child. Her classmates were questioned in regard to any knowledge they might have had involving her disappearance. Three of Kelsey's classmates reported seeing her with Savannah.

Upon Savannah's questioning, she reportedly stated that she had asked the Cowan girl if she wanted to play a game of jacks. Savannah stated that Kelsey had grown angry after losing the game and stormed away mad. Savannah said that was the last she had seen of young Kelsey Cowan.

As of now the child is still unaccounted for. The police department opened a missing persons case on Kelsey and are reviewing the location from which she disappeared. A strange feeling tells me that Savannah had something to do with this. I hate to think that my daughter has done something terrible. I can't be certain, but I can feel it.

I wish that doll of hers had never come into our lives. I feel so bad for the parents of little Kelsey Cowan. I know they're going through a tough time right now. I'm going to bake them a banana nut bread and take it by tomorrow. I want them to know that I care and that I'm there for them. I hope their daughter is found safely but I fear the worst.

Always,
Scarlette

The seventeenth of May, nineteen hundred

I took by a fresh baked banana bread along with a bouquet of flowers to Simon and Teresa Cowan. They were so thankful that someone took the time to think about them. Teresa fell apart as soon as I arrived. I could feel her pain in my soul as she stood there and cried. I know how awful it is to lose a child. I know that I didn't lose Savannah in the same way that Teresa lost Kelsey, but the understanding of what she and Simon are going through is there. She asked me several times if Savannah knew where Kelsey went after she left her side.

I've tried to comfort Teresa as best as I could. I told her that I felt Kelsey would be found; I just couldn't tell her that I feared the worst. Teresa assured me that it wasn't like Kelsey to run away. After being with Teresa and Simon for awhile several people from the neighborhood showed up carrying flowers and desserts in hand. I figured I'd let them visit with the others when I decided to leave. I gave them my best and told them both that I was there if they should need someone to talk to.

Forever,
Scarlette

The eighteenth of May, nineteen hundred

The unfortunate was revealed today. Little Kelsey Cowan's body was finally found by authorities not far from the little red school house. Upon searching a little deeper into the Clover Bluffs, Constable McPherson came across a small cave where he found young Kelsey's body resting not far from the entrance. The apparent cause of death was blunt force trauma to the back of her head. Authorities said that her head had been smashed repeatedly with a rock forcing the poor child's skull to cave in.

I went by the Cowans' house today to give them my regards and support. Both Simon and Teresa were in complete distress upon hearing the news of their daughter's misfortune. I still believe Savannah had something to do with this. If there were any way I could bring Kelsey back, I would. I'd exchange my own life in return for hers. No child should ever go through what that poor girl did. I could just imagine how alone she felt and how afraid she was during that time. I hope that poor little girl didn't have to suffer, and I pray that her passing was quick.

Forever,
Scarlette

The twentieth of May, nineteen hundred

I had gone to Mason's General Store today where I ran into Teresa Cowan. We had a brief conversation about how she and Simon were doing. The poor dear broke down and cried on my shoulder during our talk. She said she could hardly go on and felt like dying herself. Teresa told me that it feels like the sun never shines. She stated that she wished nothing more than to be with Kelsey in heaven. Hearing her say that broke me, and I began to cry with her.

Little Kelsey was Simon and Teresa's only child. Kelsey was their miracle baby, from what I can understood. Teresa and Simon tried four years to have a child. Teresa wasn't supposed to have any. She was said to have been barren. By the fifth year the Cowans got a surprise and found out that Teresa was pregnant. Nine months later Kelsey came into their lives. Teresa said that she was so happy to be a mother and that Kelsey gave her the best years of her life. Now she says she has nothing but pictures and memories of Kelsey to keep her going. She told me that if she didn't have that, she'd have nothing.

Hearing Teresa's words saddened my heart and made it feel like the weight of a brick.

Painfully yours,
Scarlette

"Andrea, my dear, is everything all right?" Tookie wondered.

"No, Mr. Blackwell, I don't think it is," she told him as she wiped tears from her eyes. "When you don't think anything could get any worse, it always does."

"What is it that has bought you to tears, my dear girl?"

"Reading this, I've come to find out that Savannah had another victim."

"Another one?"

"Her classmate, eight-year-old Kelsey Cowan."

"What drove her to killing that child?"

"I don't know. Maybe the rage that embedded itself in her heart drove her over the edge and forced her to killing Kelsey. If this is all true, Kelsey Cowan was Savannah and Illusion's first victim."

"What happened to the young girl?"

"She'd been beaten in the back of the head with a rock."

"That Savannah. She really was a monster, wasn't she?"

"Yes, Mr. Blackwell, she was."

"I'm sorry you had to come across such disturbing information, not only in that diary but with the newspaper articles as well."

"I wanted to know the truth; now I have it, or at least part of it."

"Sometimes the truth can be a scary thing, my girl, but to have the truth is better than only having the knowledge of lies. I've looked at Cyrus's journal extensively and came across some unusual symbols and diagrams that have been drawn on some of the pages. I don't have my brother's smarts to translate Latin. The sooner he can get here, the closer we are to knowing what all of this says. So if you could excuse me a moment, I'm going to give Victor a call."

Andrea looked over at John, who was still busy with his word search. "Earth to John," she said as she tried to get his attention. "John, do you hear me?"

"What is it, Andrea? Can't you see I'm busy right now?"

"I'm sorry I don't mean to disturb you. I just wanted to know if you overheard my conversation with Mr. Blackwell."

"I heard you talking about something, but honestly I wasn't paying any attention. Was it important?"

"You tell me," she challenged him. "I read that Griffin wasn't Savannah and Illusion's first victim."
"Oh, really. And who was it? The next door neighbor?"
"John, why are you getting sarcastic with me?"
"I wasn't getting sarcastic; I was just asking a question."
"Well, it sounded sarcastic to me."
"I'm sorry if it did, but we knew there were bound to be more victims, Andrea. I guess I'm just not shocked by it. So who was it?"
"A little girl. Savannah's classmate."
"She killed her classmate?"
"That's what Scarlette thought."
"But all of her victims were adults except for her brother. Isn't that what she targeted, an older crowd?"
"I guess not."
Interesting. I wonder if she had a motive for killing the girl? John thought. "You know when you think about it, you wonder, did Savannah have a motive when she killed all those other people?"
"John, you're acting weird."
"I'm just thinking. Anyway, what happened to the girl? What's her name?"
"Kelsey Cowan. She was beaten in the head with a rock," Andrea told him.
"What a shame. She was just a kid."
"Forget talking to you right now. You're too wrapped up in that word search."
"Sorry. I just don't feel like talking right now."
"Don't take it offensively, Andrea. It might be the anti-anxiety medication I gave him. His body isn't use to it," Tookie said softly.
"But he's all right?"
"I think so. Just let him be for now."
"All right."
"Well, I spoke to my brother. He told me he'd be here sometime around 6:00 p.m. I hope that'll be all right with y'all."
"That's fine."
"Good. Say now, y'all wouldn't mind joining an old man for supper now, would you?"
"We wouldn't mind. I take it that you're presenting an invitation?"
"I sure am, little lady. How does country fried steak sound along

with the fixin's? Good hot mashed potatoes with a big scoop of macaroni and cheese. It doesn't get any better then that!"

"That sounds very good. I've tasted your baked peaches, so I know you can cook."

"And that was just a dessert. Wait until supper. I'm pretty sure you won't be disappointed." Tookie stated happily. "I'm going to get to work now. You go on and read some more of that diary."

"But don't you need some help?"

"I got it."

"Are you sure?"

"Positive. Now go on."

"Well, if you need some help, please let me know."

"I shouldn't, but if I do, I'll let you know."

"All right then."

Andrea picked up the diary and started to read where she had left off.

The twenty-first of May, nineteen hundred

Around nine this morning Teresa Cowan came by for a visit in desperate need of someone to talk to. She said she felt like her marriage was falling apart because she couldn't hold herself together. She told me she'd been severely depressed and was having terrible trouble getting through each day. Teresa said she didn't feel as though she were living, but that she was just existing to some degree.

I feel such worry for her. She has sunk so deeply into depression that her life is lessening with each passing day. I tried to support her the best I could. I'm afraid if she continues to exist like this, there will be nothing left of her. I can't deny the thought; it's what I think, but it worries me so to have that conception.

Teresa had mentioned something about a silver locket missing from Kelsey's neck the day her body was found. She told me it was a gift to Kelsey on her fifth birthday and that she had worn it ever since. Teresa wanted to lie her daughter to rest with the locket around her neck. She said she had even gone to the Clover Bluffs to look for it, but came up empty. I told Teresa I'd help her search for Kelsey's necklace if she wanted my aid.

I think she was doing a little better upon the time she had left. I pray that things will work out for the best, but my worries I fear.

Until next time,
Scarlette

The twenty-fourth of May, nineteen hundred

After school Savannah came home and locked herself in her room with Illusion. As I passed down the hallway I could hear a quiet conversation from behind her doorway. I fear that I have finally heard Illusion's voice. It brought chills to my skin as I heard her speak. I do not know what the conversation was about; the words were too faint to understand. I feel as though they are planning something dreadful. I couldn't imagine what might be running through their minds. I would hate to even think about it.

    Somehow Savannah knew that I had been outside her room. Within seconds she rushed out and forced me into the wall. Savannah screamed at me for a good minute telling me that I had no right to ease drop. I didn't see the pair of scissors at first. It wasn't until she drove the scissors into my hand that I realized she had them. I cringed in pain when I felt what she had done. I looked down and saw that the object had been driven straight through my hand. My blood splattered down to the floor while Savannah stared in my face. She glared at me with her cold, dark eyes, then said this is just a taste of what I could do to you. After that she turned around and went back to her room.

    I rushed downstairs crying with pain from the scissors in my hand. Wallace heard me and came to my aid. When he saw what Savannah had done he grew sick to his stomach. He rushed off to find Dr. Richmond so he could bring him to our home. I am thankful he only lives a short way down the street. They returned quickly, and Dr. Richmond was able to tend to my hand.

    As I sit here to write this, I get a strange feeling that something unspeakable is going to occur. Unfortunately I don't believe that I harbor the power or strength to stop whatever it may be. I am, as I will always be, still waiting on a miracle to come and save my precious family. Please, God, give me strength. I'm going to need it.

Jillian Osborn

Scarlette

The twenty-sixth of May, nineteen hundred

Simon Cowan came by today crying his eyes out. He could hardly speak when he arrived at my doorstep. I tried to calm him as best as I could. I took him into the living room where he had a seat on the couch. I then went into the kitchen and poured two glasses of cold lemonade, then returned to his side. He finally told me what had been bothering him.

Simon said that during the night Teresa snuck away from their bed and committed suicide. I had been taken with such shock that I was forced to sit there beside him in silence. He said that Teresa had leaped from the balcony and broke her neck and back. I shared in Simon's pain and cried there on the couch with him. I told Simon if there were anything that Wallace or I could do to help him, to please let us know.

That poor man has lost his wife and child. What more could he go through? I knew Teresa had been experiencing such severe depression, and I worried so for her. What if I could have prevented this from happening? If only I had spent more time with her, she may still be here. I feel so terrible for what has happened. I pray that Simon will be all right. I don't think he could handle another tragedy in his life.

Forever,
Scarlette

The twenty-eighth of May, nineteen hundred

I was reading the morning paper when I came across an article on a seven-year-old boy named Owen McGregor. The article said that Owen had gone to Penny's Bakery yesterday afternoon accompanied by his older brother. On the walk home Dillon lost track of Owen. Thinking his young brother had gone back to the bakery, Dillon decided to turn around. Penny told him that she'd last seen Owen when the two brothers had left her bakery together.

Dillon searched around but was unable to find Owen in any of the shops. His last thoughts were to check around the little red school house thinking Owen had gone there to play on the swings. The playground was empty when Dillon arrived, and little Owen was nowhere in sight. As Dillon walked to the back of the school house he noticed part of a half-eaten cinnamon roll on the ground. Dillon knew his brother had been eating one as they left the bakery. Dillon then decided to search in the Clover Bluffs for his younger brother.

Not far from the cave where little Kelsey Cowan's body was found, Dillon came upon a grizzly scene. Owen's body had been thrashed into a rigid tree branch where he was impelled through the back with the remaining branch exiting out of his stomach. The article said his small body had been driven back into the tree where he clung in midair. The force from the impact was so strong that it caused the poor child's internal organs to be exposed. A look of fright had taken to the child's face, which made the scene even more disturbing. Dillon ran home to his parents and told them what had happened.

Around 1:00 p.m. yesterday afternoon Savannah had gone to Penny's bakery. I fear she was there during the time the two brothers had gone. I was bothered so by my worries that I decided to talk with Penny today. I asked if Savannah did in fact show up at the bakery yesterday afternoon. Penny said Savannah came in to order a cinnamon roll, but she had just sold the last one to little Owen McGregor. She said that Savannah seemed quite upset by not getting the last one and demanded that Owen hand it over. Owen apparently told Savannah he paid for it with his own money. After that Savannah stormed away mad and left the bakery. Not more than five minutes had passed when Dillon and Owen left Penny's shop. She told me it was the last time she had seen little Owen McGregor.

A short while later Dillon returned to the bakery looking for his younger brother. Forty-five minutes had elapsed when Penny said she heard the tragic news concerning the death of the little McGregor boy. Not even two weeks have gone by and our town has already suffered the loss of two of its children. Whose child will be next? As I write these words, I am stricken with an overflow of tears. There's a murderous soul among us, I am saddened to say, but I fear the murderer is a child, my daughter.

I'm afraid to tell Wallace. What if he thinks I'm crazy? I know he has seen the changes in Savannah. We talk about it from day to day. I just don't think Wallace could picture our eight-year-old as a brutal killer. What do I do? Should I continue to sit here in silence or do I tell someone and risk my sanity? Would anyone believe me? I know I'm not insane, but I fear this matter has driven me there. The only person I have is myself.

Scarlette

The first of June, nineteen hundred

I received the strength today to ask Savannah about Owen McGregor. She said bluntly, he went to my school, but now he can't; that little boy's dead. I couldn't believe my ears. She had not one ounce of regard for that poor child. I knew then something seemed odd. She acted like she didn't care, which she didn't. That confirmed my fears and thoughts. The only thing missing was any solid evidence that placed Savannah at both scenes at the time of the crimes. Kelsey Cowan was severely beaten in the back of the head with a rock. With each blow that she took, blood and brain matter would have splattered back onto her attacker, covering them in her blood. I don't recall seeing any blood on Savannah's dress the day Kelsey Cowan was killed, nor do I recall seeing any blood on her the day Owen McGregor was killed either.

Something doesn't make sense. I am almost certain Savannah's responsible for the deaths of those two children. I know Illusion's behind this. She's turned Savannah into the child she is today. That unholy doll goes where ever she does. They are inseparable, Savannah and Illusion. It's like they've become one. What in the world am I dealing with? Why did it attach itself to my daughter? These questions I asked with fear, for I believe I won't ever know the answer.

Always,
Scarlette

The fourth of June, nineteen hundred

I have a sense of dread that a terrible tragedy is going to fall upon my family. Every time I get these feelings something awful has happened. I may not know what it is, but I feel that something is most definitely around the corner. I wish for once that my feelings be wrong, but the intensity and dread that I feel deep in my soul make it hard to ignore. I can't keep living like this. Not only has my life and my family's lives been torn apart by the arrival of Illusion, but also some of the townspeople as well. They may not know a thing about that cursed doll, but I do. I know that things suddenly changed when Illusion came into the picture. The changes began with Savannah first, then the mutilated animal corpses which I found behind the shed, and now the murder of those two children which happened to be my daughter's classmates.

How do I stop this madness? I pray each night that my family and I could wake up from this never-ending nightmare and things be back to normal. But what is normality anymore? At times I fear I've lost all knowledge of it. My life has been spun into Illusion's web of deceptive tricks, but I will not be taken by it. Even as each day slips further from reality I must try to keep my sense and composure. I wish I were dealing with a ghost which had taken up residency in my home rather than a twisted doll with demonic tendencies.

Leave a page open for me. I know I'm going to need another come tomorrow.

Scarlette

The fifth of June, nineteen hundred

I had an odd dream last night. I'm unsure if it was my unconscious mind trying to send me a mixed message or just my imagination playing a random story as I slept. Anyway, in my dream I was in the backyard sitting in the gazebo reading a book. As I went to turn the page, I heard the most awful noise coming from beneath the azalea bush. I left the gazebo and hunted for whatever made that terrible sound. As I bent down to my knees, I could see a medium-sized racoon beneath the flowers. I was startled for a moment and afraid it was going to attack me until I realized why it was distraught. Next to its side rested a much smaller racoon, its little baby. The poor thing didn't move at all, and I feared it was dead. When the reality hit me, I began to cry. A mother coon had lost her little one. To me it was no different than a human being losing a child. Even though racoons are animals, it doesn't mean they don't feel the pain of loss. That mother racoon was beside herself in shock. There was nothing I could do to help it. Nature had merely taken its course.

I understand that people as well as animals die, but it saddens my heart so much to know that the ones living experience the pain. What once was had been taken away. I guess I might be a little more emotional than others when it comes to the death of an animal, for that matter. The one thing I could think of that might be able to relate my dream to reality is the thought that Savannah had killed a baby racoon. Maybe I'm wrong and this dream has no meaning. For now I have no certainty.

Forever,
Scarlette

The eighth of June, nineteen hundred

Savannah's fits of rage will never end. She became severely angered by Collette today for no evident reason. Seconds later, Savannah doubled up her fist and struck Collette in the mouth, knocking out a loose bottom tooth. Collette came to me crying with a mouth full of blood. She told me what Savannah had done, then I called Wallace into the room. He saw Collette's bloodied mouth, then became quite upset by Savannah's aggressive behavior. He left the room and went hunting for Savannah while I stayed at Collette's side and tended to her.

Collette is so badly bothered by Savannah. She told me how afraid she was of her older sister. That broke my heart to hear my five-year-old tell me she was that unsettled. Collette asked if she could stay with my friend Adaline for a few days. That's how scared she is to stay here. She doesn't want to be around Savannah. I told her I'd see if it was all right with Adaline first.

Wallace came back into the room and said he was unable to find Savannah anywhere in the house. He guessed that she had snuck off somewhere to avoid any trouble. I told Wallace that Collette wanted to stay at my friend's house for a couple days. He agreed and told me to take Collette there.

Adaline said it wasn't a problem, that Collette could stay for as long as she wanted. I told her that Collette and Savannah were having some problems and that Collette really didn't want to be at the house right now.

Collette told me she'd come home as soon as she felt safe enough. But I am worried. Will Collette ever feel enough security that she wants to come back? I gave my baby a hug and kiss, then told her I'd come by to visit tomorrow. At least she's in a place where she'll be safe, thank God.

Always,
Scarlette

The ninth of June, nineteen hundred

I had that strange dream again about the mother racoon and her baby. The dream was exactly the same as before. Nothing had been different. All day I've had a sense of sadness fill me. It seems as though an empty void has settled in my heart. I wander alone through the house, then for no reason begin to cry. I've tried to fight the tears, but somehow they just seem to keep coming. I feel like I've lost something or a part of me has died. Even as I went by to visit Collette today I still felt the splinters piercing my heart as I ached with an unknown loss. I don't know why I feel this way. Maybe my depression has finally taken its toll, forcing me to grow weak as the final result.

Griffin will come up to me speaking with the fullness of his heart. Mama don't be sad, my sweet child tells me. How can I be sad when my little gentleman is there? He knows when I am down so he comes around to cheer me. I feel better when I'm with my little boy. He takes away the void I feel deep within. Once he leaves my side, the sadness returns and I am back where I had originally started, moping around and being drowned by emotions as I stray from room to room.

About one-thirty this afternoon Griffin had a mild nosebleed for two minutes, then it stopped. At three-forty he had another one that lasted just a bit longer. Then between five-fifteen and nine o'clock he suffered two more. I figured his little nose was bleeding due to the dry heat. I boiled some water upon the stove, then had Griffin sit on the counter to inhale the steam. After that I applied some petroleum jelly inside his nostrils to keep his skin moistened. Griffin hasn't had a nosebleed in about two and a half hours, and he seems to be sleeping rather well. I just hope he'll be okay through the rest of the night.

Jillian Osborn

Until tomorrow,
Scarlette

The tenth of June, nineteen hundred

Oh God, my dear God, my baby has been taken from me. They killed him. They took my little Griffin's life. I can't bear this pain that has filled my heart and soul.

I woke up around three-thirty this morning to use the facilities unknowing that I would find my darling Griffin floating face-down in a tub of bloodied water. As the candlelight flickered upon the room I was taken with fright and shrieked at the sight of my son.

My cries were loud enough to awaken Wallace. By the time he entered the room I was already in the tub holding Griffin's limp body tightly in my arms as not to let go. There's no experience that's worse for a mother than to hold her dead child's body and knowing he'll never inhale another breath ever again. I fell apart with pain from the loss of my baby. They tortured him, a three-year-old. Griffin was Savannah's baby brother. How could she have done such an act of malice to him? I know he had suffered a great deal during his final moments. He had a huge gash on the front of his head and his little neck was swollen and bruised.

Authorities arrived at our home a minute shy of four a.m. Griffin's small body was placed into a shroud, then sealed inside. I fell down to the floor crying as they took my baby boy away. Wallace and I were questioned about the accident, as they called it. I know Griffin's death was no mishap. I told them it wasn't. They searched the house looking for any signs of forced entry, but found nothing. The constable asked why my gown had been soaked in blood and water. I told him that I crawled into the tub with Griffin and held him in my arms. Really, what did he expect me to do? Griffin was my son; it was my natural reaction as a mother to take him in my arms. I know the authorities think I had something to do with his death. I believe they also thought Wallace was trying to help me cover it up by the way they were talking today. That's not the truth. How do I tell them the facts? They wouldn't believe an eight-year-old could have done this terrible thing. Oh, please, God, please, I beg you, help me. I've fallen apart and there's no light for me to see. My world has grown bleak and dreary.

Signed always,
Scarlette

The eleventh of June, nineteen hundred

The constable came by today asking more questions about Griffin's death. I told him flat out Wallace nor I could have done this. He said Griffin had been murdered. That's what his medical examination showed. Then he talked about the sweep of the house and how nobody found any signs of forced entry. He told me it had to have been someone in the house who killed him. After that I couldn't take it anymore, and I broke down to him about Savannah. I told him that since we moved here she's been acting strangely.

Not long after that, Savannah came in from school, so Constable McPherson asked to speak with her. He told me Savannah was the nicest little girl, he had ever met. He said she told him that she never heard anything unusual the day that Griffin was killed. As much as I tried to make him listen to me about Savannah, he wouldn't.

Now the authorities are trying to link Wallace and me to Griffin's murder. We're being wrongfully accused for something we didn't do.

Lord save us,
Scarlette

The twelfth of June, nineteen hundred

Constable McPherson returned to the house today and asked Savannah about being at Mason's General Store. She told him she had gone there to get some candy, but when she arrived the store was empty, so she left. I asked if something were wrong, but Constable McPherson wouldn't tell me a thing. I figured he came by to talk to Wallace or me, but when he asked for Savannah, it completely shocked me.

Later in the evening I ran into my friend Adaline. I asked how Collette was doing. She said Collette was fine, then asked how I was. During our talk Adaline told me about the brutal slaying of Donald Mason. She told me she and Collette had taken a walk to the general store, but when they arrived the store was closed. She said she had a brief conversation with Ronny Mason. He told her his father had been murdered and that he was the one who had found the body in the stock room of the store.

Two witnesses said that the last person seen leaving Mason's was my Savannah. Did she have something to do with this, I wonder? Why do I even wonder? I know the truth deep in my heart, and the answer is yes. Not only is that cursed doll damned, but my daughter is, too. How do I stop this? Not just the evil that's prominent in my eyes, but these murders as well. Three children are dead, including my son, and now an old man. Savannah and Illusion have taken the lives of four people. This must stop at once. If it doesn't, I fear there will be more to come. How must I end this? Will I have to kill my own child to save the lives of others? I cannot do that, though. It is too much. No matter what Savannah has become, she is still my child. I must figure a way to stop Illusion. That might be my only hope. The doll won't break. There's no use in trying.

I'll see if Wallace would be willing to help me dispose of Illusion through one of the storm sewers. That would at least get her out and away from our home. Maybe then she'd lose the control she has over Savannah.

As always,
Scarlette

The thirteenth of June, nineteen hundred

I read an article in the newspaper concerning the brutal death of Donald Mason, the general store owner. The article said that the poor man had been violently beaten. I feel so terrible. He was such a kind man. It's disturbing to know that my daughter was the one who did this. I know it was her without a doubt; I just don't know why she'd do it. Something had to have happened for her to kill him. The same thing goes for the little Cowan girl and the little McGregor boy, maybe even Griffin. There might have been some sort of altercation or argument before their deaths, but then again I don't really know.

God, this entire situation is driving me mad. I don't have anyone to talk about this to but myself. I feel like I'm talking to a brick wall because no one is there to give me any answers. Wallace is always working odd hours; we hardly see each other. I don't know a lot of the people around here yet. This kind of stuff that's going on is what you tell your oldest friend, not just someone you've known for two months. I consider Adaline to be dear to me, yet I won't tell her the truth. I can't.

Collette came home today. She said she missed me too much to be away any longer. Starting tonight Collette will be sleeping with Wallace and me in our room. I can't bear to lose another child; I've already lost two. I must protect Collette and keep her safe. It saddens me when she asks about Griffin. She wanders through the house looking for him and calling out his name. I know she is too young to understand death. I tell her that Griffin is resting peacefully with the angels where he's waiting patiently for each of us to journey home to him.

Always,
Scarlette

The fifteenth of June, nineteen hundred

I walked upstairs this morning to gather laundry. As I passed Griffin's room, I overheard Collette talking. I opened the door and found her sitting on the floor with several of Griffin's toys. She told me they'd been playing together and asked me to join them. I was curious, so I asked Collette who she was playing with. She told me that Griffin had come home. She'd look into an empty space as though Griffin were really there and start talking to him. I figured maybe he really was there despite the fact that I couldn't see him. Children are sensitive. They see things we don't. It took a moment, but I finally told Collette to ask Griffin if he was all right, and I began to cry.

She told me that Griffin could hear me and said I should ask myself. I did, but I never heard a response. Then Collette looked into the empty area and said, mama can't hear you, but I'll tell her. She turned to me and said that Griffin was happy to be home. Collette then came up to me and said, Griffin doesn't want you to be sad. As she said that I felt little arms wrap around my leg, and my heart suddenly grew warm. It was then that I knew Griffin was actually there. I closed my eyes, then told him softly that I loved him dearly and always will.

Forever,

Jillian Osborn

Scarlette

The twenty-third of June, nineteen hundred

There was another death. This time it was Adelle Collingswood, Savannah's piano teacher. Myrtle Bristow found Adelle's body beside her beloved piano. The poor woman had two iron rods stuck through her eyes and her hands had been completely severed by piano strings. Savannah had a lesson with Adelle prior to the time that Myrtle had found her body.

I personally picked Savannah up after her lessons, and like all the other times, I never saw any blood covering her dress. I should have gone in myself to see if she was all right, but I didn't. Abby Bristow had a lesson after Savannah. That's when Myrtle found Adelle's body. Constable McPherson found Savannah's name listed in her appointment book, so he came by to have another talk with her.

Savannah told him kindly that Mrs. Collingswood appeared to be quite fine before she had left. Savannah brainwashed Constable McPherson into believing that she was a darling little girl. Afterward he dismissed the fact that Savannah had been the last person who had lessons with Adelle Collingswood before her death.

Why doesn't he see that Savannah is committing these murders? He knew she had been the last person seen coming out of Mason's General Store; now this. Why doesn't he link those facts together? Savannah should be his prime suspect; however, he won't treat her as one.

Children are not always innocent. They can be dark and disturbing. Unfortunately I had to find that out the hard way.

Forever and Always,
Scarlette

The twenty-seventh of June, nineteen hundred

Heavy showers have been toppling down from the clouds all day. I asked Wallace if he'd help me get rid of Illusion by dumping her into the storm sewer. I told him today would be perfect, that the rain could carry her away, ridding Illusion from our lives. He asked me how I expected to get Illusion away from Savannah. I told him we'd go into her room after dark and take Illusion away while she was sleeping.

Thank God, Savannah didn't wake up and we were able to get Illusion away from her. Wallace and I scurried out into the rain hunting for a storm sewer to throw her in. We must have looked like two blooming idiots, but I didn't care. As Wallace fit the doll into the sewer, a bolt of lightning struck the ground not more than five feet from where we were standing. Wallace hurried to loosen his grasp on Illusion, but as he did, the doll took his hand.

She raised her head from within the sewer and peered up to Wallace through the metal bars, laughing wickedly. I never heard anything like it. The sound scared me to death. It was as though seven men or demons had been laughing. The sound was like something straight out of hell; if not that, then something close to it.

This thing, this demon doll, began to talk. I think we heard its true voice. It seemed like all seven entities or so were all speaking at once. Between all the voices, Wallace and I were able to make out the sentence. It asked, "Why would thou do such a thing and throw me into such filthy water?" It brought chills to my spine, and I became quite nervous.

I told Wallace to get rid of it. I could see him trying to shake his hand loose from Illusion's grasp, then I heard a splatter as the doll hit the water below. For now we are safe. I don't know what Wallace or I will tell Savannah. I guess we'll have to deal with that in the morning. I pray everything goes all right.

Till then,
Scarlette

The twenty-eighth of June, nineteen hundred

It's already back. God, if I can't get rid of the thing or even break it, what do I do? Savannah came down for breakfast lugging Illusion in her arms. I don't know who was frightened more, Wallace or me? I know if I felt my heart stop, Wallace felt his. Savannah looked at us as she took a bite of her breakfast and said, "Illusion always comes back." I felt my body tremble and knew there was no hope. There's no way we can destroy that blasted doll.

Jillian Osborn

Sitting on pins and needles,
Scarlette

The third of July, nineteen hundred

Collette continues to see and play with Griffin. I believe I might have heard his voice just for a moment today. It was a blessing to hear once more. I don't see Griffin, but I can feel him in the house. When I walk into a room I can sense him there. Knowing he's around brings to me a feeling of peace.

Collette and I are always together, and she tells me Griffin is also there with us. I make sure Savannah can't harm Collette in any way. Collette stays at my side until Savannah goes to school, but once she returns, Collette comes back to me.

As I have said before, I must protect Collette and keep her safe. She is the last of my children.

Always,
Scarlette

The fourth of July, nineteen hundred

Independence Day at last! Okay, so I just wanted to say that. Anyway, it feels like any other day. Just because it's a holiday doesn't mean it will be any different than a regular one. So what if there are fireworks, parades and carnivals? None of that matters anymore. I don't have all of my family here to enjoy it the way we used to.

Last year Savannah was a sweet seven-year-old who loved and cared about everything. Griffin had his first taste of carnival food. And now what? I have a daughter who's nonexistent and a deceased son whose spirit now haunts this house. On a happier note I still have my Collette, my darling girl, and I have Wallace, my husband and friend.

I just need to get out of this depressing hole I'm in. I need to be happy; I need to start living again. How Can I, though? Our lives are still plagued by this evil. There can be no happiness anymore. What hasn't yet killed us just makes us grow weak.

Surviving each day,
Scarlette

The seventh of July, nineteen hundred

There has been yet another murder, the milkman, Cole Jameson. During his morning delivery routine, Mr. Jameson was found murdered on the steps of Kipp Radcliff's home. His mouth had been taped shut and his body was pierced full of scissor holes. Kipp found Cole's body early yesterday morning. I know Savannah is again responsible for another death. The rate is now six. Illusion has turned my daughter into a monster; they are one and the same.

Scarlette

The ninth of July, nineteen hundred

I had the most unsettling dream this morning. It was truly horrible. Words can't express the terror I felt. I was in a cemetery, and I walked upon my grave, but not just mine, my husband and children's as well. On the headstones our names were inscribed, and just below I could read the year of death on each one, nineteen hundred. I awoke crying, then Wallace heard me. I told him we were going to die as we did in my dream. Savannah's going to kill us all one of these days. This dream was too real to ignore. We're going to die if we don't find a way to stop Savannah and Illusion first.

Something I thought I'd never come to do, I am now contemplating. For this to stop, Savannah must die. I am the one who must take her life. Illusion can be buried with Savannah in her casket, then neither can harm another's life.

God, what am I saying? I can't kill my daughter, even though I must. But if I tried, how could I make it easy on her? I wouldn't want Savannah to suffer in the least. She's still my child. I have to think about this.

Jillian Osborn

Scarlette

The tenth of July, nineteen hundred

I had taken some of Savannah's things to her room. As I was putting a few blankets away in her closet I came upon her trunk. It wasn't odd that she had it there, but what bothered me was the dried blood that had crusted along the wood. I bent down to my knees and opened it. Looking back at me were six dresses, all stained in blood. I took each one out and cried terribly as I set them on the floor. Beneath the dresses I found a secret compartment which Savannah had made for herself. I scraped my fingers as I pulled the wooden trap away. Underneath I found a collection of things.

I came across a wooden bat completely saturated with dried blood. Next to the bat was a large rock that had hair and blood dried to it. I also found bloodied scissors, a bloodied brick and a broken piano string as well. There was even a splintered branch resting inside her trunk. I linked each piece of evidence to every murder that had been committed.

Kelsey Cowan's, Owen McGregor's, Donald Mason's, Adelle Collingswood's, Cole Jameson's and my own dear son, Griffin's. I have the evidence now that points Savannah to being their killer. I always felt it was her; now I have confirmation. Not only did I find the weapons that were used, I also found things that had once belonged to each victim.

The wedding ring that was missing from Donald Mason's finger, I found in Savannah's trunk along with Kelsey Cowan's locket. There was part of a cinnamon roll wrapped in a cloth, a hanky with the initials CJ, an expensive pair of earrings and Griffin's favorite wooden train. After finding everything, I became quite sick to my stomach. When Savannah came in from school I confronted her about the trophy trunk I found. She simply laughed at me then said, "Are you ashamed of me now that you found the truth? I couldn't help what I did. They all left me no choice. I asked Kelsey nicely for her locket, but she wouldn't give it to me. Then I asked Owen for his cinnamon roll, but the stupid pig started to eat it. I begged Mr. Mason for his ring, but you think that old man took it off his finger? That idiotic piano teacher was the most rude of all. She told me that little girls shouldn't wear such expensive earrings. Mr. Jameson wouldn't give me his handkerchief because his wife made it for him before she died. Really, mommy, that's stupid, don't you think? Aren't people supposed to give you things when you ask them nicely? So what they wouldn't give me, I took from them. It was simple, really. Very simple. I did not care. I'll take out anyone who gets in my way," she told me bragging. I asked Savannah why she killed Griffin. She said, "The stupid brat left his toy train on the floor in the kitchen and I slipped on it. I fell on my back, bruising my spine. After that happened, I was filled with so much anger, I went upstairs into his room, quietly put my hand around his mouth and carried him out into the backyard where I had a brick waiting for his head. I hit him, then his blood splattered into my mouth. I must say, I enjoyed it quite like candy. But the little pest wouldn't die. Then I remembered how afraid he was of water. It's a true shame you or daddy didn't hear his muffled cries when I took him into the bathroom. But I had Illusion there. She put you and daddy into a deep sleep, so deep you didn't hear a thing. But, oh, if you could have just heard Griffin. Vannah, stop, he cried to me. Then he started calling for you and daddy. That's when I grabbed his throat and held him under water. He fought pretty well for a three-year-old. You should be happy." Her words angered me as my heart filled with rage. All I can remember is smacking Savannah in the mouth. She started laughing at me, then yelled, "Is that all you got?" I asked her why I never saw the blood on her dresses. She told me Illusion has the power to make people see what's there and what's not when she wants. I told her to keep explaining, so she said, "The blood was always there, but Illusion disguised it from their eyes, concealing the truth from their sight."

    When she told me how evil she truly was, I knew I couldn't let her continue living. I have to do it come tomorrow. I'll drop Collette off at Adaline's house. I know she wouldn't mind watching her for a couple days. I'll put something in Savannah's food. Then, when she says she's not feeling well, I'll tell her to lie down in her room, and there she can peacefully transcend into death. My mind is made up. I'm going to do this. I'll make vegetable soup for tomorrow's supper. I can make a special batch just for Savannah. She'll never know. The azalea plant is known to be highly toxic. I can take some of the leaves off our bush in the backyard, cut them up, then cook them in Savannah's soup. I'll make her eat enough to cause a deadly reaction.

    God, am I a bad mother for thinking this? Am I doing the right thing in your eyes? If it is, I pray that you give me the strength to follow through with it.

Jillian Osborn

Forever,
Scarlette

The eleventh of July, nineteen hundred

I had the dream about visiting my grave again. I am alone in a dark cemetery wandering through the grounds when I come upon my grave. Wallace's headstone is to the right of mine and to my left are my children's graves lined up neatly in a perfect row. There are flowers placed all around us, and I remember smelling their perfume as I stood before each mound of earth.

This dream haunts my thoughts and terrorizes my mind. I sit here and cry my eyes out because I was a bad mother today. I put the azalea leaves into Savannah's vegetable soup. She enjoyed it so much she had two small bowls. My heart would break with each bite that she took for I knew I was killing my daughter. Tears began to stream down my face as I sat with Savannah and Wallace at the table. Wallace asked what was with the tears. I lied and told him something had gotten into my eyes.

Two hours later Savannah came to me and said her stomach was hurting. I told her she'd be fine, that it was just a little belly ache. An hour later her pains had worsened and she started throwing up. I told her to lie down and that I would come in to check on her. I locked myself in the bathroom where I cried my heart out. When I finally gathered myself, I went into Savannah's room and sat with her on the bed. She had grown weak and pale when I got there. She darted her eyes toward me and asked, "You and daddy would never hurt me, would you?" I sat there in silence for a few seconds, then responded to Savannah's question. Of course not, I told her as calmly as possible. "That's not what Illusion thinks." I asked Savannah if she believed her. She told me that Illusion never lies. I then said for her to get some sleep and that I'd be in to check on her a little later. I went downstairs and sat with Wallace to pass the time.

Later I returned to Savannah's room and checked in on her. She was sleeping soundly with hardly any breath. I felt my heart sink into my stomach as I sat there beside her in denial. I told Savannah that I loved her dearly, but it was something I had to do. I asked for her to rest peacefully with comfort as I kissed her forehead. I held her small hand in mine while

I prayed for her departure. Now may she rest soundly in the hands of God as I deliver her from evil.

I've killed my daughter tonight, and I know that my soul will never be spared for this act. But I ask for God's forgiveness. May he have mercy on my soul. I believe that the hell here is now over for Wallace, Collette and me. The last page to this journal has now been written as the chapter comes to close.

I'm going to hide my journal beneath the floor in the attic. Maybe one day someone will come across it and read my story. Now it's time. I must bury these secrets until they are unearthed once more.

With love,
Scarlette

CHAPTER SEVENTEEN

"Well, my dear, I take it you've finished with your reading?" Tookie asked Andrea as she was closing the journal.

"I read about things through somebody else's eyes that I could have never imagined." Andrea began to shake her head. "Savannah killed for the things that she wanted."

"What kind of things?"

"Jewelry, a handkerchief, even a cinnamon roll. When she didn't get what she wanted, she set out to kill. Illusion drove her into sheer madness. One thing I didn't understand was Scarlette's last entry. Scarlette decided to kill Savannah by poisoning her. The last entry was on July eleventh, 1900, the day before they were all found dead. Scarlette said, or at least came to believe, that Savannah had died from ingesting the poison. But apparently Savannah didn't die and took her vengeance out on her mother and father. Wallace didn't know anything about the poisoning, so I'm assuming that Illusion lied to Savannah and said that he did. That's why Savannah killed him. Scarlette was pushed down the attic stairs. In her last entry she said she was taking the journal into the attic where she would hide it beneath the floor. She must have been killed not long after she hid the journal. That would sound about right, don't you think?"

"I'd say so. I don't think Scarlette would have gone to the attic for anything else. It's like you said, she was killed after hiding it."

"So does that mean Wallace was Savannah's last victim before she took her own life?" Andrea wondered.

"I'd have to say that there's a possibility Wallace was killed before Scarlette, but we don't know that for certain."

"Yeah, you're right."

"What was the final death count for Savannah and Illusion?"

"Including Savannah's death, it comes out to nine," Andrea responded.

"It's disturbing to know that an eight-year-old girl had taken all those lives so long ago."

"Trust me, it baffles me as much as it does you. I hate to get off the subject, but what is John doing over there?"

"He wanted to help me fix dinner. You were so engrossed in Scarlette's diary that we left you alone to read."

"Oh, Mr. Blackwell, I'm so sorry. How rude of me."

"You have no reason to apologize, my dear girl. I figured if you wanted to finish it, now would be the time."

"I was taken with Scarlette's words. They drew me into her life, and I felt as though I were there while everything was happening to her and her family. I think her diary was the saddest true account I ever read."

"Looks like the only thing we have left to decipher is Cyrus Cornu's diary."

"I'm thankful your brother is willing to help us," Andrea told Tookie while John walked over to the table. "Are you feeling any better?" she asked her husband.

"If you're asking rather I feel normal again the answers yes."

"I was worried about you earlier. I thought you were drifting away from us."

"Thanks for worrying, but I'm fine now."

"Has anyone checked in on Chloe?"

"I've been peeping in on her from time to time. No worries. She was still asleep the last time I checked on her."

"Good," Andrea responded.

"Did that diary say anything else about Illusion?" John wondered.

"Nothing more than we already know. Scarlette did mention one thing that gave me chills."

"What was that?"

"The last time she and Wallace tried to get rid of Illusion, they heard her true voice."

"What do you mean, her true voice?"

"Scarlette described it as though seven men or demons had been talking at once. She said it sounded like something straight out of hell."

"Oh, wonderful."

"Not really, but at least we know a little something more."

"Yeah, that thing's possessed by seven men, demons or whatever you want to call them. We can't fight something that powerful, Andrea."

"We're going to have to try, John, or we'll end up like the O'Connor family. History will try to repeat itself. We know what could happen if we lose the battle."

"I wish Collette were still alive so she could tell us what to do," John told her softly.

"I wish she was, too, but I'm afraid we're on our own with this."

"Look at it this way, kids," Tookie interrupted. "Y'all still have me. You're not alone."

"I know you're with us all the way. John and I appreciate that. We just wish that somebody knew what to tell us to do in this type of situation," Andrea explained. "For now things seem bleak, like there's no end to it."

"Don't give up. There's always a way to destroy the evil that lurks among us."

Andrea shook her head as she thought about the words Tookie said.

"You're right, but it's trying to find a way to defeat it that makes this hard."

"I believe you'll find a way. It might just come to you when you least expect it."

"I should probably check in on Chloe. Will you excuse me for a moment?" Andrea got up and removed herself from the table. She walked out into Tookie's living room where she found the place to be a mess. Andrea looked over the room with disbelief.

All of Tookie and Evelyn's picture frames had been smashed into pieces and their photos were torn. The pillows on the couch had been ripped apart, with the stuffing pulled out and scattered along the room. Andrea's eyes fell upon the gift she and John had brought in for Chloe.

It was a new doll, one that was simple yet sweet. Chloe had pulled the doll from its package, then drew on its face with a black marker. Its eyes were blackened along with its lips and a pair of scissors had been driven through its head giving the doll a rather creepy appearance. Andrea picked the doll up, then returned to the kitchen. "We have a major problem here," she said just as John and Tookie spotted the doll.

"Is that the one we just brought her?" John asked.

"Yeah, but it doesn't look like it anymore."

"Why'd she do that?"

"It doesn't matter," Andrea told him, then looked at Tookie. "I'm sorry to have to say this." she paused. "Chloe destroyed the pictures you had of you and Evelyn. Mr. Blackwell, I'm so sorry. I know those can't be replaced."

Andrea walked back into the living room with Tookie and John following.

"Oh, goodness, Evelyn, our wedding pictures," Tookie stated as he held one of the broken frames. "They're all gone. All of our memories ripped to shreds."

"Oh, Tookie, I'm so sorry for this," John told him. "I can try to tape them back together for you."

"That's nice of you, son, but I'm afraid it would be somewhat of a puzzle to fix."

"Is there anything we can do?" Andrea wondered.

"Not that I can think of."

"Let us clean this mess up for you then."

"I think we need to find Chloe first," John told his wife. "Where'd she go?"

"I don't know. She was gone when I got here. I guess she could be anywhere."

"Why don't we split up to look for her? Is that okay with you, Tookie?" John wondered as he waited for permission.

"That's fine by me."

Andrea took the bottom floor and hunted for Chloe while John and Tookie went upstairs and hunted. Tookie came upon Evelyn's doll room and opened the door as he revealed the mess hidden within it. Evelyn's collection of dolls had all been broken by Chloe.

John came into the room and took in the view for himself. "Ah, gee, Tookie, everything's been destroyed. We should have never brought Chloe into your home. Look what she's done."

"Don't you worry, son. I know if your daughter was in the right state of mind she would have never done this."

"But all the money you and Evelyn invested has gone down the drain. I want to reimburse you for the damage Chloe has done here. It's the least I could do for you."

"I don't want your money, son. I have enough of my own. I just want to see an end to this madness."

"We better check your library, Tookie. Chloe may be in there."

Andrea walked up the stairs while John and Tookie were leaving Evelyn's doll room. She saw the mess from behind the door. "Oh, my God." She gasped, "Your wife's things." Andrea paused. "I can't find Chloe, but I cleaned up the mess in the living room."

"We think Chloe might be in the library," John told her.

"Well, what are we waiting for? Let's go," Andrea responded.

They started down the hallway when they heard the familiar sound of footsteps above their heads.

"She's in the attic!" Tookie told them.

"How do we get up there?" John asked.

"Follow me."

Tookie led John and Andrea over to a large wooden door, then turned the crystal knob. "Through here."

They walked up the flight of creaky stairs and opened another door which led into the open attic.

"Chloe, are you in here?" John called out.

John, Tookie and Andrea waited by the doorway for a moment.

"If you're hiding, you better come out!" John let loose and yelled, "Chloe, we know you're up here. Stop playing these games and come out!"

"Tookie and I will check out this part of the attic. You look over there," Andrea told her husband.

John walked toward the back of the room and hunted for Chloe. "Tookie, you don't have any secret crawlspaces that she could hide in, do you?"

"None that I know of," he said to John.

"We might have to search through some of this furniture. Chloe might be hiding in a wardrobe or something."

"We won't stop looking until we find her, John," Andrea told him.

"Andrea, come here. I think I've found her." Tookie said softly. "There." He pointed. "That trunk. It was moving. I think she's in it." Tookie walked over to the trunk, then stopped with Andrea beside him. Tookie looked up at John, then motioned for him to walk across the room.

"Tucker Blackwell, you let me out of this trunk right now!"

"Evelyn?"

"I can't breathe in here. Now open this trunk!"

"I won't!"

"But I can't move and it's dark."

"You aren't my Evelyn!"

A loud snarl was heard from within the trunk by Tookie, John and Andrea.

"Are you afraid to undo the lock and release me?" Evelyn asked while her eye was seen peering out through the keyhole.

"Let's just leave," John told Tookie. "It'd be better if we do."

"I agree with John, Mr. Blackwell. We know Chloe isn't up here. We have to find her."

"Yes, we must find your daughter and make sure she's safe."

"Let's check the first floor again."

"Tucker Blackwell, I said let me out of this trunk!"

"I'm not falling for your tricks, demon!"

"Then you leave me no choice. I'll blow it up and come crawling out after you."

"Such lies you speak!"

"Tookie, we have to get out of here. Ignore her. That isn't Evelyn."

"You think I lie?"

An explosive force blew the trunk into pieces, and from within it, came Evelyn. She cracked her neck from side to side as she emerged through the rubble, then took off after Tucker while she crawled quickly across the floor.

"Move!" John yelled to Tookie and Andrea as they went running from the room. Andrea lost her footing as she tripped over a storage box.

John came up behind her and stopped Andrea from falling. "Hurry! Hurry! Move!"

John was the last out of the room as he slammed the door behind him.

"Do you think she'll get out?" Tookie wondered.

"She better not. I locked the door."

"Good thinking, son."

Tookie, John and Andrea walked into the living room.

"Where else could she have gone?" Andrea wondered.

"Maybe we should check the basement," Tookie suggested.

They walked into the kitchen where they were shocked to see Chloe sitting at the table with Illusion.

"Looks like Sam drank all his water, Mr. Blackwell. You better give him more before he gets all hot again." Chloe giggled.

"You better watch that mouth of yours, Chloe Craven!" John blasted out in anger. "Why would you destroy Tookie's things?"

"I wanted to have some fun while I was here."

Andrea walked over to Chloe and popped her lightly in the mouth. "How dare you for saying that."

"Was that supposed to hurt?" Chloe laughed. "Because if it was, I'd say you're pretty weak."

"You apologize to Tookie for what you did here today or else!" John yelled.

"Or else what, daddy? You can't punish me. I won't listen to you. I follow only Illusion's command." Chloe cleared her voice. "Now, where's my supper? I'm ready to eat."

"You rude little brat!" John told her.

"And with your vocabulary, that's all you could come up with?"

"Your mother and I didn't bring you up to act like this. I think as punishment you should be denied your supper."

"But I want food. I demand to have it *now*." she yelled. "And I'm not stupid. I can smell something's cooking."

"You want your supper?" Andrea asked.

"Ah, hello! How many times do I have to tell you people?"

"Mr. Blackwell, is it okay if I fix her a little something?"

"Sure, that's fine."

"Will you show me where you keep your skillets?" she asked nicely.

"No, Andrea, don't you fix her a damn thing," John told his wife.

"Just walk with me for a second, Mr. Blackwell," she said as they went toward the sink. "She's going to have a bowl of cereal and that's all. I just wanted her to think I was making something."

"Look in that cabinet. You'll find what you need. I'll get you a bowl and spoon."

"Thank you." Andrea grabbed a box of cereal from the cabinet and poured some into the bowl Tookie had placed on the counter.

"Here's the milk," he told her.

Andrea walked over to the table and placed the bowl in front of Chloe. "Here's your supper. Now eat."

"But I didn't want any cereal! I want real food!"

"That's just too bad. Supper isn't ready yet, so do with that."

"I hate you."

"I'm sorry you feel that way."

"I'm taking my cereal and I'm going into the living room. Seeing your face just makes me sick."

"There's a bathroom upstairs if you feel like throwing up."

"Don't you get smart with me, mom. Illusion and I don't like it."

"Chloe, why do you continue to stand here if my face makes you sick?"

"Oh, brush off, you senseless, bitch."

"Don't forget to drink all your milk. You want to have strong bones when you grow up."

Chloe stomped out of the kitchen in a rage.

"Wow, honey, you handled that rather well," John told her.

"I figured she needed a dose of her own medicine for once."

"Well, I think you gave it to her. She didn't seem too happy leaving the room."

"I'm just tired of her rude remarks and spiteful tongue, John. She's turning out to be like Savannah."

"I think that's Illusion's whole point. She wants to make all children like Savannah."

"You know, John, you might just be right on that," Tookie added.

"It's just something I've been thinking about. But you do think it's pliable?"

"Absolutely. A good thinker can come up with a concept that nobody else has thought about. It just might be that Illusion is trying to make replicas of Savannah. The idea isn't as far-fetched as it may sound."

"Let's say that's what she's doing. We know Savannah was first to abide under her command; now Chloe. But why would she use children?"

"The only guess I have is that she wants to corrupt their innocence."

"But what if it's something else?"

"What do we know about Savannah that could link her and Chloe together?"

"They both live or have lived in the same house," John responded.

"That's a start, but I don't think it's the case. The other families who have lived in your house with kids of their own never had the extent of your problems you and Andrea have experienced with Chloe. I believe the bond between Savannah and Chloe, and maybe even Illusion, has to be on a more personal level."

"Personal how, Mr. Blackwell?" Andrea questioned him.

"Maybe they were born on the same day or something."

"We don't know when Savannah was born, though."

"We do know that Illusion was given life on October thirty-first, 1899," John commented.

"Oh, God, I don't know why that didn't strike me before," Andrea told them.

"And what would that be?" wondered Tookie.

"That's Chloe's birthday, October thirty-first. Oh, God, John, why didn't we ever think about that before?"

"Do you think Savannah was born on that same day?"

"She may have been, but we don't know for a fact. Did we read her obituary when we were at the library?"

"I don't think so. I just remember seeing it." John turned to Mr. Blackwell. "Tookie, do you suppose the library would still be open?"

"Yes, as a matter of fact, the library doesn't close until seven."

"I'm going back there to see if I can find Savannah's obituary again. I'll find out if she was born on October thirty-first."

"Okay then, but try to hurry back, son. Supper will be ready in a little bit."

"Can I set the table for you, Mr. Blackwell?"

"Sure, dear, if you don't mind. The plates are in that cabinet." he pointed. "And you'll find the silverware in that drawer there." Tookie took the macaroni out of the stove and set it on a burner to cool. "This looks like my best batch yet."

"Just looking at it makes me hungry."

"John helped me with the country fried steak. Come on over and take a look."

"John really helped you with this?"

"He sure did. John did pretty well for his first time."

"At home that's one thing you won't find John doing, slaving behind a stove. He likes to grill, though. That's about the only time you'll find him cooking."

"Maybe today he's learned to take up the habit."

"That would be nice for a change."

CHAPTER EIGHTEEN

"Can you excuse me for a minute, Andrea? I think I just heard the door bell." Tookie walked out to the living room and saw an image standing behind his door. "Ah, Victor, you're early."

"I'm sorry, Tucker. Is it a bad time?"

"Of course not. Come on in!"

"You, ah, you got a grandchild here I didn't know about, Tookie?" Victor asked, kidding his brother.

"This here is Chloe, John and Andrea's daughter."

"That sure is a pretty doll you got there. I'm Tookie's brother, Victor."

"I don't care who you are," Chloe said bluntly. "Now leave me be. Savannah, Illusion, and I are watching cartoons."

"I'm sorry I've distracted you, Miss Chloe."

"Did you not hear me? I said, leave me be. If you were a person of understanding you would have known that meant for you to go away."

"Come on into the kitchen, Victor. Andrea's in there."

"Is that child always that rude?" Victor wondered.

"Please except my apologies for my daughter's rudeness. I'm Andrea Craven."

"I'm terribly sorry. I didn't mean to talk so loud."

"That's okay. Chloe has been a problem for my husband and me for quite some time now. Again, please except my apologies on her behalf."

"By all means. No hard feelings, Mrs. Craven. I'm Victor Blackwell. It's nice to meet you."

"It's nice to meet you, too. You'll be meeting my husband in a little bit. He had to run back to the library," Andrea explained. "Tookie was telling us you're a retired Latin professor?"

"That's right, and I hear you have an unusual diary you'd like me to translate."

"Yes, please. Whatever you could tell us would be greatly appreciated. John and I will be happy to pay you for your time."

"That won't be necessary, Mrs. Craven, but thank you for the offer."

"We were just getting supper out of the stove, Victor, if you care to join us," Tookie said to his brother.

"What do you have made for today?"

"Homemade country fried steak, macaroni and mashed potatoes, just the way mom would fix it."

"I can't pass that by now, can I?"

"I didn't figure you would."

"All right then, you got me."

"We'll get the glasses ready when John gets back."

"We can go ahead and do that now. I see him pulling up," added Andrea.

"Perfect timing. I'll get the tea out of the fridge. Anyone care for some lemon juice?"

"Come on, Tookie, you know you can't have a glass of ice tea without some lemon!" Victor laughed. "I tell you what, if my wife knows I had supper with you, she'll have my hyde. So we'll just keep that a little secret."

"Why would your wife have your hyde, Victor?" Andrea wondered.

"The misses is found of Tucker's cooking. Today he made her favorite spread. She absolutely loves his country fried steak with all the fixin's."

"Don't you know you can't deprive a woman of good food? Especially when it's not made by her hand!" Andrea joked.

"That's why I'm not going to tell her a thing!"

"Tookie, it's just me, John," he announced as he came into the house. "I found what we were looking for," John told them as he entered the kitchen and saw Victor standing near Andrea. "Oh, hello there, I'm John Craven," he said, extending his hand.

"Victor Blackwell. Nice to meet you."

"Oh, okay, you're Tookie's brother. I should have known. You both look alike."

"Oh, no, dear boy, I don't look nothing like that old man at all!"

"Apparently you must look somewhat like me, Victor." Tookie laughed.

"Ah no, I don't see it."

"Are you two always this comical together?" Andrea wondered.

"For the most part, I'd say. I'll let you in on a secret, Mrs. Craven."

"Oh, really?"

"Our mama used to say I was the most handsome of the two."

"Oh, really, Victor. And why wouldn't mama ever give you a mirror to look into?"

"Poor Tookie. Has old age already caught up with you? As I remember it, I think it was you she wouldn't give a mirror to!"

"Would you like me to call your wife and tell her you're staying for supper?"

"Oh, okay. Mama always said you were the second cutest."

"Well, brother, if that's what you want to believe, go right ahead."

"See there, Mrs. Craven, Mr. Craven? Tucker knows I'm telling the truth!"

"Hardly! One more peep from you and I'll put you in the corner!"

"You remember I used to write on the walls and get you in trouble?"

"I most certainly do. Mama thought it was me who was doodling my name. I tell you I couldn't count on one hand how many times I had to paint that wall for you."

"You always got me back, though, didn't you?"

"Well, dear brother, you left me no choice. Now is everyone ready to eat?"

"I don't know bout y'all, but I'm starved." John said.

"I'm going to see if Chloe wants some of this food," Andrea said to everyone. "Chloe, Mr. Blackwell made us some country fried steak with mashed potatoes and macaroni. You want to come eat?"

"I don't want any of that damn food. Besides, daddy said I couldn't have supper, remember? Maybe if you're lucky I'll die of starvation."

"Chloe, I'm asking you if you want to come eat."

"I'm so tired of people who can't listen. You're all the same. I thought I told you clearly, I didn't want any of that damn food."

"Fine, whatever. Starve then. I don't think I care anymore."

"You never did. I finally realized that because Illusion told me."

"Just watch your cartoons," Andrea said before she left the room. "We don't need to worry about Chloe eating with us. She's refusing to."

"Is she still on the couch?"

"That's where I left her," Andrea told John.

"Tookie, do your doors upstairs have locks?" John asked.

"I have a master key."

"I want Chloe locked out from each room. I don't want her ruining anymore of your stuff. Can I borrow that key for a moment?"

"Here it is. The door to my study is a bit of a nuisance. Make sure you pull on the door as you're locking it."

"I'll be sure to. Be back in a moment."

"What's all this about locking doors and ruined stuff, Tucker?" Victor questioned his brother.

"Chloe went on a rampage earlier and tore up some pictures of Evelyn and me. During that time she made her way into Evelyn's doll room and broke nearly every single doll that Evelyn collected."

"What led to this behavior?" Victor queried.

"Excuse me, I don't mean to interrupt," Andrea said softly. "But didn't Tookie tell you about the problem?"

"He told me you found a journal in your home that needed to be translated. Was that not your problem?"

"I'm afraid that's just part of it," Andrea explained. "Ah, how do I tell you this without you thinking I'm crazy?"

"Feel free to speak your mind. I'll tell you after it sinks in if I think you're crazy."

"Victor, we're dealing with a serious matter at this time. Please try to act civil," Tookie told him.

"I'm terribly sorry. I didn't mean to offend anyone," Victor apologized. "Now what's bothering you, Mrs. Craven?"

Andrea went into detail about the house at seventeen-twenty-three East Waldburg Street just as John entered the room.

CHAPTER NINETEEN

"So you see why we need that journal translated?" Andrea pondered to Victor. "We all think it might explain why Illusion was created, and maybe it could give us an origin to what she is."

"We're also hoping there might be something in it that could inform us how to stop her," John added.

"I've heard some ghost stories in my time, but nothing close to this. I know my brother to be a logical man, and if he believes in this, I know that I can, too. I have no reason to doubt his logic. My brother has a brilliant mind. I know I can trust him. I also believe in what you and John have told me as well."

"Then I take it you don't think we're crazy?" Andrea asked.

"Not in the least. I won't lie and say the story doesn't sound far-fetched or unbelievable, but we need to realize that strange occurrences like this are in fact possible. I think it's more of a rarity because it's not something you hear about every day. It's not your typical haunting that you read in a book or see in film," explained Victor. "Have you thought about contacting a priest at all?"

"We've talked about it, indeed, but then your brother here told us about three holy men who dropped dead on the stairs to our home. It seems apparent that this thing clearly does not like anyone who has a connection to the church."

"Did you think about contacting someone who works in the field of parapsychology?"

"I don't know about, John, but I've given some thought to it. Then I think, what if something bad happens to them? Savannah and Illusion have a way of giving life to your worst nightmare. They use the image of someone who was once in your life, but has since passed away. They then put you through hell as they twist the personality of the person they're betraying into a grisly specter."

"It doesn't matter if that person had the kindest heart while alive?" Victor wondered.

"No, they can take on the image of the kindest person you ever knew and turn them into the darkest being you ever met," Andrea explained.

"What about the one friend of yours who saw their uncle in your home?"

"Rich," John responded.

"Yes, him. But wasn't his uncle a bit on the crazy side? The man killed his children and nearly his nephew for that account. What are your thoughts to this?"

"That's true, but his Uncle Fred wasn't always crazy. He was a civil man who once loved his kids as much as any father, maybe even a little more. He started losing it when he found out his wife wanted a divorce along with complete custody of their three kids. He was worried that she'd end up winning, so he planned on killing the kids to avoid her from getting custody. He set up a camping trip and it was then he had planned on shooting Rob, Lily and Cooper. The only thing he didn't count on was the fact that his nephew was going to be there. Rich's parents had to leave town for an emergency, so his father asked Fred if he and Eileen could drop Rich off for a few days. It was being at the wrong place at the wrong time that nearly cost Rich his life. Fred truly went mad that night. He lost touch with who he was as his personality took on a drastic change, then he turned into someone else just like that."

"May I ask a question?" Tookie wondered to John.

"Sure, what's that?"

"Did you ever wonder if the reason Fred decided to kill his kids was due to something else?"

"What do you mean, Tookie?"

"What if he killed them as punishment to his wife for leaving him?"

"Tucker, we're not in court discussing a case you're representing," Victor told his brother. "The Cravens don't need a lawyer; what they need right now is a person who knows Latin. We need to focus more on their problem at hand and not a triple homicide that took place many years ago."

"I'm sorry, you're right; even though I hate to admit it."

"But you said it anyway," Victor responded. "What'd y'all say we clear off this table? I'd like to take a crack at that journal."

Andrea carried the journal over to Victor while he unpacked a few of his things at the table, "Here it is, sir," she said as she presented the diary. "Now, I'll only give this to you if you promise me one thing."

"What's that, dear?"

"Assure me that you'll say a prayer before you open this book."

"You're worried about its contents?"

"I'm afraid the things you'll read will be dark."

"If it makes you feel better, I'll say a small prayer." Victor recited some words in his mind, then opened the journal to the first page. "I can tell you this now, this book by all means is not a regular journal. The opening page says *Mei Liber Libri Consisto Niger Deliciae,* which roughly translates to my book of black charms. It was written by Cyrus Cornu, which y'all already knew."

"What kind of journal is it?" Andrea wondered.

"It appears to be more of a *grimoire.* The word comes from the old French word *gramaire.* It's a means to invoke angels or demons, depending on the practitioner. In Egypt a similar book was written that goes by a far different name. The Necronomicon or *The Book Of The Dead.* The type of person who messed with this sort of thing had to be experienced. These books weren't made for the curious mind. It was said to be the real stuff, the true means to invoking a demon or angel."

"How do you know this?" John asked Victor.

"I have a friend who studies Theology and the different religions which people practice. He's been into that sort of thing since he was a child. He's one of the greatest experts I know."

"Do you prefer that we leave you alone so you can figure that journal out?" John asked.

"No, not at all. I can translate a sentence or paragraph as I go along. I can explain my findings as I read, and we can all talk about it as a group," Victor said as he flipped through the pages. "Mmm that's odd."

"What's odd?" wondered Andrea.

"This grimoire is not only written in Latin, there's a lot of Spanish merged into it as well. Tucker, would you mind fixin some coffee? I believe I'm going to want a cup."

"Mr. Cornu was from Spain. Would that account for the Spanish written in there?" wondered John.

"It's likely. Give me a minute here while I decipher some of this."

"Take all the time you need. We're not going anywhere."

"There are some pages that appear to be part of a diary which he was keeping. This is talking about an experiment Mr. Cornu is wanting to try. He names it The Illucious Monstrosity Experiment."

"I'm sorry, but the what?" John asked with curiosity.

"It sounds like he wants to create a monster and bestow upon it the name Illucious."

"So we're not dealing with a demon then?" John inquired.

"Monsters are demons, son," Victor added.

"Are you also saying that this thing's true name is actually Illucious?"

"I would say so. I think it adopted the name Illusion because whatever was summoned had been placed into the body of a female doll. Make any sense?"

"I suppose."

"Cyrus wanted to create something beyond evil, and he wanted to grant it life through something that seemed so innocent and trusting. What would be the most perfect idea he figured then to place the evil into a child's doll."

"Why did he want to resurrect something that terrible?"

"Hold on, hold on, I'm getting to that. He wanted to know if a demon could live in an inanimate object and be controlled by its master. There's an unusual page here dedicated to a list of demons and their correspondences, *demonio ante violencia, Bechard,* which means demon of violence and its name is Bechard. Then we have the demon of fear, Agramon."

"How many are listed in all?" Andrea wondered.

"All together there's a sum of seven."

"Scarlette said she and Wallace heard that many voices or more come from the doll. Please continue. I didn't mean to interrupt."

"I'm just going to run through this so y'all bear with me now. There's a demon of deprivation, Balberith, a demon of delusion, Balbon, the demon of tricks, Belial, the demon of deception, Jezebeth, and a demon of lies, Pytho. I think we know now who old Cyrus was invoking. Not just one, but all of them."

"You think he called upon all those demons in just one night?" Tookie asked his brother.

"I wouldn't doubt it, but I don't think he realized how much power he was summoning," Victor explained. "Here's a rather morbid take on how the doll was to be created through Cyrus's eyes. I don't think any of you are going to like what you hear, but I must continue. It says here, *sesos ante en loco, lengua ante en mentiroso, corazo ante en asesino, ojos ante en infiel, labio ante en deshonor boca, e pelo ante en puta*. Y'all really don't want to know what that says."

"No, we probably don't, but we need to know. Please tell us," John asked.

"All right, then. The doll that your daughter has is no ordinary doll, but y'all already know that. It seems as though it's far more complicated then what you think or may already know."

"How can it get anymore complicated?" Andrea questioned Victor.

"Trust me, with what I just read, it can."

"Can you please explain a little more clearly about what you revealed?" Tookie asked his brother.

"Cyrus wanted to make a doll composed of human organs and body parts. He wanted the doll to have the brains of a madman, a tongue of a liar, the heart of a killer, the eyes of the unfaithful or a deceiver if you will, and the lips of a dishonorable mouth. Right here it says that the hair of the doll was supposed to be from a tramp and soaked in the blood of a virgin, then dried. This is getting into some pretty hefty stuff. The inside of the doll is said to be painted with the blood of an innocent, a child, a baby. This man was outright insane, and you say he was a professor? He talks about robbing graves at night to obtain some of his specimens which he carefully preserves in formaldehyde. He then talks about going to the park and scoping out any mother who may not be attendant to her baby. During that time

Cyrus plans to kidnap the child and take it back to his house where he'll attempt to bleed it by slow death. Wow, I don't know if I can interpret anymore. This is a little too disturbing to read. Tucker, where's that cup of coffee I asked for?"

"In the pot. I'm sorry I didn't get it sooner. I got caught up by that book. I'll get it now. Anyone else care for a cup?" he wondered.

"Victor, is there a lot more you have to decipher?" Andrea asked.

"I think what we've learned is only the beginning. Let me see what else this says. He talks about a Madame Arabella who runs a brothel on the other side of town. She keeps a candle lit in the window to notify men that she has girls available for hire. Cyrus plans to use one of their scalps as a wig for Illucious. He states that he's going to wrap a gag around her mouth to make it seem like a kinky game, then slice her throat with one clean stroke before he takes the hair from her head."

"Does it mention where he plans to kill the girl?" Andrea asked.

"My guess is that Cyrus could have killed her in any place of his choosing. He might have taken her life while occupying one of Madame Arabella's rooms, but on the other hand, he could have simply taken her back to his house and killed her there if he paid enough."

"That's a scary thought. When I was in the hidden room, horrible visions were perceived in my mind. The blood on the table made me think of a person being tortured."

"His slayings were more than likely to be sacrificial. Cyrus probably believed if he could sacrifice human souls to those demons, they would accept him as a faithful servant and person of honor who, in return could weep rewards from those he had summoned. What Cyrus didn't know is that Illucious would come to be blessed with supreme power that couldn't be controlled by his own will. He gave life to something that was ready and willing to kill whoever it chose. Illucious is a demon of many that rules in one body, Chloe's doll. To fight this evil would be like fighting the devil himself."

"Does Cyrus speak of a way to stop it at all?" John inquired.

"If it does, it would be discussed at the back of this book. Allow me to finish translating these words, and I'll let y'all know what else Cyrus has to say." Victor studied the journal for awhile. "This part is dealing with Cyrus's notes, which he calls *The Construction*." Victor began to read below the title. *"The construction of the doll will be quite intricate as everything has to be right. I've salvaged doll parts that had been broken* and thrown away to reconstruct my own. Halloween is coming soon. I plan then to cast my spell and give Illucious life. The workings are in my favor. There's said to be a full moon on that night. I plan to make a quality doll the same way a crafted dollmaker might. There will have to be some exceptions made as for placing in the internal organs.

After the inside has been splattered and dried with the blood of an innocent, I will seal the brains of a madman within the skull. The same shall go with the heart of a killer, which will be plastered inside the chest cavity. I have already taken the glass eyes from their sockets so I may replace them with the eyes of a deceiver. A small piece of skin from a liar's tongue will be attached to the oral cavity as I use the fleshy folds of a dishonorable mouth to form lips for Illucious. After the doll is completely crafted, I will then add the donations of hair from the tramp which was soaked in virgin's blood. I've been watching a woman by the name of Cora Gairden when I visit the park. She has a nine-month-old daughter by the name of Cecily. Cora likes to read while Cecily is fast asleep in her carriage. This will make for a rather simple pick up. I always pass by Cora in plain view each day as I stroll along the way, but yet she fails to even notice I'm there. What a terrible advantage she bestows upon me, but still it's her mistake, so I mustn't care. Her fault will be my long term gain. As for my virgin, there's a young girl who walks past my home each day to and from school. It would be easy access to take her. The child is usually alone. She looks like the type of girl who is willing to help someone in need. When I see her walking down my street, I'll force myself to trip and fall. She'll ask if there's anything she could do to help me. I'll tell her to walk me into my home, then I'll have the child when I lock her in. The last person I need is a tramp, but that will be any random whore at Madame Arabella's house. My plans are coming to perfection. My dark lords shall be proud. Just a few days to go, then I can execute my intentions," Victor translated aloud to everyone.

"God this guy was one sick bastard," John interrupted.

"Yeah, a sick bastard who was messing with some pretty dark stuff," Andrea replied.

"Y'all would have that right one hundred percent. Listen, the page I'm looking at now talks about invoking the demons, Bechard, Agramon, Balberith, Balbon, Belial, Jezebeth and Pytho. Cyrus chose to summon those seven demons so he could place them into the doll under the order of possession by means of creating Illucious. His plans were to create a demon controlled by seven correspondences violence, fear, deprivation, delusion, tricks, deception and lies. It's like he wanted to create a high ranking demon of his own to control and use as his servant. Here's more of his notes on this page.

"It is now the twenty-ninth of October and I plan to take an unlucky whore's life, Gisele Whittier, a petite tramp with ivory pale skin and navy blue eyes, one of Madame Arabella's favorite dames, and quite pretty for that matter.

It leads me to shame for I had to take the life of such a beautiful face. I cut Gisele's throat from ear to ear as I felt her warm blood rush over my hand and cover my face. I hated to remove her scalp for the disturbing new look turned her into someone else. She resembled not one bit of the tramp I had first brought into my home.

Maybe I did a messy job. I'll be sure to be more careful on the next one. The thirtieth of October, little Felicia McBeth.

It was the virgin's turn to be taken by death and her blood collected as it drained from her body. My plan worked as I expected. Little Felicia was on her way to school when I met her just outside my house. I acted like I stumbled on the sidewalk before I fell to the ground. Felicia ran up to me after witnessing the accident. She helped me into my home, and it was then I locked her in.

The problem with Felicia was that she was too trusting. She fought with me as I carried her up into my attic. It wasn't until she saw the room that she became quite nerved and scare. I shackled her onto my table as she started to cry. I made small incisions on both her wrists, then inserted small tubes beneath her skin to drain the blood. I made a larger incision to her throat and placed an ample-sized tube beneath the skin and drained more. It took several hours and many more tubes to completely bleed her body dry.

I must do it faster next time when I bleed the innocent child. I filled jugs containing Felicia's excrements and labeled them virgin's blood. That is all I'll say for now.

The thirty-first of October. Today the abomination of evil will be born; its name, Illucious. I have one final sacrifice I must attend to and with luck I have her here. Cecily Gairden has an inattentive mother who at the time didn't realize her daughter was being taken along with her carriage. That was at seven-forty yesterday evening. I've come to wonder, will this child be at all missed? I guess Cora Gairden will take Cecily's loss as a punishment.

It is almost time to begin the incantations and empower my spell. It is two-thirty in the morning. We are now two and a half hours into Halloween. I will begin the ceremony at precisely three a.m. and use Cecily as my offering before I shed her blood.

The parts to the doll will be set upon the table with black candles alit. The jars containing my filthy specimens will be placed on the table as well, and then there will be Cecily. All of my supplies will be before me as I recite my words. Demons will be conjured, an offering will be made, a sacrifice will succeed and the arrival of Illucious will be achieved."

This appears to be all that was said through his words. The rest of the stuff written on these pages are the spells and incantations Cyrus used when he made Illucious. I don't think I see anything worded in here on how to stop the demon itself."

"Please keep searching. There has to be something in there that talks about it," Andrea begged.

"No, my dear, I'm afraid not," Victor told her as he turned to the last page. "The only thing left now are a few bare pages." Victor flipped through each one when a piece of loose paper slipped down to the table, "What do we have here?" he said, picking it up.

"What is it?" Tookie asked Victor.

"It's a piece of paper, Tucker. Give me a moment to open it."

"Well?" Tookie asked with anticipation.

"It says *quemadmodum ut confuto desatento daemon.*"

"What's that mean?" John inquired.

"How to stop an unruly demon, that's what it means, and that's what it says here. Why doesn't everyone take a sigh of relief, because we've found something! I believe this will tell you how to stop Illucious for good."

"Oh, please, Victor, say you're not joking," Andrea said.

"I'm not joking. This says how to stop that monstrosity."

"What do we have to do?"

"It doesn't sound easy, I'm afraid. There's a great deal of work that has to be done."

"What kind of work?" wondered John.

"Cyrus says if Illucious should become self-willed and unruly, the only way to stop her is to take out her internal organs and drive a ceremonial knife through its heart and brain. He says to toss the remaining parts of the doll into a fire to destroy and vanquish the demon."

"That sounds impossible," stated Andrea. "How are we going to do that? Illucious is unbreakable."

"I don't think the intentions were to break it, I think what you have to do is pull the doll apart. Rip its head off, you'll have easy access to the brain. Use a knife to open the chest cavity and expose the heart. It might sound crazy, but it's worth the try."

"I think Illucious would kill us before we even got its head off. Isn't there an easier way to do this?"

"I'm sorry, Andrea, but that was the only thing Cyrus had written. It's either that way or no way."

"I just don't know if we can do it. It all sounds too complicated to even try. Do you think Illucious would follow us if we decided to move?" Andrea wondered while Victor glanced toward Tookie.

"What would you say to this?"

"I would probably say yes. You see, there's a reason Illucious went after Savannah their birthday. The same goes for Chloe. They all share that one thing in common. They were all born on the same day, Halloween. If Illucious wants Chloe that bad, it'd find a way to get her, no matter where she is. If you don't try to destroy the doll, I'll try myself," he told John and Andrea.

"I'll try, but I can't promise you that I'll beat it," added John.

"I'll help you then," Tookie told John assuringly.

"No, I appreciate your offer, but Illucious and Savannah have already tried to kill you once, not to mention poor Sam. I already know what to do; I'll try to stop Illucious myself. I don't want anyone else getting hurt."

"That's just too bad, John, because I'm going to help you. There's nothing you can do or say to stop me," Andrea told him.

"I'm helping you, too, son, and that's the end of it," Tookie replied.

"I guess that just leaves me now," added Victor. "I'm in, too, and there's no way you can get rid of me. We'll have our own small legion against Illucious."

"And when do we exactly plan on doing this?" John inquired.

"Well, since I'm already here, why not tonight?" Victor announced.

"Tonight?"

"Why not?"

"It just seems a little too quick."

"John, if you wait any longer, there's no thought into what might happen to you and your family," Tookie told him.

"But we don't have a plan."

"So why don't we make one?" Andrea insisted.

"Okay, so here's the deal, Tookie. You and Victor come by our house in about an hour or so. If Chloe isn't asleep, she'll wonder why you're there. We'll tell her that Victor wanted to stop in and say goodbye before he left town. We'll wait until she falls asleep and take Illucious from her side. Does everyone agree on this so far?" John wondered.

"I'm sure we're all with you one hundred percent," Tookie told him.

"I have a question about something that's been bothering me," said Andrea. "You all remember Cyrus saying on that piece of paper that the brain and heart were to be stabbed with a ceremonial knife?"

"What about it?" John questioned her.

"We don't have a ceremonial knife. Can we use a regular one?"

"That's a good question, Andrea," Tookie told her. "Cyrus did say to use a ceremonial knife. I believe that's what we'd have to use."

"Where can we get one, though?" John pondered aloud.

"Well, son, I don't know." Tookie turned to his brother. "Victor, what about you?"

"I think I know the place where we'll find one." Andrea added.

"What store would that be?" Tookie wondered.

"I'm sure we could find one in our home. All we have to do is go into that unholy room. Cyrus should still have one in there that we could use."

"What's better then having what you need already in your home? That'll save us some time from having to search around town for one," said Victor.

"I'm just dreading having to go back in there." Andrea gasped.

"You don't have to go. The three of us men will. Just show us where the room is," John told his wife. "We should probably get Chloe home. Andrea and I will try to get her to bed. I hope that will make things much easier on us. Tookie, you and Victor come on by in about an hour. Andrea and I will see y'all then."

Andrea gathered the diaries. "Thank you, Victor, for helping us.

You've been so kind. And Tookie, anytime you want to have us over for supper again, we'd be happy to come. Thanks for everything."

"It was my pleasure, dear. I'm glad you enjoyed yourself."

"Well, should we gather Chloe from Tookie's couch, then take her, Illucious and Savannah back to our house?" John implied.

"I'll lead y'all into the living room," Tookie stated.

"Chloe, come on. Time to go home," Andrea announced as she walked toward the couch. "Oh, God, where is she?"

"She's not here?" John wondered.

"No, she's gone, and so is Illucious."

"The doors upstairs are all locked, so she can't be up there. Are there any rooms she could get into down here, Tookie?"

"I'll go and check." Tookie returned moments later. "I couldn't find her."

"Where else could she be?" Andrea worried.

"Do you suppose she went back to y'all's house?" Victor asked as he ran the question across to them.

"I don't know. I guess it's possible," Andrea stated.

"Victor and I will come with y'all then."

"Are you sure?"

"Yes, ma'am. We're coming with y'all just in case you need some help."

"I guess we'll go now." Andrea walked out the door with everyone following behind. "Was it supposed to rain today?"

"I don't recall anything being in the forecast," replied Tookie.

"Well, it sure is pouring out here. By the time we get to our house we'll all be drenched."

"A downpour of rain won't hurt us. Come on, y'all. We got to go find your daughter," Tookie said.

CHAPTER TWENTY

They all rushed over to the Craven's home. Lighting rippled in the sky behind their house.

"The place looks pretty creepy right now," added Victor. "It's like a battle's brewing."

"There is, Victor, and we're all part of it," Tookie told his brother. "Saddle up, everyone. We have a war to win."

John unlocked the front door. As they slowly crept in, the house was dark and cold. John tried to flip on the switch, but there wasn't any power.

"What are we going to do? We can't see?" Andrea asked him.

"What we're going to do is try our best to find Chloe. I'll gather some flashlights."

"What's that awful smell?" Andrea wondered.

"I smell it, too," added John.

"It smells like sulphur," Tookie told them.

"But why?" Andrea asked.

"Usually the smell of sulphur is present when a demon is around," Victor told everyone.

"It never smelt like this before. It's so bad, it's about to make me sick," Andrea commented.

"Where are those flashlights, John?"

"I'm getting them, Tookie. Be there in a minute," he yelled from the kitchen. "Here we go. I'm afraid we only had two that I could find."

"That's all right, son. It's better to have some light than no light at all."

"I'm guessing Chloe's in her room. That'll be the first place we'll check."

"Should we break into groups, John? What if Chloe's somewhere else in the house? It might be better that we pair up in teams. What do you think?"

"Tookie, I'd say you're crazy, but you might be right."

"I take it we'll break into groups then?"

"Tookie, you go with Andrea while Victor comes with me. Is that all right with everyone?"

"I don't have a problem with that."

"Okay then, Victor and I will search upstairs while you and Andrea check down here."

"What if something bad should happen to one of us, John?" Andrea asked her husband.

"Let's hope nothing does, but just in case yell and someone will come to your aid."

"That works for me," added Victor. "Shall we get a move on then?"

"Should Tookie and I check the basement, too, John?"

"Leave no room unchecked." John and Victor walked carefully up the stairs. "Victor, try to stay as close to me as possible."

"I'll be sure to. No second guesses on that."

"There's a room to our left. We'll check there first."

"I'm right behind you." John entered the dark room shining his flashlight into each corner. "It looks empty. Should we move on?" John asked Victor as he flashed his light upon him.

"Why don't we check in the closet and under the bed? You know how kids like to hide in those places," Victor told him.

"I'll check under the bed first." John got down on his knees and took in a deep breath. "Here goes nothing," he said as he lifted the cover away from the floor and peered beneath the bed. "Clear. Let's check the closet."

"Do you need a hand getting up?"

"I think I can manage." John walked over to the closet with Victor at his side. "Count of three," John said as he took a breath. "One."

"Two!"

"Three!" they yelled.

"Shine that flashlight in there!"

"It's just an empty closet. Let's check Chloe's room." John and Victor returned to the hallway and stood before Chloe's door. "Are you ready, Victor?"

"Don't you have a candle or something I can hold for light?"

"There's a candle scone by your head. You'd have to hold the candle, though."

"I don't care. That'll work for me. You got a light?"

"Here's a match." John lit Victor's candle, then opened the door to Chloe's room.

"What a horrible cold I feel."

"You don't have to go in if you don't want to, Victor."

"God, that room's like ice."

"Stay here then."

"No, son, I'm coming with you. Remember, we're to stay together."

Just as Victor finished his sentence, the door slammed shut, separating him and John.

"What? What's going on? Why did you shut the door?" Victor yelled.

"I didn't. It shut itself!"

"I can't get this door to open! Are you all right in there?"

"For now, I am. I see what you mean by it feeling like ice in here. I wish I had a coat."

"Do you see your daughter at all?"

"No, just my own breath."

"Look around. I'll see if I can get this door open!"

"What the hell is this?"

"What is it, John? What'd you find?"

"Pictures behind Chloe's door."

"Well, what are they, son?"

"Oh, God, Victor. They're diagrams."

"For what, John? What?"

"It's how Chloe plans to kill Andrea and me. Oh, God, Victor, my picture has an axe through the head." John grabbed the pictures and tore them up. "Chloe's far more gone than I thought, Victor."

"Is that doll in the room with you?"

"Not that I can see. I'm going to walk over to Chloe's bed and check."

Victor continued to stand outside the door as he waited for John's reply. He looked down the hall as a strange feeling crept over him. That's when Victor heard the sound of a child's voice crying out.

"I want my daddy!" the little girl pleaded.

"Chloe, hon, is that you?" Victor yelled.

"I want my daddy!" she cried again.

"I'm coming, dear. I'm coming. Don't be afraid." Victor followed the cries down the hall to the bathroom. "It's Victor, Tookie's brother. I'm going to take you to your daddy, Chloe." Victor opened the door. Just as he did a flash of lightning lit through the window and brightened the room. In the corner Victor saw a little girl huddled on the floor with her chin buried into her chest, hiding her face. Victor walked up to the child and put his hand on her shoulder. "It's all right now, dear. I'll take you to your daddy." Suddenly the door slammed behind Victor's back. "Don't you worry, little one. I'll get us out of here."

"We can't leave," the girl cried to him.

"When I get the door open we can."

"It's shut for a reason, daddy," the little girl explained. "The illusion is for you to be stuck in here with me." The child lifted her head slowly as she kept her eyes set on Victor. "Do you recognize me now?" she asked while getting up from the floor.

Victor shined his candle upon the child. Looking back at him were two green eyes on a swollen, blood-covered face.

"The accident did this to me, remember?"

"Hannah?" Victor asked with confusion while he backed into the door.

"You do remember me. I didn't think you would, daddy. It's been thirty-three years since you last saw my face. I guess you can say I haven't changed much. I still have the wounds that car gave me after it ran me down. The pain has never declined either. I continue to live with it. Well, you know what I mean. I continue to exist with the suffering even in death. Each minute is like being hit with the agony all over again. I can bear it no longer, daddy. I've walked around with shattered bones and lacerations long enough. The only way for this to end is to have you come with me. I need you to take care of me and comfort my cries. We can walk into the light together. Before we know it, we'll be in a place where there is no suffering."

"You let her rest in peace, you blasphemous demon!"

"Is that what you think? Daddy, it's me, Hannah. Don't shun me aside as I ask for your help."

"Open this door right now, you unclean spirit!"

"Don't you remember the promise you made to me while you held my dying body? Must I refresh your memory for you?" Hannah's voice changed as it mimicked her father's. *"I promise if I could trade places with you I would. I wish it had been myself who were hit than to see your life wither away in my arms like this."*

"I would have traded places with you, but I couldn't, Hannah! God called you home that day instead of me." Victor broke down and started crying.

"I'm not here to trade places with you, father. I've only come to bring an end to your meaningless life."

"My life has not been meaningless!"

"Denial. It's such a sad sight when someone encounters it. Let go and trust me, father. Better things await you and me," Hannah said as she raised the silver object up to his face.

— **CHAPTER TWENTY ONE** —

"Chloe, if you're hiding in here, you better come out! I'm fed up with these games you and Illusion are playing. Why don't you just come on out so I can see you both?" John asked while he noticed the bedcover moving. "I know you're here. You can't fool me. Chloe, I'm giving you ten seconds to get out from under that bed. One, two, three, four, five, six, seven, eight."

Two arms reached out from beneath Chloe's bed and grabbed onto John's ankles. "Nine! Ten!" A man's voice quickly yelled back while he pulled John to the ground. Candles quickly lit as they all sparked flames at once. "And then there was light, Jonny, boy! I didn't figure you wanted to look upon your old man in the shelter of darkness, now did ya, son? We've been seeing a lot of each other lately now, haven't we? What's wrong there, Jonny? Oh, I see, you got a nice bump on your head. Are you just going to lie there? You know it's not nice to ignore your father when he's talking to you."

"Go to hell."

"Look around, son, cause this is it." He began to drag John around the room by his feet.

"Why are you doing this?"

"Because I can! This is *my* house and I will give you hell as long as you're in it. I'm going to drag you over here now because I have something I want to show you. You stay with me, John, I don't want you falling unconscious just yet."

"Please, leave my family and me alone. We'll move. You can have your house back!"

"Nice bargain, but no. When you came here, you brought someone with you that I needed. The consequences will always be the same. Each time one of my chosen children move in with their family, that child will convert to my ways and be ruled under me. I will teach them, just as I taught Savannah. Once they've completed that test, I'll know they are truly worthy for my legion."

"And exactly how do they become part of your legion, demon?"

"Dedication to me and suicide grants them entrance into my army. But enough talk about me and my children for now. As I said earlier, I have something to show you." John's father picked something up from the windowsill. "You might be surprised with the things you could find in one's home. I figured we could play a little game before your daughter begins hers. I have some kerosene in my hand here. Found it in your basement. I bet you didn't even know it was there, did you, son? Anyway, there's a lot of candles in here. If any of this kerosene should spill and a candle falls over, we'd be in a real fix, wouldn't we? You know if Chloe could see all that blood you've put on her walls, she'd be pretty upset. Chloe keeps a clean room. Oh, except for those dirty things she hides in her closet. The dear girl has an astounding fascination with rotting animal carcasses."

"You're lying!"

"I can assure you I'm not. The bird you had her bury? She dug it up; it's in her closet. Care to see? Or maybe another time. I know you're dying to get to the game. Instead of lighting the room on fire, I thought I'd burn you. I know you hear me talking, but yet I don't feel like you hear what I'm saying. Did you hit your head that hard or what? Turn around, you bloody mess. Oh, that's good. Real good. You have a nail embedded in your head, you stupid boy. That wasn't supposed to happen. You should be putting up a fight with me right now. Instead you're just lying there. Oh, well, maybe a little fire will wake you up!"

"No, please, you don't have to do that," John said weakly while his father poured the kerosene on his son's legs.

— **CHAPTER TWENTY TWO** —

"I'll go down the stairs first, okay, dear? You just stay close behind me."

"Tookie, this storm has me too afraid to go down into that basement," Andrea told him.

"I can go by myself. I'll be all right."

"No, I won't let you go alone, and anyway, I wouldn't let you leave me here in the dark without a flashlight. Would you be mad if I held onto your shirt?"

"Of course not, Andrea. You hold on as tightly as you want. I'll admit, I'm afraid, too, but I'm happy you're with me. Now, shall we go find your daughter?" Tookie started down the stairs as Andrea clung closely to him. The stairs creaked and cracked beneath their feet with each step they took.

"Can we hurry up? I don't like it down here."

"We'll do this as fast as we can, I promise." Tookie walked Andrea further into the basement. "Look, look. I think I see a flashlight over there. Let's see if it works. Looks like you have one for yourself now, too. Does that make you feel better?"

"Only by ten percent. Right now I'm not liking this basement. Please, can we hurry?"

"Let's just check over there, then we can go."

"All right, Chloe's not here. Can we go now, please, Tookie? I don't want to be down here another minute. I can't breathe."

"Okay, dear, okay. We're going."

"Can you move a little faster, Tookie? I don't mean to be rude, but I have to get out of here. I don't feel right."

"We're almost at the top of the stairs. Then we'll be in the kitchen."

"That makes me feel better."

"All right, my dear, we made it. Now you can breathe easy." Tookie opened the door and walked into the kitchen, but before Andrea could make it through, the door slammed shut before her. Andrea began to panic when the door wouldn't open.

"Tookie, please open the door!"

"I'm trying, Andrea, but it's locked!"

"Get me out of here! I don't want to be in the basement alone! Please, get me out! Please!" Andrea started beating at the door in a frenzied panic. "Please, please, Tookie, open the door!"

"Try to calm down, dear. I'll get this door open for you in a moment."

"Please hurry. I think I hear something down here!"

"What do you hear?"

"It sounds like someone's reciting a nursery rhyme or something. Tookie, please hurry. It's getting closer! Tookie, please!"

"Is it Ivy or Adrienne..."

"Who carries an axe..."

"To hack up mommy - -wack, wack, wack."

"Tookie, it's the twins! Get me out of here now! Break the damn door, I don't care!"

"Andrea, this is solid wood. I can't break it!"

"There's a key on top of the television for this door. See if you can find!"

"Is it Ivy or Adrienne..."

"Who carries an axe..."

"To hack up mommy - - wack, wack, wack."

"You're not here! You're not here!" she yelled repeatedly. Andrea looked down and saw the twins approaching the stairwell as they continued to recite their rhyme.

"Hello, mommy."

"Looks like we have another chance encounter."
"We bet you thought..."
"You'd never see us again?" finished Adrienne.
"Ever, ever again."
"But look, we're here once more."
"Once more, mommy, once more."
"And as always..."
"We have our axe."
"This time for you..."
"The game will be over," remarked Ivy.
"You can't escape the final round."
"No escaping, mommy."
"You won't get away."
"Those are the facts."
"So, mommy..."
"Have you missed..."
"Our nicely sharpened axe?"

- CHAPTER TWENTY THREE -

"I'm coming, Andrea! I just found the key. I'm going to get you out of there!"

"Tucker Blackwell, you will do no such thing. You hear?"

"Evelyn?"

"Who'd you think I was, dear? I know for certain I ain't your mama. That old hag never liked me too much. I hope she burns in hell. Did you hear me, Tucker? I said, I hope she burns in hell because that's where she's at. She's forced to sit upon a burning pile of coal and brimstone as punishment for her sins. And you always thought your mother was perfect. The truth isn't pretty, is it, Tucker Blackwell? I don't mean to make you mad, my dear Tookie, but you had a right to know."

"You're nothing more than a liar. I don't believe a word you say."

"Tucker, you never had a problem believing me before. Why do you now?"

"What do you want with me?"

"I want to riddle your body with the pain from my cancer and let it engulf you. We can share in the same pleasurable pain as it spreads throughout your body."

"Get away from me!"

"I just want a kiss, my love."

"Get away from me this instant."

"But I didn't get one before my passing, so I think I owe this one to you."

"God, I call upon you for strength in this battle!"

"He can't hear you, Tucker Blackwell. It's no use. You're wasting your time."

"Blessed is the man who trusts in the Lord and has made the Lord his hope and confidence," Tookie said in Evelyn's face.

"Come unto me, ye who are weary and overburdened, and I will give you rest," Evelyn responded while she held Tookie against the basement door and kissed his lips.

"May you be damned back to hell," Tookie said as he slid to the floor. "Where did you come from?"

— CHAPTER TWENTY FOUR —

"We promise it'll be quick," said Ivy.
"Quick, mommy. Real quick."
"We wouldn't lie."
"Oh, never. Not to you."
"But if by some means..."
"You don't believe us..."
"Then we can show you."
"Example," Adrienne said as she held her arm out for Ivy.
"Oh, God, what are you doing?" Andrea cried.
"Showing you."
"See how quickly..."
"I cut off her arm?"
Andrea could hear the sound of Tookie's cries from behind the door as she tried to get out. "What's going on?" Andrea cried.
"Can't you see, mommy?"
"You're in a house that creates illusions."
"But don't forget..."
"There is some reality."
Andrea gathered every ounce of her strength and pushed against the door as hard as she could. Never once did she turn around to face the evil which crept up the stairs behind her. With luck Andrea was

able to get the door open and escape. She made it safely into the kitchen where she found Tookie hunched behind the door.

"No!" Andrea screamed when she took in the sight. His body looked withered and blistered beneath the flashes of light that filled the room. "Mr. Blackwell, can you hear me? Oh, God, what have they done to you?" she asked as she shined her flashlight into his face revealing the bloody mess. It was then Andrea realized Tookie was gone. She fell to the floor and started to cry uncontrollably by his feet. "We should have never gotten you involved in this. Look what it's cost you," she wailed. "Please forgive us. I'm sorry. I'm so sorry." Andrea sat on the floor for a moment to gather her thoughts. "John, Victor? God, please tell me they're safe."

Andrea looked at Tookie once more as she realized the large C carved on his neck. Then it dawned on her. Tookie's flashlight was missing. She looked around the room, but found no sign of it. As Andrea was walking past the kitchen table she heard the sound of small feet racing across the floor accompanied by an eerie laughter. Andrea grew frightened and began to walk faster just before she felt the pain in her foot. She took another step when she experienced it again.

The agony felt like scissors being jammed repeatedly through Andrea's skin. Suddenly she began to rattle her leg as she cried out in pain. As bolts of lightning lit the kitchen through the windows, Andrea was able to catch a glimpse of Illusion beneath the light gnawing away at her ankle.

"Get off of me!" she yelled in anger just before Illusion drove the scissors into her calve. Illusion slid across the room and hit the wall not more than ten feet from Andrea. "How'd you like that, you damn doll?" She kept her eyes on Illusion as she pulled the scissors out of her leg. Andrea let out her pain as the scissors dislodged. "And I thought you were some kind of almighty demon with tremendous power. But all you can do is attack me with scissors!"

"Who are you to undermine my abilities?"

"You should know my name by now! I know yours, Illucious!" Andrea limped out of the room and drug herself up the stairs.

— CHAPTER TWENTY FIVE —

"Mama's coming, Chlo! I'm going to get you out of here! John! Victor! Where are you?"

"Andrea, please help! Get me out of here!" Victor begged as he beat on the bathroom door.

"I'm coming, Victor, I'm coming!"

"Hurry, hurry, please! You have to get me out of here!"

Andrea struggled with the door as Victor continued to beat upon the walls and cry, "I promise I'll get you out!"

"Please hurry. It's dark in here!"

Andrea got the door open and shined her flashlight into the room. On the floor beneath the window Andrea saw Victor trembling with fright.

"The pain. I can't take it any longer," Victor cried.

"I've got to get you out of here. Come on, Victor!"

"My arms and face. They're burning. I feel like I'm on fire."

"Why do you feel like you're burning?" Andrea asked with concern.

"Hannah, my daughter, peeled my skin away with a straight razor."

Andrea got Victor out of the bathroom and shined her light onto his arms. "Oh, God." She gasped, "Try to hold your skin down on this arm."

"What about my face?"

"It's not as bad. Your arms are what have the deepest wounds. Let me get a towel to help cover this up."

"I'm so glad someone came along. I've been yelling and screaming for what felt like an hour."

"It's okay. We're together now," Andrea assured him.

"Is Tucker all right? Did you leave him with John?"

"Oh, God, Victor."

"What, dear? What is it? Did Tucker get hurt?"

Andrea broke down and started to cry heavily. "I'm sorry, Victor. I'm so sorry."

"Oh, no. How bad is he?" Victor panicked.

"I don't know how to tell you this."

"It's real serious, isn't it?"

Andrea tried to control her cries as she fought to say the truth. "They got him! They got him! I'm sorry, Victor, I'm sorry. I didn't know it was going to happen." Andrea continued to cry.

A saddened look took to Victor's face. "My brother's gone?"

"He's down in the kitchen. I'm sorry, Victor. I had no choice but to leave him there."

"It's okay, dear. I understand. I can see you're not in the best shape either. You were lucky like me and you escaped with your life."

"Oh, God, Victor, where's John?"

"He was locked in Chloe's room last I seen him. We got separated when the door shut after he entered."

"We have to get him out now!" Andrea raced down the hall as fast as she could with her injuries. "John! John! Oh, please be all right."

"We have to get this door open. The damn thing won't budge."

"On the count of three we'll shove our bodies into it. Ready?"

"Now! One, two, three!" The door gave way as Andrea and Victor stumbled into the room.

A horrible sight was presented before them that caused Andrea to scream when she saw her husband's lifeless body against the wall. Andrea felt a knife go through her heart as she gazed upon him. "No! John! No!" she cried.

Victor grabbed Andrea quickly to shelter her from the sight. "Don't look, my dear. John wouldn't want you to see him like this."

"He wasn't supposed to leave me!" she cried on Victor's shoulder.

"He can't be gone! He can't be gone! He just can't!" Andrea started sliding slowly through Victor's arms. "They split his head in half straight down the center of his skull," Andrea cried out. "But that wasn't enough for them, so they set his legs on fire and carved a large H onto his stomach. John didn't deserve this, Victor."

"I'm sorry for your loss. I know how you feel."

"We have to stop Illusion and find Chloe or one of us is liable to be next."

A violent crack of thunder ripped through the sky and echoed throughout Andrea's house. "I feel this battle brewing, Victor, and with it, some serious conflict is going to arise," Andrea stated as she watched out the window. "We're going to put an end to this tonight. It has to stop now. We're doing this for the O'Connor family and for all the other victims, which now include my husband and your brother."

"I think we should take a moment and gather our strength. The final battle will be the worst fight. We need to figure out what we're going to do rather than rushing into an unplanned event. Do you remember what needs to be done to destroy the doll?"

"It's all in my mind. Every last word."

"Andrea, where in this house do you think Illusion and Savannah are hiding Chloe?"

"My worst fears say the attic in the hidden room beneath the floor."

"Are you ready to do this, Andrea?"

"I never thought I would be, but I am now," she said with confidence. "What about you? Do you think you're ready, Victor?"

"We have to get this done, like you said."

"We need to find that ceremonial knife first. There should be one in that forsaken room beneath the floor."

"First check the places where you'd think it might be to save time."

"I think there may be one in the armoire."

— CHAPTER TWENTY SIX —

ANDREA AND VICTOR STOOD BEFORE THE attic.

"Scarlette O'Conner's body was found here at the place of her death. I couldn't imagine being pushed down these steep, dreadful stairs," said Andrea, reminiscing the past.

"Stay alert to all your corners. You don't want to be a victim of an attack and not know it."

"My heart's pounding so fast and exhilaration is racing through my veins. I'm more alert now then I was in the beginning. What are we waiting for? Let's open that door."

"It's locked."

"Just like all the other doors in this house. I'm not surprised."

"Wouldn't it be nice if open sesame actually worked for once?"

"I think it has. We're being invited into the room," Andrea said as the door creaked open. The attic was lit with lustrous lighting as candles burned brightly, diminishing the dark. In the center of the room Victor and Andrea found Chloe sitting poised on the floor before them.

"I wasn't expecting either of you for another ten minutes or so. I must say, you both got here quicker than I thought."

"Chloe, where's Illucious?"

"Correction! You mean *Illusion*," Chloe yelled. "She's around."

"I wasn't asking if she was around; I asked where she was. Now tell me!"

"Must you yell so loudly, mommy?"

"I will ask you once more, where is she?"

"I think we have other important issues to talk about. I can clearly see that daddy and Tucker aren't joining y'all. What a shame. Did something happen?" She giggled. "It was pretty messy on their behalf, wouldn't you say? I don't think you could get all this blood out of my clothing even if you tried! Oh, I'm sorry neither of you can see the stains, right? Should I ask Illusion to reveal them before y'all's eyes so you could see?"

"Chloe, what are you talking about? Blood-stained clothes?"

"May you be blessed with sight!" she yelled. "Reveal!"

Before Andrea and Victor's eyes came the form of a different sight. In the center of the room Chloe sat covered with the blood of her father and neighbor.

"I told you it was messy. I'm all sticky now, but I have no cares." Chloe tilted her head to the side. "You're still confused, aren't you? I thought my clues would lead you to understanding," Chloe explained. "You think Illusion and Savannah killed daddy and Tucker, but you're both wrong. Adults; you really are stupid! Illusion and Savannah helped, but I was the one who got the job done. They were only there to expose you to fear and inflict some pain. The killing part was my scenario. Do you understand now?"

"You did that to them?" Andrea cried.

"How could you?" Victor wailed.

"I'll be more clear with my speech. I found daddy sitting on the floor already dying from the nail embedded into his brain while his legs blazed with fire like a pair of burning logs!"

Chloe reached behind her back and brought something into view for Andrea and Victor to see. "Cyrus Cornu, whom I know you're familiar with, had a rather wide selection of battle axes in his personal collection. I chose to use this one on daddy. It's a rather nasty looking device now, isn't it? I think so," Chloe said as she was examining the blade. "Don't either of you try to come closer to me. Stay there. An invisible shield of energy circulates around me. If you walk into it, I guarantee you'll be shocked to death. The reason for me telling you this is because I have yet to finish talking. Mommy, wasn't it always you who said respect those that speak before you? So I invite you to listen in on my unimaginable details!"

"How could you be so malicious?"

"You're impatient, mommy. Give me time. I was just getting to the good stuff. Where was I? Oh, yes, the battle axe. That's how daddy met his demise. As his body quivered from shock I carved the H into his stomach with his very own hunting knife."

"Enough!" Andrea shouted.

"I had to leave my mark! Tucker was my first victim of the night. I had to get to him quickly in order to claim his life. Evelyn gave Tucker a gentle kiss and caused cancer to take over his body. He was already withering and blistering when I got to the kitchen. It wasn't until he dropped to the floor that he had seen me."

"Andrea, shut her up!"

"I guarantee you I took him by shock. I had seen his flashlight laying by his side so I picked it up."

"Chloe, I'm telling you once more. Enough."

"I am almost certain I broke every bone in his face. You have no idea what bones sound like when they're being smashed to dust."

"Andrea, make her shut up."

"Victor, as your brother laid there gargling on his own blood, I carved the C into his neck. My plans were to carve each letter of my name into my victims. Mommy, you were supposed to be O and Victor was supposed to be L, but somehow you both escaped. I'm to receive the final letter E just before I take my life, then I'll have honorable entrance into Illusion's legion and be of third rank. There will be others to come along who'll be assigned to their positions. But that will come later, for I am what matters now."

"You're insane! You've been taken by Illusion's twisted mind and she's brainwashed you. Chloe, you have to fight this!"

"I was chosen at birth to fulfill my right. I am destined for greatness. It's important I don't turn my back on it. I still have something to do, and that's to eliminate the both of you," Chloe said as she walked toward her mother and Victor. "I think I like this axe. It suits me quite well."

"Victor, run!" Andrea shouted.

"Where do I go?"

"Downstairs! Hurry!"

– CHAPTER TWENTY SEVEN –

THEY WERE RUSHING TO GET DOWN the attic stairs when Victor lost his footing and slipped. He landed at the foot of the stairs while Andrea helped him up. "Keep moving!" she screamed. "Hurry! Hurry! Go!"

They made it down to the first level almost out of breath with their hearts pounding heavily. Andrea stopped dead in her tracks when she saw the front door swing open. Between the frame Andrea and Victor saw an outline of a person.

"Anyone home?" the voice asked.

"Rich?"

"Yeah, Andrea, it's me!"

"We have to get out of here now!"

"What the hell? Andrea, watch out!" Rich yelled as Victor pulled her away from the blade Chloe swung upon her. "I knew things would be bad before I got here!" Rich shouted. "Come this way. Hurry!"

"This could all be over really quick if you didn't run from me!" Chloe screamed as she swung the battle axe through the air, barely missing Andrea's back. "You're making this really hard!" Chloe roared in anger.

"Andrea, watch out!" Rich yelled.

She moved out of the way long enough for Rich to get a good view of Chloe.

"Please, Andrea, forgive me!" he cried when the gun went off. Across the room Chloe's body fell to the floor.

"Rich, what have you done?" Andrea cried out.

"Oh, dear God!" Victor yelled.

"I'm sorry! Oh, God, I'm sorry! What have I done?"

Andrea ran over to Chloe's body and fell to the ground beside her. "You shot my baby!" she cried uncontrollably, "Chlo, Chlo, mommie's here, baby. I'm right here."

Victor and Rich walked over to Andrea and Chloe.

"What have I done? I didn't mean to kill her, "Rich cried. "I'm sorry, I'm sorry. I was just trying to help you."

"She's still breathing," Andrea managed to say.

"We have to get her to a hospital." Victor told them. "Chloe doesn't have enough time. She has a wound to her gut. We'll have to hurry."

Chloe gripped at the battle axe still in her hand. "I have to stay here," she said weakly. "I'm coming, Illusion."

Those were the final words from Chloe's mouth before she swung the axe into her face, taking her life.

"No!" Andrea cried. "My baby! My baby!" she repeated over and over as she began to hyperventilate.

"I have to get Andrea out of here, son. She's going into shock. Can you see about covering Chloe up?"

"Yes, sir," Rich said sadly. "I can't believe this happened. What have I done? I'm no different than my uncle. I've done as he. I've shot a child," he cried in his mind. Rich took a blanket from the couch and used it to cover Chloe. "I'm so sorry, kiddo." He cried by her side. After Rich said his condolences he walked out to the front porch where Victor had taken Andrea to get some fresh air. "I'm sorry, Andrea. Can you ever forgive me for what I've done?" Rich cried on her shoulder.

"You didn't kill her, Rich. Chloe killed herself. I don't have any hostilities toward you. I know you were just trying to help. If you didn't arrive here tonight, Victor and I might not be alive right now."

"How can I ever face John again? My best friend is going to hate me for the rest of my life. I shouldn't have come here with this gun. God, I'm such a damn screw up."

"Rich, there's something I need to tell you about John," Andrea said as she broke down to cry.

"What? What is it?"

"He's no longer with us, Rich. Chloe killed him."

"No, no, no, no, no, that's not possible!"

"I'm sorry, Rich, but he's gone." She cried, "Chloe killed Tookie, too. Oh, God, I'm so sorry. Where are my manners? Rich, this is Tookie's brother, Victor." Andrea said as she introduced them. "This is Rich. He was John's best friend."

"I'm devastated to hear all this," Rich said as Andrea and Victor saw the shock in his eyes. "I'm sorry about your loss, sir. Your brother was a respectable man," he said as he extended his hand.

"Thank you, my boy. I appreciate your sympathy as I give you mine in return."

"Rich, what made you come back?" Andrea wondered.

"I was trying to call the house all afternoon. I grew worried when I couldn't get an answer. I had this strange feeling you were all in some kind of trouble. I figured I needed to come back, so I did. Is this finally over now?"

"Not by a long shot. We have to go back into the house and find Illusion. Victor and I know a way to destroy her. Would you help us?"

"Shouldn't you both get to a hospital first? I think you need some medical attention. You're both in bad shape right now."

"Not until we finish this. I will not leave this house until I know Illusion is gone for good. That demon has destroyed our lives."

"I won't leave either. I promised Andrea that I'd help her and I will. I don't even hurt anymore. I've grown numb to the pain. I'll survive without seeing a doctor for now."

"So be it then. I'll stay here to help y'all fight this. You could use another set of eyes to keep watch in that house. Don't trust what you see."

"Actually you better trust what your eyes see. It might be an illusion but it can most definitely harm you. Andrea and I are proof of that as you can see," Victor told Rich.

"How do we destroy the doll?"

"It's complicated. It will certainly not be easy. We have to dismember the doll in some way, take out its heart and brain."

"Wait! What'd you mean, its heart and brain?"

"The doll's composed of human body parts that must be destroyed. The object is to take out its heart and brain, then pierce them with a ceremonial knife. We're to throw them into a fire along with the remaining portions of the doll itself."

"Are you sure this is going to work?"

"No, but I pray it does."

"Where are we supposed to get a ceremonial knife, especially at this time?"

"In my house. I'm pretty sure I know the place to find one, but it won't be pretty. I dared never to go back in that room."

"What room are you talking about?"

"There's a room hidden beneath the floor in the attic. We have to go there. If I had to do it by myself I don't think I could. I feel better knowing that I have the two of you with me and I don't have to go alone. The place scares me, but together I know we can get the job done."

"When should we do this?"

"Whenever we're all ready. Rich, I must warn you, there's no electricity in the house. We have to do this by flashlight."

"My uncle won't pop up, will he? I don't want to see him again. I just can't."

"I can't say he won't. I'm sorry, but know we'll all be together. I don't want anyone straying away at anytime, is that understood? We are to stick together," Andrea explained while she felt legs crawling on her back. "I feel like I have something on me. Rich, what is it?"

"Turn around so I can see." Rich spotted an ugly cicada creeping up Andrea's shirt.

"It's a bug."

"Get it off me! Get it off me! I hate bugs!"

Rich and Victor swatted their hands against Andrea's shirt.

"Yuck, it's a cicada. Step on it!"

Rich stomped on the bug; it crunched beneath his foot. "Oh, God, there's more! Those nasty things are all over the porch!"

"Where're they coming from?" Andrea panicked while Victor looked around.

"They're coming from inside the house."

"I can't go back in there if those bugs are coming out!"

"We have to, dear. Try to act like they're not there. I know you're frightened, but we have to go back into that house," Victor told her.

"I can't stand bugs. They make my flesh crawl."

"Try to put your fears aside. You can defeat this if you try," he assured her.

"Fine, fine. You're right."

"Should we go in now?" Rich wondered.

– CHAPTER TWENTY EIGHT –

"Oh, God, they're all over the place! I can't do this!"

"Yes, you can! Rich and I will be here to help you through it."

"Victor, I can't! I'm deathly afraid of cicadas!"

"You're letting Illucious defeat you if you don't try, my dear."

"Who's Illucious?" Rich asked.

"That's the birth name of Illusion," Victor explained. "It's the demon's true name given by its creator, Cyrus Cornu."

"I haven't been gone long and you guys find out all this information that I don't know about."

"It's a long story with many details. Maybe we'll tell it to you one day," Andrea told him. "Rich, make sure you bring your gun. I'm ready to do this now. Let's get it done."

"I'll go first. Y'all can follow," Rich told Andrea and Victor. "We're going to the attic, right?"

"Yeah, I'll show you where the room is."

As everybody walked through the house, the sound of bugs being crushed under their feet was heard.

"I want to turn around. I can't take this. Those cicadas are flying all around. They're going to get me!"

"Andrea, don't panic. You're doing fine," Rich told her. "Try to imagine something pretty like butterflies instead."

"I can't!"

"We're almost to the attic. You're doing fine. Just hang in there a little longer."

"I want this to be over!"

"We're here. Let's go," Rich said before he stopped in his tracks.

"Those are Vipers! Oh, God, and Cobras!" Andrea yelled as she watched them slither across the floor beneath the candlelight. "I'm not going in there! If we get bit by one of those snakes, we're dead."

"Just try to avoid them. If they come near us, I'll shoot."

"Why don't you just shoot them now?"

"I don't have enough rounds to take them all out. We'll just have to improvise. Where's this hidden room that we need to get to?"

"Over that way where that trunk's at."

"Okay, we're going now. Everyone follow me and watch where you step!" They walked carefully across the room, trying to avoid the snakes with each step. "Everyone doing all right so far?"

"I guess."

"Fine here," Victor added.

"Snake! Snake! Snake!" Andrea panicked. "It's coming for us! Quick, Rich, shoot! Shoot!" Rich turned to his side and saw the cobra charging after them. He pointed his gun directly on the beast and fired a shot straight into its head. Andrea lifted the trap door from the floor. "Hurry! Hurry!"

"Wait! Look for any snakes first before you start down those stairs!" Victor shouted.

"It looks clear. Lets go!"

"Where the hell are we? What is this place?" Rich wondered.

"This is the unholy room," Andrea told him.

"There's no time to explain. We need to find that knife," Victor said quickly. "Hurry everyone, start looking!"

Andrea ran to the armoire and opened it. Rich saw the butcher table in the center of the room and gasped.

"What's with this? Were people murdered in here?"

Victor saw a large trunk in front of him and opened it. A putrid odor escaped into the air along with dust and dirt. Victor shined his light into the trunk and was shocked when he came across the skeletal remains of Cyrus's victims. "Oh, dear God!"

"What? What is it, Victor?" Rich asked as he walked toward him. "Oh, gee, man those are bones!"

"I found it!" Andrea yelled to Victor and Rich. "This is what we were looking for!"

Victor closed the trunk while Andrea walked across the way.

"Can I see it?" Rich asked.

"Here," Andrea said as she handed it over.

Rich shined his light over the object. "This knife looks rather wicked. Y'all don't suppose that Cyrus fellow used this on his victims, do you?"

"I wouldn't be surprised," added Victor.

"I don't care to know. Let's just get the hell out of here. I don't like this room. It scares me just standing here."

"Okay, okay, we're going. We got what we needed."

"Do y'all hear something down here?" Victor wondered.

"No, why?" Rich answered.

"Wait. Shh. There it is again. Did y'all here that?"

"What was it?" Andrea wanted to know.

"I'm not sure, but you heard it?"

"Of course I did. There it is again! Where's that coming from?"

"It sounds like something's hissing, doesn't it?" stated Rich.

Victor shined his flashlight across the room. "I think something's in here with us."

"I don't see anything, do y'all?" Andrea wondered.

"I think we should get out of here now!" Victor added.

They started across the room when Rich stumbled over something and fell to the floor. He saw a large reptile standing before him hissing in his face. "Big lizard! Big lizard!" he screamed.

"Move, Rich! Move! That's a Komodo dragon!" Victor yelled as he pulled him away from the large beast. "Hurry, son, follow Andrea!"

"What the hell's that thing doing in here?"

"I don't know, but I bet it wants to eat us."

"What about the snakes, Victor? What are we going to do?" Andrea cried. "We're going from one hell to another. We're never going to make it out of here!"

"Yes, we will. Don't you say that!" Rich told her.

"Try not to get in the way of the snakes," said Victor.

"Hurry, close the door. That lizard is coming after us!" Andrea panicked. "We're surrounded by snakes! Now what do we do?"

"We're going to stay calm and walk out of here. We got in here;

we can get out, too," Victor assured everyone. "Rich, son, you got that gun of yours ready?"

"Lock, stock and barrel!"

"Shoot at any snake that comes after us."

"Oh, trust me, I will!"

"Let's go!"

"How are we going to get out? Three cobras are guarding the exit," Andrea cried.

"I'll tend to them, don't you worry." Rich fired his gun as one snake fell to the ground. That caused the others to quickly slither away and go after him.

"Watch out, Rich!"

"I know, I know, I see them!"

"What are you waiting for? Shoot!"

Another bullet raced through the air as Rich fired another shot, then another. "Go! Go! Hit the stairs!"

Andrea followed Victor as they made it out of the attic.

"Rich, hurry! Get out of there now!"

"Come on, son! You have more snakes following you!"

"Safety at last!" Rich sighed aloud.

"Quick! Shut that door fast!"

Everyone stood on the stairs as their hearts raced in their chests.

"I can't breathe. Y'all got to give me a minute." Victor stated.

"Oh, no, we're back with the cicadas."

"Hey, it's better than being in a room filled with deadly snakes!"

"Or one harboring a giant lizard that could consume an entire child in about twenty minutes, for that matter."

"Do you think it's all real? I mean, those snakes, these cicadas. What if it's just something that Illusion has put in our minds for us to believe?" Rich wondered.

"But look at all the bugs we've stepped on. We can hear their bodies breaking beneath our feet. And what about those snakes you killed, Rich? We seen them fall to the ground."

"But why are they here?"

"Maybe it's our fear that brings them."

"I'm scared of cicadas," Andrea admitted.

"I don't like poisonous snakes, especially those in that room," added Rich.

"A friend of mine was in Central Indonesia studying the *Varanus Komodoensis*, or what you may know as the Komodo dragon. He got too close to a mother guarding her eggs. The female dragon felt threatened and my friend was attacked along with another zoologist who had been with him at the time. I saw a picture of the Komodo that killed him. The thing was almost twelve feet long from head to tail. Since then I've just had a fear of those beastly lizards, even though my possibilities for seeing one were rare. Or at least that's what I had once thought."

"Damn these bugs!" Andrea shouted. "Could we start moving a little faster?"

"Where're we going?"

"I don't know. Just keep moving!"

"Go to the kitchen," Victor told Rich.

"No, Victor! You don't want to go in there!" Andrea cried. "Go to the living room," she yelled.

As they were going down the master stairs the house lit up with light.

"That's better. We finally got some power," said Victor.

"What if it goes off again?" Andrea wondered.

"Where'd all the cicadas go?"

"Oh, thank God, I didn't even notice they were gone."

"Are you more at ease now, dear?"

"Somewhat, but I still fear what's yet to come."

"I know what you mean. I fear it, too," Victor told her.

Andrea stopped on the stair and turned around. "Rich, aren't you coming?"

"Andrea, where's Snow? I can hear her in one of these rooms."

"Oh, God, I almost forgot! She's in my bedroom. We have to go back and get her!"

"Stay here. I'll only be a moment." Rich returned with Snow in his arms.

"Is she all right?"

"Yeah, she ran out as soon as I opened the door."

"Oh, thank God!"

"Here. I think she wants you."

"I'm so glad you're all right," Andrea said as she kissed the kitten on top of her head.

"We have to put her someplace where she'd be safe."

"But where?"

"What about one of those empty boxes in the living room? She couldn't jump out," added Victor.

"You think she'd be all right?"

"I'm pretty sure."

"Okay." Andrea walked into the living room and saw Chloe's body resting beneath the blanket on the floor. Her eyes grew teary as she watched the blood expand through the blanket, staining it red. "Oh, my poor baby," she cried. "I'm sorry I didn't get you away from this house. You'd still be here if we had just done the right thing and left."

Rich walked over to Andrea and put his arms around her. "I'm very sorry for what happened here tonight. I know you're hurting; so am I. I wish there was something I could do to fill your void. I hate to see you suffering like this."

"Promise me you'll help us destroy Illucious."

"I give you my word."

"Where can we find that demon?" Victor questioned everyone. "Any thoughts?"

"I don't know. We'll just have to search the house. Anyone care to take the lead?"

"We'll look down here first and check from room to room," Rich added. "Y'all ready?"

"I hope this is the last time I have to say yes." Andrea followed Rich and Victor out of the living room.

"We'll check this way first," Rich said as he was passing the staircase.

"Stop!" Andrea yelled.

Rich turned around and saw the same sight as Andrea and Victor. Sitting alone halfway between the stairs was Illusion staring down at them.

"I've claimed what was once yours," Seven disembodied voices echoed through the house. "Fear me, for I am the demon of a different kind of hell. I am the violence that produces intense force. I am the fear that brings distressing emotions. I am the deprivation that leads you to loss. I am the delusion of grandeur, the cleverness of trickery, the master of deception and the monarch of lies. Together I am Illucious. Seen as a God by some while viewed as a Grand Demon among others."

"You've taken everything from me!" Andrea cried out.

"That I have, but you must view it as a blessing."

"How is it a blessing, huh? You've taken my husband away from me, my daughter and a good friend!"

"I've presented you with an opportunity to start over again."

"You've ended my life by taking my family!"

"But I've given you a new life in return. I suggest you follow my instructions and go."

"You've given me nothing!"

"If you are so ignorant as not to see the truth, I might as well bring an end to your days. I will present you with two choices. One, I will allow you to leave my house safely, or two, you can stay here and die like the others. It's your decision. Time to make a choice."

"I'm not leaving this house until I've destroyed every last inch of you!"

"She's carrying the knife," Savannah's voice carried down the stairs as she came into view.

"You think you can harm me? You should know I am of eternal life."

"Maybe you are, but not in the body of a doll. You can be destroyed, Illucious! Unfortunately, on your behalf we're aware of the facts that will lead to your defeat." Andrea laughed. "The others in the past may not have known, but given time someone was bound to find out. I guess you can think of us as angels sent here to carry out your destruction. Where there is evil, goodness roams!"

"Silence!" Illucious roared with anger. The demon's rage shook through the walls and dismantled the chandelier hanging from the ceiling.

"Victor, watch out!" Rich yelled.

"How dare you speak of goodness in my house!"

"Mommy, please help me get it out!"

Andrea turned around to see Chloe standing in the corner of the room trying to loosen the axe she had lodged in her face.

"I think my tummy's burning, too." She giggled, "Rich, next time use a bigger gun. Maybe then the person you use it on will actually feel some pain."

Rich looked down at his .44 mag revolver and shook his head.

"What's wrong with everybody? You all look like you've seen a ghost. Oh, that's right. I keep forgetting, I'm not used to this transition thingy yet. Man, I sure did make a mess of my face. Do you think one of you could help me pull this out?"

"Andrea, we have to stop Illucious now! We're running out of time standing here!" yelled Victor. "You and Rich need to forget about Chloe. She's just a distraction."

"You screwed with the wrong people, demon. Now it's our turn to mess with you."

"You can try, but I guarantee you won't make it up the first stair."

"You wanna bet I don't?"

"Don't say I didn't warn you!" The seven voices of Illucious laughed.

Andrea started for the stairs while Victor and Rich walked behind her. She lifted her foot to the first step as it quickly vanished, followed by the second, third and fourth. "Oh, I see how you want to play! Well, you know what? I've got some tricks up my sleeve, too. Go ahead, make them all vanish! It won't stop me from coming after you! By God, I'll find a way even if it takes all night!"

"Well then, let the game begin. But let me first warn you, not a single soul has seen anything yet," Illucious said while Savannah cradled the doll in her arms.

"This is insane! We're never going to get up there without any stairs to walk on," Rich told Andrea. "It's not possible."

"I think I know a way."

"How?"

"I'll pull that chair out and place it beneath the railing on the second floor. We can climb up there, but you'd have to go first, I'm not tall enough."

"And I'm an old man. That stunt is far too dangerous for my aging body. I'll have to stay down here."

"We understand, Victor," Andrea assured him.

"Will y'all be all right?"

"I hope. Say a prayer, though, for good luck."

"Here, take this."

"What is it?"

"My cross. Hannah saw it the second time she cut my face. This cross is what drove her away. She didn't like the sight of it," Victor explained. If I didn't have this on me, I think I'd be dead, he thought. "Please, I want you to take it."

"But Victor, you're going to be down here alone. If it brings you comfort, shouldn't you keep it?"

"I'm sure you'll both be needing it more than I do. Why don't you humor an old man? Take it with you. Besides, I can watch the little kitty for you while you're up there. We'll keep each other company."

"I promise, Victor. We're going to bring this back to you."

"I know. I have faith that you will."

"We'll see you in a little bit. Take care of Snow."

"Do you remember what to do, Andrea?"

"Dismember the doll, then burn it."

"Don't forget to destroy its brain and heart."

"Trust me. Given the chance, I'll be on top of that. This demonic doll is going down once and for all. I'll make sure of it," she said.

"I will, too." Rich told him.

"Let's go!" Andrea said as she pulled the chair across the floor. "All right, Rich. All you got to do is climb up there, then help me up. Think you can do it?"

"Ah, it shouldn't be too hard." Rich climbed on the chair, then stretched his arms as he grasped for the banisters on the railing. Rich fought with his body weight as he pulled himself up. "Damn, this is harder than I thought."

"You can do it, Rich. You're almost up there."

"Almost feels like a mile away."

"Please be careful."

"I'm trying! I'm trying!" Rich pulled his body over the railing and fell to the floor.

"Are you okay?"

"I just have a few sore muscles, but I'll live."

"Is everything all right up there?"

"So far, so good."

"Here, take this knife first," Andrea yelled as she stretched out her arm.

"Got it!"

"All right, you mind helping me up now?"

"Here, give me your hand!"

"I can't reach!"

"Keep trying!"

"I can't do it! You have to lean over a little more!"

"Okay! Okay! Here, can you grab onto me now?"

"Just a little farther! There! Now pull me up!"

Rich struggled, but finally pulled Andrea over the banister, "God, that was a workout."

"Are you saying I'm fat?"

"No, Andrea, of course not. It's just that it wasn't a simple task to have to battle. What are you looking at?"

"Huh? Oh, I thought I saw something move over there on that table."

"What'd you see?"

"I don't know. It was a blur."

"But you saw something?"

"Yeah, I saw something. Forget it. Let's just go."

"Are we going to the attic again?"

"No, Chloe's room." Andrea walked past the table with Rich just as something caught her attention.

"What is it? You seeing things again?"

"Well, why don't you tell me?"

Rich turned around and looked at the table. Sitting on top was a pair of resin gargoyle statues that seemed to move with a life of their own.

"Rich, tell me I'm seeing things!"

"I'm pretty sure you're not. Have you looked at these paintings? It seems like all the flowers have died in them. Isn't that odd?"

Andrea watched the dried petals in the paintings fall down to the floor.

"Did you hear that?"

"Hear what, Rich?"

"Put your head against the wall and listen."

"I hear something, but I don't know what it is."

"Back up!"

"What?"

"Just back up!"

As soon as Andrea moved away, the light bulbs in the wall fixtures began to blow up in their sockets. "What's going on?" Andrea panicked as the walls began to crack open with hoards of rats escaping through the crevices. Some rodents had an extra set of jagged fangs that grew out from their oral cavities while others looked rabid and foamed from their mouth. Their eyes were like tiny red garnets that glowed in the night.

"What do we do, Rich? There's so many of them!"

"Run?"

"But we can't!"

"Damn it! Try to anyway! We need to get out of here!"

The wind howled outside like a pack of wild dogs while the rain beat against the windows and tapped at the glass.

"Oh, my God!" Rich said as he choked. "This has got to be a freaking joke!"

Andrea turned her head and watched as the suit of armor walked down the attic stairs. It swung its lance swiftly through the air, forcing the long sword to strike the walls with each violent blow. Andrea's eyes were wide open and taken with fright. Her mouth had dropped down to her chest as she watched the suit of armor pound heavily on the floor as it came down the stairs.

"We're goners now! You see that thing? It's gonna kill us!" exclaimed Rich.

"Quick! That door's open! Go in there!"

"Where are we?"

"The study."

"We won't be safe in here. That walking armor is going to get us."

"Try to find something long so we can knock it down!"

"Like what? All we can throw at it are books!"

"Well, you better start throwing! It's here!"

Rich began taking books from their shelves while the armor suit started toward him. "This isn't working!"

"Quick! Grab one of those pokers by the fireplace!"

"My hands are sort of occupied at the moment."

"Fine. I'll get it." Andrea yelled.

"Ow! That damn sword's sharp!"

"Are you hurt?"

"The damn thing sliced my arm!" Rich pulled out a large book from the shelf. "This thing's big enough. It should knock you down." Rich yelled as he threw the book at the armor and raced across the room. "That little poker ain't going to stop that thing."

"It's a try! You got any better ideas?"

"Yeah! Distract it to follow you over to that window."

"What're you going to do?"

"Just trust me."

The suite of armor walked toward Andrea as it swung its blade upon her. "Are you all right?" Rich cried out.

"Hurry up!" Andrea shouted as she fought the armor with her iron poker. Andrea backed away and screamed as the blade swung for her head.

"Move now!" Rich yelled as he came up behind the armor suit and gave it a firm push, then out the window the suit fell to the ground.

"You okay?"

"Yeah." Andrea gasped. "Do you see the armor down there?"

Rich turned around to peer out the window. "It's gone!" He said in a state of perplexity.

"But it should have broken with the fall."

"Do you see it?"

"No."

"Okay then!"

"Oh, my God, Rich, Victor! What if the armor goes after him?"

— CHAPTER TWENTY NINE —

Andrea ran out of the room screaming, "Victor! Victor!"

"Is that you, Andrea?"

"Oh, thank God!" she said as she came upon the banister.

Victor stood on the bottom floor as he looked up at her. "Is it over?""

"No!" Andrea cried as the front door slammed open with rain pouring in. "You and Snow have to get out of here!" she wailed as the lights down below blew out. "Oh, God, Victor, it's here! Run!"

Victor turned around and saw the suit of armor standing in the doorway. "What is that?"

"Get out of here!"

The armor stood motionless between the door frame, then with no warning began to lash out with its lance. Andrea fell to the floor crying, "Please, Victor, get out!" The armor started in through the door and went directly for Victor.

"Get out!" Rich yelled.

Victor ran to the living room and took the box Snow was in, then looked around the room trying desperately to find a way out. Then he realized the armor was standing before the living room entrance as it made no attempt to get in.

Victor started laughing as he walked up to the suit. "You see? My little plan worked! You can't come in here."

"Victor, is everything all right?"

"Yes, Andrea, I'm safe. I used one of your buckets of paint to draw crosses all along the living room walls and floor. It worked! This armor can't come in here to harm me."

"Stay in there!"

"I only left the first time because you were calling for me."

"Shit! These damn rats are attacking my ankles." Rich yelled.

"Kick them off!"

"I'm trying, but their teeth are stuck in my pants."

"Beat your leg against the wall." Andrea advised him. "Now, come on. We got to go!" They walked down to Chloe's room and stood before the door. "Try not to look at John," Andrea cried to Rich.

"He's in here?"

Tears poured down Andrea's face as she shook her head. "Victor and I didn't get a chance to cover him."

Rich ignored Andrea's words as he saw John's body. "Oh, God, Chloe did this?" Rich asked just before he threw up upon the floor.

Rats scurried in through the door and ran to the freshly thrown up vomit to have a meal.

"That's sick," Andrea said as she felt weak to her stomach.

"Wait a minute," added Rich.

"What?"

"Do you hear something? Like wings flapping? Lots of them?" Rich shined his flashlight above the door to take a look. "Oh, hell, we got bats!"

Andrea crouched down to the floor trying to avoid them. "How'd they get in here?"

"The broken window in the study."

"I don't think these bats flew in."

"Maybe it's because the lights are out again," Rich thought. "Remember, Illucious makes things appear in the dark."

"Damn it, where's that doll? I thought it'd be in here."

"But look, it's not."

"Damn it, Illucious, Illusion, whatever the hell your name is! Come out and face me!" Andrea yelled as her voice echoed throughout the house. "Where the hell are you?" The sound of Savannah's voice was heard laughing eerily through the room followed by Chloe's. "What is it? You scared to show yourself? Come on! What're you waiting for, huh? Or are you just a cowardly little demon?" Andrea yelled at the top of her lungs.

"Follow the laughter. It's going toward the attic. Listen!" Rich told Andrea.

They raced out of the room and started down the hall before they came upon the stairs. The wallpaper leading to the attic had withered and peeled while a bad odor was detected as it rolled down the stairs. Rich and Andrea tiptoed up the steps, then went into the open attic.

"You don't see any snakes, do you?" Andrea wondered.

"So far, so good. Hey, why is it raining in here? You feel that?"

Through the light of the burning candles Andrea saw black rain as it fell from the ceiling.

"Do you have a leaky roof or something?"

"It's not the roof," Andrea told him. "Look through the light. The rain's black."

"Why is it black and not clear?"

"How am I supposed to know? It's just another of Illucious's tricks."

"I don't remember it being this cold up here earlier, do you?" wondered Rich.

Andrea looked around the room while Rich watched the rats scurry along the floor, "They keep coming along with the bats."

"We're up here! Where the hell are you?" Andrea screamed.

Before she and Rich's eyes two children appeared in the center of the room, one with an axe lodged in her face while the other wore a rope around her neck as she clutched Illusion in her arms.

"I never took you for being this driven," the seven voices of Illucious spoke.

"You took my child from me! How'd you expect me to be?"

"We thought you'd be lifeless," Savannah responded.

"And never the more dull," Chloe added.

"Silence!" Illucious roared. "It is my time to speak. Now, where were we? You both may have gotten up here, but I have my ways. I can stop you, Andrea Craven, and I can stop Rich Sullivan, too. You both are human. Remember that. Neither of you has the power to fight something that is indestructible." Illucious sent out a cold blast of energy that knocked Andrea and Rich to their knees. "I can manipulate your bones as they break beneath your skin. Care for an example?"

Rich's fingers slowly began to twist on their own as he cried out in severe pain. He brought his hand to his face and watched the bones snap one by one. "Andrea, please, you got to make this stop!"

"That's enough, Illucious! You've made your point."

"You're mistaken. I have no point to make."

"Why are you doing this?"

"Don't you enjoy hearing this grown man cry?"

"Yea, though I walk through the valley of the shadow of death, I will fear no evil, for thou art with me," Rich cried as he recited those words.

Illucious began to laugh at him. "You wish to visit the valley of shadows? I am the one who can take you there."

Andrea stood from the floor and started after Savannah and Illucious.

"Back down with you!" the doll yelled in anger as another blast of energy laid Andrea to the ground. The energy wave was so powerful that it knocked over the burning candles spread out along the room. Hot wax spilt to the floor and set the attic on fire.

Andrea felt a sharp pain pierce her wrist as the nail went through and held her down. Along the attic walls Rich and Andrea heard distraught voices and the cries of a baby take to the air.

Coming out of the wood as it moved mechanically was a severely decomposed body of a woman. Her throat had been slit and her head had been scalped. The woman grasped through the air trying to touch something that wasn't there. Gurgle-like noises escaped through her throat as blood ran down the woman's neck.

Through the wall peeled away another badly decomposed body. This time it was a little girl. Her body was punctured full of draining tubes which forced her blood to splatter down to the floor. In the distance Rich and Andrea heard the continuous cries from the baby. They watched on as a fancy old carriage strolled along the way. Inside was the decapitated body of a baby girl.

"They are all under my control!" Illucious said fiercely. "And under my watch these lost souls will never find rest, for they are all apart of me," the doll spoke madly. "Claim the life that makes your own. Gisele Whittier, the tramp who donated my head of hair. My Felicia, the little virgin who bled all that she had to spare. The infant, Cecily Gairden, the purely innocent offering which was bestowed upon me so that I may bathe in her blood. And all the others who stand around you in the shadows. The madman, the liar, the killer, the deceiver and the one with a dishonorable mouth. They're all here by my request and demand. All you have to do is look around to see," Illucious said hostilely. "I gave you a chance to leave my house. Instead you refused the offer, for that my legion and slaves shall bring you down."

"I will not let that happen," Andrea stated to the demon. She pulled the nail from her wrist as her blood ran to the floor. Several rats ran up to the fallen blood while Andrea started kicking them away.

Rich walked over to Andrea and stood by her side. "We are not afraid of you!" he yelled.

"We have nothing to fear!" Andrea shouted as she unearthed the cross hidden beneath her shirt. "For everyone you've ever hurt! For every breath that you stole and took! For every nightmare you have given, I stand in your way and bid you forbidden!"

Illucious roared as all the voices shook through the house. "Put it away!" the disembodied voices spoke.

"You don't like crosses. Do you, Illucious?"

"Put it away!"

"They make you grow weak," Andrea snarrled. "All your control is gone? Isn't it? Was this the secret Collette knew about that kept you at bay? Just wave a cross into Illucious's face. Why did your legion and slaves back away from us? Are they weak like you, Illucious?" Andrea walked over and took the doll from the ground. "It looks like it's your end of days." Andrea said as she stared in its face, "What's wrong, Illucious? Why aren't you fighting? No strength? Are you powerless?" Andrea yelled as she violently ripped the doll's head from its body. "Burn in hell where you belong!" Andrea handed Rich the remaining torso of the doll. "See if you can get the heart out while I work on the brain."

Rich slashed at the doll with the knife. "This thing's heart is really lodged in here."

"Can you get it out?"

"With some effort I should be able to. God, this thing stinks."

"You're telling me," Andrea told him as she worked on the brain. "I can't believe I'm touching this."

"Someone has to do it. There, got it! Oh, hell no!"

"What?"

"Look, the heart's beating." Rich got grossed out and dropped the beating heart to the floor. Blood splattered off the internal organ as it smacked against the ground. "That's disgusting."

"So is this," Andrea said as she held Illucious's brain in her hand. "Hurry, hand me the knife!" she said. She thrust the blade deep into the corpus callosum. The brain tore open as an overflow of maggots poured out. "I think I'm going to be sick."

"I know the feeling," Rich stated. "Time for me to pierce the heart."

"I'll do it if you can't."

"I can do it," he assured her. "I want to help you destroy this thing. It messed my life up, too," stated Rich as he held the beating heart in his hand. "Knife."

"Here."

Rich took the knife from Andrea's grasp. "Lights out!" he said while plunging the blade into the beating heart. Just like the brain, maggots spilt out through the wound.

"It's finally over." Andrea gasped.

"We still have to burn the rest of this doll."

"Do we toss it in the fire that's up here?"

"Illucious said this was her house. Why not let her burn in it?"

Rich and Andrea cast the remaining parts of the doll into the flames. It all went up within seconds, forcing everything to wither and scathe to a crisp.

"We have to get out! The fire's burning out of control. We must hurry!" Rich let Andrea rush ahead as they left the attic. Heavy smoke filled the hallway burning their throat and eyes. "Faster, Andrea! These flames are spreading quickly!"

"I can't leave John here and let him burn in this house."

"We don't have a choice."

"I have to get him out!"

"Andrea, John's dead. There's nothing we can do for him. We're going to die, too, if we don't escape these flames."

"I understand, but I can't leave him like this. John was my husband. He deserves a proper burial."

"We don't have enough time. I'm sorry," Rich said as he jerked Andrea through the rest of the hallway.

"Unhand me! I need to go back!" she cried.

"You can fight with me all you want. I'm not letting you go."

"Damn it, Rich!"

"We can't battle those flames. It's too much," Rich told her. "Look, Andrea, the stairs are back! Victor, you still down there?"

"In the living room," Victor said before he walked out.

"What happened to the body of armor?" Rich wondered as he and Andrea came down the stairs.

"The darn thing fell to the floor a few minutes ago. It never got back up as you both can see. I take it this monstrosity is finally over?"

"Not until we get out of here, it ain't. There's a really bad fire that's spreading quickly. We must hurry and get out."

"It looks like those flames are stalking y'all. When you move, they follow."

"Victor, you and Andrea get out of here. I'm going to get Snow."

"Sure, sure. Come on, my dear," Victor said as he tried to lead her out of the house.

"Andrea, where are you going?" Rich wondered.

"I listened to you once and I left my husband burning upstairs. I won't do that to my daughter. I'm getting her out."

"No, Andrea, you can't do that. You heard Victor. He said those flames follow us and spread through the house. If you go in there, I might not be able to get out with Snow. The flames won't spread as fast if it's just one of us. Right, Victor?"

"That sounds reasonable."

"If you won't let me go in, will you at least bring my daughter's body out?"

"Andrea, dear, it's either Chloe or Snow. If the flames spread too quickly, there'd be no way to get them both out."

"Can't he try?"

"Well, that's up to Rich."

Andrea looked Rich in the eye. "Will you please?"

"Fine, fine, I'll try. But I'm getting Snow out first." Rich then turned to Victor. "Take her out of here."

Victor took Andrea by the arm as they walked to the front door. The flames followed Andrea as they burned through their path.

"Go to the side of the house," yelled Andrea.

Rich walked into the living room as flames snuck up behind him and spread upon the ground and walls. Victor and Andrea walked to one of the living room windows and peered in. It was all in flames as was the rest of the house. Victor took a rock from the ground and smashed the window.

"Hurry! Hurry!" he yelled.

"There's no way out of here! The place is covered in flames!" Rich panicked.

"Help me break the rest of this glass. You can climb out the window." Victor suggested.

Rich used a lamp to knock out the rest of the glass while Victor helped.

"Here, take the box!" Rich said as he handed it to Andrea.

"What about Chloe?" she cried.

"Andrea, Rich barely has enough time to get himself out."

"But he said he'd try."

"He was trying, my dear, but the flames have overpowered him."

Rich stuck his head through the window. "Hey, y'all, I hear sirens."

"Must be the fire department."

"Hey! Hey! Are y'all all right?" a voice in the distance asked.

Andrea turned around and saw a man approaching.

"Oh, dear God, we got to get that boy out!" The man said suddenly. "Here, son, I'll give you a hand." The man helped Rich through the window. "Are y'all all right?"

"Roy, is anyone hurt?" a woman's voice yelled. "The fire trucks are just down the street."

"Hurry, Bessy! Help me get these folks to the front of their house."

"Boy, that's some fire. Is everyone all right here?"

"We just barely got out," Rich told the man and woman.

"We need to move away from the house. These flames are burning out of the window," said Roy.

"Here, miss, let me help you. I'm Bessy. My husband Roy and I live across the street."

"I'm Andrea," she said softly.

"Y'all are really lucky you got out of there. This house has always been a problem for anyone who's ever lived in it," Bessy told Andrea. "Miss are you all right?"

"I've lost everything in that forsaken house. It's all gone, every last bit."

"Come, come, my girl. You can cry on my shoulder."

"What am I going to do?"

"We'll help you figure something out. Be thankful you're still alive."

"The whole house went up in flames so quickly."

"Try not to think about it right now. We need to get you to an ambulance and get these wounds taken care of. What happened in there?"

"We were all fighting for our lives."

"You know, my mother used to tell me stories about that house when I was a young girl. She was good friends with the original owner, Collette McGowan. She swore to me that place was haunted."

"Did you believe her?"

"My mother never lied. She was a truthful woman," Bessy stated as a man ran up to her and Andrea.

"I'm Captain Doyl with the Savannah Fire Department. Is everyone all right here?"

"Just shaken up," Andrea told the man.

"Is anyone else in the house that we need to know of?"

"They didn't make it out of the fire," Andrea said with a lost look in her eye.

"They? So there are two other people in that house?"

"Three, but they're already gone."

"My men are working as fast as they could to get this fire out."

"They won't be able to put it out. The house will burn to the ground, I know."

"Eric, take this lady to the paramedics. She's in need of medical attention."

"Yes, Captain. Come with me, miss."

Captain Doyl walked up to his firefighters. "All right, men, we have three bodies in that house that need to come out."

"We're on top of that, sir!"

CHAPTER THIRTY

"You both need to see the paramedics," Roy told Rich and Victor. "They're coming now."

"I'm Greg. I'll be working on you tonight," the EMT said as he walked up to Victor, "Follow us. I'll take you to Seth," he told Rich. "You're going to need some stitches." Rich and Victor followed Greg over to an ambulance. "Seth, I have a man here who needs some medical attention."

"Step into my office, sir. Okay, what do we have going on?"

"My arm was cut open and I have a few broken fingers."

"All right, let me take a look here. Did you get cut with a knife?"

"I fell into a sword."

"A sword?"

"Yeah, one of those lances that a body of armor holds."

"Ah, so you fell into it when you were trying to get out of the house?"

"Yeah, you know, with the smoke and stuff makes it hard to see."

"I have to clean your wound. This is going to sting."

"It can't hurt as bad as the cut did."

"Not as bad, but it won't feel good either."

"Just get it over."

Seth applied the alcohol to Rich's wound and cleaned it. "Okay, I have to give you a shot to numb your arm."

"Damn, that hurts."
"It's all over. Do you have any feeling here?"
"No."
"You can't feel this at all?"
"Nope."
"All right, I'm going to start stitching you up now."
"Do I need to go to the hospital or anything?"
"You're going to need some x-rays of your hand. All right, you're stitched up. Here's some ointment. I want you to apply it to the wound two to three times a day. It'll keep your wound moist and help with the scarring. Make sure you change your bandages, too. You don't want an infection."

"Two to three times a day with the ointment. What about the bandages?"

"Three to four times should be sufficient. You'll know when they need to be changed. You can take some over-the-counter pain medicine. It should help with your discomfort if the doctor doesn't prescribe anything. You'll want to see a doctor to get these stitches out in about a week."

"Thank you for your help."
"Just doing my job."
"Can I check on my friends before we leave for the hospital?"
"I see no problem with that."

Rich looked for the ambulance that Andrea was in, then rushed over to it and tapped on the glass. "Is she all right?" he asked while the paramedic opened the door.

"She'll need to go to the hospital. She has some pretty bad wounds that need to be treated by a doctor. I'm just prepping her right now."

"Can I see her?"
"Sure, come on in."
"Hi, Andrea."
"Hi, Rich."
"This guy taking good care of you?"
"So far. He's cleaned my wounds and hooked me up to an IV. I'm going to need surgery on my foot and hand. He stitched the wounds on my arm and leg and got that out of the way. The injury to my wrist is pretty severe. They'll tend to that at the hospital."

"Your hand, too?"

"My finger, really. Remember when I got bit?"
"Yeah, I remember."
"Well, it got badly infected. I might lose it."
"Oh, no, are you serious?"
"Yeah, the paramedic said I was sick due to the bite."
"That's not good."
"It's just my finger. At least I'll have the rest of my hand. Have you talked to Victor?"
"No, not yet. I wanted to check on everyone before I go to the hospital, too. I need to get my hand looked at."
"Yeah, your fingers are in bad shape. Will you check on Victor and see if he's all right?"
"Sure. I'll be back to check on you after while."
"If I don't see you when you come back, I'll see you at the hospital."
Rich left Andrea's side and went hunting for Victor.
"You looking for that man you were with?" Roy asked.
"Yeah, you know where he's at?"
"Over there. I'll take you to him. You doing all right?"
"Yes, sir. Just a couple of stitches for now. How's it going with the fire?"
"They're having trouble getting it under control."
"I figured they would."
"The gentleman you were looking for is in there."
"Thank you. Hey, if you hear anything more about the fire will you please let me know?"
"Sure. I'll let you know if I find anything out. How's the lady?"
"Andrea? She has to go to the hospital and have surgery."
"If you need anything, please let Bessy or me know."
"I will. Thank you," Rich said as he shook Roy's hand. Rich tapped the glass on the ambulance window. "I've come to check on Victor."
"Come on in. Victor's here."
"How're you doing, sir?"
"I'm in a mess, son. The paramedic here thinks I need reconstructive surgery."
"I'm sorry to hear that."
"It's either that or look this way for the rest of my life."
"It's just a shame. Are you in any pain at all?"

"Not like I was when it first happened. How's Mrs. Craven doing?"

"She needs to have surgery, too. She might lose her finger. She has a bad infection that's spreading."

"That poor dear. She really took a lot, didn't she? And how are you?"

"Surviving, I guess. I'll need to get a few x-rays of my hand to see how bad the damage is."

"You'll be all right."

"I know. It's just a few broken bones. I can live with that."

"I'm sorry to interrupt y'all, but we'll be leaving shortly," said the paramedic.

"Oh, Okay. Well, I'll see you at the hospital then, Victor."

"You, too, son."

Rich walked back to see Andrea to say his goodbyes. "Victor's going to need reconstructive surgery."

"Looks like we'll all be in the hospital together, huh?"

"Looks that way. They're leaving with him now."

"We're supposed to be going in another minute or two."

"I'll stay at the hospital until you both have your surgery."

"Thank you, Rich."

"We have to stick together, right? I wouldn't leave you guys up there."

"If John were still here, he'd thank you for your help," Andrea said sadly.

"I know he would. He's still with us, Andrea. Just in a different sense. Well, I better be getting back to my ambulance. I'm going to see if I can drive my car to the hospital. That way we'll have a ride when you and Victor get out."

— CHAPTER THIRTY ONE —

"Captain Doyl, we're not having any luck with this fire. The more water we spray, the more the flames build up. We're going to need more fire trucks out here."

"I'll call dispatch now and get some more men out here a.s.a.p."

Rich overheard the conversation as he walked up to the ambulance Seth was working in. "It's me. I'm back," Rich said as he stepped in.

"Did you find your friends?"

"Yes, Victor's on his way to the hospital now. Andrea will be leaving shortly. Would it be a problem if I drove myself to the hospital? When my friends get out, we're going to need a car."

"Are you fit enough to drive?"

"I would think so. I don't have any major problems."

"If you think you can, go ahead."

"Thanks for understanding." Rich walked back over to the ambulance holding Andrea. "Seth said I could drive my car. I'm going to follow you guys out when you leave. Don't worry. I'll be right behind you."

"Looks like the house continues to burn, doesn't it?"

"God had plans to condemn that place and destroy the evil within."

"That was also Tookie's wish, to see that house burn down one day. I just hate that he's not here to see it."

"Tookie had faith in you and John. He saw something in the both of you. I think he knew you'd try to destroy that house of Illusion's."

Andrea watched the ash fall to the ground like Snow. "At one time that was a beautiful home, but its nightmares made it a dreadful place."

Through the heavy flames, Andrea saw a woman standing before the door frame with her husband to her side. In his arms was a little boy no more than three years of age. Andrea blinked unknowing that the sight she had seen was real.

"Are they really there?"

"What? Who?"

"The O'Connor family. Can't you see them?"

Rich turned looked upon the house. "No, I don't see anyone."

"They were just there! Scarlette, Wallace and Griffin. It was almost like they came to say their goodbyes."

"Maybe they were."

"The ambulance will be leaving now. Did you want to hitch a ride, sir?" the paramedic questioned Rich.

"Oh, no, that won't be necessary. I got my car," he said as he exited the vehicle.

The paramedic yelled to the driver just as Rich walked away, "All right, Wally, let's roll on out!"

— CHAPTER THIRTY TWO —

Rich Sullivan sustained three broken fingers due to the powerful manipulation of Illucious's mind. He was released from the hospital during the early hours of June 13, 1978.

Victor Blackwell had minor reconstructive surgery to repair the inflictions Savannah and Illucious had placed upon him. He was released from the hospital on June 16, 1978.

Andrea Craven went through a tedious procedure to repair the torn ligaments and tenants in her foot. The bite mark she had received from Illucious had spread into a nasty infection that caused her finger to turn black. Doctors were left with no choice but to remove the unhealthy digit from her hand. She was also treated for Toxemia with the use of proper medications. On June 18, 1978, Andrea Craven was released from Banners Hospital.

Being the kind man that he was, Victor Blackwell persuaded Andrea into living with him and Clara until she could get a place of her own.

Rich Sullivan abandoned his tiny apartment back in Tennessee. He thought his life would be better off if he were closer to Andrea Craven and Victor Blackwell. And just as he did with Andrea, Victor persuaded Rich into staying at his house for however long he needed.

As for the Cornu House, once located at seventeen- twenty-three

East Waldburg Street, nothing remains but burnt boards and scorched grass.

The bones of John Craven, Tucker "Tookie" Blackwell and little Chloe Craven were finally removed from the rubble on June 14, 1978.

John and Chloe Craven received a closed casket, conjoined funeral the morning of June 23, 1978. Family and friends came from far and near to pay their homage and respect to the dearly departed.

Tucker "Tookie" Blackwell was at last laid to rest the day following the burial of John and Chloe Craven. He, too, received a closed casket ceremony to bid him a farewell into his afterlife.

As for Sam, Tookie's beloved companion, he found a nice home with Victor and Clara. Sam was given the same love and respect that Tookie had offered his beloved friend. Victor and his wife felt honored to have him. After all, Sam was a good old dog.

Last, we have Snow, Chloe's little white kitten. Andrea found much comfort in having her around, for Snow filled the voids in Andrea's heart and eased her depression. On August 10, 1978, Andrea found a nice local home perfect for herself and Snow. They moved in on August 12, 1978.

Rich bought a nice place not more than a block from Andrea's new home. They visit each other often, spending plenty of time together.

Victor and Clara have become Rich and Andrea's expanded family outside their own. They shared many meals and conversations among one another. During their visits, Andrea and Rich got the pleasurable opportunity of seeing Sam. Through him, they encountered the chance to remember the humble man who had once taken care of him.

In this bizarre legend of a satanic doll and her twisted legion, we have come to know many of the horrifying facts; including the thought that some tragedies tear us apart, while others bring us closer.

THE END

Made in the USA
San Bernardino, CA
15 April 2013